PRAISE FOR CAROLYN BROWN

The Wedding Pearls

"*The Wedding Pearls* by Carolyn Brown is an amazing story about family, life, love, and finding out who you are and where you came from. This book is a lot like *The Golden Girls* meet *Thelma & Louise*."

—*Harlequin Junkie*

"*The Wedding Pearls* is an absolute must-read. I cannot recommend this one enough. Grab a copy for yourself and one for a best friend or even your mother or both. This is a book that you need to read. It will make you laugh and cry. It is so sweet and wonderful and packed full of humor. I hope that when I grow up, I can be just like Ivy and Frankie."

—*Rainy Day Ramblings*

The Yellow Rose Beauty Shop

"*The Yellow Rose Beauty Shop* was hilarious, and so much fun to read. But sweet romances, strong female friendships, and family bonds make this more than just a humorous read."

—*The Readers Den*

"If you like books about small towns and how the people's lives intertwine, you will LOVE this book. I think it's probably my favorite book this year. The relationships of the three main characters, girls who have grown up together, will make you feel like you just pulled up a chair in their beauty shop with a bunch of old friends. As you meet the other people in the town, you'll wish you could move there. There are some genuine laugh-out-loud moments and then more that will just make you smile. These are real people, not the oh-so-thin-and-so-very-rich that are often the main characters in novels. This book will warm your heart, and you'll remember it after you finish the last page. That's the highest praise I can give a book."

—Reader quote

Long, Hot Texas Summer

"This is one of those lighthearted, feel-good, make-me-happy kind of stories. But, at the same time, the essence of this story is family and love with a big ol' dose of laughter and country living thrown in the mix. This is the first installment in what promises to be another fascinating series from Brown. Find a comfortable chair, sit back, and relax, because once you start reading *Long, Hot Texas Summer* you won't be able to put it down. This is a super fun and sassy romance."

—*Thoughts in Progress*

Daisies in the Canyon

"I just loved the symbolism in *Daisies in the Canyon*. As I mentioned before, Carolyn Brown has a way with character development with few if any contemporaries. I am sure there are more stories to tell in this series. Brown just touched the surface first with *Long, Hot Texas Summer* and now continuing on with *Daisies in the Canyon*."

—*Fresh Fiction*

The
Lullaby Sky

ALSO BY CAROLYN BROWN

The Lullaby Sky

CAROLYN BROWN

Published by Montlake Romance, Seattle

www.apub.com

Amazon, the Amazon logo, and Montlake Romance are trademarks of Amazon.com, Inc., or its affiliates.

ISBN-13: 9781503937802
ISBN-10: 1503937801

Cover design by Laura Klynstra

Printed in the United States of America

This book is dedicated to all shelters for abused women and to the volunteers who help to keep them running. You know where you are and who you are, but please know that words cannot begin to tell you how much you are appreciated.

CHAPTER ONE

The table gave Hannah something stable to hold on to as the old white-haired judge took his place at the highly polished bench. A river of sweat trickled between her breasts, but it would all be over within an hour. Seven years of misery was about to come to an end. Feeling four sets of eyes scrutinizing her, she stole a quick glance at the other side of the courtroom.

Marty and his lawyer were conversing in whispers, but his cold green eyes locked on her, disapproving as always. She shrank inside her skin and wished she'd worn the little black suit and high heels, that she'd swept her hair up into a twist at the back and not used so much smoky eye shadow. This wasn't the day to take a stand for independence and wear skinny jeans, a western-cut shirt with pearl snaps, or cowboy boots. The papers weren't signed and sealed yet, and her soon-to-be ex hated cowboy boots.

A hand came from behind to rest on her shoulder, and she tensed; then Travis patted her gently and she relaxed—at least enough to breathe again. With her four friends behind her, she could draw on their strength to get her through this day. Aunt Birdie, her great-aunt, and Miss Rosie, Travis's grandmother, had wanted to be there for her also, but Hannah had convinced them to stay home and babysit her daughter, Sophie. Besides, those two old gals said exactly what they wanted when they wanted. Not what she needed in this courtroom.

People were sitting now that the judge had settled into his chair, but Hannah's feet remained glued to the floor. Her hands had a death grip on the table. If she let go, would she faint? What if the judge said no? What if he made them wait another three months? What if Marty changed his mind and wanted visitation or even full custody of Sophie?

"You may be seated, Mrs. Ellis." The judge nodded toward her.

The lawyer tugged on her arm, and she let go of the table and slid down into the wooden chair. "Sorry," she whispered.

"It'll be over in a little while," he whispered. "You aren't contesting anything, so there's nothing to fight about, and from the looks of his girlfriend, he wants this divorce as much as you do."

Though the old oak benches in the small courtroom were polished to a glowing sheen, a bit of dust lingered on the end of the table where Hannah and her lawyer sat in two straight-back chairs. Would Marty see that and go into a rage right there in front of his parents, his pregnant new girlfriend, and the judge? Marty did not abide a speck of dust on anything. But for him that was minor. Leaving a hair in the bathroom sink, or worse yet, a single wrinkle in the bedsheets—those were sure to set him off into a screaming rage. Instinctively, she wrapped her arms around her body to protect her ribs.

The judge fanned through the papers before him. Hannah remembered to take breaths, but they were shallow. Afraid to blink for fear she'd wake up and this would be a dream, she felt her eyes become so dry that they ached.

"Approach please, sir?" Marty's lawyer asked.

The judge motioned him and Hannah's lawyer forward, leaving Hannah unprotected except for her three friends. Darcy, sitting behind her and beside Calvin, mumbled something under her breath. Outgoing, bubbly Darcy with her spiky, blonde hair was the vice president of a bank in Gainesville, but Hannah had no doubt that the mumbling contained words that would fry the hair off Lucifer's pointy little chin.

Cal laid a hand on Hannah's shoulder. Having seen him in his starched jeans, white pearl-snapped shirt, big belt buckle, and polished boots, Hannah knew most folks in the room would think the tall blond was a bull rider or a rancher. Truth was, Cal was a fashion designer— sewing was his passion.

Travis was often every bit as misjudged as Calvin. Tall, lanky, and studious-looking with his wire-rimmed glasses and dark-brown hair that was always too long, he was often mistaken for a schoolteacher. In reality he could wield a hammer or run carpentry equipment with finesse. He'd left Crossing right after high school and had come home only for holidays until last year, when he came back for good. It helped to have some men on her side with Marty glaring at her.

Then there was Liz, the other target of Marty's glares. He hated quiet, sweet Liz, because she'd given Hannah a job, and he despised the little bit of independence that job had brought into her life. Liz had pressured Hannah into working as a teacher's aide the past several years at the school where she acted as principal. Liz should be in a court of law for the same reason Hannah was, but Liz was still making excuses for her son-of-a-bitch husband.

The whispering in front of the judge ceased, and the two lawyers returned to their clients' tables. Hannah's heart skipped a beat when she saw the smug expression on Marty's lawyer's face. She whipped around to try to read his parents' body language, but both of them were looking straight ahead. His pregnant girlfriend, a tall redhead, laid a hand on her baby bump. She had that look in her eyes reserved for deer in the headlights and women who're scared senseless of the man they are with. She blinked and looked away quickly.

A diamond the size of a dime on her hand glinted in the sunlight flowing into the room from the single window. Marty turned toward the woman and flashed one of those brilliant smiles that had endeared him to Hannah back in the beginning of their relationship. Marty wasn't handsome, just generic—medium height, light-brown hair, green eyes. But when he walked into a room, that fake charm drew women to him. Looking back, Hannah realized now that his smile never reached his eyes unless he was slapping her around or yelling at her.

Hannah had fallen for his charisma. By the time she realized it was all a game to him, it was too late to turn around and go back. She was pregnant and then she had a daughter that he constantly threatened to take away from her. That poor red-haired woman sitting behind him was number two in what would probably be a long line of women that Marty would try to break with his "training."

If only she could yell at her to run away and never sign the papers to marry him. Hannah glanced back at her again, but she was staring straight ahead as if she was afraid to look anywhere else. Hannah was the past; the redhead was the present. And someday when Marty decided he couldn't train the new woman any better than he could the one he had in the past, he'd move on to the future. Nothing would ever change him.

Her lawyer checked a page on the papers in front of him and leaned toward her. He smelled like coffee and cigarettes with a hint of spicy aftershave thrown into the mix. "Are you sure that you don't want to ask for more? This whole thing is pitiful. Your daughter deserves more, and so do you."

She shook her head. "He didn't change his mind about Sophie, did he?"

Her lawyer shook his head. "No, he is relinquishing all rights to his daughter, but for God's sake, Hannah, he married you without a prenup. He owes you more than the piddling amount he's offering as child support. You also deserve alimony."

She shook her head. "Just get it over with and let me sign the divorce papers. I don't want anything from him."

"Are we ready?" the judge asked.

"Yes, sir," both lawyers said in unison.

"Is there anything else that Mr. Ellis would like to say?" the judge asked.

Cal wiggled in the pew behind Hannah. Without looking she knew he'd propped his left foot on his right knee and folded his arms across his chest, daring Marty to say a word.

No, they aren't pews. That isn't right. Hannah frowned. She had to get it right. If she didn't, then there would be consequences. Churches had pews, and this did not resemble a church in any sense of the word, unless one took into account that the devil incarnate sat at the other table. In the courtroom they were benches.

They still looked like pews to Hannah, but then, she'd been in church a lot more often than she'd ever been in a courtroom.

"My client has nothing else to add to his petition," Marty's lawyer said.

"And you, Mrs. Ellis?" The judge nodded toward Hannah.

Hannah spoke before the lawyer could open his mouth. "I want to be clear on this. I get my child, my house, and the land that goes with it in this settlement."

The judge nodded. "Do you agree with this? And are you willing to take a onetime payment in lieu of a monthly child support check, half today and half of which will be set up in a trust fund to be given to the child on her twenty-fifth birthday? And you will not revisit this issue at any time in the future?"

"Yes, sir." Hannah nodded.

"According to this, you will have the deed to the house and all the contents thereof, the airplane hangar and what is in it, the property it sits on, and the 2004 Chevrolet that is on that property. Is that agreeable?"

"Yes, sir." The lawyer finally got a word in ahead of her.

"Are you aware that since there was no prenuptial agreement you are entitled to a lot more?" the judge asked.

Marty's lawyer moved in a blur as he pushed back his chair and stood to his feet.

The judge pointed at him. "Sit down. I want this young woman to know without a doubt what she is signing today."

"I am aware. I will not ask for anything more from Marty in the future, and I understand what I am signing," Hannah said.

"Martin or James, not Marty," the lawyer muttered.

"What was that?" the judge asked.

"His name is Martin, James, or Mr. Ellis, not Marty. He does not like to be addressed as Marty," the lawyer said coldly.

"Noted. Okay, I'm going to grant this divorce contingent upon the transfer of deeds and titles." The judge picked up the gavel, but Marty's lawyer jumped up again and asked if he could approach.

The judge sighed and laid the wooden hammer back down.

Calvin leaned forward and whispered, "It's almost over, darlin'. Just a few more minutes."

"I have all those documents right here. We would like to have this totally finalized today," Marty's lawyer said.

"I suppose you would." The judge narrowed his eyes at Marty. "And one more time: Martin James Ellis, you are fully aware that you are signing away all parental rights, and that includes the right for another man to adopt her if Mrs. Ellis should remarry?"

"Yes, sir," Marty said without hesitation. "Hannah can have her maiden name back if she wants it and give that to her daughter. I don't want anything to do with this woman or her child again. Marrying her and trying to give her a better life was a mistake."

The judge shook his head slowly. "I don't want to see you back in my courtroom in six months or six years crying the blues about visitation." He shifted his gaze to Hannah. "Do you want it entered into the divorce decree that you and your child will take back your maiden name?"

Hannah whispered to her lawyer as she nodded. "If it can be done right now, I do want my name back and for Sophie's to be O'Malley instead of Ellis. If it's going to prolong things, I'll keep the Ellis name."

"My client would like to have her name back and change the name of the child, but only if this can be done today," the lawyer answered for her.

"Okay?" He turned to Marty. "You sure about this, Mr. Ellis?"

Marty's head bobbed up and down as he conferred with his lawyer.

"My client says that he is fully aware of what he will be signing and he is fine with letting his wife have her name back and to give that name to the child." His lawyer looked like a model for a toothpaste ad when he grinned.

Hannah could feel the touch of someone's angry gaze and glanced over her shoulder at the pregnant woman behind Marty. This glare was cold as icicles. Cool as a cucumber sandwich on a hot July day, his girlfriend sat there with her chin up, but her eyes swam in fear and sadness. Marty was starting with better material this time. This one came from money, so he wouldn't have to work so hard to get her fit for proper society, those words whispered so many times that they were branded in Hannah's brain.

But maybe, just maybe, this woman could get away from him. Hannah would even help her if she could. Not only this poor woman who was about to endure the blazes of hell, but every woman who needed to get away from an abusive relationship. Hannah would be willing to do whatever she could to help them.

The judge slammed the gavel down and startled Hannah so badly that she whipped her head around, shoulders involuntarily shuddering and eyes blinking several times. When she could focus again, there was movement all around her.

Marty hugged his parents, kissed his girlfriend, and shook hands with the lawyer. Liz, Darcy, Travis, and Calvin leaned over the rail separating them from her and enfolded her into a group hug.

Hannah's lawyer gathered up the papers and shook her hand when the hug finally ended. "I hope that you don't regret this, Mrs. Ellis."

"Miss O'Malley," Liz said quickly. "And believe me, sir, the only regret she has is that she was ever Mrs. Ellis to start with."

Hannah was no longer Mrs. Martin James Ellis IV, from the rich and famous Ellis family in Dallas, Texas. She was once again Hannah O'Malley from Crossing, Texas, and her daughter was now Sophie O'Malley, not Sophie Ellis.

Sophie!

Hannah couldn't wait to get home to her daughter. Aunt Birdie and Miss Rosie were watching her, just like they did every day during the school year while Hannah worked. But today was special. Today Sophie belonged exclusively to her, and Marty could never again threaten to take her away.

Mark it down. Write it on stone. This is the best of all the thirty-eight Christmases I've ever had all rolled into one. The first day of June will never pass again without a celebration. She felt like skipping from the somber room and doing cartwheels down the courthouse hallway.

The euphoria ended abruptly, and she frowned. There should be at least one tear and a whole bucket full of guilt at ending a marriage. She'd cried when she had to shoot a poisonous snake, so where in the hell was the guilt for not being able to make her marriage work? Or the guilt over letting Marty prevent it from working?

Marty's lawyer carried a whole stack of papers to Hannah's lawyer. He handed her a pen and pointed to the places where she should sign. With a few signatures, it was done. The lawyers would still have to have it all recorded at the Cooke County Courthouse, but it was finished. She had a place to live, an old car, and a daughter that no one could ever again threaten to take away from her. She still had a job as a teacher's aide when school started if she wanted it. She didn't have a controlling, abusive husband who looked for reasons to slap her around or put her down. It seemed like a damn good trade-off to Hannah.

Her friends gathered around her and, acting like bodyguards, they ushered her out of the courtroom and outside.

"Whoa, that sun is bright," Calvin said as they all stopped on the courthouse lawn to put on their sunglasses. "It reminds me of Cancún. I'm going to design a clothing line with bright island colors, darlin' Hannah, and I want you to model them for me."

"I'm not tall enough to pull off your wild designs. I'm barely five foot three, but thank you for trying to make me smile," Hannah told him.

A loud pop off to their right stopped Hannah in her tracks. She rolled her shoulders forward and threw her hands over her eyes. Travis gently draped his arm around Hannah's shoulders, and she tensed up even tighter.

"It's all right. You have the right to a case of nerves today. Marty isn't shootin' at you. That was only a car backfiring," Liz said softly.

"Calvin, sweetheart." Darcy batted her chocolate-brown eyes up at him. "When you start designing clothes for size-sixteen women, I'll gladly be your runway model."

Calvin crooked his arm and tucked Hannah's arm into it. "Darcy, I might just call upon you to do that. We could use a fan to blow your long hair back and give the illusion of you walking on the beaches and enjoying the cool ocean breezes."

"Oh, so you like my hair long, do you?" Darcy asked.

"I love your hair long and in its natural brown color," he answered.

"Hell, Calvin, the way you paint that picture, I'd model for you," Travis drawled.

"You, my friend, would not look good in my designs." Calvin laughed. "The limousine awaits, my sweethearts." He led the way down the sidewalk. "And Hannah, please don't let this whole ugly mess get you down. Looks like he's been cheating on you for a very long time. That woman had to be six months pregnant, and I'd bet she's not the first one he's screwed around with. Poor thing has no idea what she's getting herself into, and"—he lowered his deep voice—"black is not her color. Lord, honey, she looked like she was going to a funeral."

Liz shivered in spite of the heat. "I hate funerals."

It had been a funeral of sorts. A marriage had died, and as a result there should be a dark cloud somewhere. All she could see in the sky was a bank of pretty white clouds slowly moving northeast. Sophie would call it a lullaby sky. The vision of sitting on the porch swing singing lullabies to her dark-haired daughter put a smile on Hannah's face. Sophie was a ball of fire unless Marty was home. Then she turned into a shy little girl who was afraid of her own shadow. That's when she clung to Hannah and wanted to go outside.

Hannah didn't like the horrible strain in the house on the weekends when Marty came home, so she'd take Sophie out to the porch swing and tell her stories about the clouds and sing lullabies to her. Now when Sophie got a boo-boo on her knee or couldn't sleep she'd ask for "lullaby skies"—puffy clouds and "Twinkle, Twinkle Little Star." Those two things made everything in life all right again.

"What are you thinking about? You look like you are a million miles away," Travis asked.

"The lullaby sky. It and Sophie," she answered with honesty.

"Yes. We can talk about clouds or twinkle stars or anything but funerals," Liz said. "I'm glad school is out. Playground duty in this kind of heat drains me. And besides, Hannah needs the summer to regroup and get settled into being a single mother. Are you really going to remodel your old big house into an inn? I'll miss you at the school."

"The principal, and I mean you, Liz, shouldn't have playground duty. She should sit behind a desk in an air-conditioned office and be dressed like a . . ." Calvin paused and changed the subject. "An inn, huh? Well, now, I might be your first customer when you get it ready to rent out. And are you going to serve food?"

"I've got another idea for my house, but I need to think about it before I say a word," Hannah said, glad for anything to get her mind off the whole courtroom scene.

Liz regained the conversation. "At any school I run, people pull the same duty no matter what the work title is."

Calvin chuckled. "Looks like I kicked a hornet's nest, but I got y'all to thinkin' about something other than that ridiculous settlement."

"It wasn't ridiculous. I got more than what I wanted. I got my name back, and Sophie is now an O'Malley, too. That means more to me than money ever could. And now I can really do anything I want with that hangar and the house," Hannah said.

Darcy kept in step with Hannah. "Why not make it into a wedding chapel? The living room and dining room are big enough to host maybe fifty people, and the bride could come down the stairs. There could even be a bride's room in one of the four bedrooms up there and a groom's room in another."

The biological clock had been ticking very loudly in Darcy's ears this past year. The closer she got to forty, the more everything was about wedding books, wedding cakes, and cute baby names with her. Hannah had told her repeatedly that settling was never better than singledom. Only in Hollywood was thirty-eight considered old.

"What if I thought the groom was another Marty and I talked the bride out of marrying him? Now that would be a fiasco, wouldn't it?" Hannah said.

Single mother? The two words bounced around in Hannah's head.

She'd been that since the day Sophie was born. No, that wasn't right. It went back to the day the ultrasound said Hannah was carrying a baby girl. Two months after the quick courthouse wedding so his parents wouldn't know until it was over—that's the day everything started downhill. Right after that his parents decided that maybe she should move into her grandmother's old house in Crossing. It had been sitting empty for ten years, and after all, the baby would be better growing up in a rural community rather than a penthouse in downtown Dallas.

She'd thought it was wonderful at first, and then in a fit of anger just before Sophie was born, Marty told her that she wasn't and never would be Ellis quality. The whole reason he'd agreed to let her live in her grandmother's house was to keep his life with her and his real life in two separate boxes. She'd cried and told him that she would learn to be a better wife. That maybe it was her fault for having been single for so long. And when he'd thrown the next tantrum she'd cried again.

Looking back, she realized that making her cry was part of his plan. When his verbal abuse didn't produce tears anymore, he'd started grabbing her arm and jerking her around while he whispered threats. When she jerked away from him, the fists came out. He'd reminded her that she could shed tears, but if she made a sound, he'd walk out of the house with Sophie.

In the beginning he came home a couple of nights a week and on weekends, but even before Sophie was born, she hadn't looked forward to seeing those days arrive. Then it became only weekends and then only a couple of weekends a month, and she still didn't miss him when he was gone. The past year, he'd been to Crossing exactly four times, and all four times he'd left her with bruises.

"You were off in la-la land again." Darcy patted her hand and jerked her back to the present. "I'm starving. Call Aunt Birdie and tell her we'll be there in twenty minutes."

"Soon as we get into Calvin's van." Hannah headed around the corner of the courthouse to where Calvin's bright-red rental van was parked.

"Whoa, Miss O'Malley . . ." He pointed at a white limousine sitting at the curb. "I arranged for this to be waiting for us after the hearing. The driver will take us to Crossing and bring me and Darcy back here when we finish dinner. We'll show those sons a bitches that we are not poor white trash."

"But we are," Hannah disagreed. "You can put a hog in a satin ball gown, and it's still a hog."

"Some people don't have the sense to appreciate a good country hog," Calvin teased and then grew serious. "Or a good woman. You deserve a limo, and Marty deserves a bullet. It's against the law for me to do one of those things."

Hannah forced a smile as the driver of the limo opened the door, and Calvin stood to one side to let the ladies enter first. As she looked out the tinted window, she saw Marty Ellis with his parents on one side and his girlfriend on the other getting into a shiny black Caddy. Hannah would be willing to bet that the girlfriend didn't know how to fold a napkin right but that the people she hired to do it for Marty—or James, as she called him—would do a damn fine job.

Travis covered Hannah's eyes with his hands. "Don't look at her."

Liz laid a hand on her knee. "You're better off without a lyin', cheatin' son of a bitch."

And you should know, my friend, Hannah thought. *You are living in the same kind of situation that I was before today. I pray every day that you finally wake up and realize that you need to get away from Wyatt before you have kids with him.*

Calvin crawled into the limo and sat beside Darcy, right across from Hannah, Travis, and Liz. "I hope that woman puts a ring in his nose and leads him around by it. It's okay, honey, it'll come back around and bite him right on the ass. I only hope we all get to see him yelping with pain."

"I'd just as soon never see him again," Hannah said as the limo driver pulled away from the curb and headed out to the highway. She had no urge to look back at Marty, his parents, or his new woman. She wiped a tear of pure relief from her cheek.

"You okay? Please tell me those are tears of joy," Liz said.

"Honest, y'all, I am fine. I'm glad you were with me today. I couldn't have made it without you. And now you can all come to see me in my house, not just visit with me over at Aunt Birdie's."

"That's what friends are for," Calvin said. "But, honey, he will get tired of that hoity-toity redhead and he will go looking for another woman. And as far as coming to see you in your house, well . . ." He stammered.

"It was strange going in there. We were afraid we'd leave a mess and . . ." Liz inhaled deeply. "We knew he was OCD and it made you nervous. We didn't want to add to it. But Cal is right. We're here because we love you."

"Hear, hear!" Darcy raised an imaginary glass.

"Hey, now." Calvin pulled a bottle of expensive champagne from an icy bucket. "Let's use the real stuff to celebrate this glorious day. I'll pour if Darcy will hold the glasses."

Darcy picked up the first flute. "With pleasure, but I have to work this afternoon, so I can only have a little bit."

As Calvin poured, she passed the stemmed glasses to her friends. When he'd finished she held up her glass. "To happiness."

Liz touched hers with Darcy's. "To the beginning of something new and wonderful."

Travis added his glass. "To a beautiful change."

Calvin touched his to the other four. "What Travis said, only double."

Hannah raised hers to clink with the rest of them. "To my amazing friends, who have helped me get through this day."

"Hear, hear!" Darcy said a second time.

Hannah sipped the champagne, but she didn't feel free—not yet—hopefully it would come after the dust settled, as Aunt Birdie said.

Chapter Two

Hannah crawled out of the limo and stepped onto the lush green grass on Aunt Birdie's lawn. Thanks to Travis, the flower beds, the rose bushes, and everything else were kept in pristine condition. He'd also been working on the house. A little paint on the porch railings and repairs here and there—general maintenance, he called it.

Miss Rosie, a short lady almost as round as she was tall, waved from a rocking chair on the front porch. In reality she was Travis's grandmother, but everyone in town had referred to her as Miss Rosie since she was a young Sunday school teacher down at the church. Miss Rosie removed her big pink eyeglasses and cleaned them on the tail of her checkered gingham apron. "Did you get that in the settlement?"

"What?" Hannah asked.

Miss Rosie pointed. "That limo. Did it come in the settlement?"

"No, it did not. I got my twelve-year-old Chevy," Hannah answered. "Sophie?" she asked.

"Is mine and the judge says it's irrevocable." She smiled.

"Then all is good." Miss Rosie nodded. "Birdie is around back with Sophie. She'll be glad that you're home safe and that it's all over."

Hannah bent and gave Miss Rosie a quick hug. "Me, too. I hope I never see him again."

Miss Rosie wrapped her arms around Hannah and held on for an extra few seconds. "We promised your mama we'd watch out for you. We didn't do such a good job. We should've shot that son of a bitch long ago."

Hannah patted her on the back and straightened up. "Then you'd have been hauled off to jail. Neither Sophie nor I would have you here in Crossing."

Miss Rosie stuck a finger up under her glasses and wiped away a tear. "Go on and let Birdie and Sophie know you're home so we can have dinner."

Hannah gave her a brief nod and headed down the steps and around the house. No one could remember when Birdie Wilson didn't live in Crossing, Texas, or when Miss Rosie Johnson didn't live in the little white frame house with a picket fence right beside her. They'd been best friends since they were babies, and the two of them were the very reason that Hannah's mother, Patsy, felt comfortable moving away from the area ten years ago. Aunt Birdie—who was really Hannah's great-aunt on her father's side—and Miss Rosie would watch out for the house Patsy was leaving, and they'd take care of Hannah across the street.

"My backyard or this one?" Hannah asked.

"This one. That baby girl knows something isn't right today, and she's taken her old quilt out there to look at the sky. You know what that means. Sophie's worried. Birdie is telling her stories about the clouds, and then they are going to sing the twinkle star song and everything will be all right."

"Miss Rosie." Calvin tipped his hat.

"Calvin. I'm glad you came back for this. Hannah needs her friends around her. Dirty sumbitch should be shot for what he's caused her and that precious baby. Y'all come right on in and Hannah can go get Birdie and Sophie. Food is on the buffet."

Hannah raced around the house. Aunt Birdie and Sophie were stretched out flat on their backs on an old patchwork quilt Hannah's grandma had made years ago. Hannah leaned against the edge of the house and drank the scene in.

They were staring up at the pretty white clouds in the sky with a shotgun between them. Sophie's dark hair made a halo around her delicate features. She'd always been small, like Hannah's mother, Patsy, but her attitude came from Aunt Birdie.

Hannah had always wished she could be as strong and as outspoken as Aunt Birdie and Miss Rosie. History said that the town had been named Crossing because it had sprung up at a time when folks thought a bridge would be built across the Red River right there. But the people who made those decisions had decided to build the bridge on down the river near Gainesville. The old-timers in Crossing said that getting across the river had nothing to do with the town's name—it had been given that name because everyone knew better than to cross a Wilson or a Johnson.

"Mama!" Sophie squealed when she saw Hannah. "Take off your boots and come lie on the quilt with us. It's almost time to sing."

Hannah sat down on the back porch, removed her boots and socks, and hurried across the grassy lawn. She stretched out beside Sophie and took her daughter's little hand in hers. Tears dammed up behind her eyelids when Sophie squeezed her hand. "I love you, Mama. I missed you today."

"I missed you, too, but I had to take care of some business," Hannah said around the lump in her throat.

No child should have to endure the stress that Sophie had when Marty was home. Someday, somehow, Hannah was going to help other women who had lived in fear, but right now the time with her daughter was what was important and precious. She pointed to the clouds. "That one is an angel, right?"

"No, Mama!" Sophie laughed. "That is Cinderella's coach."

"Is it all done?" Aunt Birdie whispered.

"Yes," Hannah said.

"Good. I wasn't lookin' forward to jail, but I'm old and that sumbitch wasn't takin' Sophie," Aunt Birdie said.

"So that thing is loaded?" Hannah gasped.

"You bet your sweet ass it is. Rosie's got a pistol in her apron pocket, too. If that sorry scoundrel got past her, then I'd take him out with old Betsy here." She patted the shotgun like it was a child. "Everyone in the house and ready for dinner?"

"Dinner!" Sophie was a blur as she went from lying on her back to standing in a flash. "Aunt Birdie made roast beef and she let me help her cook pies. I got to poke holes in the crusts. Where is Aunt Liz and Darcy and Calvin and Travis? We can sing another time. This is a good day, Mama." She started off in a run, like most kids who are eager to get somewhere fast. Her pink shorts and tie-dyed T-shirt reminded Hannah of a rainbow as she disappeared around the house.

"You could go in the back door," Hannah called after her, but it was too late.

"So?" Aunt Birdie rolled to one side and eased her way to a sitting position. A tiny, wiry woman, aptly named, she wouldn't tip the scales at a hundred pounds with rocks in her pockets. Her short, kinky gray hair looked a lot like a poodle's just before it went to the groomers.

"I signed the papers as they were. I didn't fight him or ask for anything other than what he was willing to give."

"For Sophie?" Her dark eyes narrowed amid a bed of wrinkles.

"I would have given up the property, the car, and the child support for him to let me have all rights to her, but he sat there like a king on a throne and thought he was taking everything from me. It's all just stuff except for Sophie."

Aunt Birdie picked up the gun. "Me and this could have made sure there were no rights to have. But I want to know how you are."

Hannah stood and extended a hand to Aunt Birdie. "My insides are still in a jitter. I keep thinkin' I'll wake up from this dream and it will be a day when he's coming home. I got my maiden name back and the right to give it to Sophie. Or keep it if I marry again." Hannah shuddered. "Which I will never do, but if I did, the new husband could adopt her and Marty would have nothing to say or do about it. I can have her birth certificate amended to remove Marty's name as soon as I get the finalized divorce papers in the mail next week."

Aunt Birdie put her veined hand into Hannah's and groaned on her way up. "Takes a lot to haul an eighty-year-old woman from ground to upright. Hannah, this was never Marty's home. It was just a place he came once in a while because he had to. Leave this quilt. It's not supposed to rain, and you know she'll be back out here on it after we eat."

Travis came out the back door and crossed the yard in long strides. "I've been sent by the royal princess to request that y'all come on to dinner. She refuses to eat until you arrive."

Aunt Birdie laughed. "That's my Sophie."

"What the . . ." Travis picked up the shotgun and ejected both shells. "Aunt Birdie, you brought a loaded gun over here with that baby?"

"She'll be six years old in a few weeks. And there ain't a way in hell I can kill a man with an unloaded gun. I don't have the strength to beat him to death with the butt," Aunt Birdie fussed.

"Lord!" He rolled his eyes upward.

"*You* probably can't kill him with an unloaded gun, either," Aunt Birdie said.

"Raising two old women is worse than raising kids," he murmured.

"Nothing wrong with my ears, and you ain't never raised a kid. Clock's tickin' on that, too," Aunt Birdie scolded.

"Mama, Mama!" Sophie bailed off the porch, hit the ground running, and threw herself into Hannah's arms. "Did you see the princess car? Uncle Cal says I can ride in it later if it's okay with you. Please, Mama, please!"

Hannah sank her face into Sophie's wild mane of curly black hair and inhaled deeply. Her daughter smelled like hot summer, green apple shampoo, giggles, and innocence, all mixed together in a wiggly five-year-old little girl. Never again would she have to retreat into a clingy little girl filled with fear. She could always be that wild, rambunctious child who loved life. Maybe someday she wouldn't even remember Marty or the angst he brought with him when he walked through the back door.

"Well? Can I go in the big car with Uncle Calvin?" Sophie asked.

"Of course you can."

"Good." Sophie giggled and wiggled free of her mother's arms.

Hannah followed Sophie through the front door and into the living room. The little girl skipped across the room, through the arch, and into the dining room. She loved the swinging doors separating the dining room from the kitchen and made two trips back and forth through them before she slipped her small hand into Hannah's and held on tightly.

"Is there someone still out there in that big car?" Aunt Birdie asked.

"The driver is waiting to take Cal and Darcy back to Gainesville," Travis answered.

"Well, you go invite him in to dinner. It's noon, and he's got to be hungry," Aunt Birdie said.

Calvin picked Sophie up and carried her to the dining room. "The driver brought his lunch. It's against the limo policy for him to eat with us."

"Why didn't you drive the car, Uncle Cal?" Sophie asked.

"Did Cinderella drive her coach?"

"No, silly." Sophie giggled.

"So you like my new car?" Cal asked.

"It's 'tentious," Sophie said seriously as she wiggled free from his arms and raced into the kitchen. "But to be a princess you got to be a little bit 'tentious."

"Pretentious," Aunt Birdie said. "That's our word for today, and that policy should be changed. Come on now. The roast will be getting cold." Travis held the door for the ladies, and Calvin stepped back to the side.

"And what does *pretentious* mean, Sophie?" Liz asked.

"It means 'puttin' on airs.' Aunt Birdie told me all about that this mornin'," Sophie said.

"That's right," Darcy said. "But today we needed to put on some airs. After we eat, the driver is taking Calvin and Darcy back to town, but not before he lets you ride around Crossing in it."

"Why do we need to put on airs today? Is this a special day? I set the table all by myself." Sophie pushed her way past everyone and was first in the kitchen. "Look, Mama, at the table. Aunt Birdie says I did it perfect."

"Of course you did." Calvin winked at Hannah.

A moment of panic struck Hannah. The napkins, straight from the roll of paper towels, were folded haphazardly. The knife blades weren't facing the plate on a couple of settings, and all but one tea glass was on the wrong side. She took a deep breath and forced herself to relax. It was going to take a lot more than signing her name to a thick document to get Marty out of her life.

"It looks beautiful," Hannah said.

Sophie beamed. "It's my first time and I wanted it to be pretty for all y'all today."

"I declare this table fit for a queen," Darcy said.

"I love pot roast. There's not a restaurant in New York that can make it like yours, Aunt Birdie," Calvin said.

"It's just dinner, but it's gettin' cold and there ain't nothing in the world worse than cold carrots. Let me bless the food and y'all best get on to eatin'. Sophie has been starving nigh unto death for half an hour." Birdie stopped talking to them, bowed her head, and started talking to God in the next instant. "Father, bless this food and thank you for this day. I know that you say that vengeance is yours and your time ain't like our time, but I'd be much obliged if I could see a little of that vengeance before my last breath. If not, we'll discuss it when I get there. Amen."

"What is vengeance?" Sophie asked.

"That's our word for another day. For now, let's get into this dinner," Aunt Birdie said.

Liz watched the clock during the meal, getting more jittery when it passed twelve thirty. Hannah recognized that scared-bunny look all too well and wished that Liz would open up to her about what was going on between her and her husband, Wyatt. Hannah knew everything that Liz would say and at least some of what she was likely going through, but until she admitted she had a problem, there was no way Hannah could help her.

Darcy kept a running conversation going with Sophie about food and the fact that Sophie would be in kindergarten when school started. Calvin never talked much when good food was in front of him, but several times he caught Hannah's eye and winked.

"Thank you, Aunt Birdie, for doing this," Hannah said.

"Wasn't nothing." She waved it away with a flick of her bony wrist. "I like to cook, and every now and then it's fun for me and Rosie to have a big crowd around the table. Besides, Travis helped me get it all ready. He's every bit as good in the kitchen as he is with a hammer and screwdriver, if you can get his nose out of a book."

Birdie's salt-and-pepper hair had once been jet-black. She liked to brag that she was a quarter Native American and descended from the Seminole tribe in central Oklahoma, but Hannah figured it wasn't one of the Five Civilized Tribes that Aunt Birdie sprang from but one of the warring tribes—maybe Apache or Comanche. Like those fierce Native Americans, she'd always had a fight in her, and getting older hadn't diminished it one single bit. Hannah had no doubt Aunt Birdie and Miss Rosie would wade into a forest fire with a cup of water and put the damn thing out. Hannah had often wished she'd gotten more of her great-aunt's and neighbor's spunk and a lot less of her father's shy nature.

"So what's on everyone's agenda this week?" Hannah asked.

"First week out of school, there's no school for me. I do have to go in a few hours a day after this week, but my secretary will man the phones for July. This week I'm deep cleaning the house." Liz glanced at the clock again. "Speaking of that. I hate to eat and run, but Wyatt will be home in about half an hour and I should be there."

Wyatt Pope was a long-distance truck driver, and most of the time he was on the road a week at a time and then home for a few days. But if he was coming through Dallas, he often made a detour up through Crossing and spent a night at home.

"Take him a plate. There's lots of leftovers," Birdie said.

"Thank you." Liz smiled. "That is so sweet. I'd love to. Mind if I take both kinds of dessert? He does love his sweets."

"Of course you can have both kinds of pies. That way he can have a night snack, too," Birdie answered.

"I should be going," Darcy said. "I promised I'd be back by one thirty so the tellers wouldn't have to rearrange their lunch schedule. I'll be back over the weekend, Hannah. Thanks for the dinner. I'm not taking a plate or they'll all converge upon me like flies on honey." She planted a kiss on Birdie's forehead.

"Flies on honey?" Sophie's little forehead wrinkled.

"Flies like sweet things. I'm surprised you aren't covered up in them," Calvin said quickly. "Turn that frown upside down into a smile."

Sophie looked around the room. "I don't see any flies. I must not be sweet as you think. Daddy said I was just like my mama. He didn't think we were sweet."

Calvin laid his paper towel napkin to the side and pushed back his chair. "Your daddy won't be coming around anymore, honey."

"Promise?" Sophie's dark eyes grew bigger and bigger. "For real. He's not going to make Mama—" She tapped her finger against her head.

"Jittery?" Darcy asked.

"Crazy." Travis grinned.

"That's it. Crazy. Daddy made Mama crazy, and the only thing that I could do to make her happy was take her out on the porch and let her tell me stories about the clouds, and then we would sing 'Twinkle, Twinkle.' We call those kind of days 'lullaby sky,'" Sophie said seriously. "Mama, can we still go see our lullaby sky when I get a boo-boo?"

"Of course we can," Hannah said. "But maybe you should start telling me stories."

"I'm a big girl now. I can do that," Sophie said with a stoic sigh.

Calvin hugged Sophie. "Yes, you are a big girl. And since I'm riding back in the limo with Darcy, I should be going, too. Thanks for dinner, Aunt Birdie. I'll return from New York City in a couple of weeks, Hannah, but I'll call you every chance I get. However, before we leave Crossing, the princess here has a ride coming in the limo. Come on, Sophie O'Malley."

"I'm not Sophie O'Malley. I am Sophie Ellis," she protested.

"Would you like to be Sophie O'Malley?" Hannah held her breath.

"Your mama has changed her name to Hannah O'Malley," Aunt Birdie said.

"Well, then I want to be Sophie O'Malley, because I want to be just like my mama. But it does sound funny, Uncle Cal." Sophie giggled. "I like it, though. Even better than I like Sophie Ellis."

Hannah followed them all out to the porch. "I cannot thank all y'all enough for today."

"You'd be there for us in the same situation," Calvin said. "Let me know if you or Sophie need anything. I mean it. Money, food, a few days away from Crossing, shotgun shells."

Hannah air-slapped his arm. "You are totally badass."

"I know." He laughed. "Wait right here and I'll send Princess Sophie back to you in about five minutes."

For the first time since she got into the van with her friends that morning to go to the courthouse, she was alone. She stared at her house across the street. Would she feel different when she walked into it in a few minutes? Would the stress that lurked in every corner be gone? Could it ever return to the happy place that she'd visited as a child when her grandmother O'Malley lived there?

It looked the same as it had that morning when she walked out of it—a rambling old house that had been built decades ago and still had the wallpaper in the six upstairs bedrooms to testify to its age. A big, square house built for a big family, opening up into a huge living room with an archway into a formal dining room and a kitchen beyond that. The other side of the ground floor held the master bedroom and Sophie's bedroom right beside it.

The master bedroom had the best king-size bed that money could buy, along with furniture Hannah absolutely hated, but she only used the room when Marty was home. Most of the time, Hannah slept in one of the bedrooms upstairs.

She'd paid for her marriage to Marty in nerves, nausea, and migraines. She wrapped her arms around her body and shivered—never again would she have to worry about him arriving unexpectedly and finding things out of order. Never would she have to send Sophie outside to play so she wouldn't witness his wicked temper.

"It really is over," she whispered. "So why don't I feel like it is?"

"Because it'll take time," Travis whispered.

Startled, she jumped and shivered. "I'm sorry. I didn't hear you come out of the house."

"It's okay, Hannah. You never have to apologize to me." He smiled.

The limo came to a slow stop in front of the house, and Sophie shot out the door and jumped into her mother's arms for the second—or was it the third?—time that day. She wrapped her legs around Hannah's waist and hugged her, planting dozens of kisses on her face.

"I liked the 'tentious car, Mama, but it's too big for us. I like our car and Travis's truck and Aunt Birdie's van better than the big princess car." She leaned back and looked Hannah right in the eye. "Did I really get a new name today or was you teasin' me?"

"You really did. So did I. We are now Hannah and Sophie O'Malley," Hannah answered.

"Sophie O'Malley," Sophie whispered. "I like it. Do you like it, Travis?"

"Oh, yes, I do. It sounds just like a princess name."

"Sophie O'Malley, princess of Aunt Birdie's castle and queen of Hannah O'Malley's house." Sophie's pecan-colored eyes danced with merriment.

"Oh, no, you don't, young lady," Hannah said. "You might be princess of Aunt Birdie's house and mine, but I'm the queen and don't you forget it."

Sophie hopped down and ran into the house, no doubt to tell Aunt Birdie all about the limo. Travis kept his distance, but his eyes locked with Hannah's.

"What?" She wiped her cheek. "Do I have chocolate pie on my face?"

"No, I was thinkin' maybe *you* shouldn't forget it," Travis said.

"Forget what?"

"Who's queen of your house," he said.

"Are you saying that I spoil Sophie too much?" Hannah asked.

"No, I'm saying that you've been spoiled too little, Hannah O'Malley." He grinned.

Chapter Three

Friday afternoon Hannah stood in the doorway of Sophie's bedroom, her eyes instinctively scanning the room to be sure everything was in place. Barbie dolls put away in the old suitcase that had belonged to Hannah's mother when she was a child. Books arranged from tallest to shortest with all the spines the right way so that the titles were upright. She noticed a wrinkle in the bedspread and a throw pillow that was slightly off kilter and quickly crossed the room to fix both. She'd smoothed out the wrinkle and rearranged the pillows when it dawned on her that Marty would not fly that little airplane of his to Crossing—not ever again.

She sat down on the edge of the bed and remembered the day Marty had taken her to meet his parents. It was a few days after their courthouse marriage, that spring before Sophie was born in July. A disaster from day one. She wasn't a total country bumpkin, and she'd been taught table manners, but the way their noses twitched when she sat down at the restaurant with them—well, it looked as if they'd stepped in fresh cow crap out in the pasture.

Marty wanted to live in the city. Hannah wanted to move into her grandmother's house in Crossing, which had been deeded to her when her father died. Marty said he needed to be near his job and his life was in Dallas, but they would compromise—she could live in Crossing and raise the baby in a rural community. He would build a hangar and a small landing strip on the back of the property for his little private plane, and he would fly in and out on weekends and whenever he could get away through the week.

Then he talked her into putting the title to the place in his name. For the baby's sake, he'd said, and she signed the papers without even thinking about it. Then he had even more than Sophie to hold over her head. He could take her child and her familial home. He could leave her with nothing but the old car that she'd been driving when he married her and what clothing was on her back at the time. Her substitute teaching and waitress gigs had not given her much of a financial foundation.

The front door opened, and Hannah jumped up, straightened the bedspread, and scanned the room for anything that might be out of place. She took a deep breath and tried to remember if there was more than one book on the coffee table and if it was centered properly. She and Sophie had had ice cream for a midafternoon snack, and she'd left the dirty dishes in the sink.

"Hey, where are you? I've got a terrific idea for our first weekend project," Darcy yelled from the living room as she arrived.

Hannah exhaled slowly and braced a hand on the wall for a second before she put a smile on her face and headed for the living room. It was only Darcy, not Marty. *He was not coming back, not ever,* she thought with each step.

Darcy had kicked her shoes off in the middle of the floor, left her suitcase beside the sofa, and thrown herself back in the recliner. "I need sweet tea," she said as she popped the chair into a sitting position. "I'll make us both a glass. You got fresh lemons, right?"

"Always." Hannah's hands itched to pick up Darcy's high heels and carry them up to a guest bedroom. "What's this big idea of yours, anyway?"

Darcy hopped up out of the chair and followed Hannah into the kitchen. She removed a gallon jug of tea from the refrigerator, set it on the cabinet, filled two glasses with ice, and carefully poured them full. Hannah rolled a lemon on the cabinet until it was soft, sliced it into wedges, added two to each glass, and put the rest into a bowl for later use.

"Sophie has ratted you out, girlfriend." She set them on the table. "I know that you sleep in the guest room and that neither of you go into the master bedroom except when I'm here. So we're going to clean out that room and paint it tonight. Then tomorrow we'll go to town and get a new bedroom outfit and whatever else you need to redo it." She pulled out a chair, sat down, and propped her feet in another one. "Give me time to drink this and we'll get started. Travis is bringing his truck over to take all that furniture down to the hangar to store until you decide what to do with it."

"And the paint?"

"It's pale blue, like your room when you were a teenager. I picked it up after work, and yes, I remembered two rollers and the brushes and the whole nine yards. Travis doesn't know it, but he's going to do the part up close to the ceiling."

"Aunt Darcy!" Sophie ran into the room from the back door. "Travis said he's moving stuff for Mama today. What is it?"

"We're going to redo my old bedroom." Hannah smiled. "Darcy thinks it should be pale blue."

"Me, too. I wish we had one of them windows in the ceiling but we can 'tend, can't we?"

Hannah opened her arms, and Sophie walked into them. "Yes, we can pretend. We'll curl up in my new bed and pretend that there's a window up there and we can see the clouds. We'll even sing."

Her child smelled like a sweaty five-year-old who'd been playing tag with an imaginary friend in the backyard. Another split second of panic set in—Sophie's face was not clean and her hair not brushed out, plus the tea glasses were sweating onto the tablecloth. *Oh. Sweet. Jesus.* Darcy was there—Marty hated Darcy more than any of her friends.

"What?" Darcy asked. "You went pale as a ghost."

"How pale is a ghost, Aunt Darcy?"

"They're white like bedsheets." Darcy laughed.

"My sheets are pink, but Mama's are red silky stuff in Father's room. Upstairs in her other room, they're white. Aunt Birdie has white sheets and I like the way they smell." Sophie wiggled free of her mother's embrace. "I'm going back outside. Nadine is waiting for me."

"Want to explain all that?" Darcy asked.

"Sophie's sheets are pink. Those in the master bedroom, the ones I only slept in when Marty was home, are red satin. But I really like plain old white cotton sheets, so that's what I use in my bedroom, which is upstairs."

"Now it makes sense. And what happened to Anna Lou? She didn't quite fill me in," Darcy said.

"She has the bumps so she can't come out and play today. Nadine is playing with me," Sophie said as she ran out the back door, yelling to the imaginary Nadine that she was back and ready to play chase.

"Nadine? Bumps?" Darcy asked Hannah.

"Mumps. She saw something on one of her cartoon shows about the mumps and instantly Anna Lou had them. I had to tell her ten times last night that she'd had shots for mumps when she was just a baby so she probably wouldn't get them. Nadine was the little girl on the show who was the next-door neighbor," Hannah explained.

"You've done well with her," Darcy said. "You almost had a panic attack there. Was it because you forgot that Marty was gone and thought since this is Friday he might be flying in?"

Hannah nodded. "Exactly. Please tell me that her imaginary friends aren't something that will show up later in the form of OCD or temper fits?"

Darcy giggled. "She's got Marty's DNA, but honey, she's also got yours, and environment plays a big part in every person's life. How have you been these past couple of days? Has it become real that it's over?"

Hannah slowly shook her head. "Aunt Birdie said this antsy feeling inside me took six years to build and I shouldn't expect it to leave in three days."

"I hate him for what he did to you. We all thought it was mental abuse. Was there more? Did he hit you? Please tell me he never laid a hand on Sophie." Darcy looked as if she could break into tears.

Hannah reached across the table and laid a hand on Darcy's. "I sent Sophie to the backyard or the porch or even to Aunt Birdie's when he got mad. He didn't know much about being a father, because he always had a nanny and his dad was too busy to pay much attention to him." Hannah's words came out slowly.

"He did beat you, didn't he? Just like we think Wyatt slaps Liz around. God, I'm going to rethink ever trusting a man."

Hannah sipped her tea. "He could get very angry, and he left bruises more than once. If I hadn't been such a country bumpkin . . ." She hesitated. "It's in the past. Let's leave it there. At least there were no broken bones and he never laid a hand on Sophie."

"Aunt Birdie is right about it taking time, but why didn't you tell me he was doing more than yelling and threatening?" Darcy frowned.

"It wasn't your burden to carry. I made the mistake of trusting him, of getting pregnant, and of marrying him. And he wasn't always physically violent. Most of the time it *was* mental abuse. I couldn't ever do anything right. But now it's in the past. Now, tell me more about what you've got in mind for my room. Do I get a say-so?" Hannah removed her hand and picked up her glass of tea.

"Of course you do. I picked out the paint, and I'm supplying part of the elbow grease. Liz will be here in about half an hour, and Travis said he'll be here when you get your underwear drawers cleaned out. He doesn't want to embarrass you." Darcy grinned. "Like at thirty-eight, he's never seen a women's underbritches!" She giggled. "So let's take this tea to your room, strip down the bed, and then start packing all your dresser drawers into boxes. We'll move them into the dining room for tonight, and by tomorrow night, the room won't look the same." Darcy squeezed her arm gently. "I'm your friend, Hannah O'Malley—we share burdens as well as joys. And now I'm going to put on my paintin' clothes and you should do the same."

"Thank you." Hannah swallowed hard, but the lump in her throat didn't budge very much. "I'll do that after we get the drawers emptied and the room ready to paint. Am I really going to put perfectly good furniture in storage and buy new? It sounds extravagant."

Darcy moved from kitchen to living room. "Yes, you are. Anything in this house that was Marty's or reminds you of him, we'll throw away, give away, sell. It doesn't matter. You need a fresh start."

Darcy set her tea on the coffee table, threw her suitcase onto a chair in the corner, and unzipped it. She'd been wearing a cute little jacket, a straight skirt, and a silk shell. It all came off in a blur and landed on the recliner in a pile. She dug around in the messy suitcase and brought out a pair of paint-stained jean shorts and a button-up shirt with ragged arm holes where the sleeves had been cut out.

Hannah followed her from one room to the other and tensed at the mess. "Want me to take your things up to one of the bedrooms while you change?"

"They're okay here until we get done with cleaning out your room. I'll tote them up there, then. I'm surprised that you sleep upstairs, as protective as you are," Darcy answered as she wrapped a stretchy hot-pink headband around her hair.

"I still have a baby monitor in her room. I know when she rolls over in bed," Hannah answered.

"Well, okay then. Let's go reclaim your property."

Hannah led the way across the foyer, took a deep breath, and opened the bedroom door. Flashbacks stopped her right inside the door. This was where Marty had beaten her down with his words and sometimes his fists. Either way, it was always her fault. If she hadn't folded the napkins wrong, if Sophie's toy hadn't been left on the coffee table, if she'd been raised in the right circles, if he'd only known that she was nothing but low-class white trash—then she would understand what he needed in a wife and she wouldn't be living in the backwoods where he had to train her even to be able to take her to a Christmas party.

Darcy went straight to the shiny black dresser with nine drawers and pulled out the bottom one on the right side. Carrying it to the bed, she gasped. "Sweet Lord! Do they all look this neat?"

Hannah nodded. "I told you that Marty is OCD."

"This goes beyond OCD, Hannah. Did you iron these socks?" Darcy dumped the whole drawer on the bed.

Hannah blushed and took a deep breath. "What should I do with all of his things?"

"You own them. The judge said everything in this house. What do you think? A bonfire?"

"No!" Hannah said quickly. "If we did that, Sophie would want to roast marshmallows."

"And I damn sure don't want her to eat anything that comes from the flames from this stuff," Darcy said. "It might poison the child. I vote we put all of his stuff in a big black garbage bag and store it with the furniture."

The idea came to Hannah in the form of a picture of a sign outside a women's shelter in Gainesville. She'd made it to that shelter once, but Marty had figured out where she was within five minutes of the time she walked through the doors. Why not donate all of this stuff to that shelter that helped abused women? They could sell whatever they couldn't use and keep the money. She whipped her phone from her hip pocket and clicked on the phone number highlighted on their website.

"Patchwork Home. Gina speaking," a brisk voice answered.

"This is Hannah O'Malley. I came to your place a while back, but only stayed about five minutes. I live in Crossing, and I've got some things I would like to donate."

"I remember you. You are kin to Birdie Wilson, right?"

"Yes, ma'am."

"And you had a little dark-haired girl with you?"

"Yes, that's right."

"Did you resolve that abuse issue?"

"Divorce was signed on Wednesday."

"Good for you. Now, about this stuff you want to donate?"

Hannah sat down on the edge of the bed. "A complete bedroom suite, sheets, comforters. How much can you handle? And what about men's clothing?"

"All of it, and we'll be glad to get it. Sometimes women show up here with teenage boys in tow, and we seldom have anything that they can wear."

Darcy sat down beside her, picking up the tail of the conversation. "Great idea."

"My ex-husband wasn't a very big man, so these things should work for a teenage boy. Socks and underwear?" she asked.

"Honey, sometimes they arrive in nothing but their pajama pants, and even barefoot if their mama has left in a hurry. I can round up some volunteers to come and get it," Gina said.

"No, we'll bring it to you. Is tonight all right?"

"Of course. I've got two volunteers here now who'll help unload and then get the clothing organized," Gina said. "I'll be expecting you."

"I never knew that you went to the shelter," Darcy said after Hannah hung up.

"I tried, but he figured out where I was." Hannah stood up, threw open the closet doors, and tossed three expensive suits on the bed. "This stuff needs to be gone, not just stored, and I'm glad that I can donate it to the shelter."

"Hey." Travis rapped on the doorjamb. "Sophie said it was all right for me to come in through the back door."

Hannah reminded herself to breathe. Long, deep breaths. That would still her racing heart. No one had sneaked up on her in a long time. She'd had to be vigilant to live with Marty, especially the last two years.

"Sure it is, but what in the devil would a battered-women's shelter want with men's T-shirts? They are ironed and ready for use, folded even neater than they were the day they were bought." Darcy held one up. "And probably the best that money can buy."

"Gina, the lady who runs the Patchwork House, says that the abused women don't always arrive alone. Same way I did. Sometimes they bring teenage boys with them, and ninety percent of the time, they only have the clothes on their backs."

"Then you are giving all this to the women's shelter?" Travis asked. "Furniture, too? Hannah, it's only been a couple of days, and this is very nice furniture. Don't do anything that you'll regret later. You could sell this stuff and make a few dollars."

"Like Darcy said, if it's in this house, it belongs to me, and believe me, there will be no regrets. And this is what I want to do with it—all of it," Hannah said with conviction.

"Holy smoke, Hannah, you weren't kiddin'," Darcy exclaimed when she opened the next drawer. "You really did iron his underwear."

"By choice?" Travis asked.

"For survival," Hannah whispered as she headed to the kitchen. She took a moment to rein in her thoughts. Pure fire would pour from Marty's eyes and steam from his ears if he knew all his clothing was going to be stuffed into a garbage bag and sent to a battered-women's shelter.

He hated women's shelters. She'd had the bruises to prove it, because when he came home the weekend after she'd tried to leave, he'd made sure she understood that was the last chance she'd ever get to try to run away with Sophie again. Next time he would take the child and she'd never see her again.

But there had been no next time, because Hannah was terrified of losing Sophie. She peeled off two garbage bags—one for the things in the dresser drawers, another for the things in the closet. She smiled at the poetic justice of sending it all to the women's shelter. Everything that had been Marty's. That's what Darcy had said. The shelter could have that damned leather recliner in the living room and the table beside it and the lamp, too. That had been Marty's, and no one had better sit in it or move that lamp a fraction of an inch. When she dusted Hannah used a tape measure to be sure it was put back exactly where he liked it.

"You might need to hook up that trailer that you cart around your lawn mower on when you take it down to the church to take care of the landscaping," she said as she shook out a plastic bag, picked up a fistful of snowy-white T-shirts, and tossed them inside. When that was done, she started on the underwear and then the silk pajama pants and the matching robes. By the time she put the last pair of socks into the bag, there was barely enough room to tie it shut.

"Now what?" Darcy asked.

"There are two drawers of my things. Dump them on the sofa in the living room and I'll take care of them after a while," Hannah said, amazed at how much lighter her heart felt already. She picked up the second bag and shook it open. "Next is all the clothing he left behind and his shoes. Travis, you might want to hitch up the trailer."

"Yes, ma'am." He grinned. "I'll back it up to the front door and start taking things out of here soon as you're ready."

"This stuff is pretty heavy. You'll need some help," Hannah said.

"Aunt Birdie has a furniture dolly out in her storage shed. I used it when I moved my stuff into the house last year. Everyone in town borrows the thing when they move. See y'all in a few minutes."

Sophie came bouncing down the hall, singing "I'll Fly Away" so loud that it echoed all through the house. She made up words that she didn't know and the new lyrics said that she would fly away, oh, glory, if Jesus would just send her some wings.

Hannah giggled.

Darcy laughed out loud.

Travis picked up Sophie and swung her around until she squealed.

When her feet were on the ground, she ran to Hannah's side, her eyes darting around the room. "Mama," she whispered. "Father will be so mad."

"Your father said that he doesn't want any of this stuff," Hannah said. She didn't say that Sophie's father—not her daddy by any means—didn't want either of them, either.

Travis hurried across the room, picked Sophie up, and tossed her onto the bed. "It's a trampoline! See how high you can jump."

Hannah nodded. "It's okay. Your father isn't ever coming back here again, so we don't have to worry about him getting angry. So bounce away, because this bed will be gone in an hour."

Sophie bent her knees and jumped several times before she fell backward on the bed. "I didn't think you meant it when you said you were fixin' the room all over. Why isn't he comin' back?"

"Because we got a divorce and he let us have a new name, remember?" Hannah answered.

"What's a divorce?" Sophie asked.

"It's when a man and his wife decide they can't live together anymore." Hannah struggled to keep it as simple as possible.

"And the judge in the court signs a paper and they aren't married anymore," Darcy said to help her out.

"Then I like a divorce. Can that be our word for today?" She pointed toward the air-conditioning vent at the top of the wall. "What is that, Mama?"

"It's where the cold air comes out in the summertime and the warm air comes out in the winter," Hannah said.

Sophie continued to point. "No, not that. You got a spider eye, too. I wonder if there's one at Aunt Birdie's house."

"What?" Hannah asked.

"Lie down right here with me and you can see it. It's little bitty and it's red like a little spider eye."

"Why didn't you tell me that you'd found a spider eye in your ceiling?" Hannah asked. *Who knew when the exterminator could get out here?*

"I thought it was like the thing in the living room that you turn on to get cold air or hot air. Or"—Sophie giggled—"it was really like Charlotte in the book you read to me. Oh, I forgot to tell Nadine about Charlotte and her web. I got to go tell her." Sophie bounded off the bed and down the hall.

Darcy followed her and returned with a kitchen chair and a dinner knife. "If that's what I think it is, Marty should be shot."

Hannah covered her face with her hands. "Please tell me it's insects and not a camera. I feel violated even though . . . oh . . . my . . . God." She felt the fire glowing in her cheeks. He'd filmed the abuse so he could watch it over and over again.

Darcy crawled up on the chair and undid the screws. "It's a nanny cam. Why would he do this?"

Hannah went straight to the third step in the grief cycle that she'd read about concerning divorcing an abusive husband. Anger, as hot as a Texas wildfire, raged from her toes to the ends of her jet-black hair. "Hand it down to me, Darcy. And let's go see how many more are in the house."

"I'll take it to the bank with me on Monday and put everything we find in my safe deposit box. You're already listed as the only other person who can open it if something happens to me, so if you ever need them for proof of anything . . ." She paused and handed the tiny camera down to Hannah. "I promise I won't look at what's on there. Since he hasn't been home in months, it's probably run out anyway. Besides, if there's footage of him hitting you, I'd be tempted to kill the bastard."

There was one in Sophie's bedroom and one in the living room aimed right at his recliner. None in the kitchen or the bathroom.

"I guess he was only making sure his possessions were where he could check up on them," Darcy said through clenched teeth.

Hannah immediately began checking under lamps and in the corners of the cabinets. "What if he's bugged other places in the house?"

Darcy slipped all three cameras into a zippered compartment of her suitcase. "I'll help you. Mostly those things are hidden and they have a live feed into something . . . and here's a little something different." She'd removed the back of the telephone, and there another electronic device blinked away. She held it up to her mouth and whispered, "Hello, Marty! This is Darcy and we have your nanny cams. I'd say that they have enough evidence on them that you'd best keep your sorry ass in Dallas, or else there'll be a stink attached to the Ellis name that folks will smell all across the country."

The blinking light went off immediately.

"Now, it's just a matter of finding the rest of them. Probably one in each room," Darcy said as she unzipped the suitcase and added the little thing, along with its spindly wires, to the stash.

"Here's the second one." Hannah found one in the kitchen phone.

"Did you have a phone in the bedroom?"

Hannah nodded. "He insisted on one in Sophie's room and in all the bedrooms upstairs, supposedly to be there when his parents came to visit, which they never did. The only place there isn't one is in the master bathroom." Hannah shivered from her head to her toes. "I'm buying new phones tomorrow and having my number changed on Monday. And a new cell phone, too," she said. "Oh, Darcy, what would have happened if I'd ever talked about him in this house?"

"The good Lord was protecting you for sure."

"I was so embarrassed that I'd let myself fall into that hornet's nest. The only people that knew nearly everything were Aunt Birdie and my mama. Thank God, I always talked to Mama at her house and not this one," she said.

"Why didn't you call her from here?" Darcy asked.

"When Liz and I shared an apartment in Gainesville, I always talked to Mama on Monday night right after supper. It was our time, and we enjoyed catching up on everything then. After Marty and I married and I moved back here, it was just easier to call Mama over at Aunt Birdie's. She held the baby and let me have an hour to visit. Then it got to be habit, I guess. I'm convinced today that it was guardian angels watching over me. I said things to her that if Marty had heard, he would have killed me for telling anyone," Hannah answered.

"Thank God that you never had an affair or we'd have never found your body. This is horrible, Hannah."

"What's horrible?" Travis asked as he and Sophie came into the room from the front porch. "Trailer is ready. What goes first? Sorry I took so long, but with what all y'all have to move out of here I decided to bring the work truck."

"That recliner, table, and lamp." Hannah pointed.

"I bet the shelter will be glad to get it even if Marty's sorry old ass has sat in it. We'll tell them to wipe it down with bleach before they let anyone else use it." Darcy winked at Travis and mouthed, "Later."

Hannah eased down onto the sofa. Would it ever be completely over and done with? She wanted to be angry, to recapture that moment when it had washed over her in the bedroom when she'd discovered the nanny cam. But all she felt was disgust and emptiness.

Travis sat down beside her. "You okay?"

"I will be, and getting rid of all this stuff will help tremendously."

He jumped up and nodded. "Then let's get this crap out of here. We'll slide this dolly right up under the back side of the chair, rope it down, and roll it right out there onto the trailer, then up into the truck bed," Travis said as he worked. "Table and lamp will fit into the backseat along with those garbage bags. Is the dresser ready to go after that?"

"Yes, it is. Just tell us what to do to help. Lord, I wish I could do more for women who are still suffering like I did," she said.

You can. The voice in her head sounded a lot like her grandmother's. *There are four bedrooms upstairs that will be sitting empty. Use them to help those women. Call the shelter and offer your services.*

Hannah picked up her cell phone and then threw it back down on the sofa. "I need to make a phone call."

Darcy put a finger to her lips and whispered. "Just to be on the safe side, I'd take it out to the yard."

Hannah carried it out into the middle of the road separating her house and Aunt Birdie's and called the phone number to the Patchwork House.

"Hello," Gina answered.

"This is Hannah O'Malley again. I have four bedrooms upstairs that I would like to offer to you to use if you run out of room, or however else you'd like to use them. Overnight. Hideaways for abused women. I want to help other women who are going through what I did. I will convert one into a living room for my guests so that they won't feel so cooped up, because I do know they aren't supposed to be outside a lot when they are in a shelter," Hannah said.

"There would need to be home visits, and we'd have to do paperwork to vet you, since we get state aid."

"Then get it started. I have a good friend and neighbor who would be glad to serve as a bodyguard when there are guests in my house."

"Thank you, Hannah. This idea could be therapeutic for you and for the women. But even a bodyguard wouldn't keep the women from being at risk. Let's give it a few days, and I'll come over to your place and we'll talk about it then."

Hannah sat down on the grass and stared up at the big, round moon, hanging in the sky like a queen surrounded by her subjects. "Twinkle, twinkle little star," she hummed.

"Everything all right? I got worried about you." Darcy extended a hand toward Hannah.

Hannah patted the grass beside her. "Sit down and hear me out. I've made up my mind what I want to do. I'm offering my place as a safe house for abused women. I've talked to the lady at the shelter about it. Not on a long-term basis, but only when Gina's is full and she needs help, or when she needs to put someone in a secret place for a few days. But first there's paperwork and interviews and things."

"Oh, sweet Jesus! Do you realize what you are doing? Bringing those kind of women in here will bring all the ugly right back into your life with every one. You need to forget it, not bring it home for dinner," Darcy said.

"What are you two fighting about?" Travis sat down beside Hannah.

"We are not fighting," Hannah said.

"Darcy's tone says otherwise."

Darcy shrugged. "She wants to turn this place into a safe house for abused women. Tell her not to do it, Travis."

"I think it's a wonderful idea, but when you have women living here, I will be staying in one of the bedrooms as a bodyguard," he said.

"Thank you." Hannah smiled. "I kind of volunteered you already."

"What about Sophie? You know that your guests will have to be snuck inside the house and not leave until someone comes to get them. And Sophie will tell everyone in church that she's got friends living with her," Darcy argued.

"Sophie has so many imaginary friends that no one will think twice when she tells them about new ones," Hannah answered. "Are you with me or against me?"

"With you, all the way." Darcy nodded with a degree of hesitation. "I don't think it will help you, but if it's what you want to do, you've got my support. Now, we've got work to do."

Sophie rounded the side of the house and threw herself down in Travis's lap. "Work? I can help. Nadine had to go home and it's starting to get dark." She jumped up and laid a hand on her tummy. "I'm getting hungry, Mama. What's for supper?"

Travis led the way back into the house. "Aunt Birdie made a pot of potato soup, and she said when y'all got to a stopping place to come on over and help her eat up the leftovers."

"Let's get all this stuff that we don't want anymore out of the house, and then we'll take a break and eat before we start painting. Think you can wait that long?" Darcy asked.

Sophie nodded. "If you give me a job to do."

"Could you sort through what I tossed on the sofa and put my socks in one pile, my pajamas in a pile, and . . ."

Sophie held up a hand. "I can do that, Mama. I'll get three laundry baskets from the 'tility room and put your stuff in them." Like always, she took off in a dead run from the bedroom, down the foyer, and into the living room.

"We'll get through this," Darcy said.

"I'm so grateful that I have y'all to help me," Hannah whispered. "And Travis, I'm going with you to the shelter. I want to talk to Gina again, even if it's only for a few minutes. My mind is made up and I really want to do this."

He hugged her, drawing her close to his side. "Then it's what you should do."

Chapter Four

Sunlight streamed into the room through the sparkling-clean windows, waking Hannah with its warmth. She stretched, working the kinks from lifting and painting out of her back and neck. There was a whole new, empty room waiting for furniture downstairs. It was painted a soft blue, and no doubt the sun was pouring through those windows also.

She'd even taken down the blinds and drapes and taken them to the shelter. While Travis loaded them, she'd popped open another garbage bag and filled it with six sets of king-size satin sheets along with the comforter, the pillows, and the throw pillows. Then at the last minute she decided she didn't want the pale-gray carpet, either, so Travis yanked it up, rolled it into a long tube and loaded it on the trailer also.

She sat up in bed and drew her knees up so she could wrap her arms around them. "I love the way that paint transformed the room from cold to warm."

When she redid the rest of the house, she would use a Texas bluebonnet theme in one of the guest rooms and maybe a morning glory theme in another. Her house would have a calm, soft effect on the abused women and kids who visited. Gina would let her do this, she was sure of it. There weren't many places in a small, secluded town like Crossing that would be as perfect as Hannah's.

"And I'm going to get out the sewing machine and make valances for the rooms, throw pillows for the beds and for the new living room. Travis can take the bedroom furniture in that room to the shelter, and I'll buy a small sofa that could be let out into a bed if necessary and put a television in there." She made plans out loud as they came to mind. "I can see one room in gingham checks," she murmured. "And another in wildflowers."

The aroma of coffee wafted across the room, and her chest tightened. It was Saturday. Marty was home, and he'd be furious that she'd slept in. He liked his coffee made with the french press and his breakfast on the table promptly at seven o'clock. She glanced at the clock beside her bed. Seven fifteen. Adrenaline rushed through her body as she threw back the covers. And then she reminded herself that Marty was not in Crossing.

"Good morning!" Travis said. "I brought you a cup of coffee. Figured you might need it after that late night we all put in."

Her eyes darted around the room and finally settled on him in the landing right outside her open bedroom door. "Thank you. How long have you been here?"

He handed her the mug, his warm skin brushing hers, and sat down on the edge of the bed. "Long enough to locate the extra key under that flowerpot with dead plants on the back porch and make coffee. You really have to start hiding that better."

His brown hair looked like it had been combed with his fingertips that morning, with one strand resting on the thin metal nosepiece of his wire-rimmed glasses. His grin shone genuine and sweet beneath his summer sky-blue eyes.

"Tell you what. You keep that key, and if I ever lock myself out, I'll come and find you," she said.

"Sounds like a solid plan to me." He nodded. "I'll put it on my key ring and keep it safe."

She straightened her legs and scooted to one side so that she could prop her back on the wall. Hannah could hear every movement—from the squeak of the bed across the hall where Darcy was sleeping to the sound of a lonesome cricket singing a solo somewhere in the downstairs bathroom. She'd learned to be very aware of her surroundings and Marty's body language through the years. Turning it off wasn't as easy as flipping a light switch. So how in the hell had Travis sneaked into her house, made coffee, come up those stairs—especially the noisy one three up from the bottom—and gotten into her room without her knowing it?

"The whole house smells fresh and new," Travis said.

That was the answer. The paint smell in the house had thrown off her other senses, including the instinct that told her when someone was near.

"I love it." She sipped the coffee.

"How'd you sleep last night?" Travis asked. "Sore this morning from all that work?"

"Yes, I am, but I have a pretty new room for all the aches and pains. And I never sleep past six and here it is after seven, if that answers your question. How about you?"

He reached over and touched her on the foot. "I feel better and sleep better knowing this is over for you."

"Y'all keep telling me it's over. Why don't I feel like it is, Travis?" she asked.

"This is your first weekend as a single parent. Ten weekends from now won't be as tough."

"Promise?" she asked.

He set his coffee cup on the floor, raised his right hand, and placed the left one on an imaginary book. "I do hereby swear that each week will be easier than the last one. In six months you won't even remember these tough times. Hallelujah. Amen. Praise the Lord."

"You better move to the other side of the room, Travis Johnson. When that lightning bolt shoots though the window and zaps you dead for blaspheming, I don't want to be too close." She giggled.

"I'll die a happy man, because I saw a twinkle in your eye for the first time in a long time." He grinned. "I like the new room a lot, Hannah."

"I was sitting here thinking that I might paint every room in the house just like it and do all the woodwork in white."

"It will be like a sky full of fluffy white clouds. Sophie will love it." His grin widened.

"That's a phase with her. It'll fade when something new comes along. At least I'm not painting all the walls like that patchwork quilt she drags around with her. Now that I've decided to do this, I'm getting so excited about it."

Travis chuckled. "I'm so glad to see you happy, Hannah. But you better whisper about that quilt idea, because if she hears you say that in your sleep, she'll want her room to be done in a patchwork design. And remember, darlin', this cloud phase has lasted more than a year. She made me lie in the grass last summer when she called them 'crowds' instead of clouds. So we might have a few more years of guessing what the clouds are before she outgrows her love for her lullaby sky." He hesitated, but the silence in the room felt comfortable between them. "I bet when she's a grown woman with kids of her own, she takes them out to look at the clouds whenever they get a boo-boo. It's ingrained in her. It's her safety net."

Travis, dependable, sweet man that he was, could find good in everyone. Hannah hoped that someday when the right woman came along, she'd realize that she'd found real gold and not fool's gold.

"You are thinking of the past again."

"What makes you say that?" Hannah asked.

"It's the sadness in your eyes. I wish I had a mental 'Dead End' sign to put in your mind so that every time that happened, it would make you turn around and forget that there was even a man named Marty in the world," he said.

"That is so sweet, Travis." She smiled. "So you agree I should paint the whole house that pretty shade of blue? I could pick up the paint while Darcy and I are shopping for new furniture today."

"I think it would be beautiful."

"What if I don't like it in a week?"

He chuckled. "Then repaint it. This is your house. You can paint the rooms a different color every week if that makes you happy. Darcy never got a chance to tell me what was really horrible last night, you know."

"Bugs and spider eyes."

"Want to elaborate just a little?" Travis asked.

"It all started when you let Sophie bounce on the bed. We found nanny cams in three different vents where Marty had been recording and watching us. And listening devices on the phones," she answered.

☙

Travis squeezed the coffee mug every bit as tight as his chest felt. He'd always known Marty was an egotistical son of a bitch with OCD and a god complex, but this strayed into the area right before a true sociopath came out of the closet. Hannah would be a long time getting over his mental abuse, but hopefully she'd been saved from suffering something worse.

"Did you check your cell phone?" he asked.

Hannah shook her head. "There's not room for a bug in that phone, is there?" She picked up her phone from the nightstand beside the bed. She removed the cover and then the back and handed it to Travis. "Can you take that thing apart and tell me if there's a device of any kind in the back?"

"No, I can't, but we can take it to the phone place tomorrow when we go shopping for new furniture," he said.

"Take it outside and leave it on the back porch until we can get it seen about."

Travis handed the phone back to her. "I don't know how he could have gotten anything into the telephone. It takes a tech person to get inside one of those smartphones. But your car, now that's a different story. He's probably got some kind of tracker on it, and we will check it out tomorrow."

"I bet you are right. That makes more sense, anyway. When Sophie was two, I packed a suitcase, crammed a tote bag full of her favorite toys, and we left. We'd gotten about fifty miles down the road heading east. We were going to Virginia to live with my mother and grandmother until I could find a job and get on my feet."

"And?" Travis asked.

"And Marty called, told me that I would turn around and go back home, or else."

"Else?"

"He had lots of money behind him, Travis. I figured someone in town had seen us loading the suitcases and tattled on me. I always blamed Wyatt, because he was the only person in Crossing that Marty even talked to. I waited six months. That time I didn't take a thing from the house. For anyone looking on, I was going out to do my Thursday evening grocery shopping. I drove straight to the shelter in Gainesville and . . ." She paused.

"And he called you, right?" Travis said.

"He did. He said it was the last chance he would ever give me. That I belonged to him and Sophie belonged to him, but it could be arranged that I wouldn't be in the picture anymore. If I wanted to raise my daughter, I'd better go home and stay there."

"Did he come home that weekend?"

Hannah nodded. "Oh, yes, and he brought Sophie a Barbie dollhouse and played with her all weekend. It was probably the most attention he'd ever paid the child, and she wasn't quite sure how to take it all in. But I knew it was a message to me so I didn't run again. That along with the threats and the bruises that he put on me. My car"—she paused—"was why I couldn't leave. If only I'd known, I would have left it at home and gotten someone to drive me."

"Marty is going to fall over the edge one of these days and do something really bad to someone. I'm just glad he's out of your life, Hannah, and it won't be you or Sophie in front of him when he cracks." He held up his hand. "Dead end! Let's go get another cup of coffee and imagine your kitchen painted blue with red-checkered curtains on the windows."

"Not red with this shade of blue," she said. "I'm going to sew them, so maybe pure white in the living room and kitchen. I want lots of sunshine to pour into the house, especially in the morning. I can pull the shades in the afternoon to ward off the heat."

Travis's heart kicked in a little extra beat at her enthusiasm. It might take six months—it might take a couple of years, even—but someday she was again going to be that cute little dark-haired girl with big brown eyes that he'd had a crush on in elementary school. She'd been shy even back then, but there was sparkle in her eyes and a bounce in her step. When he'd come back to Crossing the year before, he'd figured he'd stay in his grandmother's spare bedroom, but Aunt Birdie had insisted he take a couple of rooms in her house on the second floor. That way he wouldn't be so cramped. There was already a small sitting room up there and he could have his choice of bedrooms. And he'd have his own bathroom and not have to share.

At first he thought he'd stay three months and finish the latest novel he was working on, but then the time stretched out and now a year had passed.

"And"—her eyes started to twinkle—"when we go pick out furniture, I'm going by the fabric store to buy stuff for all the windows downstairs." She giggled and it came from all the way down inside her heart. "Calvin would call them window treatments, not valances." She slung her legs over the side of the bed and stood up with the grace of a ballerina.

"You could call them Hannah's creations. Want some help painting and getting a bedroom transformed into a living area this week?"

"I never turn down help," she said.

"Good, then, I'll be here early Monday morning, and by nightfall we'll have the walls done. On Tuesday we can do the woodwork, and Wednesday you'll be ready to drag out that sewing machine." He grinned.

"How about on Monday, I do some sewing, and we start painting on Tuesday? That way the window treatments"—her eyes twinkled—"will be done when all the paint dries and we can hang them up. Besides, I'm itching to do some sewing now that I thought of it."

"You are the queen of this castle, despite Sophie's take on things." Travis led the way down to the kitchen. He poured two more cups of coffee and handed one to her.

Darcy made her way into the living room and fell back onto the sofa, pulling a red-and-white throw over her eyes. "It's too early to be up. The sun is barely awake. I need coffee."

"Rise and shine, Valentine!" Aunt Birdie sang at the top of her lungs as she entered through the kitchen door.

Darcy peeled back a corner of the throw, glanced at Travis and then at Hannah and Aunt Birdie before falling back on the throw pillows and covering her head again. "It's June, not February, Aunt Birdie." She groaned.

Sophie made her way to the sofa and curled up beside Darcy, yanking part of the pillow over her eyes. "Is it morning? Do we get pancakes with chocolate chips?"

"Yes, you do, and they are right here on a platter waiting for you," Aunt Birdie answered. "Already slathered with melted butter and ready for syrup."

Hannah hugged Aunt Birdie. "This is so sweet of you."

"Ain't nothing. I made a stack with chocolate chips and a stack of buckwheat and one of plain old pancakes so y'all can mix or match. That way you can get on about the business of buying new furniture." Aunt Birdie opened the cabinet doors and took down four plates. "Gina, from down at the shelter, called me first thing this morning to tell me how much they appreciate the donations and to talk about your offer, Hannah. It's a good thing you are doing."

"What's a good thing?" Sophie asked.

"Giving away those things to the shelter," Aunt Birdie answered. "Most folks don't think to send men's stuff. Some of those boys will use those nice shoes for things like the prom."

Hannah pulled syrup from the pantry and milk from the refrigerator and set both on the table. "If you don't come out from under that pillow, Sophie Arlene O'Malley, I intend to eat all these chocolate chip pancakes myself."

"And I'm going to eat the buckwheat ones," Travis called out.

The pillow flew across the room, and both Darcy and Sophie sat straight up. Darcy tossed the throw to one side, jerked a thigh-length nightshirt down, and made her way to the kitchen. With one leap and a few steps, Sophie was sitting at the kitchen table in her usual spot, eyeing the platter of pancakes.

"Mama, grace this so I can eat before it gets cold . . . please," she added as an afterthought.

Hannah squeezed syrup from the bottle into a coffee mug and set it in the microwave, poked the buttons, and laid a hand on Sophie's shoulder as she bowed her head. "Why don't you say the grace, since this is your favorite Saturday morning breakfast?"

"Father up in the sky, thank you for these pancakes and for Aunt Birdie. She is the bestest, and you need to give her a blessing today. Amen," Sophie said loud and clear.

"And you thought the clouds were a passing thing?" Travis whispered. "I believe they might be with us longer than that old quilt. They might even last through eternity."

Hannah flashed a smile reminiscent of when she was in elementary school. There was his Hannah, the one he'd had the crush on.

Aunt Birdie headed toward the bedroom. "While y'all eat, I'm going to take a peek at this new room.

"Well, isn't this beautiful. You should do the whole house like this, Hannah," she called out from the room. "I like the way the sun comes right into the room. You should paint all the woodwork and your kitchen cabinets white."

"I agree." Darcy forked three buckwheat pancakes onto her plate and covered them with the warm maple syrup the second it came out of the microwave. "Hey, I could drive over after work each evening next week and we could do a room a night?"

"I've offered to help, too." Travis stacked up three pancakes, one of each kind, on his plate.

"Darcy, you can come stay any time you want. Any evening that you want to drive over here from Gainesville, feel free," Hannah said.

"My room, too!" Sophie's eyes bugged out. "I get blue in my room?"

"Do you want your room to be blue?" Darcy asked.

Sophie's dark curls wiggled as her head bobbed up and down. "And can I have a rainbow on the wall with white clouds all around it? Then I can put my quilt on the bed and 'tend I'm outside even when it's raining."

"Travis?" Darcy glanced his way.

A wide grin split his face. "Don't ask me. The queen of this castle is sitting on the throne."

"Queen? You mean Mama?" Sophie giggled.

"Yes, ma'am." Travis nodded.

"Then Queen Mama, can I have a rainbow on my wall?"

"Travis?" Hannah flashed a brilliant smile, her brown eyes all aglitter.

"Why Travis?" Sophie asked.

"Because he's real good at painting. He painted the mascot for our high school basketball team on the wall in the gym, and he was always the one who built and painted the props for plays and the floats for the parades," Darcy explained.

"You never told me that," Sophie said.

"You never told me that you like rainbows," Travis said.

"Well, I do like them. Can I have a rainbow on my wall, please, Travis?"

"I will be honored to paint a rainbow and some clouds on your wall, ma'am," Travis answered.

Sophie threw her hand over her mouth, but the little girl giggles escaped around it. "I'm not a ma'am. That's for old women, and I'm just a little girl."

"And it's not for all old women." Aunt Birdie's smile erased a few wrinkles but not many.

"I will try to remember that," Travis said seriously. "Do you ladies want me to follow you into town this morning with my truck and trailer so we can bring whatever furniture you buy home today?"

"Can I ride in the truck with you?" Sophie asked.

"That's up to your mama," Travis answered. "But if she doesn't mind, I would sure enough love the company. It gets awful lonely in the truck when I'm all alone."

"Can I please, please?" Sophie locked gazes with Hannah. "And can we get the paint for my rainbow today and can we paint my room next and can I have a poster of *Frozen* on my wall and—"

"You better catch a breath," Hannah butted in. "Yes, you can ride with Travis, and thank you for offering to go with us, Travis. And yes, we can get the paint for your rainbow, and yes, you can have your room done next. But we'll see about the poster later."

"Done with the wisdom of a queen," Travis whispered.

Hannah's phone buzzed before she could answer. She fished it out of her pocket, hit a button, read a text message, and all the color drained from her face. Her fork hit the floor with a clatter and landed under the table. Travis leaned to pick it up at the same time she did, and their heads bumped together.

"Are you okay?" he asked.

She rubbed her forehead and handed him the phone as she picked up the fork and then took it to the kitchen sink. Travis followed her, the phone in his hand and cold chills shooting up his spine.

The text message read: Chocolate chip pancakes. Rainbows. Blue walls. White trash.

Hannah pulled the magnetized grocery list pad from the refrigerator door and wrote on the top sheet:

Bugs. More, but where? What do we do?

Travis scribbled on the bottom of the pad:

I'll get a bug detector and go over every inch of this house, inside and out and your car as well.

Hannah laid a hand on his and squeezed. That was enough fuel to keep Travis going for the rest of the week. Damn that man for taking the sparkle out of Hannah's eyes and putting fear right back in.

"What's wrong?" Aunt Birdie asked.

"Not a thing," Hannah said with a forced giggle. "Clumsy old me dropped a pancake on the floor. I was going to clean it up, but there might be some little starving ants that would enjoy it for breakfast. Anyone want more coffee while I am up?"

With a frown on her face, Darcy held up her cup and glanced down at the floor.

Hannah carried the pot to the table and laid her phone beside Darcy's plate. Darcy's whole body stiffened as she handed the phone to Aunt Birdie.

"Stalker!" Aunt Birdie said loudly.

"Is that our new word for today?" Sophie asked.

"No, our word for today is *rainbows*."

"Then why did you say *stalker*? Is that like Jack's beanstalk that you read to me about?" Sophie asked.

"Something like that. A stalker is like that giant who climbed up the beanstalk so he could do mean things. Remember what happened to him?" Aunt Birdie talked more loudly than normal.

Sophie's black curls bounced when she nodded. "Jack chopped down the beanstalk and the giant got dead."

"That's what happens to stalkers. Someone comes along and chops down the beanstalk and they get dead." Immediately the phone buzzed in Aunt Birdie's hand, and she handed it to Hannah. "It's time to get out the ax," she whispered.

The text message was from Liz. Wyatt got called out early. Are you awake? I'll bring muffins if you've got coffee ready.

Hannah's thumbs quickly typed something back, and then she laid the phone on the counter. "That was Liz. She's coming over with muffins."

"Yay!" Sophie pumped her fist in the air. "I got a new name and Aunt Birdie made me pancakes and Aunt Liz is bringing muffins and Darcy is here. I love this day. Oh, and I get rainbows on my wall. You are the best mama in the whole wide world. This is the best Saturday of my whole life."

Travis almost choked on a sip of coffee before he got it swallowed. "Out of the mouths of babes," the old saying went. And what Sophie had just said so innocently aloud was far better than all the threats and cussing any of the adults around the table could have ever done.

Chapter Five

Sometimes Sophie referred to Hannah's four friends as aunt or uncle, but that morning, as she ran from one piece of furniture to another, she'd dropped all the aunt and uncle titles in her excitement.

"Liz, look at this fancy princess bed," she squealed.

"Lie down on it and tell me if you really want it," Liz said.

Sophie glanced at her mother, and Hannah nodded. People tested the furniture every single day, so it shouldn't cause the sun to fall from the sky if a five-year-old stretched out on a canopy bed.

All four of the adults watched her kick off her flip-flops and lie down. Her eyes darted to the ruffled eyelet canopy and then to each white bedpost, and finally she popped up her knees and shook her head dramatically.

"I don't want this thing," she said as she put her flip-flops back on.

"Why? It's a princess bed," Travis said.

"Because I couldn't see my rainbows and clouds if I was in that bed and besides, it feels like I'm in a cage," Sophie declared. "I'll just keep my bed and it can be in the middle of the rainbow." She made a sweeping arch with her slender arm. "And the clouds can be on either side and when I wake up I can just see them right there on my blue wall. They can keep this bed. I don't want it."

"Lord, she's making me want a rainbow on my wall," Hannah whispered.

Travis slung a friendly arm around her shoulders. "All you have to do is say the word."

She didn't flinch or tense at his touch. This was Travis, her friend, who would move mountains for her and Sophie and never, ever hurt either of them. His arm felt comfortable, like a warm blanket on a cold winter night at a football game. She inhaled and caught a whiff of his shaving lotion. Was that Stetson? She loved that scent. But when did he start wearing it?

Maybe he always did and you're just now noticing, the voice in her head said.

"So which one? The white slatted headboard and matching dresser or the oak four-poster bed? Those seem to be the two you keep going back and forth between," Liz noted.

Liz's questions took Hannah's thoughts away from Travis, and she studied the two choices, finally pointing toward the white bedroom set. "I like this one. It's airy, and the white would match the woodwork."

"I agree." Liz pointed at the oak. "The oak one would overpower the size of your bedroom. I like the simple lines of the white and no footboard. I hate those things. The only thing they are good for is keeping your knees bruised up. Are you going to replace all the furniture upstairs?"

Hannah noticed the bruise on Liz's arm. The five-finger shape couldn't be very old, because it was still purple. In a couple of days, it would be yellow and green, but it had probably happened sometime yesterday. It was just further proof that all that nervousness Liz displayed had little to do with the stress of her school job and everything to do with an abusive husband.

"No, just the one bedroom so it will be a living area. And I like that sofa bed right there." Hannah nodded at a microfiber love seat in a dark brown. "It won't show dirt, and it turns into a bed. Aunt Birdie said she's got an old coffee table and a card table with four folding chairs I can use, so I only need that thing."

"So your mind is made up?" Travis moved to the area where the bedroom had been set up. "This goes in your room and rainbows go on your walls?"

"No, just this goes in my room and rainbows go on Sophie's walls and that sofa goes in my new little room upstairs. What do you think, Sophie?"

"I love it, Mama. Can we go home now and paint my walls?"

"We will paint your walls on Tuesday. Now we're going to the fabric store to buy material for new valances."

"What's a bay-lance? Is that kind of like a ballerina?" Sophie asked.

"It's a little short curtain like Aunt Birdie has in her kitchen window, only yours won't be yellow with hummingbirds on them," Travis explained. "How about a trip to McDonald's for burgers and fries on the way to the fabric store? It's almost dinnertime."

"I do love their fish sandwiches," Darcy said and pointed at the white furniture Hannah had picked out. "I'd buy that same furniture for my bedroom if I was replacing things, Hannah. You made a good choice. Totally different from what you had, and it can be the start of a new life."

"And now McDonald's." Sophie sighed. "It really is the most wonderful day of my life."

"That kid has stolen my heart," Travis whispered in Hannah's ear.

"No kiddin'." She feigned surprise. "You and Aunt Birdie both."

"Oh, yeah," he said as the corners of his mouth turned up in a brilliant smile. "And we love it. McDonald's, and then while y'all are deciding on fabric, I'm going to find a can of bug spray." He winked. "And then come back here, get this furniture loaded onto the trailer. It will save a little money if we take it rather than have it delivered."

"Thank you, Travis. Y'all have truly all been lifesavers through all this. But I'm really glad that y'all didn't feel comfortable with all those bugs in the house," she said.

"Bugs! Spiders, too? Where? Is it Charlotte?" Sophie picked up the bed skirt on the canopy bed and looked under it.

"Little corn has big ears," Liz said. "Honey, they weren't talking about real spiders."

Sophie crossed her arms and dropped her chin to her chest. She looked up at them through a furrowed brow and shook her head in disapproval. "You are doing that big-people talk, aren't you?"

"Yes, they are, darlin' girl," Darcy said.

Travis gave Hannah a gentle side hug and then stepped away. "We should maybe make a stop between McDonald's and the fabric store and then make a stop for a new phone?"

Hannah's head bobbed once as she headed toward the checkout counter. "Yes, definitely, and then let's go by the landline folks to change my number there, also."

Darcy followed right behind her. "And you're going to need to run into a department store for sheets and a bedspread or comforter for your new bed, too. You have nothing for a queen-size bed."

Hannah had a complete panic attack. This little foray into town was going to cut a chunk out of her savings account. Marty had always given her what he called "her allowance." It was to be used for Sophie's clothing, utility bills, and groceries, and he expected a full accounting for all of it in the form of receipts. If there was anything left at the end of the month, he gave her less the next month, so she'd learned to account for it all down to the penny.

He tried to control the money she made at her teaching aide job, but she'd stood her ground on that, even if it did cost a few bruises and a lot of hateful remarks. That money she'd put away in case she did find a way to escape. It was still sitting in the bank. The day might yet come when he lost his mind completely and she would need to move far away and start over, so she needed to be very careful. Plus, there was no more money from Marty for living expenses.

"I can't do this," she said. "I should go to a secondhand store and get something that I can refinish."

Darcy laid a hand on Hannah's shoulder. "Yes, you can. Suck it up and write the check. This costs a hell of a lot less than therapy. Besides"—she lowered her voice to barely a whisper—"did you see those bruises on Liz? She needs to see that you are surviving."

"How long have you known?" Hannah sucked in a lungful of air and let it out very slowly as she pulled her checkbook from her purse.

"Awhile, but she's in denial, just like you were at first."

"You knew even before I was willing to talk to you about it?"

"Of course! I'm like God. I know everything." Darcy's dark-brown eyes twinkled. "Thank the Lord above that you opened up to me the first time out in Aunt Birdie's backyard. Now that we know he was watching and listening to everything that went on in that house, it's a good thing. Maybe that's why we all felt so uncomfortable in there. God was telling us to get out so you wouldn't get into trouble."

"I wish I'd never met that man or married him even if I was pregnant," Hannah said through clenched teeth.

"But you did, and without him, you wouldn't have that precious child." Darcy toyed with a big gold hoop earring. "Someday I'm going to get me one of those daughter things, and I hope she's as sassy as Sophie."

Hannah took a deep breath, wrote out the check to cover her purchases, and slipped the checkbook back into her purse. "When is all this going to happen?"

"When I get over Calvin," she whispered.

"You still have a crush on Calvin?" Hannah gasped.

"Can't seem to get past it. All muscled up and tanned and famous. Then look at me. Average height, overweight, and no one he'd want to hang on his arm at one of those fancy showings for his new line."

Liz put an arm around both of them. "Darcy, you are beautiful. Don't talk about yourself like that. And Hannah, Darcy will always be in love with Calvin. You know what they say about first loves."

"Liz, what is that bruise on your arm?" Hannah said, abruptly changing the subject and wishing the instant that the words were out of her mouth that she could take them back.

"You know how clumsy I am. I tripped and almost fell, but Wyatt caught me." The excuse came out slicker than a country road covered in ice. "If he hadn't, I would have broken my arm or split my head open on a doorjamb. Now, let's go have some lunch and do some more shopping. Lord, I wish I could remodel my bedroom. I'm so tired of that heavy furniture."

Darcy shot a sly wink Hannah's way. "Let's get Hannah all settled into her new life and maybe then we can redo your place."

"Wyatt would go into spasms if I changed a single thing. He doesn't even like it when I rearrange the pantry." Liz laughed, but it was too brittle to be real.

❧

Hannah stood in the doorway of her bedroom that evening and could hardly believe the transformation that had taken place in only twenty-four hours. If only she could erase all the anxiety from the past six years as easily as she'd gotten rid of everything in the bedroom in one fell swoop, then she would fall asleep on that strange bed and wake up with no memories of what she'd lived through.

"Looks nice," Darcy said at her elbow.

"I love it."

"Me, too," Liz said from the other side. "But now I'm going home. I'll see you both in church tomorrow morning, right?"

"Oh, yeah," Darcy said. "Aunt Birdie would cut a switch from the pecan tree if we missed church. We'll be right there on the pew with her. What are you bringing to the potluck? Since Wyatt is out of pocket, you are coming to her house, aren't you?"

Liz tucked her hands into the hip pockets of her jeans. "Of course. I'm going to make a banana pudding in the morning. What are y'all taking?"

"Aunt Birdie told us to bring a salad and a loaf of french bread," Darcy said. "Sophie asked for lasagna to celebrate her new name and her new room."

Liz yawned and rubbed her eyes. "Aunt Birdie can't tell that child no, but who am I to talk. I would've bought her that canopy bed if she'd said she wanted it."

"We all love that sweet girl, Hannah." Darcy yawned. "Hey, Liz, why don't you stay the night here? Travis assures us there are no more bugs or cameras in this place. He gave it a good going-over with his magic wand thing. I've got an extra nightshirt in my suitcase. We haven't all three had a slumber party in years."

"Thanks, but I'd better go on home. Wyatt calls at ten thirty every night while he's away," Liz answered.

"Give me your cell phone. I can reroute all your calls from your house to it and you can talk to him right here," Darcy offered.

Hannah could feel her friend's pain. The quickening of her pulse. The extra thump in her heart. The way her hand went instantly to the bruises on her arm—*cover them up; then no one will know.* Thoughts must be running through Liz's head in a continuous circle—what if someone saw her car at Hannah's all night? Would Wyatt think that Travis or Calvin had been there and Liz had been flirting with him? Would he be angry because she wasn't home? Good Lord, what if he had cameras and listening bugs in her house like Marty had put in Hannah's?

Liz's eyes darted around the new room, to the ceiling, to the windows. She wanted to stay, because she wanted to be anywhere but in that house where she had to walk on eggshells every day. But if she did and it made Wyatt angry, she'd suffer the consequences. Hannah knew all too well.

Hannah took a few steps toward her and hugged her. "Go home, darlin'. All we're going to do is sleep anyway, as tired as we are. We'll see you in church and spend the afternoon at Aunt Birdie's."

Liz hesitated long enough to draw another breath. "I'll come over Monday morning and we'll work on making a houseful of pretty valances. I can't believe you found blue material with white clouds on it for Sophie's room. When you tuck Sophie in tonight, give her a kiss on the forehead for me."

"Will do," Hannah said.

Liz disappeared out into the night. A squeak from the front door, the sound of a car's engine, and the flash of headlights through the slats in the blinds let them know that Liz had driven away.

"I know she really wanted to stay, and she might have if you hadn't given her that way out," Darcy said.

"Think!" Hannah flicked Darcy on the forehead. "If her car was seen here all night then Wyatt would know before breakfast in the morning. And that's if he doesn't have her house bugged like mine was. If he hasn't got the money or the sense to do that, you can bet your sweet ass that he's got someone spying for him. Abusers are control freaks."

Darcy's hands went to her cheeks. "Thank God you know the ropes. I would have felt terrible if we'd gotten her in more trouble. I want to ask her outright about it, Hannah."

"But you won't. You'll give her all the support she needs and when she's ready to talk, she will. Until then, she'll only make excuses."

Darcy turned around and headed out of the room. "The voice of experience."

"You got it." Hannah slipped into Sophie's room, pulled the soft sheet up over her body, and kissed her twice on the forehead. She tiptoed next door and eased the door of her new bedroom shut.

She picked up her phone and hit the speed-dial button for her mother. A sleepy voice answered on the fifth ring.

"You were right, Mama," she said.

"About?"

"Everything."

"Is it over? Can I call your phone now?"

"You can call the house phone or my cell phone. The house phone was bugged, but we took my cell phone to the store and they checked it out. It was fine. It was my car that he had the tracker on. Get a pen and paper and I'll give you my new phone numbers." Hannah kicked off her shoes and stretched out on the bed. "Thank goodness we got in the habit of talking at Aunt Birdie's. He had this whole house bugged for sound and video."

"I'm not a bit surprised. I've read everything I could on men like Marty. What now?"

"I've offered to run a safe house for abused women when the one in Gainesville gets overloaded," Hannah spit out quickly.

"Do you think that's wise? You just came out of a situation like they all are running from," Patsy said with worry in her tone.

"I want to help other women get away from their abusers, Mama."

"But will it be safe for Sophie? What if one of those men tracks them to your house and—"

Hannah didn't let her finish the sentence. "Travis will stay here and be our bodyguard when I have visitors."

"Did you do all right in the courtroom? Were you awfully nervous?"

"I did fine, though my nerves were shot. Marty glared at me most of the time. But, Mama, I felt so sorry for the woman Marty'll probably marry next." She went on to tell her mother every single detail. "So you are welcome to come here to visit anytime you want."

"I'd like that very much," her mother said. "Maybe one of my friends could help out with your grandmother and I could fly to Texas for a long weekend real soon."

"We'll hope so," Hannah said. "This is nice, being able to talk to you any time I want."

"Yes, it is." Her mother yawned. "I'm sorry, honey, but it is midnight in my world."

"Good night, Mama," Hannah said.

"Good night, and Hannah, I wish I hadn't been right. I wish he'd been a wonderful husband. You didn't deserve a man like that."

"Thanks, Mama. You sleep well now."

Hannah stood up and dropped her cotton housecoat on the floor with a smile and sighed as she slipped between the soft cotton sheets. In seconds she was asleep. No dreams of whether she'd left bread crumbs on the kitchen cabinet. No nightmares about Marty ripping Sophie from her arms. For the first time in six years, Hannah slept the sleep usually reserved for overactive children at the end of a long day.

CHAPTER SIX

Aunt Birdie had claimed the second pew on the left side of Crossing Community Church practically the day the church was built. Travis stood up and allowed the ladies to settle in before he took his seat that Sunday morning. As luck would have it, Darcy went first and sat beside Liz, leaving Hannah to slide in last, which meant that she sat so close to Travis that she could smell his aftershave. *And is that a new shirt he's wearing this morning?* The baby-blue-and-white pinstripe was the same color as his eyes.

"Well, dammit!" Aunt Birdie's voice echoed off the walls of the church. "Forgive me, Lord, I dropped my songbook."

Sophie hopped down off the pew and handed Aunt Birdie the hymnal. Then she wiggled her way in between Liz and Aunt Birdie, set her tote bag down, and brought out a coloring book and crayons. "After we sing, you can pick out the colors for me," she whispered.

Aunt Birdie hugged her closely and whispered, "Maybe I'll even color with you."

Travis leaned close enough to Hannah that she could feel his warm breath on her neck. "I bet she dropped the book on purpose so Sophie would pick it up and sit beside her."

Something happened right there as the preacher took his place in church that first Sunday in June. Hannah felt a stirring inside her heart that she'd thought was dead and buried. It wasn't like she wanted to throw Travis down on the pew and make out with him. But there was hope that there were men out there that could be trusted. Maybe one rotten apple in the barrel hadn't tainted all the men.

"Aunt Birdie will cuss in church for a chance at a box of crayons," Hannah said softly. "Who knew?"

"I wish I'd have thought of that," Darcy said. "I'd rather color as listen to a sermon any old day of the week."

The preacher tapped on the microphone, and the whole sanctuary went quiet. A couple of whining toddlers could be heard in the nursery located at the back of the room, but other than that, the congregation had settled in.

"Good morning. I'm glad to see the pews are filled today. This morning I'm going to talk to you about the spirit of a child. When the disciples wanted to send the children away, Jesus delivered a pretty potent message," the preacher said.

"Think he knows about what happened this week?" Travis asked out of the side of his mouth.

"Everyone in town knows. There are no secrets in Crossing."

Hannah tried to listen. She really did, but her mind wandered back to that delicious little stirring in her heart, to the stillness in her soul, to the lack of guilt that she should be feeling for both. Going in circles, dancing from one topic to another, it was hard to control excitement that she hadn't felt in years.

She was jerked back into reality when the preacher asked Andy Bob Richards to deliver the benediction. She'd tuned the preacher out after his opening statement when he opened the Bible and read, "Whoever welcomes one of these little children in my name welcomes me; and whoever welcomes me does not welcome me but the one who sent me."

His opening statement solidified the whole idea. To see a child with a happy spirit and no fear would make every bit of her service a pure joy.

Her stomach growled loudly, and Travis laid a hand on her shoulder. "Andy Bob's prayers are short. We'll get home for dinner before we starve plumb to death."

&

Travis moved his hand away only with a great deal of willpower. Knowing now that Marty had actually bruised Hannah made Travis's gut draw up in knots. He wanted to draw her close and assure her that he'd never ever hurt her like Marty had done. That anyone could ever say a bad word to his Hannah, much less abuse her, put vengeful thoughts in his head.

She looked absolutely stunning that morning in her pink-and-white sundress. Her toenails were polished in a shade darker than her dress, and her hair floated down her back in big waves. He shut his eyes for the benediction, but a picture of her was branded in his mind.

As he'd predicted, the words between Andy Bob's "Our Father in heaven" and his "Amen" were pretty scarce. Immediately folks began to stand and shuffle their way out to the aisles. Travis had done his duty and been in church. He'd sung songs whose titles he couldn't even remember, and he'd tried to listen to the sermon, but other than something about children that reminded him of Sophie, it had basically gone in one ear and out the other.

"See you at Aunt Birdie's for dinner, right?" he asked as he stood to one side of the pew and let the ladies all file out.

"Just have to run by the house and pick up the pudding," Liz answered.

"And we have to go get the salad and bread at my house. Damn, 'my house' sounded good to say," Hannah said and then clamped a hand over her mouth. "Aunt Birdie, you are a bad influence. I just cussed in church."

"The devil made you do it." Aunt Birdie smiled.

"In church?"

"Oh, darlin', this is his favorite place on Sunday morning. He's here to steal souls," Aunt Birdie whispered and changed the subject. "I love it when the pew is full and when Liz is free to join us for our Sunday potluck. Only person missing is Calvin. I keep prayin' that he'll come on back to Crossing someday so you kids will all be together again."

"When angels set up snow-cone stands in hell, he might come home," Darcy said seriously. "Calvin Winters is too big a name in clothing to be based out of a little backwater town like Crossing."

Travis's phone buzzed in his hip pocket. He checked the ID and frowned. "Hello," he said and nodded several times before he handed the phone to Hannah.

&

"Hello," she said cautiously as she made her way slowly toward the church doors.

"This is Gina from the shelter in Gainesville, and I thought if you had time this afternoon I'd come by and bring some papers to get things started."

"Okay," Hannah said. "What time?"

"Two o'clock all right with you?"

"Yes, ma'am. I will have the coffee on, unless you'd rather have sweet tea?"

"Coffee is fine," Gina said. "Filling out the paperwork will take about an hour, and I will have to fingerprint you and check the house to be sure it's safe. But the house could wait."

"No secrets hidden in my place. You can check it today if you have time," Hannah said.

"That would be good. Then I could send in my whole report in a day or so and we'd be ready in a couple of weeks, maybe sooner. See you at two, then. Thanks again for all you did for us, but most of all for what you are offering," Gina said. "Have a lovely Sunday. 'Bye now."

If Hannah had had doubts about what she was about to do, they vanished that second. She was standing in church. God had spoken and given her his blessing.

Hannah handed the phone back to Travis. "How did she get your number?"

"I gave it to her when we delivered the stuff, because I knew you were going to change your numbers. Are you absolutely sure about this, Hannah? I'll worry about you even if I'm in the house."

"I've never been more sure of anything," she answered.

"You haven't gotten over the trauma of divorce yet. What if she sends you an abused woman with a teenage son? Will you be comfortable with a boy of that age with abuse issues being around Sophie? There's a lot to think about." Travis's brow furrowed deeply.

"You will be there, and it feels right." She stuck out her hand to shake with the preacher. "Nice sermon."

"Thank you, Hannah. If you need to talk, please call me. I know that you are going through a tough time." He smiled.

"Thank you," she said.

Travis quickly shook hands with the preacher, and then they were outside in the bright sunshine. Birds chirped in the pecan trees surrounding the little white community church. Kids were still chasing after one another, expending all that pent-up energy from sitting still for half an hour's preaching. Old folks made their way to their vehicles, stopping along the way to visit with one another or give a few hugs.

Sophie tucked her sweaty hand into her mother's. "I beat Josh in a race. He's slower than an old grandpa. I got to the tree and back before he even made it to the tree."

"Well, I wouldn't race against someone as fast as you. Who is Josh? Is he like Anna Lou?" Travis asked seriously.

Sophie giggled. "Oh, Uncle Travis. You got long legs and you can run fast. Josh has short legs like me, and he's in my Sunday school class. Anna Lou don't go to this church. Neither does Nadine. I'm hungry. Can we go to Aunt Birdie's now? Is Miss Rosie coming to dinner with us?"

"Yes, she is, and I heard that she might be bringing pink cupcakes," Travis whispered. "But it could be a surprise, so don't tell anyone."

Sophie pulled at Hannah's arm. "Hurry, Mama. Miss Rosie makes the best pink cupcakes in the whole world and she puts a strawberry right on the top."

The church was four blocks from her house, and when the weather was pretty, she and Sophie often walked, but that morning they'd been rushed so they'd all ridden together in Darcy's car. Hannah would have liked a five-minute walk back to her house to clear her mind so she could think about what Gina Lawson had suggested. But that wasn't happening today, not when there were pink cupcakes and a little dark-haired imp who'd have to be coerced into eating her dinner before she could have one.

"The lady from the shelter called me." She slid into the seat and went on to tell Darcy what she'd said.

"And can you afford extra mouths to feed?" Darcy asked.

"I own the house free and clear, so I can live on what I make as a teacher's aide and still help women who weren't as lucky as I was. Maybe it will even help Liz," Hannah said.

"You consider yourself lucky?" Darcy frowned.

"I'm alive," Hannah answered. "I have a home, good friends, and food on the table. I'm really lucky, considering where I could be."

Darcy backed out of the parking lot and drove right to Aunt Birdie's. When she saw the extra car in the driveway, she slapped the steering wheel and squealed with excitement. "It's Calvin's car. He must have had business in Dallas. Dammit! I should have worn something nicer."

"You look great. Stop fretting." Hannah grinned. "You need to tell him how you feel. None of us are getting any younger."

"Don't remind me." Darcy flipped the rearview mirror around so she could see her reflection, fluffed out her hair, and reapplied lipstick. "Oh, God! I see crow's-feet around my eyes."

Sophie had been sitting quietly, but now she propped both elbows on the back of the front seat and peered at Darcy. "You're jokin' me. There ain't no bird feet on your eyes. Besides, how would they get there? The windows were all rolled up."

"It's just an expression." Darcy laughed.

"And little girl, you might be big enough to give up your car seat, but you do have to use a seat belt, so scoot on back there and get it fastened," Hannah said.

"Okay." Sophie sighed. "Y'all are doing that big-people talk, aren't you?"

"So?" Darcy parked the car in front of Aunt Birdie's, dropped the keys in her purse, and opened the door.

"You look beautiful," Hannah answered. "Dammit! I forgot that we have to get our food from my house. Sophie, do you want to go on inside and see Uncle Cal?"

"Yes, I do, and I won't even tell Miss Rosie that you said a bad word, Mama." With those words, Sophie marched across the lawn.

"I'll go with you," Darcy said. "I'll support you in this shelter thing, my friend, but it doesn't mean I won't worry about you."

"I love you, Darcy." Hannah laughed.

"More than your new blue bedroom?" Darcy teased.

Hannah bumped her with her hip as they started up the porch steps. "More than chocolate, darlin'."

They quickly gathered up the salad and bread and toted it across the road. Calvin swung Aunt Birdie's door open with a dramatic sweep.

"What's this I hear about you putting in a shelter for crows or birds of some kind? Sophie said it was big-people talk, but that you were going to do something with a shelter because the crows were attacking Darcy's eyes."

Travis stepped around from behind Calvin and took the bowl of salad and bread from their hands. "I'll take those things to the dining room so y'all can get your huggin' done."

Calvin drew Hannah to his chest tightly. "How have you been?"

"I'm better than I was on Wednesday, and Travis promises that by the end of the summer I will be really good," she answered and took a step back. "I wasn't expecting you to come back this soon, but I'm so glad to see you."

Calvin pulled her in for one last squeeze before he said, "Darcy, darlin', you dyed your hair back to its natural color! Now let it grow out by December and you can model my spring line for me."

"Yeah, right!" She wrapped her arms around him and winked at Hannah.

"Y'all going to stand in the foyer all day gawkin' at one another while the lasagna gets colder than a dead skunk in the middle of the road, or are you goin' to come on in here and eat dinner?" Aunt Birdie asked.

"I intend to eat dinner. I'm finished gawkin' for a little while." Calvin headed into the dining room. "This looks awesome, Aunt Birdie."

Miss Rosie carried a basket of thick-cut french bread to the table. "Don't go givin' her all the credit. I made the noodles. Those dried-out things you buy at the store ain't fit to feed the hogs."

"Miss Rosie, darlin'," Calvin said, "I'm absolutely sure this will outdo the lasagna they serve in Italy. Here, let me seat you."

"That's better." She sniffed the air in a pout, but her blue eyes sparkled. "You can say grace and then you will be forgiven for leaving me out."

"Yes, ma'am." Calvin nodded.

Aunt Birdie and Miss Rosie had the two end seats on either side of the long oak dining room table. Liz and Sophie flanked Calvin on one side, with Sophie at Aunt Birdie's right hand. Travis was between Darcy and Hannah on the other side of the table. After grace Aunt Birdie asked Liz to serve the lasagna and Hannah to start the salad around the table.

Sophie started to hum "Twinkle, Twinkle Little Star" and wiggled her small shoulders to keep time with the notes. "This is a happy song, Mama, for a happy day."

"And we shouldn't hum or sing at the table, remember?"

"That's Father's rule, but he ain't here." Sophie smiled brightly.

"And it is a happy song." Miss Rosie broke into the full song in her lovely soprano voice. When she got to the fourth verse, Aunt Birdie harmonized with her as they sang, "Then the traveler in the dark / Thanks you for your tiny spark / He could not see which way to go / If you did not twinkle so."

Every single thing, even the lyrics of the song, kept telling Hannah that she was doing the right thing. She would keep a house for that weary traveler in the dark, the woman who couldn't endure another beating or who was taking her children away from a horrible home. Every poor soul who'd been abused needed one tiny spark to give her hope, to show her which way to go, and Hannah was going to do her damnedest to be just that small light at the end of the dark tunnel.

CHAPTER SEVEN

Calvin began the applause when the song ended, and everyone else joined him. He paused and took a bite of the lasagna. "Oh. My. God. You ladies should start a restaurant."

"At our age!" Miss Rosie giggled. "Eighty is too old to start a new business. You come on back to Crossing and we'll give you our recipes, and you and Travis can build a fancy café. We're too damned old for that shit."

"Rosie Johnson! This is Sunday," Aunt Birdie scolded.

"Then we're too old for that holy shit." She smiled in all innocence.

"You need to go back to church," Aunt Birdie said staunchly.

"Me? I didn't cuss in church this morning, but I know someone who did."

"Ladies, that was lovely dinner music," Calvin interrupted. "And while I have all of you together, I have to tell you a couple of very well-known New York clothiers for plus-size women have approached me for a spring line."

Darcy clamped a hand over her mouth. "You weren't joking about me walking on the runway."

Calvin nodded. "You and Liz both."

It took three big gulps of sweet tea to get the chunk of lettuce to go down when Hannah choked. After a few seconds, her eyes stopped watering, and her ability to speak returned.

"Are you serious?" Hannah asked. "Does this mean you're going to move your business closer to us and we can see you more often?"

"Yes, I am," Calvin said. "And Darcy and Liz, it's only walking down a long stage, making a graceful turn and going back to get dressed again."

"And Hannah?" Travis asked.

"Sweet Hannah is too small for this line. Later I might contract for a petite line or, I'm hoping, a children's line so I can feature our Sophie, but this year it will be for women size sixteen to twenty-six," Calvin answered.

"Have you started designing?" asked Hannah.

Calvin's head bobbed up and down. "I've been working on this for a couple of years. I have a request, Hannah."

"I told you I'm too short to model for you."

"Not that. I want to buy your land. Not your house. I'll leave you a nice-size yard, but I want the rest of your property plus the airplane hangar. I've talked to Travis, and he said as soon as he's finished helping you, he can take on the job of turning that hangar into my studio. We'll turn the loft into living quarters, the old office will be my new office, and the hangar is going to be my sewing factory. The new showing will be in Dallas, of course, but I'll have more space and time to work if I live in Crossing."

"We can have it done in a month," Travis said. "It's not hard to get summer help when school is out and teenage boys are looking for jobs."

"And if you'll sell me your land, I plan to beg Aunt Birdie to let me rent one of her upstairs rooms to live in so I can help Travis with the remodeling and keep sketching out new designs," he said.

Hannah was totally speechless, and then the tune to the English lullaby started playing in her head, the fourth verse playing over and over on a continuous loop. Finally, she nodded. She'd gotten the message. The money from this sale would allow her to run a shelter for women for a long time.

"Well, you've got sh—crap for brains if you think I'd charge you a dime to stay with me," Aunt Birdie huffed. "You can move in today or next week or whenever you want to, but don't insult me by trying to rent a room. You are family, boy, and don't you forget it."

Calvin got up, rounded the table, and bent low to give Aunt Birdie a hug. "Thank you so much. I could live in a hotel, but it would mean driving back and forth every day. And besides, I like your cooking much better than fast food."

"You've always been a sweet-talker. Now eat your dinner and pretend that you are in a fancy restaurant with violins playin' over there in the corner. Besides, all this business of movin' to Crossing ain't a done deal until Hannah agrees," Aunt Birdie said.

"I agree," Hannah said simply.

A deep frown created furrows in Liz's forehead. "Don't you want to think about it, Hannah?"

"No, I do not." She shook her head. "Gina is coming today at two to start the procedure to use my place as a safe house," she said and went on to tell them what she'd decided, even adding the bit about the song that had been sung that very morning. "I'm going to do this, because it's been laid on my heart and I want to help others get away from abusive spouses. And Travis, I don't expect that women in those kinds of circumstances care if those upstairs bedrooms are gorgeous. They want a safe haven, not a five-star hotel, so after you get Sophie's room done, please go on and help Calvin."

"And when you have guests, Travis will be staying over at your place. You never know when a crazy husband or boyfriend might find his way to your place," Aunt Birdie said authoritatively. "It's either him or me and my shotgun. Take your pick."

"Okay, then," Hannah said. "But Aunt Birdie, Travis and I already discussed this and decided that he would stay with us during those times."

"Yay!" Sophie pumped her fist again. "Someone special is coming to our house and Uncle Travis can have my bed and I'll sleep with Mama. You will love sleeping in my rainbow room with the clouds and the sky in there with you. And Uncle Travis"—her expression went totally serious—"can I have a star in the sky, too?"

"Of course you can, sweet baby girl, but I'll be staying in one of the rooms upstairs. Your rainbow room is yours," he said.

"My room is going to be like the lullabies Mama sings to me like 'Twinkle, Twinkle Little Star' and 'Too-Ra-Loo,' isn't it, Mama?" she asked.

"That's right," Hannah agreed.

Calvin held his empty plate out toward Liz. "More please, ma'am. What is too-ra-loo, Sophie?"

"It's what Mama sings to me when I can't sleep. It's something Irish because we're Irish folks. Father didn't like us being Irish, but it didn't make us stop singing our song."

"It's an old Irish lullaby that goes back generations in our family," Aunt Birdie said. "I remember when my mama sang it to me."

Hannah pushed a strand of hair back behind her ear. "I'm excited about this. When something is laid upon an Irish girl's heart, she can either fight with it or listen to it. I'm tired of fighting, so I listened. There's a reason for everything. In a few years or maybe even in a few months, I'll understand better what the reason for this is, but right now I'm going to follow my heart."

"That's the Hannah we all know and love." Calvin held up his tea glass in a toast. "May we all find new beginnings that bring us great happiness."

Hannah noticed that Liz was the last one to raise her glass, and when she did it was with sadness still in her eyes.

Sophie used both hands to lift up her glass. "What y'all said sounds like big-people talk to me, but I want us all to be happy."

Travis draped a hand around Hannah's shoulders. "She's a brilliant child. I wouldn't mind having half a dozen just like her."

❧

Hannah slid a pan of brownies in the oven as soon as she got home and put a pot of coffee on. Just in case Gina changed her mind, she made a pitcher of sweet tea and sliced up a lemon. She was in the process of arranging the pieces in a pretty bowl when the doorbell rang.

"Oh, my, this place smells wonderful," Gina said.

She was a tall, rawboned woman with red hair worn in a bob right below her ears. Her green eyes and thin mouth were set in a long, narrow face with a kind expression.

"Come right on in." Hannah threw open the screen door and stepped to one side. "Coffee and brownies are ready. I hope you like chocolate."

"It's a sin not to like chocolate. I'm not sure that you can get into heaven if you don't like it." Gina laughed. "Shall we set up at the kitchen table, then?"

"Yes, that would be great. I've got a couple of pens and two pencils sharpened. Which one should I use?" Hannah asked.

"None of the above. I brought my laptop and you'll do your questionnaire on it, and then we'll take care of your fingerprints and I'll plug them into the system. Might as well tell me right now if you've got a record and save us both some time." Gina's eyes darted around the spotless living room as she made her way to the kitchen. "You keep a nice home."

"Thank you. It's habit, but I'm trying to be more flexible," Hannah said.

"I understand." Gina removed a small laptop from her briefcase and hit several keys before she turned it around.

"Coffee or sweet tea?" Hannah asked.

"Coffee to go with those brownies."

"Perfect. They are ready to come out of the oven." Hannah brought the pan out with a couple of hot pads and set it in the middle of the table. Before she sat down at the computer, she put two small plates, a couple of forks, and a knife on the table. "Now coffee," she said as she filled two mugs and handed one off to Gina. "Tell me what I need to do while you have the first warm brownie."

"Just sit down and start filling out the form. It doesn't take nearly as long on the computer as it does on paper. Mainly after the first page, when it asks for all your information, it's checking boxes." Gina groaned when she took the first bite of the hot brownie. "Lord, these are good. I'm going to gain ten pounds this afternoon."

Hannah smiled and started typing. Name, Social Security number, address, and all kinds of other questions, some pretty damned personal. Why did they need to know how much she weighed? Only God and her doctor knew that information! Half an hour later, she looked up from the screen to find Gina reading a thick romance book with a cowboy on the cover.

"I don't get to read very often, and your house is so quiet." She smiled. "All done with the questions?"

"Yes, ma'am. Now what?" Hannah asked. "Do you want to see the house?"

"Not just yet. Your fingerprints next." Gina turned the computer around, clicked a few keys, took a small device about half the size of a mouse pad from her purse, and plugged the USB port right into the computer. "Just lay your whole hand down on this and wait until the light turns green to remove it."

"Pretty fancy," Hannah said as the machine transferred her prints to the screen.

When it finished, Gina tapped a few more keys and then put the device and the computer back into her case. "That's it. Didn't hurt too bad, did it?"

"Not at all," Hannah said.

"Now let's take a look at this place. I can already tell you that if the rest looks like your living room and kitchen, the ladies I send here will be in good hands," Gina said.

"Thank you. Let's start at the top and work our way down." Hannah led the way up to the second floor. "This was my grandmother's house. We lived down the street in a smaller place, but I was here a lot as a kid. She died years ago, and then my father passed away and I inherited it. I'm glad that it can be used to help others."

"It looks like a perfect place for a safe house," Gina said.

"This is the room I intend to make into a sitting room," Hannah said, pointing to one on the left.

"Excellent idea," Gina said. "I don't think you'll have a bit of problem. We need more just like you who are willing to volunteer their homes for safe houses. Everything should be cleared in a week to ten days, and I'll call you as soon as I get word. You've already got a rail for the porch steps, and I won't send anyone who can't maneuver the stairs."

"If you do, they can have the master bedroom and I will stay in one of the rooms up here," Hannah said.

"Thank you," Gina said.

Hannah's heart felt lighter than it had in years. Tears formed behind her thick lashes, but she wouldn't let them fall. This was not a time of sadness. She had just passed the first step in doing something important with her life. Joy surged.

As soon as Gina was out the door, she called her mother. Patsy answered on the fourth ring.

"Hello," she said breathlessly. "Are you okay?"

"I'm fine, Mama. I just did all the paperwork for the safe house. Were you running?"

"Left my phone on the table, and Mama and I were watching a movie in her room," Patsy explained. "But tell me all about this new thing."

Hannah rattled on for ten minutes talking about the fancy fingerprint machine, the song at the dinner table, what the preacher talked about, and every other detail she could think of. "Mama, please come for the Fourth of July. Last time I saw you was Easter, and that was only for the weekend. Besides, you had to stay with Aunt Birdie because of the problem here."

"We had a great time dyeing eggs with Sophie. I'll do my best, kiddo," Patsy said. "Love you and see you in a few weeks, hopefully. Your grandmother is yelling for me."

Hannah hit the "End" button and slumped down on the sofa. "I want my mama," she whined.

"So does this little girl," Miss Rosie said as she and Sophie came in the back door. "I think what she really wants is a nap, but she's like a worm in hot ashes when I try to lie down with her."

"Come here, sweetheart." Hannah opened her arms.

Sophie walked into them and laid her head on Hannah's shoulder. "Why do you want your mama?" She yawned.

"Because I need a nap, too," Hannah said. "Thanks for watching her while I got that job done, Miss Rosie."

"Anytime, honey. I'm going to scoot on back to my house and get my Sunday afternoon snooze. I'll see y'all later," Miss Rosie said.

"Sing to me, Mama," Sophie whispered.

Hannah started the twinkle song, and Sophie was sound asleep before she got through the first chorus. Hannah shifted her over to the sofa and spread a throw over her bare feet.

"Changes are coming, Sophie. Big ones. Your grandma is going to visit and stay with us for the first time in your life. We're going to have guests that need a safe place. And there's more on the wind. I can feel the changes, even if I don't know what they are. I think they're going to be exciting," Hannah whispered.

CHAPTER EIGHT

A week later, Sophie's room had been painted blue and Travis was busy putting a rainbow, clouds, and twinkle star mural on the wall. Hannah had set up the sewing machine again and was making the last set of valances for the downstairs windows.

Travis did his best plotting for his novels when he was busy with something other than staring at the computer screen. The book was soon put on a back burner as his thoughts focused on Hannah. He wanted so badly to tell her about his career as an author but was afraid that she'd be angry that he had kept a secret that big from her all these years.

He had just dipped his brush in purple paint when the house went silent except for two sets of bare feet on hardwood. He looked up to see Sophie dragging her mother through the door by the hand. "Look, Mama. You made curtains and Travis made a rainbow. You just have to see how pretty it is."

Travis laid the brush down and enjoyed the warmth of Hannah's smile. His Hannah was truly coming back to him, one day at a time, one blue room at a time.

"It's going to be beautiful, isn't it?" Hannah whispered.

"Yes, it is." Sophie let go of her mother's hand and sat down in the middle of the floor. "Where are the clouds going? And the twinkle star? Mama, does the Irish see the same stars we do?"

Travis sat down beside her and pointed to three different places. "How about a cloud right there above your pillow and your twinkle star over by where your mama lies when she sings you to sleep? And then we could put another low cloud on each side so you could raise your hand and touch it even when you are in bed. Does that sound good?"

Sophie cocked her head to one side and then the other. "I like it just like you said, but could we have just a little bit of clouds on that wall around my dresser so when I wake up in the morning, I can see them?"

"Of course you can," Travis said without hesitation.

"That's a lot of work," Hannah said from the doorway. "And Calvin needs you to be ready to work on Wednesday. Have y'all even gone down there to measure and look at the hangar yet?"

"No, but I know from how many pieces of metal are on the outside about how big it is, so I've got a rough idea. We'll get the keys from you and unlock it Wednesday morning," Travis said. "And then the fun will begin. I'm glad he's coming back to Crossing. It brings us full circle." He paused and pointed toward the mirror above Sophie's dresser. "How about one more star, right up there?"

Sophie clapped her hands and jumped up. "I've got to go tell Aunt Birdie all about it."

"Look both ways before you cross the street," Hannah said.

"I will, but, Mama, don't nobody ever come down this road. It just ends at the river."

"Ain't that the truth." Hannah nodded.

Travis rolled up on his feet and picked up the paintbrush.

"Kind of like my life. It looked like a dead end, but now there's a possibility of a flood of good things," Hannah said to Travis.

"Amen, darlin'. Nothing but good things in your future, with lots of twinkle stars and rainbows."

"You've always been positive." She pulled the plastic cover from a rocking chair and sat down. "Hey, what happened to that woman you were so serious about a few years ago? Angela, right? You brought her home for Christmas one year and we all thought you'd marry her, and then boom, you didn't say much about her anymore."

"The problem is that another woman caught my eye years ago. Angela was the one who told me that before I could move on to the future, I had to get over the past."

"Why didn't you tell the other woman or ask her out or do something?" Hannah asked.

"Because I was too shy to tell her at first, and then she was out of my reach. Is that your phone?" he deflected.

"No, must be yours. I'll get back to the sewing so we'll have the curtains done when you finish and her room will be ready tonight." Hannah disappeared down the hallway and back into the dining room, where the noise of the sewing machine again filled the house.

Travis pulled the phone from his shirt pocket and smiled. "Hello, Patsy."

"I'm calling to get your take on how my daughter is really doing. She sounds euphoric when I talk to her, but we all know that when a person is flying that high, they'll crash. Do I need to make arrangements to come to Texas before Independence Day?" Hannah's mother asked.

"She'd love to see you anytime, but in my opinion she's doing better every day. I'm here as well as Aunt Birdie. We'll all support her any way we can," Travis said.

"I'm glad to hear that. What is that noise?"

"Sewing machine."

"Oh, that's right. She told me she was going to make some valances. And what do you think about this abused-women thing?"

Travis laid the brush across the paint can and sat down in the rocking chair. "I think it might be just the therapy that she needs.

Helping women to find a way out of a situation like she was in or maybe even worse might be the very thing that brings her closure, Patsy," Travis said.

"I'm not nearly as worried about her as I used to be. We get to talk when we want now, and hearing her voice is a blessing. And Travis, thank you."

"If it's a help to you or Hannah, I'm all for anything," he said softly.

"I know, and I appreciate it. I'll talk to her later this evening. Right now Mama is hollerin' that it's time for our game show that we watch together every morning, so 'bye for now."

"'Bye, Patsy." Travis hit the "End" button and slipped the phone back in his pocket.

The sewing machine stopped, and Hannah yelled, asking him if he wanted something to drink.

"Sweet tea, please." He picked up the brush and went back to work on the rainbow.

She brought two glasses into the room and handed him one. "I need to talk."

"About?"

"I don't know."

He picked up the cold sweet tea and took a long drink. "Then how do you even know you need to talk?"

"Because these feelings inside me are too heavy. I can't talk to Liz, because she's got enough on her plate. Cal is all busy getting ready to move. And besides, you've always been the one of us who . . ." She paused.

Travis's heart jumped up into his throat. He'd been the one who what? Was the sucker because he was too shy to tell Hannah that he'd loved her when they were kids? Was like a brother?

Just don't let her say that brother thing, he thought. *I can work with almost anything but that.*

The pregnant silence hung over the room like smoke in an old honky-tonk. Travis didn't realize he was holding his breath until she finally inhaled deeply and started to talk again.

"You're the one I could bring my problems to when we were kids. I love our other friends, I really do, but you were my one person."

His heart settled back into place in his chest. If he was her person, then maybe someday she'd see him as more than that. "And what's this problem today?"

"I don't feel guilty, and yet I do."

"About what?" he asked.

"I just got a divorce a week ago, and there should be at least a little bit of guilt for not trying harder to make it work. If I'd been what Marty needed in his life, Sophie wouldn't be growing up without a father. But I didn't try very hard. I didn't like the big-city life, and I did like living here in Crossing. I'd make things nice for him here, but I didn't push for him to take me to Dallas for his fancy dinners and parties. Lord, Travis, I felt so out of place at those things that sometimes I hid out in the bathroom. After Sophie was born, I didn't really care if he came home or not."

"There was a reason for all that," Travis said.

Hannah nodded. "I know, but still, shouldn't there be some remorse somewhere? All I feel is relief that it's over. I'll never make that mistake again."

"As in never trusting another man?" Travis asked.

"No, not that. One rotten man shouldn't ruin it for every other man on Earth," she answered. "I told you I didn't know how to even talk about this."

"You feel guilty because you don't feel guilty," he said simply.

"Yes!" she answered. "That's it, and I can't shake it."

"Maybe helping other women will give you some closure," he suggested.

"I hope so." Hannah shook her head as if to clear it. "Thanks, Travis. I'll get back to sewing. Aunt Birdie called a little bit ago and said that dinner would be ready at straight up noon, so that gives us half an hour. The way you're throwing those clouds on the wall, I'd say you'll have your end of the bargain done by then."

"I'm surprised that Sophie didn't stick around longer." He didn't want Hannah to leave. "I figured she'd be sitting right beside me while I painted until it was totally finished."

"She'll be back soon, but right now she and Miss Rosie are in a heated game of Old Maid. Sophie was winning, last I heard. They'll keep her busy until after we eat, and then we can surprise her with the new room."

"One more cloud and one twinkle star and it'll be done." He grinned.

ా

When Travis smiled, Hannah's heart threw in an extra beat. It had always been that way, even back when they were kids. Talking to him made things better, because he listened and then she got a clear picture of how to fix things.

And what about that woman that stole his heart all those years ago, she wondered. Was it right after he left Crossing to go on the construction road with his dad? A little streak of jealousy shot down her spine. Why hadn't he confided in her about this woman? And would he ever get over that first love?

You didn't tell him the whole story about Marty. All he knew was that the man was mentally abusive, the voice in her head said very bluntly. *So don't expect him to tell you about the woman who still holds his heart.*

"Okay, then, back to the noisy sewing machine." She blinked her way back to the present.

"We'll get it all done by Wednesday"—there was that grin again—"and when Cal gets here with his truckload of stuff, I'll be ready to start helping him lay out his new designing place. We've been talking on the phone a lot. I kind of know what he's got in mind."

She didn't want to leave, yet she really did need to get back to the sewing business, so she whipped around and went back to the dining room.

She'd finished another valance when Liz called to apologize for not showing up to help. Wyatt had come home unexpectedly. She'd be able to help after he left on Wednesday morning. His route would take him north, so he'd be gone a week this time.

"Are you okay? You sound like you are losing your voice," Hannah said.

"I'm fine. Wyatt is watching a movie, and he doesn't like me to talk very loud. Got to go. He's motioning for me to refill his tea glass. See you Wednesday," Liz said.

Hannah's hands were shaking when she hit the "End" button on her phone. For a long minute, she wished that it wasn't against the law to shoot an abusive man. Wouldn't it be wonderful if they made it legal just one day out of the year?

They could even issue hunting licenses and make some money for the state, like they did with those tags that hunters hung on deer when they shot one. Only this time it would be something to hang on the abuser's toe. Then whoever got to the station first to check in their dead husband would get a big, gold-plated trophy.

To take her mind off what was going on right down the street at Liz's house, she stretched out another length of white fabric on the dining room table and cut it into the right lengths for the living room window valances. She was working on the last cut when the doorbell rang. Figuring it was Sophie, sent by Aunt Birdie, to tell them to come on to dinner, she didn't answer it. Sophie liked to play visitor, but Hannah was busy.

It rang again, and she hurried from the dining room across to the foyer. Expecting to see Sophie with a big grin on her face, she slung it open, but it wasn't her daughter on the other side of the screen door. Gina was standing there with a strange woman beside her.

"I tried to call, but you must have not heard your phone. Can we please get inside?"

"Yes, of course." Hannah threw open the door.

The petite lady that followed Gina into the house was smaller than Hannah by at least fifteen pounds and looked like she'd been dragged through a hedge backward.

"I'm sorry. This sewing machine sounds like a threshing machine." Hannah motioned them inside.

Gina nodded toward the lady. "This is Elaine, and she's twenty-one. She walked into the shelter this morning. You have been approved, and the paperwork is in the mail. Patchwork House is completely full. I don't even have a sofa to put her on. I'll let her tell you her story, if it's all right if I leave her with you."

"Of course it's all right." Hannah held out a hand, and the younger woman bypassed it and hugged her tightly.

"Thank you so much. I walked ten miles to get to that shelter, hiding in the weeds every time a car came by," Elaine whispered. "I can't go back. He'll kill me."

Travis poked his head out of the dining room. "Aunt Birdie called. Dinner is ready. Oh, I'm sorry, I didn't . . ."

Elaine jumped back two feet, hit the door with her bony shoulders, and slapped her hands over her eyes. Her slim body quivered all over.

Hannah rushed to her side and laid a hand on her shoulder, which only made the situation worse until Elaine uncovered her eyes. "It's okay. Travis is one of the good guys. He won't hurt you. Travis, this is Elaine, and she's going to stay here a few days."

"I'm so sorry I scared you," Travis said. "I was coming out to tell Hannah that it was time for dinner. You are both welcome to join us, Gina."

"Thank you, but I have to get back." Gina smiled. "And it's best if Elaine stays inside. You did read that handbook I left for you, right?"

"Every word—twice." Hannah nodded seriously and then turned to Travis. "Tell Aunt Birdie I won't be there. I'll just make a couple of sandwiches here."

"How about I bring some food for you and Elaine?" Travis said.

"That would be great, and Gina, Elaine can stay here as long as she needs to," Hannah said.

"I appreciate your generosity," Gina said.

Hannah heard the kitchen door open and close and hugged Travis in her mind for being so kind. She laced her fingers in Elaine's and led her to the kitchen, where she pulled out a chair for her at the table.

"Hungry?" Hannah asked.

"I ate breakfast yesterday. He said I didn't deserve dinner or supper since I hadn't ironed his shirts right. When he caught me sneaking a few cookies out of the jar, well . . ." She stopped.

Words weren't necessary. The bruises on her arms and her legs were definitely belt marks, and the black eye said he'd used his fists as well.

"Travis is my friend, and he's helping me do some painting. He'll be back soon with dinner and we'll eat. Then you can take a good, warm bath and a long nap," Hannah said.

Elaine looked like she needed it. Her cheekbones were hollow. Her blonde hair hung in oily strings around her gaunt face, and her eyes darted around the room as if she was afraid it would disappear.

"He'll be out huntin' for me. I'll work. You just tell me what to do and I'll do it. I can clean and iron, and I'm good with kids. Gina said you got a little girl."

"Yes, I do. Her name is Sophie, and she's going to love having company," Hannah said.

Elaine jumped and shivered when someone knocked on the kitchen door. Hannah laid a hand on her shoulder as she passed. "It's okay. I imagine it's Travis bringing us some food, but I'll make sure before I open it."

"I'm sorry," Elaine whispered.

"It's okay." Hannah gently patted her before she pulled back the curtain over the window.

She opened the door and stood back for Travis to bring in a cardboard box with covered dishes inside.

"Aunt Birdie said that she and Sophie are going to read some books and take a long nap and then she'll bring Sophie home. This is baked potato soup, hot bread, and peach cobbler for dessert. Do you still want me to come over and help get Sophie's room put to rights?"

"Yes, please." Hannah nodded. "And tell Aunt Birdie thank you for everything."

Travis set the box on the table and smiled at Elaine. "I'm the resident handyman for Crossing. Welcome to the Lullaby Sky."

"What?" Hannah asked.

"Sophie just now informed me that was the new name of this house. So you two are the first to know the formal name."

Elaine's mouth turned up slightly. "I like it. It's calm in this place— like looking at the sky on a dark night. The stars give us hope."

"Okay, then, I'm going back across the street to eat a couple of bowls of my favorite soup. You ladies have a good dinner and visit." He left the same way he came in, easing the door shut so softly that it didn't make a sound.

Hannah uncovered the bowls and shoved the first one across the table toward Elaine so she could get a whiff of the delicious aroma. Then she pushed back her chair, stood up, and went to the cabinet for silverware and the butter. When she turned around, Elaine had her head bowed and her lips moved silently. She raised her head after a few seconds and blushed.

"Amen," Hannah said.

"I didn't know if you was a prayin' woman, and I didn't want to offend. Can't eat this good food in a house this nice without thanking God for getting me here safely," Elaine said.

"We do say grace, and I am a prayin' woman." Hannah laid out the cutlery beside Elaine's bowl and handed her a paper towel to use as a napkin. "Eat slowly. If you go too fast, it might make you sick."

Hannah wanted to hear more of her story, help her heal, until a little voice inside her head told her to be patient and let Elaine tell what she wanted when she wanted. So they ate in silence, Elaine finishing only a third of her soup before she ate three or four bites of the peach cobbler.

"Don't throw any of it away. I'll eat it for supper," Elaine said.

"Or maybe some of the cobbler after your nap? You must have walked all night."

Elaine shook her head. "Only about half of it was in the dark. The rest was daylight. I got to the shelter about ten, and that nice lady brought me here. You reckon I could have that bath now?"

Hannah wanted to weep for this poor woman. "Of course you can. There are towels and washcloths on the chair beside the tub. Bubble bath and salts are there, along with shampoo and conditioner. Help yourself to any of it. And I will leave clean underwear and a nightshirt beside the door. If you'll put your clothes on the top step, I'll pitch them in the washer and dryer for you. When you wake, they should be clean. Follow me, and you can pick out which of the bedrooms you want to claim while you are here."

"You choose for me," Elaine said.

Hannah threw open the doors for all three bedrooms as they passed by them on the way to the bathroom. Elaine didn't react to the first three, but the last one brought half a smile to her face.

"When you finish your bath, use this one. You're looking toward the river, and on the other side of it is Oklahoma," Hannah said. "You can have the run of the house, though if someone knocks on the door, you should hurry up here and hide. Gina says as little exposure as possible is necessary. I have four friends plus two neighbors, Aunt Birdie and Miss Rosie, that you don't need to worry about."

"Thank you, Hannah. You are an angel." Elaine swiped at tears and disappeared into the bathroom.

Hannah had set aside a few sets of clothes, and she fished through them for a nightshirt and a pair of underpants. She laid them beside the bathroom door, through which she could hear the sound of water running in the deep, old claw-foot tub as she crossed the landing into the room where Elaine would stay a few days. She pulled the chain to turn on the ceiling fan and quickly changed the bedsheets so they'd smell fresh.

That finished, and with nothing else she could do to make Elaine more comfortable and feel safer, she headed down the stairs. She found Miss Rosie and Travis sitting at the kitchen table, each with a glass of sweet tea in front of them.

"Her name is Elaine, and she is having a bath. Since she walked all night and half the morning, the next thing she wants is a nap," Hannah said.

"Clothing?" Miss Rosie asked.

"I would guess what she has on her back. I didn't even see a purse."

"I'll go down to our church clothes closet and fix her up with some things. What size would you think?"

"Have no idea about size, but I think she's about my height and maybe fifteen or twenty pounds lighter."

Miss Rosie nodded. "This is going to be a joint effort, Hannah. I talked to Gina after she got back to the shelter, and she's in agreement."

"You know Gina?"

Miss Rosie sipped her tea. "Oh, yes. I'm the one who got her the job and helps her write the grant requests from the government. She called me after she talked to you about offering to be a safe house."

Travis laid a hand on Hannah's. "She is really nervous, so I'll stay out of the way as much as possible."

"Poor thing. That's probably a good idea. Why don't you take the downstairs bedroom and I'll sleep upstairs while she is here? If it was me in her shoes, that would make me more comfortable," Hannah said.

"That sounds like a good idea," Miss Rosie said quickly. "I'm thinking this one is going to need a fresh start. I'll start putting out feelers and get with Gina about new papers."

"You can do that?" Travis asked.

"Oh, yes, we can. We'll find a place far away and give her a whole new name and identity so that bastard can't find her ever again. But it can't be done overnight, and we'll need to bring in the therapist to talk to her a couple of times to be sure that when she gets to her new location, she doesn't get crazy and call him."

Hannah's dark brows became a solid line and deep wrinkle furrowed across her forehead. "I didn't know that you . . ."

Miss Rosie smiled. "I've been trying to ferret out who was the snitch for years when it came to your situation. If I could have figured out who was telling Marty every single time you drove out of town, I would have fixed things for you. Had no idea that it wasn't a person at all, just technology. But things work out for the best, Hannah, and now you are right where you need to be to help others."

Hannah glanced over at Travis. "Did you know that she was involved with helping abused women?"

He shrugged.

"He knew. He even volunteers when Gina needs someone to talk to the older boys. My grandson makes a pretty good therapist," Miss Rosie said with pride.

"Why didn't you tell me?" Hannah asked Travis.

"I guess I'm telling you now, or rather, Miss Rosie is." Travis grinned as he slid his hand from Hannah's and drank the sweet tea. For the first time since the divorce, she hadn't flinched when he put his hand on hers, but she did feel empty when he removed it. Did that mean that she was healing? She'd expected it to take months, maybe even years before she stopped jumping when someone touched her.

"Let's get Sophie's room ready," Travis suggested. "She's itching to come home and see it."

Hannah's soft giggle filled the room. "That's my Sophie."

Travis pushed up out of the chair and held out a hand. "That's our girl, all right."

Hannah put hers in it, and together they walked to Sophie's room. He didn't let go until they were inside the room where clouds and the twinkle star greeted them. And somehow it wasn't uncomfortable or weird. It felt just right.

Chapter Nine

There wasn't even a faint little wispy cloud in the sky on Wednesday morning when Liz showed up wearing faded jeans, an oversize T-shirt, and flip-flops. She came through the door fanning herself with the back of her hand.

"It's going to be a hot one," she said. "Oh. My. Goodness—this doesn't look like the same place. It's so airy and beautiful and I love it. And I had looked forward to helping, but"—she paused—"you know how it goes. Wyatt was home a lot longer than I expected."

Yes, Hannah knew exactly how it went. She didn't need a map to know what Liz was going through. But was Liz reaching out to her with that last statement? If so, Hannah should do something to encourage her to open up. Where did she start?

"You are here now, and that's all that matters." Hannah said the first thing that came to her mind and hoped that God would give her the right words to say next. "Why don't we paint your house while Wyatt is gone? It would be a surprise for him when he comes home." Holy hell! That wasn't the right thing to say at all. Had those words really come out of Hannah's mouth?

"Oh, no!" Liz waved both her hands. "That's his house, remember. It belonged to his grandmother, and the place has to remain a shrine to her. I'm sure the world would come to an abrupt end if I even moved a picture on the wall."

Hannah pushed ahead. "Then let's just do your bedroom." If God wanted her to talk about redoing a room, then he must have a purpose.

Liz shook her head. "That was his bedroom as a child. I'd love to have a king-size bed, but even mentioning it makes him angry. That full-size one that we are sleeping on is lumpy, and Wyatt takes up three-fourths of it."

A picture of the sign at the Patchwork House flashed in Hannah's mind. *God, if you're trying to tell me something, I sure wish you'd spit it out a lot plainer,* she thought. *Patchwork. House. Quilts. Do you want us to make a quilt, or should I hog-tie Liz and take her to the shelter against her will?*

"If we can't redo your house, then let's make a quilt. The sewing machine is set up and we've got some scraps from the valances, and I know Aunt Birdie has lots of leftovers from her quilting days out in her storage shed. That can be our project for the rest of the summer," Hannah said.

"We could even borrow her quilting frame after we piece it together." Liz sounded really excited.

Maybe Hannah had finally found her way through the maze that God had thrown her into. The peaceful rhythm of working together might help Liz share some of her thoughts.

Liz poured two glasses of tea and handed one to Hannah. "I've never quilted anything by hand, but it sounds like fun. Let's go over there and see what she's got. I bet she can even help us pick out a pattern."

Hannah shook her head slowly from side to side. "I know you. You'll pick out something so difficult it'll take us a year to piece together. So before we go, let's decide to start out with an easy pattern."

"What's the fun in that?" Liz's grin reached her eyes for the first time in months.

"Aunt Liz!" Sophie squealed as she pulled Elaine into the room by the hand. "I have a new friend. Her name is Laney."

Hannah watched Liz's smile fade and her eyes mist as she took in the bruises on Elaine's face, arms, and legs. Time froze. Hannah saw herself in the past, and from the pained look on Liz's face, she was looking at herself in the present and possibly even the future.

"Liz, meet Elaine. Elaine, this is my friend Liz. She's also my boss—I'm a teacher's aide at the school where she's the principal," Hannah said.

"Sophie has told me all about you," Elaine said with shy hesitation.

Never before had Hannah wanted to fix things so much, both for her old friend and for her new one, but she was helpless in a hopeless situation. Elaine had taken the first step, and there would be help for her. But Liz was a different story. Hannah felt totally helpless to lend a hand to her friend when Liz wouldn't admit she needed it.

"I'm pleased to meet you, Laney," Liz finally said, hoarsely, as she pulled the sleeve of her T-shirt down to cover a yellow-and-green bruise.

Elaine nodded and smiled. "Sophie did a good job of describing you."

A rap on the door broke the intense aura in the room. Elaine took a couple of steps back toward the stairs. Hinges squeaked, and Calvin's big, booming voice filled the house.

"I have arrived. It took a week longer than I'd thought it would, but I'm here! The moving van is down at the hangar right now, but I had to come see everyone before I tell them where to put things. Sophie, my beautiful princess, I'm waiting for my hug."

Sophie threw herself into Cal's arms. He swung her around the room twice before he set her down and wrapped both Liz and Hannah into a three-way embrace.

"Uncle Calvin, this is Laney. She was supposed to stay with us one day, but she got to stay longer. But"—Sophie lowered her voice—"she can't go outside. I think that she's afraid Nadine will give her the bumps."

"Mumps," Hannah said. "Anna Lou had them last week, and now Nadine has got them." She lowered her voice so only he could hear. "And Cal, Elaine is one of my guests." She raised an eyebrow. "She's still jittery and jumpy, so . . ."

"Enough said," Cal said from the side of his mouth.

"I'll go on up to my room." Elaine slunk off in that direction, fear and intimidation in her body language.

"I'm Calvin Winters. I'm sorry I barged in here like a bull in a china closet," Cal said in a soft tone. "I'm so excited to be back in Crossing that I didn't think. Don't go, Elaine. Do you like it here?"

"Oh, yes." Elaine turned with a smile. "I love it here."

"So do I." Cal flashed his warmest smile. "That's why I'm coming home. I sure hope that things work out well for you. Maybe our paths will cross again, and next time I'll be a little less blustery."

"Thank you," Elaine said.

"I was only checking in before I go down to the hangar and start unpacking, so I'll see all y'all later. Nice meeting you, Miz Elaine."

"You, too," Elaine answered.

He'd opened the door to leave, but Aunt Birdie pushed her way inside and rolled up on her toes to kiss Cal on the cheek. "I thought that was your van out there. I been tellin' you for years that you could design your clothing line anywhere in the world, so why live in a big city?"

"You are so right." Calvin nodded.

Sophie crossed the room to grab Calvin's hand. "Can I go with y'all to see what you are doing with Father's airplane place?"

"No, you are going with me," Hannah said. "You would get in the way down at the hangar. And besides, I might need help picking out scraps if Aunt Birdie don't mind us taking some for a quilt."

"Well, hot damn." Aunt Birdie grinned. "Y'all are making a quilt? What size bed? Calvin, get on out of here so us ladies can talk sewing projects."

Calvin's chuckle turned into a full-fledged laugh. "Now, Aunt Birdie, you know that I love to talk about fabrics and sewing."

"But you are going to be hammering nails and building walls the next few weeks instead of making dresses, right?" Hannah asked.

"I can do that, too, but my first love is the sewing machine." Calvin sighed.

"Don't know the size of the quilts or who they are for, Aunt Birdie," Hannah answered. "But Liz and I need a project."

"Then make them in throw size and I'll get Travis to put together a rack that sits on the floor to hold them," Calvin said.

"Liz and I are both making one, and we'll both need a rack," Hannah said.

"I bet Travis won't mind making two." He nodded.

"Just one," Liz said. "I told you—I can't add to or take from that house I'm in, or it would cause the beginning of the next world war."

Aunt Birdie pulled out a chair and eased down into it. "You could piece together throws instead of full-size quilts if you want a project that would go faster. And to answer your question, I'd be glad to get rid of whatever scraps you want to take out of my storage shed."

"You are welcome to my scraps, too," Cal said. "I've got at least a dozen boxes being unloaded right now."

Aunt Birdie pointed at Sophie and then at Liz. "Y'all two go on over to my storage building. Take a couple of garbage bags with you. Sophie can pick out colors for Hannah, and you can find what you'd like to work with. Pattern books are on the shelf above the boxes."

"Can Elaine go with us?" Sophie asked. "We won't go through the backyard, so she won't get the bumps."

"Sorry, darlin', but Elaine has to stay inside," Aunt Birdie said. "But I bet she'll help y'all cut out the pieces for the quilt when you get back."

"Can we look at Uncle Cal's stuff first?" Sophie asked.

"No, because it isn't unloaded yet. When we do the second one, we'll go through his scraps," Liz said. "Come on, baby girl, let's get the stuff to go into the quilting business. We need to think about a pretty throw for the rocking chair in your room. I'm making mine special for you," Liz said. "What colors do you think would be pretty?"

"Blue and yellow and white, like my new walls. And can it have stars and clouds on it?" Sophie put her small hand in Liz's, and the two of them left by the front door.

"And I have to go down to the hangar," Cal said. "That invitation to lunch still standing, Aunt Birdie?"

"No, but it is for dinner. You are in the backwoods, Calvin, not the city. Here we have dinner and supper. And dinner is at noon, straight up. Today we are having chili and corn bread," she answered.

"Yes, ma'am," he said.

ℂℂ

When everyone had disappeared, Hannah looked over at Elaine. "Let's make tea and talk."

"Hot tea with cream and sugar." Elaine smiled.

"Yes," Hannah said as she made two cups of tea and carried them to the living room. "Even though it means we didn't get to talk, I'm glad you had time to sleep and begin to recover. Gina said she's coming to take you back to the shelter tonight."

Elaine sank into the sofa and sipped the hot tea. "I need to be there to get my new paperwork done, but it scares me to leave here. I feel safe here at your Lullaby Sky."

"I'm glad that you feel safe, but don't be scared. Gina will take good care of you," Hannah said. "How long were you married?"

"Oh, he never married me. He just sweet-talked me into moving in with him and then treated me like shit. I was sixteen and my stepdad threw me out after my mama died. I got on a bus and came to Texas from up in northern Oklahoma to stay with my brother, but he'd moved and I didn't know where to go. I slept on the streets for a few nights, then Jimmy come along and offered to let me stay at his trailer."

Hannah shivered. "You've put up with this for five years?"

"And I might've put up with it longer, but he brought a new girl in last week and told his friends that he'd sell me to the highest bidder," Elaine said. "I stood up to him, and he damn near beat me to death."

"I am so sorry," Hannah said.

"Me, too, but only that I didn't leave sooner."

A gentle rap on the door took their attention that way. Hannah got up, pulled back the curtain, and motioned for Liz to come on inside.

Liz looked as if she would burst into tears any second. Her breath was coming in short bursts like she'd jogged from Aunt Birdie's back to Hannah's house. She leaned against the cabinet and kept clasping her hands and then dropping them to her sides.

"Is Sophie all right?" Hannah asked.

"Yes, why?"

"You look like you are about to deliver bad news," Elaine said.

"It's not Sophie. She's fine. She's with Aunt Birdie picking out scraps," Liz said.

"Talk to me," Hannah said.

"I'm scared out of my mind. Wyatt wants a baby," Liz blurted out.

Hannah held her breath until her ribs ached. Her first impulse was to jump up, cross the room, and hug her—assure her that she'd be a wonderful mother and not to be scared. But it was as if she was held to the sofa with ropes and chains and could not move.

"Don't do it," Elaine said. "It'll be one more reason to beat you."

"He doesn't . . . ," Liz started.

"You can lie, but it don't make it the truth," Elaine said.

Hannah opened her mouth, but no words came out. She swallowed twice and patted the sofa between her and Elaine. "Sit down and let's talk about this."

"You know how it is. You lived through it. For me, meeting Elaine has brought it all home to me. If I have Wyatt's child, he'll threaten me with it like Marty did you, and I'll wind up just like both of you. I don't know how much more I can stand," Liz whispered.

"What are you going to do?" Hannah asked.

"She's going to leave him," Elaine said. "She's got friends and a place to go, so there's no reason not to leave."

Liz inhaled deeply and let it out slowly, as if getting up the courage to even speak the words. "I have to pick my moment."

"You know I'm here if you need me, and I happen to know a really good shelter over in Gainesville if you want to hide out for a few days. I've known for a long time that Wyatt was abusive, but you have to realize you have a problem before you can solve it," Hannah said.

Liz sat down on the sofa. Tears flowed down her cheeks and left wet circles on her shirt as they dripped from her chin. "You tried and failed, and you are stronger than I am. Always have been. It's going to get rough. Wyatt doesn't let go of his possessions easily."

"Is that what you feel like you are? Just a possession?" Hannah asked.

"It's not a feeling. It's a fact. It's written in stone," she said simply. "I've started making a plan, though, and just that much and telling you makes me feel like there is a future outside of humiliation and bruises."

"The sooner you put that plan into place, the better," Hannah said. "And I'm right here any time you need me. We all are."

"Thank you." Liz wiped away the tears.

"For?"

"Not pushing me and just being my friend."

Hannah smiled through the tears that wanted to escape from her eyes. She had to be strong or Liz might take two steps backward. "I had no right to push anyone. I've got two good sharp shovels down in the hangar. If bad comes to worst, they'll never find his body."

Elaine giggled and then laughed, and then it became a guffaw that not even the universe could contain when they all started laughing. They'd barely gotten it under control when Travis stuck his head in the back door.

"Got a few minutes, Hannah?" Travis asked. "Cal wants you to come down to the hangar."

"I'll keep an eye on Sophie if Aunt Birdie brings her home before you get back," Liz said.

"And maybe me and Liz can visit some more about sorry men." Elaine nodded.

"Okay, then, but if Gina shows up early, don't let her take you away before I return, Elaine," Hannah said.

"I sure won't leave without telling y'all good-bye, and thanks for letting me talk, Hannah. It did help," Elaine answered.

Travis held the door for her, and she headed off toward the hangar for the first time in six months. She was at the edge of her yard when her phone rang. She fished it out of the hip pocket of her khaki shorts and frowned when she saw her divorce lawyer's number pop up under a picture of the front of his building.

Her heart stopped, and her hands went clammy. She didn't want to answer, but not knowing was worse than facing her greatest fear—that Marty would find a way to get back into her life.

"Hello," she said cautiously.

"Mrs. Ellis? This is Rayford Dillard, your lawyer for the divorce."

"No, this is Miss O'Malley, remember. I thought we'd finalized everything," she said.

"Sorry if I startled you. Everything is finalized and filed at the courthouse, yes. Copies are in the mail to you."

Part of the stress eased out of her body. "Thank you for letting me know."

"But we have another problem—or blessing, whichever way you look at it." He chuckled.

The word that stood out in bold italics was *problem*, not *blessing*, in Hannah's mind. "Just spit it out."

The lawyer laughed again. "Your ex forgot that his airplane was parked on your property and now he wants it back. It's a stupid thing for him to forget something that big, but he did in his haste to get the papers signed. Now it legally belongs to you. What do you want to do about it? This is damned funny."

She sat down hard on the ground. She was totally stunned. "How in the devil did he forget something as big as an airplane? Rayford, I've sold that hangar intact with everything that was in it. If Marty wants his plane, he'll have to get in touch with Calvin Winters's lawyers. But as OCD as he is, I'm still in shock that he forgot that his plane was parked here and not in Dallas."

"I asked his lawyer the same question. Do you remember him saying something about having trouble with the landing gear?"

"Yes, but I thought he'd gotten it fixed. He said he was calling a repairman and that he'd give him the key so I wouldn't even know when he came and went. He called his driver to come get him that weekend."

"Well, there was a communication problem. The guy who fixed it was supposed to fly it back to Dallas and put it in the Ellis hangar. He didn't get that part of the message, so he fixed it and left it right where it sits. All this time, the Ellises have thought the plane was in Dallas. I guess since Martin's new girlfriend lives right there, he didn't need to fly the thing. I do think it's funny as hell that karma has bit him on the ass for the way he treated you in that courtroom," Rayford said with more laughter.

"The matter is out of my hands." Hannah giggled. "Winters, Grayson, and Drury out of Denton represent Calvin, if you want to get in touch with them. And before you ask, that's his father and his two sisters, and they are partners in that firm. I don't think Marty is going to be happy, and I feel sorry for that redhead who's now with him. When he gets mad, it's not a pretty scene."

Rayford had stopped laughing, but now he had the hiccups. "I will definitely tell him that. Have you had any problems?"

"No, sir. I cleared out all his hidden cameras, listening devices, and GPS trackers and changed my phone number. I did keep all the camera stuff. How did you get my number, anyway?"

"I went through Aunt Birdie. Remember, she's the one who recommended me to you. But never fear, I would never give the number to anyone. And Hannah, hang on to everything that you found. If he ever makes trouble, it might be helpful. You have a good day. This has certainly made mine better."

"Thank you and mine, too." She hit the "End" button and blinked a dozen times to be sure she wasn't dreaming.

Travis sat down beside her. "I got one side of that conversation and I know there's an airplane in the hangar. So what are you going to do?"

She fell back on the grass and laughed until tears streamed down her face for the second time in less than an hour. "Not one damn thing," she said between chortles. "It's no longer my plane, and Cal can push it off into the Red River if he wants to, or he can sell it to the highest bidder to reclaim some of the money that he paid me for the place. I knew he was overpaying me and now I don't feel so bad."

Travis pushed back a strand of her hair stuck to the moisture on her cheek. "I like it when you laugh like that."

She looked up into his eyes, rimmed with lashes so thick that most women would sell their souls to have them. How had she never realized how pretty his eyes were or how handsome he was? And when in the devil had his touch caused a catch in her chest and a little flutter in her heart?

Chapter Ten

Aunt Birdie poured two shots of Pappy Van Winkle into a couple of recycled jelly glasses and held hers up in a toast. "To karma and the future. Both of us old coots are going to live to see our dreams come true before we die. It's happening before our eyes."

"Don't you call me an old coot. I'm a full-fledged bitch, and I got the background to prove it." Miss Rosie sipped the amber liquid, holding it on her tongue a full minute before she swallowed. "Damn fine stuff. You did well to hang onto it until our victory dance."

"Oh, honey, this is just the twelve-year-old stuff. I'm hanging onto that prime bottle until we cross the finish line," Aunt Birdie said. "I told you when that damned old plane sat there a month that he'd forgotten about it. Now we know why. He was out tomcattin' in a sandbox he didn't have no right to play in. Well, here's to you, you rotten sumbitch." She held up her glass again, then downed the last dregs and poured another shot.

"I wonder if this shit burns?" Miss Rosie asked.

"Why would you want to use something this wonderful to set fire to something? You could buy twenty gallons of gasoline for what this bottle cost me."

Miss Rosie's plump shoulders rose a few inches in a shrug. "Might be worth it to take care of Wyatt. I'm so old I remember when God created dirt, so I don't mind spending the rest of my days in prison for setting a worthless man on fire and roasting marshmallows with the flames."

"Marshmallows toasted off someone that wicked would poison you," Aunt Birdie scolded.

"But what a way to go." Miss Rosie held her glass toward Aunt Birdie. "Hit me one more time."

Aunt Birdie poured a healthy two fingers into the glass. "To the future, and may it all turn out the way we want before we die or go to prison."

Miss Rosie giggled. "Now that's something we can agree on for sure. Just giving you a forewarning that Travis will be spending the nights over there again starting on Saturday."

"And how do you know that?" Aunt Birdie lowered her chin nearly to her chest and looked up at Miss Rosie. "We agreed not to meddle."

"It's not really meddling. Not any more than you do when you make sure they're sitting beside each other at the dinner table," Miss Rosie protested. "There's a new woman at the shelter, and they'll be another week getting her papers ready. She has a couple of little girls. I think they'd benefit from a kind of halfway house like Hannah's place before they're sent to Florida to help run a T-shirt shop on the beach."

"Darcy and Cal?" Aunt Birdie asked.

"What about them?"

"You don't have inside connections with anything to help them," Aunt Birdie said.

"I'll leave that up to you, and you are welcome." Miss Rosie giggled again. "Hot damn! This stuff packs a wallop. I'd best be getting on home while I can still walk across our yards."

Aunt Birdie put the top back on the bottle. "You never could hold your liquor."

"It's the Indian blood in me. No, that's not politically correct. It's the Native American blood in me. We like the booze, but we don't do too damn well with holding it. That damned old Irish your mother gave you means you could drink a barrel of cheap whiskey and still dance the jitterbug." Miss Rosie tossed back the last of what was in her glass.

Aunt Birdie did the same and pushed back her chair. "I'll walk you home."

"I ain't that drunk," Miss Rosie protested.

"And I ain't listenin' to you. If you fell and broke a hip, I'd have to stay with you at the hospital until you got well, and then all our plannin' would go down the Red River." She looped her arm into Miss Rosie's.

When they reached the back door, Aunt Birdie flipped on the porch light. "Only got a sliver of moon tonight, so we'd best have some artificial light."

"We've been across these two yards so many times in our life we could do it blindfolded."

Aunt Birdie gripped her best friend's arm tighter. "But not blindfolded and drunk."

"Is that a skunk or did you . . ." Miss Rosie stopped suddenly and pointed.

Aunt Birdie saw the skunk at the same time she stepped in a gopher hole and stumbled, taking both her and Miss Rosie to the ground. They lay there on their backs, arms still locked together and the skunk parading past their feet, taking his time to stop and check out each blade of grass on the way.

"Be very still. He ain't got his tail up," Miss Rosie whispered from the side of her mouth.

"Yet," Aunt Birdie said softly. "Are you hurt?"

"Hell, no! Drunks are limber as cooked noodles. Lord, that thing stinks. I wonder how in the devil he gets a lady skunk to lift her tail for him," Miss Rosie said.

"Shhh, he'll hear you and spray us."

"Don't shush me. If he sprays me, I'll wring his sorry neck right here."

The skunk tipped his nose up in the air and sniffed for several seconds, then moved on into the darkness. Aunt Birdie waited a little longer and then sat up, unhooked her arm from Miss Rosie and smelled the sleeve of her shirt.

"Dammit! He left his scent on the grass. We'll have to burn our clothes."

Miss Rosie pursed her mouth tightly and then huffed. "I guess it's a small price to pay for not breaking a bone, but I did like this shirt. Oh, well, I don't expect they'd let me keep it in prison anyway."

Aunt Birdie giggled and then guffawed. "Ain't life grand."

"Even with skunks!" Miss Rosie joined in the laughter. "At least I can strip off naked as a newborn baby and leave my clothes on the back porch. You got to wear yours in the house and smell up the whole place."

"Not if you loan me a robe. I can strip off mine on your porch, take a shower in your house, and wear one of your robes back home."

"Better go by the way of the road when you go home. If you bring my robe back smelling like skunk, I'll never drink with you again," Miss Rosie told her.

☙

Travis left the computer and pulled back the curtains so he could see across the street. The lights in Hannah's bedroom cast a yellow glow out into the yard, but then they went out. He went back to the computer and typed in another scene in his newest book.

He'd set out to write mystery, but so much of life and love came through in his voice that his agent told him that he was actually writing romantic suspense. His father was a big, burly carpenter with clear lines about what men and women did with their lives. Writing books was pretty much on the side of a sissy. Writing romance, even suspense, was not in the masculine wheelhouse. So he and his agent created a pseudonym for him at the beginning. He was Teresa Walters on the front of the book, and an actress's picture graced the back. She also was paid to sign books for him when necessary, although the agent was pretty good at making up excuses for public appearances. Cal was the only person in the whole world who knew that he'd made enough money to retire by the time he was thirty-five.

And yet he was driven to keep writing. He promised himself that when he finished each book he would take a whole week and do nothing but what he wanted to do. The first day went fine, but by the second evening he was pacing the floor, and by the third day he already had his notebook out, plotting the next book.

What would Hannah think of his secret identity? She'd always accepted Cal's fashion business, so maybe she wouldn't think he was less of a man because he wrote romance books.

He'd written two pages when he pushed back from the laptop. He needed a break, and Aunt Birdie's chocolate cake called to him from the kitchen. The light was still on under Cal's door, so he knocked gently. It swung open immediately.

"Hey, want to join me in the kitchen for chocolate cake?" he asked.

Cal raked his fingers through his hair. "I was just trying to decide if it would be wrong to go raid the refrigerator. I'm having trouble on my next design, and sometimes walking away from it is the only thing that helps. So yes, and besides, I would appreciate the company."

The light was still on in the kitchen, and there was a bottle of Pappy Van Winkle and two jelly glasses sitting on the table when they arrived. Travis laughed down deep in his chest at the expression on Cal's face.

"Looks like the two old gals have been celebrating something. Usually if they're going to have a snort, they get out the Jack Daniel's. This is only for really special times." Travis took the cover from the chocolate cake pan.

Cal reached for two plates and a couple of forks and carried them to the table. "So what could be that special? If it was me coming back to Crossing, then they should have at least invited me to have a shot with them. If it was Marty finding out about that airplane in the hangar, they should have invited all of us to have a shot with them."

"Who knows with those gals? It could be that they were celebrating the fact that they'd lived through another day. Big chunk of cake or just a little one? Milk, tea, or beer?"

Cal pointed to the milk jug. "Milk. We have beer?"

Travis nodded. "Aunt Birdie likes one every so often, and I still love a cold one on a hot night, so there's always beer in the fridge and liquor behind the doors of the buffet in the dining room. But don't touch the Pappy.

"So are you going to finally tell Darcy that you've been in love with her since grade school?" Travis grinned.

"Darcy deserves a big old he-man type, not a fashion designer. She could never hold her head up in front of her friends with the likes of me. Can't you just hear all the arguments she'd face? 'No, he's not gay. No, I didn't marry him to give him an alibi. Yes, he really does make a living with a sewing machine.'"

Travis nodded. "I understand. 'He writes romance novels, so he must not be a real man. He makes his money telling stories about love and life, but he does do some carpentry on the side.'"

"Does that mean you are in love with Darcy, too?" Cal asked.

Travis set two plates of cake and two glasses of milk on the table. "Only as a friend."

"I can only hope and dream," Cal said.

"Hope and dream what?" Aunt Birdie brought a blast of hot air with her when she came through the back door.

"Is that skunk I smell?" Cal asked. "I can't remember the last time I got a whiff of that horrible scent."

"It is." Aunt Birdie wrapped a big pale-pink chenille robe tighter around her thin body. "And this is Miss Rosie's robe. We got a little smell on us when I was walking her home, and I don't want to hear another word about it. Eat your chocolate cake and drink your milk like good boys. Good night!"

She disappeared in a flash of pink, and then a loud voice filtered back down across the foyer. "And don't you touch that Pappy Van Winkle. If you want a shot of something, get out Jack or Jim or even Johnnie Walker Red, but that Pappy isn't for you."

"And my mouth had begun to water for a taste of Pappy." Cal laughed.

"Living in Crossing ain't always easy, but it's never dull." Travis forked a chunk of chocolate cake into his mouth.

∾

The clock said it was well past midnight, but Liz continued to pace from one room to the other, from the living room into the kitchen, where she made a U-turn to go through the living room and down the hall to both bedrooms again and again.

If it hadn't been so late she would have called Travis. She touched her arm, remembering the way Wyatt had reacted when he went through her phone and found she'd talked to Travis one night. The bruises had been bad enough that time that she'd had to wear a different dress from the new, sleeveless one she'd bought for the school Christmas party. Wyatt didn't even listen to her when she told him that she'd been talking to Travis about building a gun rack for his Christmas present. Oh, no! He'd just gone off on a tangent about her making a fool of him by talking to a man behind his back.

Wyatt didn't mind her visiting with Hannah, but he didn't like Darcy and he'd never liked Travis, not even in high school. It was going to be a nightmare when he found out Cal was back in Crossing. She stopped by the refrigerator, but nothing looked good. Besides, her stomach felt like gypsies were dancing around a bonfire inside it.

Now that she'd admitted that she was thinking about leaving Wyatt, she couldn't think of anything else. The pictures of his family hanging on the hallway walls glared at her. That sheep in that painting above the sofa had eyes that moved so eerily that she'd taken it down and checked to see if there were hidden cameras. After what they'd found at Hannah's place, she wouldn't have been surprised at anything.

When she couldn't take the jitters any longer, she turned out all the lights, picked up her purse with both phones tucked inside, and made her way across the backyards to Hannah's house. She rapped on the bedroom window and waited. In a few seconds, Hannah peeked out and motioned her around to the back door.

"Are you all right? Did Wyatt come home early?" The questions started the moment Hannah swung open the door.

"I'm fine, but I can't sleep in that house tonight. Can I borrow your sofa?"

"No, but you can take one of the rooms upstairs. First, let's have a cup of hot tea to settle your nerves." Hannah threw an arm around Liz's shoulders. "You are shaking like a leaf in a tornado."

"I can't live like this much longer," Liz whispered.

Hannah steered her into the kitchen, turned on the light, and pulled out a chair for her. "I'm here for you. Do I smell skunk?"

"Probably. I got a whiff of one when I was crossing through Aunt Birdie's and Miss Rosie's backyards. Do I need to take another shower to get it off me?"

"After the tea, a long, soaking bubble bath might do you a world of good, and then a really good night's sleep. Don't set an alarm and sleep as long as you can tomorrow." Hannah set about filling a pan with water and taking down a diffuser pot. She added two tablespoons of loose chamomile tea to the basket, and when the water boiled, poured it over the top.

"You were the lucky one, Hannah. Marty never came home through the week and then this last while he didn't even come around on weekends," Liz said.

"Yes, I was, but when he was here, it was miserable. I couldn't even fold a napkin right, but then I was only poor white trash and he couldn't expect anything more from me. And we won't talk about a speck of dust on the chair rungs or folding the towels the wrong way."

"Mind if I join you? I know exactly what you are talking about," Elaine said from the doorway.

"Come right in," Liz said. "We'll call it midnight group therapy. I thought you had moved to the shelter last night."

"Thank you. Gina is coming for me early in the morning. They had a glitch with the room I'll be staying in. The lady who's in there couldn't leave until the morning. Seems like all I want to do since I got here is eat." Elaine opened the cookie jar and took out half a dozen. "Dust on the chair rungs didn't bother Jimmy. But he could go off in a rage over not folding the towels with the tags turned to the inside."

"That is page one in *Abuse for Dummies*," Hannah said. "I got my first slap across the face over not placing the silverware on the table just right."

"My first whipping with his belt was over beer," Elaine said. "Even an idiot child with an IQ less than a slug should know to buy beer before anything else at the grocery store."

"Page two is the control of everything," Liz volunteered. "Like the checkbook and the phone and . . ." She paused and blushed, as if she'd said too much already.

Hannah patted her friend on the back. "You can talk freely here, Liz. It's okay. Consider this house Las Vegas."

"Anything that's said in Lullaby Sky stays in Lullaby Sky." Elaine sat up straight and nodded. "And the amount of shampoo it takes to wash my hair. The bottle holds sixteen ounces and I should make it last a whole month. If it runs out before, then I'm being extravagant and the next month I have to wash my hair with hand soap to learn my lesson." Elaine sipped her tea, and silence hung over the room for a moment before she went on. "I swear to God and the angels, he was worse than my stepfather. I jumped right out of the frying pan into the blue blazes. I'm so damned happy to be getting a new life that I pinch myself every now and then to be sure I'm not dreaming."

"We won't talk about even glancing at a book with a man on the cover. That means we're lusting after someone else," Liz said. "And if we argue, it's an automatic fight and then apologies with vows that it will never happen again. By the end of summer, I will be Miss Andrews again and not Mrs. Pope."

"And how does that make you feel?" Elaine asked.

"I can't even explain it," Liz said. "It must be what you felt when you saw the shelter sign after walking all night. Deep, deep relief, but even that doesn't come close to the feeling."

"It was one pretty sight, for sure. If I could just get through the door of that house, I knew there was a chance I wouldn't die. And"— she tucked her chin to her chest—"before tomorrow I want to thank you two especially for all you've done for me. I'm not good with words, but I can't thank you enough."

"I should be thanking you, Elaine. You gave me this courage, and Hannah gave me the willpower to do this," Liz said.

"And you both are helping me," Hannah said. "So this is a win-win-win situation."

Hannah sent up a silent prayer of thanks to Gina for going with her gut feeling and bringing Elaine to her house.

CHAPTER ELEVEN

On Thursday morning Hannah was up at the crack of dawn so she could tell Elaine good-bye. Sophie hated good-byes, so Travis promised her that they would grill hot dogs and hamburgers that evening out in the backyard. And when she asked for a movie under the stars, he said they could set up the television on a couple of sawhorses on the back porch. But when Hannah made her way to the kitchen, she caught a flash of lightning.

She pulled the window blinds up to see a slow, soft rain was falling. She found the remote and turned on the television, found The Weather Channel, and learned that the storm had settled right over Crossing. Rain with occasional lightning but no chance of a tornado was the forecast.

Time to change plans. They would have a picnic in the house with the red-and-white plastic tablecloth on the kitchen table instead of the picnic table in the backyard. She'd make the hot dogs on the cast-iron griddle and they'd have a movie in the living room. She lifted a window so she could smell the rain.

"You didn't have to get up this early." Elaine carried a used suitcase that Miss Rosie had brought over into the kitchen. She set it on the floor and hugged Hannah tightly. "Gina says I've got a good job waiting and a new name with a new driver's license. You all have given me courage. I feel like God has smiled on me."

"He has," Hannah said. "We probably won't ever meet again, but I'll always remember you, Elaine."

"I'm hoping when it's been six months that I will be like you." Elaine was a pretty woman, but she'd be even more striking when she had the self-confidence to back up that sweet smile.

Hannah looked at the time and date on the bottom of the television screen. "Today is June 16," she said. "My husband made excuses not to come home for six months, but it's been only two weeks and one day since I faced him in court. You'll be surprised how much strength you get every single day."

"I hate good-byes," Elaine said.

"Me, too, and I hear a car pulling up by the back porch. I guess it's time."

Elaine picked up the suitcase. "We've already had a hug, so don't walk me to the door and I won't look back. When I think of Lullaby Sky, I will smile," Elaine said as she closed the door gently behind her.

Hannah sat down on the sofa, put her head in her hands, and reminded herself that this was part of the job of helping other women. Good-byes had to be said in order for them to move on with their lives.

But I'm supposed to be helping them, and I feel like Elaine helped me more than I did her, she thought.

And that is the beauty of this service, the voice in her head said.

"Mama, Mama!" Sophie bounced into the room. She wrapped her arms around her mother's waist and hugged her tightly. "Since it's rainin', does that mean Laney gets to stay another day?"

Hannah bent to kiss Sophie on the top of her head. "No, baby girl, it means that we can't have our movie under the stars outside, but we can have a party in our house and everyone can come. Have you invited Nadine and Anna Lou?"

"No, silly Mama. They can't come in the house." Sophie giggled.

Hannah took a deep breath and let it out slowly. "Elaine has already gone. You told her good-bye last night, remember? Have you done your job and picked out the perfect movie for us to watch?"

"I'm workin' on it. I've got two lyin' on my dresser. I really liked her, Mama. Will she come back someday?"

"I don't think so, but we have two whole days' worth of memories with her, don't we?" Hannah answered.

"It don't seem like she was here that long."

"She slept the whole first day and stayed in her room. That's why it doesn't seem like we got to keep her longer, but . . ." Hannah paused.

"I love it when you say *but*." Sophie grinned. "That means something good is going to happen, right?"

"Aunt Darcy is coming to the party tonight and so is Aunt Liz."

"Yes, yes, yes!" Sophie pumped her little fist in the air. "Can Aunt Darcy spend the night?"

"You can ask her." Hannah hugged her daughter closer to her side. "Let's go make breakfast. A rainy day calls for oatmeal with raisins and pecans and brown sugar."

"And toast with peanut butter and bacon?"

"You got it. Race you to the kitchen," Hannah said.

Sophie put her small hand in Hannah's. "Let's just walk, Mama, and have breakfast with just us like we used to. But when it's over, can I go over to Aunt Birdie's and see if she wants to play cards with me this morning?"

"We'll call her and see if she has something else planned, but if she doesn't, I bet she'd love to play cards with you this old rainy morning," Hannah said.

After breakfast Hannah donned a bright-yellow raincoat, kicked off her shoes, and headed toward the hangar in her bare feet. The wet grass felt like velvet between her toes, and the scent of wet dirt was as intoxicating as a double shot of Jack Daniel's on the rocks. She stopped and held out her hands, letting the soft rain fill them until there was enough to bring to her nose to smell it up close and personal. No chlorine. No artificial flavor enhancers. Just plain old rain, straight from heaven, to nourish the earth.

"That's what I want if I ever go into another relationship. I don't want a husband with money. I don't want fancy frills. I just want someone who loves to walk barefoot in the rain and smell the wet dirt with me." She splayed open her fingers and let the water run through to trickle onto her feet with the other raindrops.

"Which will never happen." She sighed and started walking again toward the hangar.

She expected to hear the noise of hammers and buzz saws, yet there was nothing but crickets complaining about getting wet and tree frogs singing songs of praise for the glorious rain.

"It's all in how you look at it and how you study it, as Aunt Birdie says. What is one person's blessing is another's nightmare," she said as she swung open the door into the office and stepped inside for the first time in a year.

"Who's having nightmares? Is Sophie all right?" Travis looked up from a roll of papers stretched out across Marty's oversize oak desk.

"She's fine. I was philosophizing to myself," Hannah said.

The office had been built according to Marty's specifications. Like everything he had a hand in doing, it was either big or bust. Given how little he used it, he could have easily been comfortable with a small desk, a phone, and maybe one metal file cabinet. But that was not Marty's style. An oversize desk that probably cost more than Hannah made in a year at her teacher's aide job sat in the middle of the floor.

And yet that wasn't the way to describe it, either. It sat *perfectly* in the middle of the room. The distance from one wall to the center of the thing equaled the distance from the far wall to the center. Behind it stood two tall matching oak file cabinets, the keys to the locks hanging on the handles of the top drawers. A desk chair that was probably fancier than the president used in the Oval Office had been shoved over into a corner, and two burgundy leather chairs faced the desk.

No one had ever sat in those chairs. Not Sophie, who wasn't allowed to enter the hangar or the office. Certainly not Hannah. Unless . . .

She gasped so loudly that Travis jerked his head up to check on her. "Are you okay? Does this room bring painful memories? We can go out into the hangar if it does. That's where Calvin is working with a tape measure so he'll know how many bins we can put in for his fabrics."

"I'm fine," she murmured. But that wasn't the truth—not at all. She'd gotten a vision of the pregnant redhead she'd seen in the courtroom sitting in one of those chairs. Had she and Marty made the baby on that desk? The last few times he'd been home, he'd spent more time than usual in his office. She shook her head. Marty might be manipulative and controlling, but he wouldn't bring a woman to his office in Crossing, because he'd have to explain why he even had a place in such a tiny town. It was far more likely he spent time in his office talking to his new girlfriend on the phone, telling her lies about how he had to work late and couldn't see her that night.

Travis rounded the end of the desk and put his hands on her shoulders. "Don't go to that bad place."

"What makes you—" she started.

He put a finger on her lips. "Trust me, darlin'. I can tell when you are going there even if I don't know all of what happened in those times and places. I care too much about you to ever want you to go back. Shake it off and look forward. Leave the past in a fog where even memories don't exist."

She wrapped her arms around him and leaned into his chest, her ear against his steady heartbeat. "Travis, have I told you today that I love you?"

Holy smokin' hell! Had she really said those words out loud? Hannah pulled back and stammered, "I'm sorry . . . I mean . . . I do love . . ."

"It's okay, and darlin', I love you, too. We all do." He grinned as he pushed his glasses up on his nose. "And I was really getting worried that you didn't love me at all."

"Whoa! Get a room!" Calvin pushed his way into the room.

Hannah giggled and took a couple of steps back. "Travis was interrupting my trip into the dark world of the past. He deserved a hug for pulling me from the abyss."

"Well, dammit!" Cal chuckled. "I thought maybe Cupid made his way through the rain and shot you both with one of his darts. Darts!" His eyes twinkled. "Little silver darts printed on black chiffon layered over a brilliant blue that would make the darts sparkle in the light. You two are an inspiration." He quickly removed a notebook, wrote down a few words, and shoved it back into the pocket of his khaki cargo shorts.

"So I should hug Travis more, right?" Hannah asked.

"Oh, yes, darlin'. If I can get a glorious revelation from one hug, just think what I could get if you—"

She slapped a hand over his mouth. "Don't go there, Calvin Winters."

He removed her hand and kissed her knuckles. "Too soon?"

"Definitely too soon," she whispered back.

Travis chuckled. "He's in love with Darcy and all this new stuff he's designing for his next show, so he's got cupids on the brain."

"Maybe I should tell you to get a room." Hannah cocked her head to one side.

Cal's gaze caught hers and held. "I know how close y'all are, but please don't say anything."

"I'll keep your secret." Hannah wanted to hug herself. Darcy loved him. He loved Darcy. Until it was revealed, Hannah would simply enjoy knowing that it would happen.

"Let's change the subject," Cal said. "I love this big office. It's twice the size of the one I had in the city. I've already unloaded my files into the cabinets and there's still an empty drawer. Marty must have known he was leaving. He cleaned all that out. I can't believe he forgot the airplane."

"To my knowledge, those cabinets were never used," Hannah said, eyeing the phone on the desk. She unplugged the thing from the wall. "Where's your bug zapper, Travis?"

"It's at the house, but I can take a look inside that phone without it." He checked the outlet first, then went on to the phone, where he found and removed the dime-size device hiding in the mouthpiece.

"One down," he said. "I guess he wanted to be sure you weren't using this to make calls to anyone."

"Looks like we'd better sweep the office," Cal said. "And if you are listening right now, Marty, call me if you are interested in buying this airplane that I own. This phone will stay hooked up for two more days. Then the company is coming to remove it and put in a better one with my business number attached to it. So you've got two days to call me, then I intend to put the damn thing on Craigslist."

"And now"—Travis tucked Hannah's arm into his—"we will step out of here and into the hangar, where we know we have privacy."

"How?" Hannah asked.

He led her through the open door and nodded toward Calvin, who picked up a remote and hit a few buttons. "Redneck Woman" by Gretchen Wilson blared through two speakers Calvin had set up.

"With that playing and the rain on the metal roof, he can't hear anything," Travis answered. "Where is Sophie?"

"Aunt Birdie wants to keep her and let me have a day to myself. So I came down here to see y'all and to walk in the rain. I love the feel of wet green grass on my bare feet."

He looked down at her toes. "And such lovely feet, too."

"Yes, they are. Yes, yes!" Calvin clapped his hands. "I'm going to design a line of clothing and instead of high heels on my runway models, they are going to wear ankle bracelets and toe rings and go in their bare feet. Who'd have thought I could get so much inspiration from Crossing, Texas?" He pulled the notebook out of his pocket again and wrote a few phrases.

"Don't get him started on the rain. He's already got visions of something that Darcy will model that involves raindrops on chalice," Travis said from the corner of his mouth.

"You mean challis?" Hannah asked.

"Yeah, that's it. Sha-lee, cha-lice. It all sounds the same to me. I know the difference between denim and T-shirt knit, and that's about it." Travis grinned.

"Hey, if you've got a few more minutes, I could use a woman's ideas when it comes to my own loft design. I'm seeing a wide-open space, but Travis thinks I need walls in the bedroom area."

"From here it doesn't even look like it's been floored. It just looks like rafters to me."

"It hasn't, but this is how it will be once it's got a floor and stairs leading up to it." Travis rolled out a length of paper on a worktable and laid scissors on either end. "Once this plane is out of here, I won't need all the space from here to the ceiling to make Cal's working room. So we can put up eight-foot walls and the top can be his new apartment. Look at this and imagine a wide-open space up there."

Hannah stared at the rough drawing Travis had made, but her mind went back to the early days when Marty's parents had hired a professional team of carpenters out of Dallas to build the hangar. She'd been excited about the whole thing. Marty wouldn't have that hour-long drive to his office just south of Dallas, along with the frustrations of the traffic. He would simply fly down to the Ellises' private airport, one of the company drivers would pick him up and take him to the offices, and then in the evening the process would be reversed.

It worked that way for a few months, and then Sophie was born and everything went downhill from there. He'd been so disappointed that he didn't have a son that Hannah promised him one the next year.

God must've seen the future much better than Hannah, because there were no more children. Possibly because Marty started staying away so much that it would have been hit or miss with ovulation.

"So what do you think?" Cal asked.

Hannah sneezed three times in quick succession. Travis quickly pulled a white handkerchief from his pocket and handed it to her. "It's dusty in here, but when we get finished it'll be a fine place for Cal to design, develop his creations, and live in."

She blew her nose and then didn't know what to do with the hanky. It seemed gross to hand it back to him. Should she take it with her, wash it, and then return it?

"If you're done with that, I feel one coming on, too," Travis said.

She'd barely got it in his hand before he rattled the walls with a big, manly sneeze. "Ragweed must be getting ready to hit all of us with allergies," he said as he shoved the hanky back into his hip pocket.

Now that's a true friend, Hannah thought. *Marty would have never shared one of his high-dollar hankies with me. Lord, he would have thrown a fit if I sneezed in the same room with him. But why am I letting him into my head this morning?*

"So what do you think, darlin'?" Cal asked.

"Truth is I can't tell heads or tails from this paper, but I'm going to agree with Travis about walls for your bedroom. The rest could be open space, though there will probably come a time when you want privacy." She jumped to one side and shivered when something gray and furry brushed against her leg. "You've got a rat in here."

"Not a rat, a stray kitten. It's gray, and I've been putting food out for it. You just spooked her," Cal said. "Here, kitty, kitty. Come here, pretty girl. Hannah wouldn't hurt a fly, I promise."

Two dark-blue eyes peered out around a stud and blinked several times before the kitten inched her way toward Cal's outstretched hand.

"Oh!" Hannah clasped her hands together.

"We've about got her tamed enough that we can give her to Sophie. That way she won't be so sad about Elaine leaving. She'll have a kitten to take her mind off the disappointment," Travis said.

Cal picked the kitten up and held it close to his chest. "I guess we should ask you if it's okay to let her have a pet."

"She's wanted a kitten for a long time, but y'all know that Marty was . . . is . . . Lord, I keep talking about him like he's dead. He *is* allergic to cats and dogs." Hannah reached out to touch the little gray kitten.

Travis threw an arm around her shoulders. "You can hold it, Hannah, and it's okay to put Marty in the past. It means you are finding a little bit of closure."

Cal put the gray fur ball in Hannah's hands, and it didn't miss a single second of purring. She held it close to her chest and stroked its soft fur, all the time letting Travis's words sink in. It might take a while, but closure was happening. Marty had been such a huge part of her life and fears for so long that she couldn't expect him to disappear all at once. But right at that moment, she forgot all about him as she kissed the kitten on the top of its head.

Travis removed his arm from her shoulders and started back down the ladder. "Bring the kitten with you. We'll keep her in the office tonight and give her to Sophie tomorrow right before Elaine leaves."

"Her?" Hannah asked.

"Yep." Cal started down the ladder behind Travis. "You'll need to get her fixed in a few months or else she'll have kittens. I bagged up some more fabric scraps for you, by the way. You need to have a quilting party when everyone arrives."

"Good point. But think about Sophie with a bunch of sweet kittens to play with. And you should know, Elaine has already left." Hannah eased down the ladder using one hand. When she reached the bottom, both guys were smiling like a couple of possums eating grapes through a barbed-wire fence.

"What?" she asked.

"Nothing," Cal chuckled.

"Nothing doesn't put grins like that on your faces."

"We like seeing you happy like you were when we were kids, back before you met Marty," Travis said. "And sometimes all it takes is something simple, like a kitten or—"

"Or having a whole support group of good friends," she interjected with a smile.

Chapter Twelve

Travis heard a crash somewhere in the kitchen that startled him in the middle of writing an intense scene for his new book. For a split second, he wondered if he'd imagined it, but then a second crash followed. Leaving his characters in the middle of a crisis, he took the stairs two at a time as he hurried down them.

With visions of either Hannah or Sophie lying on the floor with a broken arm or worse yet, a broken neck, he rounded the kitchen table so fast that it made him slightly dizzy. His eyes darted around the room. Where were they? Had Marty come back and kidnapped Sophie?

A sob near the sink caught his attention, and that's when he saw Hannah sitting on the floor, her knees drawn up and her face in her hands. She held the handle of a broken cup in her hand, and sobs racked her body.

"Are you okay?" Travis asked breathlessly.

The floor was covered with glass. "I dropped a coffee cup, and when I reached for it, I knocked two more off the cabinet," Hannah said through tears. "I know Marty isn't here. I know he isn't coming back, but my brain went into instant fear."

Travis scooped her up like a new bride and carried her to the living room, where he sat down on the sofa with her in his lap.

"A broken cup means getting told how stupid and clumsy I am, but if he's really angry, it can mean slaps or even fists," Hannah said. "Am I ever going to be normal, Travis?"

"Yes, you are," he said. "Things like this will happen, but don't let it affect you like this. Tell yourself that he's gone and it's over every day. Hell, every hour if you need to."

One step forward, two back, he thought. *But I'm willing to give it time.*

Liz knocked on the back door but didn't wait for an invitation. She carried a whole platter of decorated cupcakes into the room and set them on the cabinet. "What's going on in here? Did someone die?"

"Broken cups," Hannah said.

"I understand." Liz smiled weakly. "But don't let it ruin your day or jack your blood pressure up too high. I brought cupcakes to go with our ice cream. Aunt Birdie and Miss Rosie are on their way across the street, each of them carrying a casserole dish."

Hannah jumped up from Travis's lap and wiped her eyes with the back of her hand.

"Go on to the bathroom and wash your face," Liz said. "I'll clean up the broken glass."

"And I'll help," Travis said.

"Hey, hey, we're here," Miss Rosie yelled as they came through the kitchen door. "We brought baked beans and potato salad to go with the burgers and hot dogs and Sophie said there is a movie in the living room after we eat. Mercy, did someone get mad and start throwing things in here?"

"No, Hannah knocked a few mugs off the cabinet," Travis said.

"Did she get cut?"

"Not a bit. Don't step right there just yet, Miss Rosie." Liz quickly swept all the broken shards into a dustpan. "Now it's all gone. Whatever you've got in that dish sure smells good."

"Yes, it does," Hannah said as she reentered the room. "Y'all didn't have to go to all this much trouble."

"Thank you," she mouthed to Travis and Liz.

Travis barely nodded as he took the dishes from both the women and set them on the cabinet. "I can't believe that Cal insisted on grilling the hot dogs and hamburgers outside in the rain."

"He says it's not raining under the porch roof, and besides, he has an umbrella," Hannah said.

Sophie arrived in a blur of blue, wearing last year's Halloween costume that was only slightly too short.

"Looks like you are Elsa tonight," Aunt Birdie said.

"Yes, I am." Sophie twirled around. "And Elsa likes hot dogs and sweet baked beans and, oh, cupcakes!" she squealed.

"You are far more beautiful than Elsa," Travis said. "Can you spin one more time just for me?"

Sophie giggled and did a double twirl, then swiped her finger across the icing on one of the cupcakes and licked it off. "Good! My favorite! That can be my cupcake." Her words came out in snatches as she licked her fingers again.

"What if I want that cupcake?" Travis asked. "It'll be the sweetest one, since it's had your finger on it."

"Uncle Travis." She giggled. "I'm not that sweet."

"Depends on who you are asking. I think you are sweeter than sugar and honey mixed up together," he teased.

"Oh, Uncle Travis, I love you!" She threw her arms around his waist.

"Not as much as I love you." Travis's drawl was even deeper than usual.

Birdie removed the lid from the container of baked beans. "Okay, ladies, let's get all this put on the table so we can fill up our plates and go to the living room to watch the movie."

Miss Rosie opened the refrigerator and took out the container holding ice cubes. "I'll make the sweet tea while y'all get the rest of the stuff on the table."

"Right on time!" The rich aroma of grilled food filled the house as Cal carried a platter of hot dogs and hamburger patties into the house. "See, I told you I could grill on the back porch even if it is raining."

"I smelled charcoal cookin' a block away." Darcy threw the back door open and entered the kitchen. "I'm starving. I didn't even get a lunch break today, and that one little package of peanut butter crackers that I ate on the run is failing me." She sniffed and headed toward the table. "Oh. My. God. Sophie, you are adorable in that outfit."

Sophie did a lovely curtsy and bowed. "If that's as good as pretty, then thank you, Aunt Darcy."

Conversation swirled around him. He heard Darcy tell Cal that she'd had no idea he knew his way around a grill. Sophie was explaining who Elsa was to Miss Rosie. But the aftershock of holding Hannah in his lap and listening to her heart beat in unison with his almost let a full pitcher of sweet tea drop from Travis's hands. He had to get a grip on more than the glass pitcher.

⁓

Hannah helped Sophie fix her hot dogs and carried them to the living room for her. Miss Rosie and Aunt Birdie were already on the sofa, their plates on the coffee table. Darcy had spread Sophie's old quilt out on the floor, and she and Cal were sitting off to one side of it.

"It's a real picnic," Sophie said. "With a quilt and everything. Uncle Travis, you can sit right here and Mama can sit by you and I get to sit in the middle of all y'all."

"Yes, ma'am," Travis said as he sat in the spot he'd been assigned. "I will save your place, Hannah."

Hannah liked her hamburger the same way every time—mustard, pickles, tomatoes, and lettuce. But she forgot all about the burger when she sat down beside Travis and sparks danced around them on the quilt.

"Good, huh?" Travis asked.

She nodded, really looking at Travis as a man rather than a friend. It had to be that episode with the broken cups and him responding with kindness that triggered the sparks. He was Travis, for mercy's sake—her friend for their whole lives. Besides, she'd been divorced less than a month.

"The best part is that I didn't have to cook them or worry about getting them perfect," Liz declared.

"I think you should be moved out by the time Wyatt comes home. You can have a bedroom upstairs," Hannah said as the music for the movie started.

Liz smiled. "Thanks, but your aunt Birdie says I can have one of her spare bedrooms, so I'll be staying with her through the summer until I can find a place of my own."

"Yes, I did, and I'll be glad to have her staying with me," Aunt Birdie piped up from the sofa.

"I wanted her to stay with me," Miss Rosie said.

"But I've got more room. She will have to share the upstairs bathroom with Calvin since he's living there, too."

"No problem with that," Calvin said. "I lived with sisters, and we had to share a bathroom."

"I hope it all goes smooth," Hannah said. "Need any help?"

"Yes, I do. He's gone for a couple of days this week. Could you come over and help me pack my things? I can do it, but I'd sure like your support," Liz answered.

"Just tell me when and I'll be there." Hannah smiled.

"Shhhh. The movie is about to begin and I've spent far too much time in the land of adults," Cal said. "I haven't even seen this wonderful show."

"Oh, Uncle Cal." Sophie giggled. "Since you live so close to me now, you can watch my shows any old time."

Cal hugged her so tight that her dark curls bounced. "Thank you, baby girl."

Sophie wiggled out of his embrace and huffed, "I'm not a baby."

"No, you are not," Cal said. "But you'll always be my baby girl."

"Even when I grow up? How can I be a baby girl when I'm a big girl like Mama?"

"Baby girl just means that you are special," Travis said.

Sophie giggled and scooted over to sit beside Liz. "Then I'll be all y'all's baby girl."

Travis laid a hand on Hannah's leg and squeezed. "She is adorable. You've done such a good job with her, Hannah."

Hannah placed her hand over Travis's, and a tingle shot through her heart. What in the devil was going on in her body? She'd vowed to never trust a man again. But this was Travis. Good, dependable, trustworthy Travis.

Chapter Thirteen

On Saturday morning, Hannah slept poorly, and finally, at six thirty, she got out of bed and padded into the kitchen, where she found Darcy sitting in the dark with a glass of sweet tea in her hands. "So you couldn't sleep, either?"

Darcy shook her head. "I thought it would be wonderful to have Calvin this close, but it's not. I can't get past this thing I have for him. I've tried and tried, dated other men, but none of them measure up or make me feel like he does. I have made up my mind to be single forever and dote on Sophie." Darcy shrugged. "Why couldn't you sleep?"

"Travis." Hannah set about making a pot of coffee.

"He's always been in love with you. Since grade school," Darcy said.

"But that's when we were kids. There's been a lot of water under the bridge since those days." Hannah's chest tightened. Could she be the woman that he'd never gotten over? She couldn't be, because she was past thirty before she got tangled up with Marty. That would have given Travis years to open up about his feelings.

Darcy shrugged. "The heart knows what it wants. Now what?" She threw up her hands and sighed.

"Now we be patient and see what happens."

"Do you know what *wait* is? It's a four-letter word and they are all awful." Darcy groaned.

"So is love," Hannah reminded her. "Hey, you remember when we all went to the park after graduation and Cal pushed you on the swings?"

Darcy nodded. "That was years ago, but I still remember it like yesterday. I wanted him to kiss me so badly that night."

"Why didn't you kiss him?"

"Fear, I guess."

"Well, we're all older now, and you should tell him how you feel."

Darcy's cheeks turned scarlet. "It would make things awkward. I'd rather have him as a friend than lose him forever."

"But think how glorious it would be. What if *he* was afraid to tell *you*?"

"I'll play devil's advocate and ask him if he has feelings for you," Liz said from the back door. "We'll talk about it later, Darcy," she mouthed with a backward nod at Aunt Birdie and Miss Rosie arriving right behind her.

A few strands of gray hair had escaped Miss Rosie's bun, and she pulled a bobby pin from her pocket and fixed it. She wore a wildly colored caftan and bright-orange flip-flops that morning. Aunt Birdie set a paper bag filled with groceries on the cabinet and removed a cast-iron skillet from the cabinet. Her jeans hung on her fanny like a sack on a broomstick, and her red T-shirt sported Rudolph all tangled up in Christmas lights.

"We are here and we're going to make a big breakfast. Sausage gravy and hot biscuits and scrambled eggs and blueberry muffins," Aunt Birdie said.

"Thank you," Hannah said. "I was going to make pancakes, but your breakfast sounds a lot better."

"You can still get out the griddle and make pancakes for whosoever wants them. Being able to run in and out of your house is so much fun,

Hannah," Aunt Birdie said. "It reminds me of when your grandma, my sister, was alive. We used to do so many meals together, and it brings back memories for me. Built our houses pretty much off the same plan right across the street from each other. I still miss her."

Miss Rosie cracked a dozen eggs into a bowl she removed from the cabinet. "Well, holy smokes, Hannah! Your cabinet isn't all perfect."

"It's not easy, but I'm working on that." Hannah was glad that someone noticed she was trying to get out of the deep rut Marty had dug.

"Aunt Birdie!" Sophie ran across the floor and wrapped her arms around the older woman. "I love it that you are coming over here so much. Are you cooking? Can I set the table?"

"Yes, darlin' girl, you can set the table. Me and Miss Rosie are making breakfast and you do a wonderful job of helping." Aunt Birdie pointed at the drawer where the cutlery was stored. "We'll need six of each."

"But what about Uncle Cal and Uncle Travis?"

"This is a ladies' breakfast. The boys have already had breakfast and are down at the hangar working," Miss Rosie answered.

Liz poured three cups of coffee and handed one to Miss Rosie and one to Aunt Birdie. "I love this feeling. Being free to come and go as we want and not worry about anything. This is the kind of home I want."

"Then get out of your situation and make a home like this. I like that the boys aren't coming to breakfast this morning. Y'all all looked like warmed-over hell on Sunday morning, and that's a good thing. You don't feel like you have to go rushin' around tryin' to look decent. Only strong women who are comfortable in their faded pj's are allowed in this house right now." Aunt Birdie crumbled sausage into the iron skillet and stirred it with a wooden spoon.

༄

Travis put the last nail in the cat carrier at eight thirty that morning. It was just a wooden frame covered with chicken wire, but it held the gray kitten and could be used to take her to the vet.

He and Cal had made a trip into Gainesville that morning and picked up litter and a pan to put it in and cat food, both dry and canned, specially formulated for kittens, plus half a dozen cat toys.

"Are we going to do something every single time a guest leaves Hannah's place?" Cal asked as he put the gray kitten into the carrier and shut the door.

"If necessary. But Elaine left Thursday and this is Saturday, so it's really not a present for that reason. Besides, the kitten needed just a little more taming before we gave her to Sophie. We didn't want it to scratch her," Travis said.

"Party on Thursday after Elaine left that morning. Darcy arrived last night. Kitten today. What happens tomorrow?" Cal asked.

"Church," Travis said.

"We shouldn't spoil her with things, but with love," Cal said.

"You preachin' to you or to me?"

Cal picked up the loaded pink litter pan. "Both of us. You can't imagine how much I love that baby girl."

"I think I can. I'd cut out my heart with a rusty butter knife for her or Hannah."

"Give Hannah some healing time, but not too much," Cal said. "Then sweep in and give her a life of happiness forever."

"Being with her would sure give *me* a life of happiness forever." Travis sighed as he eased the kitten inside. She instantly set up a howl, and he started talking to her in a high-pitched voice. "It's okay, little girl. It's only for a few minutes, and then you'll be carried around all day."

"Don't ever use that voice on Hannah," Cal said.

"Do you intend to use your kitten voice on Darcy?" Travis asked.

"Hell, no." Travis picked up the carrier, and they walked side by side from the hangar toward the house. "How much time does it take to heal? A year?"

"Good Lord, not at all!" Cal exclaimed. "What we saw at the courthouse at the first of the month was just the paperwork. The marriage has been over a long time. You'll know when the time is right."

"And you?" Travis asked.

"I hope I do," Cal drawled. "The attraction is there. I can feel it, but . . ."

"But what?" Travis asked when his friend stopped walking and paused.

"I'm scared out of my mind to tell her how I really feel."

"Join the club, bro," Travis drawled.

Cal's phone rang at the same time Travis's did.

Travis set the cat carrier down and pulled his phone from his hip pocket.

"Hey, Dad. Did you pop the question?" he asked.

"Not yet. Did you find what you were looking for at Pete's place?"

Travis smiled. "I did, and it picked up all kinds of bugs. We've got them all taken care of and Hannah has new phone numbers now."

"Good. I was just calling to check on you kids."

"We're taking it a day at a time. Tell Linda happy birthday. I was planning on calling your future fiancée first thing this morning, but—"

"Well, shit!" John butted in before Travis could finish his sentence. "I forgot that today was her birthday. Thanks for reminding me, son. I'll get off here and make a reservation at Margaritaville in Panama City Beach and make an excuse to go buy her a present."

"You've got the perfect present in your pocket," Travis said.

"Naw, I'm saving that for the right moment. It shouldn't be on her birthday. 'Bye now," John said.

"Your dad?" Calvin asked.

"Yep."

Travis picked up the kitten and they headed toward the house again.

Sophie was sitting on the sofa watching Saturday morning cartoons when Cal and Travis brought the kitten in through the back door and into the living room. She looked up and gasped.

"Is that really a kitten?" she squealed.

"It is, and she says that she needs a home. You reckon she could find one in this house?" Travis set the carrier down at Sophie's feet. "She's sure been crying for a friend. I don't expect you'd know anyone who might be her new buddy, would you?"

"I can be her friend." Sophie left the sofa and dropped down on her knees by the carrier. "Can I get her out of that cage?"

"Of course you can," Hannah answered. "She's a beautiful kitten. You reckon you could share with me?"

"I sure will share, Mama, but can I hold her first?" Sophie asked.

Travis quickly crossed the room and slung an arm around Hannah's shoulders. "I'm sorry I don't have a kitten to give to you."

"Someday she'll have babies and I'll get my own kitten then. Maybe I'll be the crazy old cat woman and I'll have a dozen old mama cats who have babies two or three times a year."

"And I will sit on the porch and let them crawl all over me." Travis chuckled.

Chapter Fourteen

"Good mornin', folks." The preacher's big booming voice filled the little white church that morning. "I'm glad to see all the pews comin' close to being full. It's a lot easier to preach to a crowd than to one or two folks falling asleep on the back row."

A few muffled giggles floated above Hannah's head, but she didn't hear them. She was too busy trying to make sense of the sparks that sizzled every time her knee or her arm brushed against Travis. There was no avoiding it. He was sitting right beside her, and since she was on the very end of a full pew, there was nowhere to go.

She'd known him since they were babies in the church nursery. They'd gone through thirteen years of school together, and there had never been anything like this. So why now? Besides, the way he sat there so cool and never flinching must mean that he didn't feel the heat.

"I'm going to read a few passages from the thirteenth chapter of First Corinthians. Paul was writing to these folks concerning loving one another. It caused me to think of the love that Ruth had for Naomi, when she followed her into a strange land after both of their husbands had died. I think, and this is my opinion only, that there are many ways of marital death. God did not intend for a husband to mistreat his wife or for him to be lord and master over her. When that happens, the husband is killing the marriage as surely as if he shot the wife between the eyes with his deer-huntin' rifle," the preacher said.

Without taking his eyes from the pulpit, Travis reached over and nudged Hannah's shoulder. "He's preachin' to Liz this mornin'," he whispered.

"Ruth followed Naomi into a strange land. That's where a wife is when she leaves a husband who has not appreciated the fact that his wife should walk beside him and not two steps behind him."

A few shuffles said that the preacher was stepping on sore toes. Evidently he had some knowledge of other men in the community who weren't showing their wives the love and respect that they should. Hannah chanced a peek down the pew at Liz. Two high spots of crimson dotted her cheeks, but she was nodding in agreement.

"And in that strange land she will find God and happiness." The preacher went on with the sermon about love, but Hannah's mind wandered. Sitting in church should bring quietness to the soul, but that morning all it brought to Hannah was more questions without answers as she sat beside Travis and tried to figure out what this chemistry was that she felt.

After the last amen was said, Miss Rosie announced that dinner was at her house that day, and she wasn't taking excuses from anyone. As they were filing out of the church, she looped her arm into Hannah's. "And after dinner you can go over to Liz's and help her pack, right? Darcy can play with Sophie while me and Birdie catch our Sunday afternoon nap, and the guys will go to the hangar, I'm sure."

"I'm praying that things will go smooth," Hannah said.

"I'm not. If he hurts her again, I'm going to shoot the bastard," Miss Rosie said seriously, then turned to shake the preacher's hand and smiled brightly. "Lovely sermon this morning. A lot of men are going home with sore toes, I'm sure."

"I hope they go home with heavy hearts and repent if they've been treating their wives with anything other than respect." The preacher nodded.

"That, too," Miss Rosie said and moved on so the next person could shake his hand.

☙

Liz kept telling herself that she was a grown woman and this was simply a stepping-stone. Wyatt was coming back to Crossing tomorrow, and she would tell him that she'd already moved her things over to Aunt Birdie's place. She unlocked the door and threw it open. She stepped inside the house, and Hannah followed her.

"Come in. I've got boxes in the spare bedroom and it shouldn't take us long to get them loaded and out of here since we've got two cars we can use."

"Have you checked the place for . . . you know?" Hannah rolled her eyes toward the ceiling.

"Travis did. We are fine. Wyatt isn't as crafty as Marty or as willing to put out money for fancy devices. He just checks my call log when he gets home and fumes if I've talked to anyone too long."

Hannah glanced around the living room and shivered. "Why don't you delete the call log?"

"Tried that. Cost me dearly," Liz said. "Entering this place is like walking into a tomb, isn't it? No need to lie. I saw your reaction and feel the same every day. Like all the ghosts of his relatives are watching me and tattling to him."

"I haven't been in here since you moved in. Strange, but probably for the same reason I would meet all y'all over at Aunt Birdie's house. It is spooky, Liz. It hasn't changed since his mother lived here," Hannah said.

Liz eased down on the sofa, circa 1980, with its wagon wheel arms and orange-and-brown upholstery. "What happened to us? We were happy roommates for more than ten years and then everything went to hell in a handbasket."

"Thirty happened to us. We both felt like the chance for a marriage and a family was passing us by. You got involved with Wyatt and I met Marty. We went forward, only we chose the wrong path," Hannah said.

"Wyatt was charming at first," Liz said.

"So was Marty. That's the way abusive men are. They draw their prey in and then torture it." Hannah sat down in a wooden rocking chair. "This is the right thing to do, Liz. Don't think about his charm and change your mind."

"I have to leave. I'm to the point I'm afraid he's going to kill me. His anger gets worse and worse every time he comes home," Liz said.

"Then let's get this done, and you'll be gone when he arrives. All you'll have to do is tell him, and I'll even come with you to do that," Hannah said.

"I need to do it by myself to show him that I'm independent and I can do what I damn well please with my life. That I can live without him," Liz said. "It'll be scary, but if things start to get out of hand, I've got you and Travis both on speed dial. I think I brought less out than I took in." She wrapped her arms around her midriff and reminded herself that tomorrow it would be all over. Hannah would be there for her to talk to and Miss Rosie would be a wonderful roommate for the rest of the summer.

❧

Hannah had never done a job so fast in her life. She wouldn't have been a bit surprised to have long, bony hands shoot out from behind the door and drag them back into the house when they started carrying boxes out to their vehicles. How Liz had lived in the house for the past seven years was a mystery and a miracle rolled up into one.

"I really, really don't like the feeling in that place," she said. Hannah could practically hear eerie music coming from the shadows, and every creak from the floorboards made her wonder if ghosts didn't live under the house as well as inside it.

"It gets worse when Wyatt is home," Liz said. "Right now it's just spooky. Add the tension and fear on top of that. If it hadn't been for y'all and my job, I would have put a gun to my head a long time ago."

"God, Liz, now I feel guilty. I should have barged in here and visited with you after you moved in. I would have put you in a straitjacket and hauled you out of here."

Liz leaned against her car. "Don't beat yourself up. I had to get to this point before I'd stay gone when I left, even if it was in a straitjacket. Let's get the rest of it out and I'll lock the door. Tomorrow I'll give him my key and it will be done."

Hannah braced herself against the feel of the house when she went back inside and made short order of getting all the boxes and clothing out to the cars. She didn't breathe easy until they were parked in Aunt Birdie's driveway.

Sophie was at her side the second she was out of the car. "Mama! Aunt Darcy says that Aunt Liz is moving in with Aunt Birdie. Why can't she come live with us? We've got a big house, too."

"Because Aunt Birdie asked her first," Hannah said.

Sophie crossed her arms over her chest. "It's not fair. I would have asked her if y'all would stop talking big-people stuff and tell me things."

Darcy came out the door and picked up several hangers with clothing still on them from the backseat of Liz's car. "I'll help take things inside. Aunt Birdie decided to take her Sunday nap at Miss Rosie's and sent me over here with Sophie so we could do this job together. So you've left Egypt and you are returning to the promised land, Liz?" Darcy smiled.

"I can't believe that you were paying attention to the preacher when Calvin was that close to you, Darcy," Hannah said.

"Had to." Darcy held the door for them to bring in two boxes each. "I was afraid if I looked at him, I'd go up in flames and there wouldn't be nothing left of me but the smell of scorched linen. Why I ever bought this dress is a mystery. Damn thing has to be hand washed and ironed and it wrinkles something awful."

"But it looks beautiful on you, and that shade of peach is so pretty with your complexion." Hannah took her load to the spare bedroom and set it on the floor.

"I went through every dress in my closet before I chose this one. And did Cal even notice? No, sir! He was so intrigued with the preacher or one of those women in the choir wearing a shapeless choir robe that he couldn't even see me. God, why did I have to fall in love with Calvin Winters when we were kids?" Darcy hung the clothing in the closet. "We can sort this later. For now, I'll just get it all in here."

Hannah giggled. "Don't ask God. Ask your heart."

They all three trudged up the stairs together to the bedroom Liz would be using. "The heart is a fickle thing. It will steer you wrong. God won't."

"I think the heart tells us what it wants, but when we don't listen, that's when we get into trouble," Hannah shot right back. "Be honest. Did you have any doubts on your wedding day? I did, but then I was pregnant and felt like my baby deserved a good name. Look what that got me."

Liz nodded slowly. "I did have doubts, but they'd already given us a shower and parties and it would create a stink in the whole town if I backed out on the wedding day. Besides, if I was honest with myself, I was a little afraid of what Wyatt would do if I did. You are so right, Hannah. The heart doesn't steer us wrong. We do that to ourselves."

Sophie followed all three women into the room. "You want Travis to paint a rainbow and a twinkle star on your wall?"

Liz wrapped both arms around Sophie. "Maybe when I get my own house."

Sophie's dark brows knit together in a thinking frown. "How would you paint a lullaby sky? I think we should fix a sign for our house and hang it on the porch so people will know what to call it." She paused and stuck a finger above her upper lip. "Would it have clouds or not?"

Liz looked at Hannah and raised an eyebrow.

"Remember the preacher talking about happiness and peace this morning in church, Sophie?" Hannah asked.

"I was coloring, so I didn't listen to him," Sophie answered.

"Well, peace is when there is nothing in the house that makes you unhappy or sad. Our house is like that. But you can't make a picture of it to put on a sign, because it's a feeling down deep in your heart, not a picture in your mind," Hannah explained.

Sophie smiled sweetly. "Oh, like the way Uncle Cal looks when he sees Aunt Darcy."

"What?" Darcy spun around.

"Uncle Cal likes Aunt Darcy, like Tommy at the church likes me. But I don't like him back, so I renore him. That's what you have to do to Uncle Cal if you don't like him back. Just renore him."

She left the room with her chin in the air, and in a few seconds they heard her flipping through the channels on the television set.

"Renore?" Darcy asked.

"Ignore," Hannah told them.

Two circles of crimson dotted Darcy's cheeks. "Does anything get past her?"

"Not much." Liz stood up and headed toward the door. "But rest assured, men are blind to what kids see, so you have time to get your 'I've loved you forever' speech honed and fine-tuned before you present it to one of the biggest names in the clothing industry."

When Liz was out of sight, Hannah fanned Darcy with her hands in a dramatic gesture to ease the fire still burning in her cheeks. "Sophie will forget all about this by evening, and if she starts to bring it up, I will steer her toward her new kitten, which she's also named Lullaby. That is probably going to be the word of the summer instead of the day. And don't tell her I let the cat's name out of the bag. She's going to announce it at dinner this evening in what I'm sure will be a dramatic move. Tell me something. You've been in Liz's place more than any of us. What kind of feeling do you get over there?"

"Like I'm in an evil place and the devil is about to come up through the floorboards," Darcy said honestly.

"Then it wasn't just me," Hannah said.

"No, ma'am. But I remember his grandma who lived there from back when we were kids. She was nice and the house didn't feel like that then. I think Wyatt is pure evil and his aura is in that place."

"Maybe so. I'll help unload the rest of the boxes from out in our cars. You can start unpacking and putting them away," Hannah said.

❧

Hannah caught Cal's expression as she, Liz, and Darcy made their way into the dining room at Miss Rosie's that Sunday evening. Sophie had called it right on the money. He absolutely looked like he could sweep Darcy off her feet like a knight in shining armor on a big white horse and carry her off to live in a prince's castle.

From the looks of it, Sophie had set the table again. The napkins were askew and the knives weren't all turned the right way, but Hannah didn't have the urge to fix it. That was a big step in the right direction, wasn't it?

"Okay, folks, it's plain fare tonight since we had a big dinner. Pinto beans with the ham hock that I had left over from a church dinner, fried potatoes, fried okra, and tomatoes from Mr. Taybor's garden down the street and fresh strawberry shortcakes for dessert."

"This isn't plain, and getting to eat here twice in one day is pure heaven," Cal declared. "This is the food of the gods. Please tell me that you fried the potatoes in bacon drippings."

"Of course, is there any other way?" Miss Rosie beamed.

The dining room was small, and the table usually only seated six, but Miss Rosie had brought in two metal folding chairs that she used around the card table on canasta night with her church ladies. That cramped the two sides, but no one complained, least of all Darcy, sitting between Liz and Calvin.

"I'll say grace because I will keep it short and I'm hungry." Miss Rosie bowed her head and said a few sentences followed by a loud amen. Then she picked up the platter of corn bread, put a square on her plate, and sent it around the table.

"I liked what the preacher said this morning. Seemed right fittin'." Aunt Birdie followed Miss Rosie's lead and, after helping herself to a good-size portion of fried okra, handed it off to Hannah.

"Yes, it did," Liz agreed.

"I have named my kitten," Sophie said.

"And?" Travis asked.

"Her name is Lullaby and sometimes I might call her Lully for short," Sophie announced.

"Well, I think that's a perfect name, but I thought for sure you'd name her Twinkle or Star," Travis said.

"Those are her middle names," Sophie said. "Lullaby Twinkle Star. But I will only call her all of them when she's been bad. Do you know that cat crap really stinks? I have to hold my nose when I scoop out the litter pan."

"Sophie!" Hannah scolded.

"The truth is the truth. Don't matter if you put sugar on it or cat crap, it's still the truth." Aunt Birdie chuckled. "And it does stink. That, my sweet little girl, is your first lesson in having a pet to take care of. There's good jobs and bad jobs whether it's a kitten or a little baby."

"She's worth it." Sophie shrugged and set about eating her Sunday supper.

Sophie was between Travis and Hannah, which gave her more space than she'd had when she was sitting so close to him in church that morning. Yet when their hands brushed together as they passed the bowls and platters, the sparks were still there. She was elated when her cell phone started playing "Twinkle, Twinkle Little Star" in her purse. She pushed back her chair and answered it on the fourth ring just before it went to voice mail.

"Hannah, this is Gina. I've got a woman with two little children who needs a place for a few days. I'm full to capacity. The only problem is that she has a broken leg and can't do stairs and will need a baby bed in whatever room you give her. You offered your downstairs bedroom. Is that still available?" Gina asked.

"Yes, ma'am, any time you need it," Hannah said.

"It's two daughters, by the way. Age five and three months. Within a week her brother will come to get her, but he's out on a ship with the navy right now," Gina said. "I'm just reminding you again. They should stay in the house."

"I understand. I can get Sophie's baby bed out of the attic and set it up. When will you be here?"

"In an hour," Gina said.

"I'll be home and waiting. Might not completely have the baby bed set up, but we'll be working on it. Does she need clothing, diapers, or anything for the children? I'm sure Aunt Birdie could find things for her at the church."

"We've got all that covered at least for the first few days. You might need to furnish some diapers and laundry soap between now and next Saturday, when her brother will come for her."

"Has she had supper?"

"They are eating right now."

"Then we will see you in an hour." She hit the "End" button and went back to the table. "We have guests. Travis, could I borrow you after dinner to help me put Sophie's baby bed up in my bedroom?"

"Baby bed? Am I getting a sister or a brother?" Sophie's big brown eyes glittered.

"You, sweetheart," Hannah answered, "are getting a little girl who is your age to play with for a whole week. Once you get acquainted you might even get to have a sleepover in your room. But Sophie, when we get this kind of company, you need to know that they cannot go outside, so you will have to stay in the house if you want to play with the little girl."

Sophie's hands flew to her cheeks in a dramatic gesture. "You mean it? My very first sleepover in my whole life."

"But only if the little girl's mama says it's okay," Hannah said.

"I hope she likes Lullaby and my room," Sophie said. "Is she coming right now?"

"In about an hour, so you better clean up that plate. Especially if you want to have time for strawberry shortcake," Hannah said.

"Why does the baby bed go in your room?" Travis asked.

"She has a broken leg and can't climb stairs, especially with a new baby. I'll take one of the upstairs rooms," she answered.

"And I'll take one of the others," he said. "I'll move back tonight."

"That's not necessary," Hannah argued.

"Yes, it is," Aunt Birdie said. "And I'll feel better if he's there, so do it for my sake if not for yours."

"Okay." She couldn't tell Aunt Birdie no, not after all the wiry little lady had done for her through the years.

Travis, sleeping in the room across the hall or right next to her. Travis, using the same bathroom she did. Travis, leaving the scent of his aftershave lingering behind him. It scared her, and yet, it kicked an extra little thump into her heartbeat at the same time.

CHAPTER FIFTEEN

The woman hardly looked old enough to have produced two children. She towered above Hannah, and although she couldn't be classified as overweight, she was certainly one large woman. Hannah wondered what man would have the nerve to hit her.

Where fear had filled every fiber of Elaine's body, this young mother looked like she could chew up railroad ties and spit out toothpicks. She held her baby with one arm and had a crutch firmly planted under the other one. Her older child had a firm grip on the crossbar of the crutch and kept her eyes on her mother.

"I'm Jodie and this is Laurel and the baby is Bella. Thank you for letting us stay here." Her eyes bored right into Hannah's.

Every situation was sure enough going to be different, Hannah decided. "We are glad to have you. This is my daughter, Sophie, who is very excited to have a playmate this week, and this is Travis, our bodyguard."

Jodie scanned Travis from boots to hair and then back down. "Brad will eat him for lunch and still be hungry."

"He's a lot stronger and meaner than you think," Hannah said. "And there's a shotgun in his bedroom that could even the score pretty quickly. You don't worry about a thing. We're out in the boondocks, and the only way anyone comes here is if they live here. You will be safe."

"I'm Sophie. Would you like to come and see my new room? It's got a rainbow and a star on the wall and I've got Barbie dolls if you want to play." Sophie took the little blonde-haired girl's other hand in hers.

Blue eyes, as big as saucers, looked up at her mother for an answer.

"It's right next door from where you and the baby will be staying, and we'll leave both doors open," Hannah said quickly.

A slight smile turned up the corners of Jodie's wide lips. "You can go play, Laurel."

"Here's her suitcase and a package of diapers for the baby," Gina said. "I should be getting back."

"Thank you," Hannah said. "Now let's get you settled, Jodie. Maybe you and Miss Bella would like a nap?"

Jodie's whole demeanor changed. "It's been months since I've slept without worry. He's crazy when he's mad, and the last time he threw Laurel across the room and gave me a choice. She could take the whipping for my sass or he'd give it to her," Jodie said. "That's when I'd had enough and started making plans to leave him. But I shouldn't be whining. I got away. Now if only he don't find me for a week, I might even get back to Kentucky in one piece."

Hannah said, "You can tell as much or as little as you want. We can sit up with sweet tea or hot coffee until midnight or you can keep it all to yourself. But know one thing—I've walked that mile in your shoes. My divorce isn't even a month old."

"You are so lucky that it's over," Jodie said. "When my brother gets me back into those Kentucky hills, I'll feel a lot better. Brad knows better than to come after me there. Those folks don't mess around with men like him."

"Then we'll keep you safe until then. Travis, will you get that suitcase?" Hannah led the way to her bedroom.

Jodie gasped. "This is so beautiful and quiet."

Two little girls' giggles wafted from the next room.

Jodie stopped in her tracks and spun around, baby still in her arms. "I haven't heard her giggle like that in a long time."

"It's the house." Travis smiled.

The baby started to wiggle and fuss. Travis held out his hands, and Jodie hesitated.

"I love babies." Travis's smile was so honest and kind that Jodie turned her baby over to him.

I have done that, Hannah thought. *Travis is just that trustworthy.*

Bella gave him a toothless grin and cooed.

"He's like that with children." Hannah laughed. "But rest assured he can shoot the eyes out of a rattlesnake at thirty yards."

"My daddy got upset if I wasted ammo," Travis said as he sat down on the edge of the bed. "And Miz Bella, when you get into the hills of Kentucky, I bet you've got a grandpa who will teach you how to shoot."

"No grandpa, but she's got a great-granny and tons of cousins and great-uncles. We'll be living in my old home," Jodie said.

"She'll have folks to love her, and that's what's important. Would it be all right for Travis to take Bella over to Sophie's room and give you some privacy to unpack?" Hannah asked.

Jodie nodded but didn't take her eyes off Travis as he carried her baby into Sophie's room. "It's hard to trust. I put my faith in Brad, and look what it got me." She leaned her crutch against one side of the bed and hobbled over to open the suitcase. "Should I leave this stuff in here?"

"I've cleaned out two drawers for you, and there's space in the closet for your things. And Jodie," Hannah said, "we'll get you through this week and you can go home to your Kentucky home and heal."

Laurel dashed into the bedroom with the kitten hanging over her arm like a limp dishrag. "Mama, Mama, look, Sophie's got a kitten and its name is Lullaby."

Jodie rubbed the gray fur. "She is a beautiful kitty cat. And I like her name."

"Sophie says it's because this house is named Lullaby Sky, but they can't make a sign for the porch. Sophie has her room all fancy. Come and see. Can I paint my room when we get to 'Tucky?" Laurel tugged at her mother's hand.

Jodie picked up her crutch and hobbled to Sophie's bedroom. "Oh. My. Goodness. What a lovely room. And I think you should have a rainbow and clouds and a star on your wall in Kentucky."

Hannah followed, awe filling her just as it had Jodie, only for different reasons. There was big, tall, strapping Travis sitting in the rocking chair humming a lullaby to the baby. He looked up and winked at her, and Hannah's heart melted. Someday a woman would come along and Travis would fall in love with her. She'd get the best man on Earth, and he'd be a wonderful husband and father.

A shot of pure old green jealousy danced down Hannah's spine. She wasn't sure she could ever be friends with a woman who got the privilege of his love.

"Look, Mama." Laurel pointed. "Sophie's got Barbies like the ones I had, and now we're going to play with them."

"That's my cue to take Bella to the living room. She's too little to play with Barbies and the girls need their privacy. Is that all right with you, Jodie?" Travis drawled.

Jodie nodded without hesitation this time. "I can unpack my few things if you want to go with him." She glanced at Hannah.

"I'll make a fresh pitcher of sweet tea and a pot of coffee. There's some leftover cupcakes, too," Hannah said.

"Laurel will love that. She's got a sweet tooth just like my brother's. I'm so glad that he can take a two-week leave from the service and help me go home. Should've never left." Jodie sighed.

"Hindsight and all that . . ." Hannah paused.

"Shit!" Jodie said under her breath.

"Yes, ma'am." Hannah nodded.

Hannah had just gotten the tea made when Jodie showed up in the kitchen. Without a baby in her arms, she looked even taller. Her blonde hair had been short at one time, but it had grown out into several different lengths. Brown eyes were set into a round face that could be pretty if it didn't have so many worry lines etched into it.

"Tea?" Hannah asked.

"Yes, please and maybe one of those cupcakes. I didn't have much supper. I don't like to take charity, but I couldn't figure out another way to get back to Kentucky without going through the shelter." Jodie pushed up the sleeves of a knit shirt that were frayed at the wrists.

"It's a good sign that you're hungry now. And this is not charity, Jodie, so get that idea out of your head." Travis had brought a wooden rocker from the living room and was letting Bella chew on his cell phone.

"She'll ruin your phone," Jodie said.

"Who cares? She's teething. Got one of them ring things for her?" Travis asked.

Jodie shook her head. "Left everything behind. Walked out without even a diaper bag, caught a bus to Gainesville, and called Gina. I have a friend who works at a health clinic. She noticed some bruises and handed me a phone number. I kept it for over a month before I finally had enough of his shit."

"Smart woman," Hannah said. "I've still got a couple of those rings that you freeze. I found them shoved back behind a bag of frozen peas the other day. My ex-husband did not like canned peas, so I kept frozen ones for him at all times. Long story short, there are two in the freezer. Do you mind if I let her chew on one?"

"Not a bit. It'll feel good on those swollen gums." Jodie sipped her tea as she slumped down in a kitchen chair.

Carolyn Brown

Hannah dug around in the freezer side of her refrigerator and handed a pink pretzel-shaped teething ring to Travis. He put it in Bella's chubby little fingers, and she promptly stuck it in her mouth.

"How old is she?" Travis asked.

"Three months. She was a big accident. I didn't want any more kids when I found out what I'd gotten into, but the pill failed. Even so, I wouldn't want things different. She and Laurel are the reason I found the courage to leave. I couldn't stay and put them in harm's way every single day."

Hannah could hear the Kentucky accent coming through in Jodie's voice as she got a little more comfortable in her surroundings.

Hannah wished she had half of Jodie's spunk and sass. "I was lucky. My abusive husband decided he wanted out of the marriage and divorced me. But I did try to run twice. He caught me both times and threatened to take Sophie from me."

"That's why I'm going home. If he ever shows up there, well, it'll be like the lyrics of that old song—he'll never leave Harlan alive. If I can make it through this week and get home, I'll be safe," she said.

"Does he know that?" Travis asked.

"Oh, yes. He's terrified of my relatives. He could never survive the wilds. Lord, he can't even shoot a gun," Jodie said. "He's a big man. Six feet, five inches and broad across the shoulders. That's what drew me to him, I guess. I didn't feel like a big giant sunflower in a bed of pretty little delicate flowers when I was with him. I found out real quick that I wasn't any match for his fists when he was mad, even if I am a big girl."

"How did you meet?" Travis asked.

"He was in Kentucky doing construction work on a bridge. He came into the café where I worked and I came back to Texas with him when he left. I was six months pregnant with Laurel when we married."

"So you do have a place to live when you get to Kentucky?" Hannah asked.

Jodie nodded. "I've got a two-bedroom cabin, and my brother will be taking care of us until I get my first paycheck. My granny has a job lined up for me at the café where I used to work."

"We could fix you up with some clothing to take along from our church clothes closet. It'll be used stuff, but it's been washed and it's clean," Hannah said.

Jodie inhaled. "I guess that would be all right. I wasn't raised to take charity, but it's nice of you to offer and to take us in like this. Maybe someday if you are in Kentucky I can repay you with some fine home cookin' and a room to stay in."

"Maybe you can." Hannah smiled.

೦⁄౨

It was well past midnight when Hannah heard a strange sound and sat straight up in bed. What if Jodie's sorry ex-bastard had gotten into the house? From what she'd said, Travis wouldn't be a match for him. Hannah wasn't even sure a bullet could put a man like that down.

Her feet were on the floor and she was halfway across the room when she realized what she'd heard was Travis's deep voice right outside her door.

"Okay, but I really think I should go, too," he said.

And then he rapped on her door.

She swung it open immediately, and the look on his face, lit up only by the screen of his phone, said something was badly wrong. "Is it Aunt Birdie?" she asked.

"No, it's Liz. The ambulance is on the way to the hospital with her, and the police have Wyatt in custody. She keeps asking for you. Aunt Birdie is already dressed and waiting on her porch, so I'll stay here until Miss Rosie arrives. That way there will be a lady in the house when Jodie wakes up in the morning," he said.

"Oh, Travis," she said with a heavy heart.

He opened his arms, and she walked right into them. He rubbed her back and hushed her with soft sounds that spread warmth to her neck and face. "I'm so sorry, darlin'. I should have been staying with them at Miss Rosie's house tonight instead of here."

"Hindsight," she murmured.

"Get dressed. We'll hold the fort down until you come home. If Liz needs you, stay with her as long as necessary." Travis tipped her chin up.

She saw worry for Liz in his eyes, but something else, too. She didn't have time to analyze it, because his lips met hers in a kiss that made the house tilt under her feet. Her arms snaked up around his neck, and she rolled up on her toes for a second kiss. A rap on the back door made her step back, and Travis headed down the steps to let Miss Rosie inside.

"We'll talk later," he threw over his shoulder as he disappeared into the darkness.

She hurriedly threw off her nightshirt, suddenly blushing at how little she was wearing when she'd pressed up against him so tightly. Shoving a leg down into the jeans that she'd worn that afternoon, she hoped that Jodie wasn't uncomfortable with Miss Rosie and Travis. By the time she started zipping her pants, anger had set in.

"It's a damn good thing that Wyatt is in jail. If Aunt Birdie didn't shoot the sorry sucker, I would," she said aloud to herself.

Miss Rosie shuffled into the bedroom with her. "You've got a daughter to raise. I'd do the shootin' if there's any to be done. Now get on a bra and a shirt and get out of here." She wore a bright-red sweater over a floral nightgown and a pink-checkered cotton robe and carried a tote bag full of clothing. "I'm going to sleep right there." She pointed at the unmade bed. "You call me, no matter what time it is when you find out how Liz is. I want to know if she is dead. If the latter is the case, then Travis will have to cook breakfast for your guests, because I'm going to the jail with my pistol in my purse, and honey, it will be loaded."

"Let's hope you cook breakfast instead." Hannah put on a bra and grabbed the first T-shirt out of her dresser drawer. "Lord, I'm glad I brought a few clothes up here. It would terrify Jodie if I had to go into her room in the middle of the night."

"Birdie is waiting, so hurry up, child." Miss Rosie dropped the sweater and housecoat and crawled into the bed.

Hannah did hurry, but she stopped long enough to plant a kiss on Miss Rosie's forehead before she left the room.

"Take a sweater. Them hospitals is always cold," Miss Rosie said.

"I can't. They are all in my room and I don't want to wake Jodie," she answered.

"Then take mine. I can get dressed before I go down to make breakfast. And don't worry about what goes on here. Me and Travis can take care of things just fine."

Travis was in the kitchen, and as she passed through he handed her an insulated cup of coffee. "Call me as soon as you know something. I'll have the phone right by my side. Aunt Birdie said that she left a note for Cal. I expect he'll be at the hospital as soon as he wakes up. Darcy will meet y'all there."

"Thanks, Travis, for everything."

He brushed a quick kiss across her lips. "You drive safe and call me when you get there."

Aunt Birdie was waiting on the porch, just like Travis said. When she saw Hannah back the car out of the driveway, she hurried out to the side of the road and had the passenger's door open before the car even came to a complete stop.

"I packed us a few things in case we have to spend the rest of the night and tomorrow at the hospital." She slipped the tote bag through the space in the front seats and gave it a shove. "Don't matter if it falls out. I can put it all back in a jiffy."

"What do you know?" Hannah asked.

"He was supposed to be home tomorrow, but he called about ten when me and Liz were about to go to bed and said he was coming in early and he'd be here at eleven. I had a bad feelin', so I called Rosie and we waited up for Liz after she went to the house. At eleven thirty Rosie got worried and drove down to check on things. I should've gone with her, but we figured I'd stay at the house. That way if Liz came back I'd call Rosie and she could turn around and come on back home. She found Liz in her front yard with Wyatt still beating and kicking her, even when she was down. Rosie called nine-one-one and held him off with her pistol until the cops and ambulance got there."

"Is she going to live?" Hannah asked.

"Rosie said that she looked like warmed-over hell on Sunday morning. He'd used the buckle end of his belt and steel-toed boots. If she dies, he does. Plain and simple. I don't mind spending the rest of my days in prison," Aunt Birdie said.

Chapter Sixteen

I t looks worse than it is," Liz said through a lip with three stitches. "They won't let me go home, Hannah. It's going to be all over school and the county."

"It needs to be." Darcy had a firm hold on Liz's left hand. "And you will press charges. Rosie heard him say that he'd kill you before he let you leave him."

Hannah reached through the bedrails and held Liz's right hand. Not crying was even tougher than that day in the courtroom. If she broke down, Liz would be compelled to comfort her, and this wasn't about Hannah. She'd had her day of friends gathering around for support. Now it was Liz's turn. Still, seeing Liz with taped ribs, butterfly strips on her forehead and cheek, and a busted lip brought tears to her soul.

Liz squeezed Hannah's hand. "It's all right, Hannah. I was never unconscious. I faked it so he'd stop and so he wouldn't overpower Miss Rosie and kill her."

"Why didn't you fight him harder?" Aunt Birdie asked.

"He said Hannah getting a divorce caused this and he was going to take care of her and Sophie next. I still had my phone in my hip pocket, so I dialed nine-one-one. I couldn't let him hurt that precious baby girl," Liz answered.

"Miss Rosie called them," Hannah said.

"She was only there five minutes before they arrived." Liz tried to smile and flinched. "Don't tell her."

"Enough talk. You sleep and we'll be right here when you wake up," Aunt Birdie said.

Liz nodded once and shut her eyes, but she did not let go of either Darcy's or Hannah's hand.

☙

Travis awoke to the aroma of coffee and bacon. He couldn't sleep the night before, so he'd written two chapters on his work in progress. He was ahead of schedule despite the construction job, and that made his agent and publishers very happy. He liked writing, all of it, from the beginning sentence in a novel to the last page. What he didn't like was not being able to talk about it with Hannah. But it was best this way. Only his agent, his editor, and his publisher knew his real identity. Hannah would look at him with disgust if she knew the whole reason he was independent and could work at whatever he wanted was because he wrote romantic suspense novels.

He hurriedly shaved and dressed in a pair of better jeans and what he deemed a decent T-shirt and made his way to the kitchen. Cal looked up from the waffle maker and nodded toward the coffeepot.

"How are we going to play this one?" he asked.

"You mean as in temporarily or permanently?" Travis poured a cup of coffee and took a stack of plates down from the cabinet.

"For today, right now. We'll worry about the other if they let him out of jail."

"I thought maybe you and I would go to the hospital for an hour or so." Cal removed a waffle from the iron and laid it onto a plate. Miss Rosie added half a dozen strips of crisp bacon to the side.

She pointed toward the waffle maker. "You can make yours now, Travis. I'll keep frying bacon."

Travis poured half a cup of batter into the iron. "The folks here will be fine for a couple of hours with Miss Rosie. Then I'll bring Aunt Birdie home with me and you can stay with Hannah through today. Darcy had to go in to work this morning, but she's making arrangements to leave as soon as she can and stay the night."

"I figured you'd want to stay with Hannah yourself," Cal said.

"I do, more than anything in the world, but Hannah will want me to be here as much as possible. Maybe Liz will only have to be there for a day or two."

"And Hannah," Miss Rosie said, "is Liz's strength right now. She'll want her by her side until she comes home."

Jodie yawned as she made her way across the kitchen toward the coffeepot. "Good mornin'. I'm sorry I wasn't up to help, but I haven't slept like that in years. Bella only woke up one time all through the night, and she's still asleep. It's amazing."

Miss Rosie smiled at her. "A place without fear does that to a person. You can have the waffle machine after Travis gets done." She went on to tell her where Hannah was that morning and the plans for the day.

"No." Jodie shook her head. "You stay with Hannah, Travis, and you, too, Cal, if you want to. I'm very comfortable with Miss Rosie and Aunt Birdie. For that matter, I could take care of myself in this wonderful house. But I think that Sophie will be happier if someone she knows well is here. I'd feel better if y'all don't treat me like company. Please let me help out so I'll feel like I'm earning my keep around here. I may have a busted leg, but I can still work."

"Are you sure?" Cal asked.

"Very. I haven't felt like this since I left the hills of Kentucky. I had a gut feeling that I was making a mistake when we crossed the border into Tennessee, but I wanted my baby to have a father. I've found out since there's worse things for a child."

Travis removed his waffle, and Jodie started another one.

"I'm so, so sorry about your friend—Liz, right? It must be big comfort to have all of you to help her through this mess. I hope her husband dies in prison."

Miss Rosie chuckled. "I like you, girl."

"The way I see it is like this," Jodie said. "The Good Book says, 'Do not kill,' but that was a commandment for a man's family, for his brethren that he was traveling across the desert to the promised land with. It was not given for his enemies, and anyone trying to kick a woman to death is an enemy."

"Amen," Travis said.

❧

Darcy sneaked back into the room in the middle of the morning. "Is she going to be all right?"

"Of course I am." Liz opened her eyes. "I just have to heal and then this will never happen again."

Darcy clenched her hands into fists. "I should have gone with you to tell him that you'd left him. We never should have let you go alone."

"Shhh," Liz said. "It's over. I'm glad you are here, but I'm so sleepy. It must be the medicine they keep putting in that IV."

Darcy gently patted her shoulder. "You need to rest so you will heal."

Liz shut her eyes again and began to snore softly. Darcy pulled up a chair and sat down beside her, taking Liz's left hand in hers.

"Thank you," Hannah said very softly. "I need to go to the bathroom, and every time I let go of her hand she gets agitated." Hannah eased her hand out away from Liz's and tiptoed out of the room.

All the stalls in the bathroom were empty, so she chose the one closest to the door and sat there with her head in her hands long after she'd finished using the toilet. Tears bathed her face as she prayed desperately for Liz to be all right, to move on past this horrible experience.

Finally, she pulled up her underpants and jeans and left the stall to wash her hands. Holding them under the warm water, she noticed that they were still shaking. She was one of the lucky ones. She'd only gone to the emergency room one time with cracked ribs. That time she'd lied and told people that she'd fallen down the stairs. After that, Marty was careful with his abuse, leaving bruises only where most folks couldn't see them. She looked at her reflection in the mirror and immediately reached for paper towels. She couldn't go back into the room with tearstained cheeks and swollen eyes. Liz didn't need that on her plate in addition to all the emotional baggage she would be carrying around for months, maybe years.

She finally got control of herself enough to push open the bathroom door and head back down the hallway to Liz's room. She'd only taken two steps when the sound of the elevator doors opening caused her to look over her shoulder. There was still a fear in her heart that Wyatt would make bail and come back to finish what he'd started.

But two policemen, along with Cal and Travis, stepped out. Travis caught her eye immediately and waved. She stopped walking, and they quickly caught up to her.

"We thought we'd let Aunt Birdie go home and stay awhile with y'all," Cal said.

Travis nodded toward the police. "This is Officer Dale and Officer Brody. They are here to talk to Liz."

Hannah nodded. "Aunt Birdie does look tired. It's been a long night."

The four men crowded into the small hospital room. Liz opened her eyes and sighed. "He made bail, didn't he?"

One officer nodded his head. "We booked him on domestic abuse, and his girlfriend showed up and bailed him out."

The tears dried up, and Liz's jaw worked like she was chewing bubblegum for a few seconds before she spoke. "I feel sorry for his girlfriend. I want a restraining order, and I have faith that karma will come around and bite him on the butt. Maybe this girlfriend has more fire than I did and she'll shoot him the first time he whips off his belt."

"That's not good enough. Rosie was there and gave you her statement. He would have killed Liz if she hadn't held that man off with a gun." Aunt Birdie's voice had gone high and squeaky, which meant she was about to blow.

"He says that Liz brought that gun to the house and threatened him with it. He threw her off the porch and the gun went flying out into the yard. Then the elderly lady picked it up and held it on him until we got there. I don't believe a word of it, but that's his statement. Have you filed on him before for abuse?"

Liz shook her head.

"I don't give a damn. I want him tried for attempted murder," Aunt Birdie said. "Not pay a fine for domestic violence and do a few hours of community work."

"Let it be," Liz said. "He can sweet-talk the pantyhose off a nun, Aunt Birdie. If he's got a girlfriend, he'll stay away from Crossing. I'm good with him being out of my life forever."

"But I'm not," Aunt Birdie huffed. "He should be dead or in prison."

"Ma'am," Officer Brody said, "if it helps any, the woman who bailed him out of jail didn't look to me like she'd take sass off nobody. He might end up dead if he does this kind of thing to her."

"And if you want to go through with it, you've got a good chance of putting him away with the pictures the doctors took and that lady's testimony about the gun. She seemed like a credible witness to me," Officer Dale said.

"I'll think about it. Right now I just want to sleep." Liz flinched when she yawned.

"You let us know. If you want to proceed with it, we'll bring the papers when you go home, along with the restraining order," Officer Dale said.

Liz nodded and drifted back to sleep as the officers exited the room.

"Give me your keys, Hannah," Aunt Birdie said when the officers left. "I'll drive myself back to Crossing. Y'all have got two vehicles here, so you'll be fine. And two people at a time are enough in this room. Travis, you take Hannah to get some food in the cafeteria and let her rest an hour or so out in one of the cars. She's not even closed her eyes all night."

"Yes, ma'am," Travis said.

"And when y'all get back, Cal and Darcy can go out for two hours. That way you all won't get plumb wore out."

Hannah fished in her purse for the keys and handed them to Aunt Birdie. "Thank you for staying with me all night. I really thought he'd go to jail for this."

"I had my doubts. I've worked with Gina a long time." Aunt Birdie shook her head. "One set of y'all come home tonight. She don't need a roomful with her. Since Sophie is going to need you, Hannah, you might come with Travis tonight and then let Darcy and Cal have tomorrow off while you stay with Liz."

"You sure are bossy." Hannah smiled.

"Yes, I am. It takes a bossy person to take care of the bunch of you."

"I love you, Aunt Birdie. I'm so glad that . . ."

Aunt Birdie threw up a hand. "I love you—all of you. Now do what I say or I might change my mind." Her tired old eyes glittered as she left the room.

"So, are you going to listen to her?" Cal asked.

"Yes, we are." Hannah yawned. "It's ten thirty. Aunt Birdie left her tote bag, and it's full of cookies and goodies if y'all get hungry. We'll be back at one and you can leave for a couple of hours."

"A word?" Darcy asked. "Alone."

The two guys stepped out into the hallway.

"Why don't I go with you," Darcy said. "I'm not sure about spending so much time in the room with Cal."

"This might be a blessing. How often do you two get to spend time alone?" Hannah said.

Darcy wiggled in her chair and skewed up her face. "I'm scared."

"Fear begets fear. Shake it off. I'll see you in a couple of hours." Hannah left the room and motioned for Cal to go back inside. "Just call if Liz needs us."

Cal handed Travis his van keys and went back into the room. Travis pocketed them and then picked up Hannah's arm and looped it in his, keeping his hand over hers afterward. "I've had breakfast, but I could sure use a cup of coffee while you eat."

Just the touch of his hand on hers erased the anxiety in her heart. "She's strong, right? She'll pull through this."

"She will. Even though it doesn't look like it, it could be worse. The busted ribs didn't pierce her lungs or rupture any internal organs. The rest will heal. There might be a few faint scars, but the bruises will go away." He pushed the "Down" elevator button. "It's not the physical that worries me about her any more than it does about you. It's the way it's affected y'all in other ways."

They joined an elderly couple in the elevator, who smiled sweetly at them. "We pushed the wrong button for the maternity place. Our great-grandson was born last night. Y'all here to see a baby?" the gray-haired lady said.

"No, ma'am. Just here for a friend," Travis said.

"Well, you sure make a cute couple," the lady said. "Maybe someday you'll be here havin' a baby of your own."

"Now wouldn't that be something." Travis grinned.

The elevator stopped, and the old couple got off, leaving Travis and Hannah alone. She wanted to say something—to tell him that she had developed something akin to feelings for him, but the words stuck in her throat. Even though she trusted him, anything concerning that kind of relationship terrified her.

"Cute old folks," Travis said.

Saved by the elevator doors and the scent of food coming from the cafeteria not far from them, she sniffed the air. "I think that's hamburgers I'm getting a whiff of. I bet they've stopped serving breakfast altogether. I'd rather have a cheeseburger and fries anyway. Didn't realize I was hungry until now."

"Don't be so nervous." Travis led her in the direction of the aroma of fried onions.

"I'm not nervous," she protested.

"Yes, you are. You talk too fast when you are, just like you did when we were kids."

"You know me too well," she said.

"We need to talk, but you are too tired to discuss anything. Let's get you fed and then go out to Cal's van. I'll put all the backseats down and you can stretch out for a nap."

She didn't realize how tired she was until she started to chew. Her eyes grew heavier and heavier, and she had to force herself to stay awake to finish half the burger and a few fries. "I'm so sorry. The adrenaline rush is circling the drain," she said. "Oh! I need to call Miss Rosie and check on Sophie."

"I did that just before we got to the hospital. She and Laurel had breakfast together and now they are dressed in *Frozen* costumes and playing in her room. She's in good hands," Travis said. "And so are you, Hannah. I'm going to take care of you, I promise."

He cleared her tray, then returned and held out his hand to her. "Nap time. I don't think I'll even have to tell you a story."

"Not today." She put her hand in his and wasn't a bit surprised at the little twinge of heat that crept up her neck.

A nice breeze ruffled the leaves of the trees around the hospital as they stepped outside. The warmth felt good on her face, but Miss

Rosie's sweater was suddenly way too hot. She removed it and threw it over her shoulder.

"I've got an idea." Travis unlocked the vehicle and got in. "Wait right here while I turn this rig around."

She leaned against the big tree trunk and watched him pull the van out and then back it into the parking spot.

"Aha," she said.

"We can catch the breeze. I don't think anyone will bother us," he said as he circled around to the back. He swung the doors open wide and quickly pushed the seats down. "Our first time to sleep together. I had something different in mind, but it is what it is."

She giggled. "That's a horrible pickup line. No wonder you don't have a woman in your life."

"I've been waiting a long time for the right woman, darlin'," he answered as he motioned for her to crawl in first. "Sorry I don't have a pillow, but I can offer you my arm."

"I could sleep standing up in a broom closet right now." She put a knee on the hard carpeted surface and crawled inside. Then she stopped and turned to look over her shoulder. "What did you just say?"

He came in right behind her and stretched his long, lanky frame out on the other side. "You heard me. I don't want just any woman in my life. I want the woman of my dreams, and if I can't have that person, I will do without." He slipped an arm under her and pulled her effortlessly to his side. It felt right and comfortable to lie on his chest and shut her eyes, to listen to his heart beat steadily.

For the second time in only days, she wondered if she was that woman. It simply couldn't be. If that was the case, he would have spoken up years ago, wouldn't he?

There were no answers, but she did wonder as she shut her eyes and fell asleep what it would be like to have a man like Travis in her life forever.

CHAPTER SEVENTEEN

"Darcy . . . ," Cal started.

"Cal . . . ," she said at the same time.

"You go first," he said.

"She could have died. He might have killed her if Miss Rosie hadn't gone down there with a gun in her pocket," Darcy said.

Cal nodded.

"While I was getting my job stuff done so I could leave for the rest of the week, I kept thinking about how quick life can end," Darcy said.

"You took the whole week off?" Cal asked.

"It's supposed to be family emergency time. But the folks at the bank know that Liz and Hannah are even closer than sisters to me and that I don't have real family anymore, so they cut me some slack." She paused, and the silence in the room was so heavy that it hung right above their heads like smoke in an old cowboy bar. "Being an only child sucked when we were growing up. If it hadn't been for Liz and Hannah, I'd have lost my mind when my parents died."

Cal scooted his chair over close enough that he could hold the hand that wasn't stuck through the bars and clasping Liz's. "I can't even imagine life without my two overbearing sisters and my dad."

Darcy shrugged. "We've all had our crosses to bear, but today I'm . . ."

Another long, pregnant silence.

"My turn," Cal said. "I've had some time to think, too, and to hell with the crosses that we've all had to bear. We've been there for each other since we started school. Today I'm going to go past the cross and bare my soul, Darcy, so get ready to either laugh at me or hug me."

Darcy took a deep breath. Was he about to tell her that she was his best friend and like a sister? That he'd found the woman of his dreams and wanted to bring her to Crossing to live forever?

"Here goes," Cal said. "I've been in love with you since first grade, maybe before that. I want us to date—to find out if it's real or imagined or maybe a little of both—but I've been terrified to even ask you to dinner. But I'm asking now. Life is short and I need . . ." He paused again and looked right into her eyes.

Darcy was totally speechless.

He leaned in slightly and brushed a sweet kiss across her lips.

What a time to have both her hands out of commission. She wanted to touch his face, tell him she felt the same way, but she couldn't do either.

"Me, too," she said breathlessly.

"You, too, what?" he asked.

"I can't remember when I wasn't in love with you. This is all backward. We should date for months and then say those three magic words," she answered.

"None of us ever do things the conventional way, do we?" He cupped her chin and brought her lips to his for a passionate kiss that set every nerve in her body to humming. And the sparks didn't stop when he moved away. "Why did we wait this long?" he asked.

"Because you deserve one of those pretty trophy wives," she said.

"And you deserve a man who is not a fashion designer."

"Who says?"

"Right back at you," he said. "This does mean you'll go to dinner with me, right? And that we might be dating?"

"This means that yes to dinner and hell, yes, to dating." She grinned.

"About damn time," Liz said strongly, but she didn't open her eyes.

♋

Hannah slept with no dreams—bad or good. When she first awoke, she had no idea if she was really awake or still asleep, not even when she looked up into Travis's eyes. It came back in short flashes—the kiss from the night before, Liz was in the hospital, and she was cuddled up next Travis.

"Feel better?" he asked.

"Much, but it's been more than two hours, I'm sure. We should go back inside and let Darcy and Cal leave for a little while," she said.

"But I like it right here, all alone with you to myself," he said.

"Me, too, but we have to play fair," she said. "I should call the house again and check on Sophie and our guests on the way back inside."

"You'll feel better if you talk to Sophie, but I'll guarantee you that she's being well taken care of," Travis answered. "Aunt Birdie would have called you if Sophie so much as skinned a knee."

"I know, but I want to talk to her." Hannah pulled the phone from her hip pocket and hit the right number to call the house phone.

She sat up and then scooted out of the van and leaned against the tree. Miss Rosie picked up on the fourth ring and gave her all the news from Crossing. A moving van was sitting in the front of Wyatt's house, and two men were loading it with all the contents. A Realtor sign from Denton was in the front yard.

Then Hannah told her about the policemen and the story Wyatt had told them.

"Sorry sumbitch is going to walk free, ain't he?" Miss Rosie said.

"Oh, he'll have a day in court for assault, but I reckon he'll get a fine and maybe community service or probation, since it's his first offense. If Liz had documented the other abuses or went to the hospital before, things might be different. The policeman told us that his girlfriend didn't look like she'd take crap off him. I hope he's right. How's Sophie?"

"In hog heaven. She's got a playmate and me and Birdie have a baby to go all gaga over. Jodie has been cleaning all day. I worried about her on that crutch, but she gets around real good with it and she says that cleaning is the least she can do. I'd take her home with me to live forever, but she needs to get back to her people. I called the hospital a while ago and talked to the charge nurse. They're going to release Liz into Birdie's care after ten tonight, so y'all bring her on to the house," Miss Rosie said.

"Shouldn't they keep her another day?" Hannah asked.

"We can take care of her better than they can. She needs lots of sleep, a pain pill every four hours, and good food. I've got to go. It's my turn to rock that precious little Bella."

The phone went dark and the doors of the van slammed at the same time.

"Everything all right?" Travis asked.

"Oh, yes. The universe does not mess with Aunt Birdie and Miss Rosie," she said. "And they are going to let us take Liz home tonight after ten."

He put an arm around her shoulders and together they went back into the lobby of the hospital and caught the elevator up to Liz's floor. Hannah was so shocked when she walked into the room that Travis pulled her tightly to his side to keep her from falling.

Liz was sitting up in the bed with a tray of food in front of her. "Hello. Did y'all have a good rest? I was starving, so I ran Cal and Darcy out of here to the cafeteria."

"Holy smoke!" Hannah said.

"I look like hammered owl shit, but I assure you, darlin', I've been through this before. Maybe not as bad, but at least I can know this is the last time." She gently put a forkful of mashed potatoes into her mouth, swallowed, and then said, "And something good is coming out of this. Darcy and Cal have admitted that they've been in love with each other for years. I think they're dating now."

Hannah quickly crossed the room. "I'm in shock that you are even able to sit up."

"Just don't make me laugh. It hurts my ribs," Liz said.

"Stop talking and eat before your food gets cold," Travis said.

Liz shook a fork at him. "No man will ever boss me around again, not even you, darlin'."

Travis chuckled. "That's the Liz I knew in school."

"Are you sure you feel up to going home?" Hannah asked.

"Honey, this time I even get the good pain pills. Always before I had to make do with over-the-counter stuff." Liz's attempt at a grin turned into a grimace. "Besides, my insurance will fuss if I lie up in this bed too many days."

Hannah smiled and changed the subject. "Tell me more about Darcy and Cal."

"Nothing more to tell." Liz said. "Six more hours and I can go home. Let's send Darcy and Cal out on their first date, and we'll watch reruns of *NCIS* until they release me. I love Gibbs."

"I still can't believe you've made this kind of turnaround since we left a few hours ago," Travis said.

"It was that good stuff they put in the IV. I asked if I could take a bottle of it home with me, but they said I'd have to make do with pills," Liz said between bites of mashed potatoes and meat loaf. "This isn't nearly as good as what you make, Hannah, but it'll do in a pinch. How's your new guests? Is Sophie all right?"

"Doin' great. You worry about you," Hannah answered quickly.

"I don't have to worry anymore. I'll heal just like you are doing. With the support of y'all, I can do this and come out on the other side stronger and wiser," Liz said.

"Yes, you can," Travis said.

Hannah could have hugged Travis right there for those three words of confidence in her and Liz.

❧

The next morning, Hannah stretched and rolled her neck from side to side, shifted from her back to her side, and pulled the cool sheet up over her shoulder, all without opening her eyes. She liked sleeping in the guest room even better than the new bedroom. Her eyes popped open with a sense of violation all over again. Marty had known from the cameras that she didn't sleep in their marital bedroom when he wasn't there.

She threw the covers back, slid out of bed, and shivered. *With his oversize ego, he probably told himself that it was because I couldn't stand to be in there without him. But good grief! I read* Fifty Shades of Grey *in that room, and he would have seen that.*

Giggles out in the yard made her go to the window and pull back the curtains. A blast of sun hit her in the face like an old-time flashbulb on one of those square cameras. She blinked several times and whipped around to look at the clock beside her bed. Surely that wasn't right. It couldn't be ten o'clock. She hadn't slept past six thirty in years.

She looked out the window again. The sun was already halfway to the top of the sky, and it, unlike clocks, did not lie. The laughter grew louder, and then Travis came into view on a riding lawn mower. He'd hitched up the trailer behind the mower, and Sophie and Laurel were riding in it. Two glittery masks from a kindergarten party covered their upper faces, and they held up a couple of brightly colored whirligigs in the air to catch the morning breeze. Lord, have mercy! That child was not supposed to be outside.

She rushed down the stairs to find Jodie and Cal deep in conversation at the kitchen table. "The girls are outside." She panted.

"But they have on masks. No one knows who Laurel is but one of Sophie's church friends," Cal said. "It's okay, Hannah. Travis is going to make them come inside after a couple of rounds."

Hannah went to the back door to watch them, her heart still racing in her chest. The giggles stopped, and suddenly two girly voices and a deep drawl drowned out the sound of the mower engine with the lyrics of "Twinkle, Twinkle Little Star." The little girls looked up at the sky and held their sticks even higher. "He can't do that. He cannot take Laurel outside."

Cal stepped out on the porch and motioned at Travis to bring them inside. "Hannah is worried," he yelled loud enough for the whole county to hear.

Travis brought the mower around and helped the little girls out. They whined for one more ride, but he shook his head.

"You girls come on in and play in your room a little while," Hannah said.

Travis had a puzzled expression. "What are you worried about? I give Sophie rides all the time."

"You know the rules. Laurel can't be outside," she said.

"I got permission from Gina. She said if the girls were wearing costumes and masks it would be all right, but not to keep them out more than a few minutes. She said that it might be best if Sophie was outside some each day so things wouldn't look suspicious," Travis said. "I would never do anything to jeopardize Sophie or any of the folks that come here, Hannah. Trust me."

"I was so scared." She shivered in spite of the summer heat.

Travis laid a hand on her shoulder. "I can imagine. Gina called to ask me to come to the shelter today and talk to a teenage boy who stepped in when he caught his father beating on his mother. The man turned on the boy, who got whipped pretty badly. She thinks that I can help. While I was talking to her, I asked about the ride. I never thought of you waking up and being afraid. I'm sorry."

Two words Hannah had never heard from Marty. Not once. It was always her fault that she got hit. Sometimes he kissed her afterward and said that it would never happen again if she'd learn her job as his wife, but he'd never given her an apology. Her pulse settled down enough that she could breathe.

"Are we okay?" he asked.

"Yes, we are okay. I need a cup of coffee." She turned around and went back inside the house.

"Muffins are under the tea towel and the third pot of coffee is going. I slept in late, too," Aunt Birdie said from the kitchen table.

"How late?"

"All the way to seven o'clock. Thought my alarm clock was broke. Darcy and Liz were still asleep, so I left a note on the table for one of them to call me when they get up. I think they need a little time to talk without me hovering around." She folded the paper neatly and slammed it down on the table. "Not one damn word about Wyatt in today's paper. Has he got connections with the mob or something? They should be sharpening up the guillotine to chop his sorry head off this morning. Not even a mention in the police blotter."

Hannah carried the plate of muffins and a cup of coffee to the table. "Wyatt knows everyone in Cooke County. Remember, he was a policeman for a while before he and Liz got married and he started driving trucks."

Miss Rosie came into the house by the front door in a huff. "Did you see the morning paper? I can't believe this."

"He'll get his just due. He'll buck up against the wrong woman and that will be the end of it." Hannah buttered a blueberry muffin and bit into it. A month ago if someone had told her that her friends would come and go in her house like this, she'd have thought they should be committed to an asylum.

"Well, bring on the woman," Miss Rosie said.

Aunt Birdie's phone rang, and she pulled it out of the bibbed pocket of her overalls. "Just push the button on the coffeepot, sweetheart. It's all ready to go, and there's muffins on the counter. Bacon and sausage is in the refrigerator if you want to cook. I'll be home in a little bit."

Hannah pushed the plate of muffins toward Aunt Birdie. "Blueberry is my favorite and then cranberry with a touch of orange juice in the dough."

"Mine, too. Where's Jodie? I want to hold that baby. Birdie gets more time with the baby than I do," Miss Rosie said.

"I'm not sure where she is."

"In Sophie's room," Travis supplied.

Aunt Birdie shook her finger at Rosie. "I do not hog that baby. You're the one who always whines when your time is up with her." Aunt Birdie poured a cup of coffee and sat down at the table. "Are you all right, Hannah? I been thinkin' maybe this thing about having abused women in your house ain't such a good idea. It brings back all the pain and fear that you had when Marty was around. I saw how you was with Liz."

Before she could answer, Sophie and Laurel blew into the kitchen like a small Texas tornado, giggling and twirling and asking for a cookie. She handed them each one and they took off back to the bedroom.

"Well?" Aunt Birdie asked.

Hannah gave her a blank look and then remembered the conversation they'd been having before the kids romped inside. "Oh, that. I think it's helping, actually. Even though it breaks my heart to see

Liz like that and to see Jodie with a broken leg, it's bringing closure—maybe only a half an inch at a time, but it helps."

Wiping sweat from his forehead with a red bandanna, Cal came into the house, bypassed the coffeepot, and headed straight for the refrigerator. "Sweet tea?"

"In the pitcher. Help yourself," Hannah said.

"I'll stick to designing clothes. It's hot out there on that mower," Cal said. "You can have it back, Travis."

Aunt Birdie reached for another muffin. "I'm going home. Oh, and one more thing. Liz says that she's not leaving the house until her face is back to normal and that Sophie is not to see her until then. You can come and go, but leave Sophie at home. She doesn't want her to get scared. This week won't be a problem. She's got a new kitten and a new friend, but next week you might have your hands full with her."

"Send her to me if she wants to get out. We'll tell her that Birdie has the mumps." Miss Rosie smiled.

"Don't you dare." Aunt Birdie gasped. "I ain't never had them or the chicken pox neither, and you saying that might jinx me. Lord, I don't need them crazy things when I'm eighty years old."

"I'll plan some things to keep her busy." Travis poured a glass of tea and downed it all without coming up for air.

"Looks like it." Aunt Birdie waved over her shoulder as she left.

Travis leaned against the cabinet. Sweat plastered his dark hair to his neck and forehead. His glasses were smeared, but his blue eyes searched hers as if asking permission to open the doors into her heart. "With that in mind, we should plan to take Sophie into town on Saturday after Jodie's brother takes her away from here. We could go to the zoo and maybe to that new kids' movie and then for pizza."

"You should keep working on Cal's new apartment and work space," Hannah said. "We can't give her special things every time someone leaves."

"But this is her first live-in little friend, and she'll be very sad. Next time we won't do something big. Please, Hannah." He grinned.

"If we work two extra hours each day, it would make up for the eight hours we'll lose on Saturday and give our construction crew a whole weekend to waste their paycheck," Cal said. "I bet we could get more work out of them if they know they've got two days off and money in their hot little hands."

Her dark brows knit together, and she tried to think of one good reason not to let either of them tell her what to do. But this was Sophie and they were right—she would be lonely when Laurel left. And they hadn't had a fun day away from Crossing since the divorce, so it would be a good thing.

"I'm not bossing you," Travis said softly. "I'm not Marty."

"No, you are not," Hannah said after a moment. "And yes, she will miss Laurel. Let's not tell her until they are gone that morning, because I don't want Laurel to feel left out."

"Have I told you lately that you are an amazing woman?" Travis said. "You have the heart and soul of an angel."

Hannah blushed crimson. "You need your glasses cleaned. Hand them over and I'll do the job myself so that all that rose color is washed away. You can't see me real good through those things."

He jerked them off and laid them on the cabinet. "Nope, I still see the same thing, and now you are even more beautiful without all the smears and bits of grass."

She picked them up and squirted a drop of dish soap on each lens and then rinsed them under warm water. After drying them with a paper towel, she handed them back to him, her eyes coming to rest on his lips. She thought about that kiss, and heat crawled up her neck to her cheeks. She tried shutting her eyes for a second, but when she opened them again, he was smiling and the fire in her face got even hotter.

He put them back on and blinked a few times. "You must've left a lot of that rose color in them. You are even prettier now, and I didn't even think that was possible."

She tried to remember the last time that Marty said a kind word about her. It had to be the day they were married, when he'd told her that he hoped she made as pretty a wife as she did a bride.

"Travis, you are good for my ego and my heart," she said.

"Then I'm happy."

CHAPTER EIGHTEEN

Hannah shook her head slowly when Liz and Darcy arrived that Tuesday evening. "I'm so sorry. I thought the bruises would be healed better by now."

"Me, too, but they're changing colors so they'll disappear before long. Lord, it's good to get out of the house and come down here. I was getting cabin fever. You must be Jodie. I'm Liz," she said. "If either of those little girls needs to come out of their room to go to the bathroom, I'll step outside."

"I told you that we could take care of it. You'll only be here half an hour and Aunt Birdie is reading stories to the girls," Hannah assured her.

"Pleased to meet you, Liz," Jodie said. "Holy shit, woman. What'd he use on you? I thought I got it bad, but that bastard nearly killed you, didn't he? You make me thankful that I left without talking to him about it."

"Our own little support group right here. Shall I call it to order?" Liz asked.

"I think you just did. How does a group work, anyway?"

"We tell our stories and hope that by getting them out in the open that it helps heal us and other people, kind of like Alcoholics Anonymous," Liz answered.

"Okay, then we'll hold hands." Jodie held hers out.

Liz took one and Hannah the other, then Liz and Hannah clasped hands.

"I'll pray rather than us saying that thing they say in AA, since we're a little different. We got tangled up with sorry men, not alcohol."

Hannah nodded and closed her eyes.

"Lord, us three women need some help," Jodie said.

Her Kentucky accent seemed even stronger when Hannah had her eyes shut.

"We're askin' you to heal our bodies, but even more so our minds. We want you to put boils on the men who hurt us. You can even pick the spot. Or you can put a woman in their lives who will deal them even more misery than they have dealt us. We'll leave that decision up to you. As for us, we want to be able to trust again, not real soon, but someday. We'd like to cast our love upon the waters and have it come back to us at least sevenfold and without any form of ugly abuse. That's all we'll ask today. Amen."

"A-blessed-men," Liz said with a crooked smile.

"You sure know how to pray," Hannah said.

"I was raised to believe that if we pray, it will be answered. I kinda gave up on it after I married, but I'm rememberin' my roots now. Can we sit down and have a real visit now that we got the prayin' done?" Jodie asked. "So, you are a principal at the Crossing school, Liz, and you're a teacher's aide, Hannah?" She eased down into the rocking chair and laid her crutch beside it.

"That's right. I have to go back to work after July Fourth, so I'm hoping that I'm healed enough by then not to scare off anyone who comes into my office," Liz said.

"That's still two weeks away, so you will be fine. See this little scar right here"—Jodie pointed to her upper lip—"that's what happens when you get hit with a beer bottle. Five stitches. I told the emergency room people that I dropped a glass and then fell on it when I was trying to clean up the mess. It happened on Thanksgiving last year and I was pretty healed up by Christmas."

"Why did we get tangled up with men like that? It has to be a flaw in us," Hannah said.

"You have a good, strong, male role model in your house?" Jodie asked.

"My dad died when I was pretty young, and Mama raised me right here in Crossing. She moved back to Virginia to take care of her mother when I was in college," Hannah answered. "Liz, she says that Wyatt should be fed to the coyotes. Dead or alive—either one."

Liz nodded. "You tell Miz Patsy that I won't argue with that dead or alive. If I ever did love him, it died a long time ago."

"I will do it," Hannah said.

"My parents died within six weeks of each other, when I was in college." Liz propped her leg on the coffee table. "Mama with a brain tumor and Daddy from a work accident. But Daddy was never around much. He was a long-haul trucker and came home on weekends, kind of like Wyatt does—did. It takes a while to get the past and the present figured out, doesn't it? Anyway, when Daddy could, he came home a week at Christmas, but not every year," Liz said.

"I think that figures into it. We don't know how to pick a man and we are too damn trusting. We believe their lies," Jodie said. "Men who hurt women know how to make us feel all special. Then when they have us in their net like a floppin' catfish, they gut us."

"How'd you get to be so smart when you are so young?" Liz asked.

"Being through what we all have will knock the youth right out of you," Jodie answered. "My granny lives next door to the place where I'll be livin' again. I'm glad she'll be takin' care of my girls while I work at the café. I won't have to be afraid that one of my kids is going to"—she paused and swallowed hard—"that my kids are going to see me die or that I will see one of them killed by his hand."

She wiped tears away with the back of her hand. "Dammit! I don't take charity and I don't cry. Hill women are bred to be tough, and here I sit cryin' like a baby."

"We are all tough, Jodie. If we weren't, we wouldn't be here in this room right now," Hannah said.

Jodie stiffened her spine. "Damn straight, Hannah! Damn straight! And ain't no man ever going to take our strength away from us again."

"Okay, meeting adjourned." Hannah glanced at Darcy. "Now I want to hear all about your date with Calvin."

"Which one? The Monday-afternoon burger date or the Monday-night date for pizza at the hangar?"

"All of the above," Liz said. "Give us something juicy."

Darcy's eyes glittered. "I don't kiss and tell, but I can tell you that my toenails curled and my bikini underbritches tried to crawl down to my ankles, my heart went into a-fib—or maybe it was d-fib, one of those fib things—and my knees turned to jelly."

"And that was a kiss. God almighty, girl, what will the sex be like?" Jodie giggled.

"I may not survive, but what a way to die." Darcy laughed.

જી

The sounds of saws and hammers off in the distance Wednesday morning meant that Travis and Cal had gotten serious about the remodeling business. Travis had hired five local high school boys to help him with the job, and every so often she could hear their laughter traveling toward the house on the slight summer breeze.

The two girls had asked for a tent that day, so she'd draped two sheets over the dining room table and set the chairs on the top to keep it from sliding off, and they were now playing with a couple of baby dolls.

The baby thankfully was content to crawl around on the living room floor and chase Lullaby, who managed to stay a foot away from her most of the time. Jodie had picked up a romance book and was propped up on the sofa.

Everything was fine, so Hannah wondered why she felt like she was sitting on a whole keg of dynamite. The last time she'd had this much pressure in her chest was the day of the divorce.

Travis was what was twisting her up in knots—this newfound chemistry between them. Every time he walked into a room, she got a little extra kick in her heartbeat, and when he touched her, the sparks flew. But then, why wouldn't she react to him like that? He was Marty's exact opposite. Travis was encouraging, loving, kind, and happy. Any woman would respond to that kind of man in her life.

She tried reading, but after five pages she couldn't even remember the character names, so she put the book aside. She thought about making cookies, but she'd burn them for sure the way her mind was jumping from one past incident to the other.

Someone knocked on the door at exactly 11:11 a.m. She would always remember it, because when all the ones lined up, it was supposed to be a moment to make a wish and it would come true. Before she slung open the door, she shut her eyes and wished that the feeling inside her heart would go away.

Her wish was not granted.

"Hello, Hannah. I've come to take my airplane home where it belongs," Marty said on the other side of the old-fashioned screen door.

"That is between you and Calvin Winters. I sold the hangar, the land it sits on, and even the landing strip to him, complete with all the contents. He's down at the hangar, and you are not welcome here." Her insides were churning and her head spun, but by damn she intended to bluff her way through this. Marty Ellis would not intimidate her ever again.

"I have brought my lawyer and a signed check. I can see just by looking through the door that you've gone back to your white-trash ways. Toys everywhere and nothing in place. I couldn't bear to come inside," he said.

"I did not intend to invite you. My daughter doesn't need to ever see you again and I damn sure don't want to have a cup of coffee with you," she said.

Marty's eyes were absolutely full of evil. "I tried. God knows I tried to make a lady out of you."

"Good-bye, Marty." She slammed the door so hard that the chairs on the dining room table wobbled, bringing both girls out to see what happened.

"Mama!" Sophie yelled. "Did I hear Father out there? I thought I heard him talking to you."

"You did," Hannah said, unwilling to be dishonest. Screw him. "Did you want to see him or talk to him?"

"Nope," Sophie said. "I like things the way they are better."

"Then that's the way they will stay," Hannah said.

Sophie went back to her room.

"You okay?" Jodie poked her head out of the kitchen.

"I need a meeting," Hannah said with clenched teeth and knotted fists.

"Then call Aunt Birdie and the girls." Jodie knocked on the top of the table where the tent had been arranged. "Sophie and Laurel, would y'all like Aunt Birdie to come have a picnic in your room with you?"

Two heads, one blonde and one black haired, popped out from behind the split in the sheets and nodded. "Peanut butter cookies?" Sophie asked.

"And sandwiches and soup." Hannah tried to keep her voice normal, but even she could hear the icicles hanging on her words. Through the window she could see one of Marty's family's black Caddys driving slowly down the road as they left the house and crossed the yard and road.

Three minutes after Hannah made the call, Aunt Birdie came through the front door. "Was that Marty? I was just reading in the Good Book this morning about how God told Moses to wipe out all them enemies in the promised land. I think this here might be my sign to wipe him out in Crossing."

"He's come to make a deal with Cal about that airplane. I need to talk and . . ."

"Y'all go on into the bedroom that Jodie is using for your meeting. I'll make sandwiches and tomato soup and I'll read to them afterward in Sophie's room to get them ready for a nap," Aunt Birdie said and lowered her voice to a whisper that only Hannah could hear. "And don't you worry. That scoundrel don't get out of town real fast, me and my shotgun will have a come-to-Jesus talk with him. I don't think God wants him, so we'll just bypass the pearly gates and send him on to hell."

"Sandwiches? Like tuna fish?" Sophie tuned back in.

"Your choice. Peanut butter, tuna fish, or egg salad. I have all of it ready," Hannah said.

"We'll just have to heat up the tomato soup and shake some parmesan cheese over the top," Aunt Birdie said. "And Travis and Cal will be here right at noon, so they might even read you a story, too."

"Can me and Laurel each pick out two books?" Sophie asked.

"Of course you can. Just go right on in there and y'all get your nap-time books," Aunt Birdie answered and then motioned for Hannah and Jodie to be on their way by flapping her hands like she was shooing away a couple of birds. "This is my time with the girls. Darcy went on back to work this morning, since Liz is healing up. Have you called her for this meeting?"

"Yes, and she's on the way," Hannah said.

"And Darcy?"

"No need for her to leave work," Hannah answered.

"Okay, little girls. It's time for us to let these womenfolks do that big-people talk," Aunt Birdie said.

"She reminds me of my granny. I bet she and Aunt Birdie would be good friends," Jodie said.

The front door opened, and Miss Rosie came inside ahead of Liz. "Was that Marty driving into town? Lord, he's not wanting to come back, is he?"

"No, he just wants his plane. Forget the prayer," Hannah said as she led the way back to Jodie's room. "Just get out the bucket of water to cool me down. I'm so mad I could digest bullets."

"Looks like you've hit the third step in the stages of grief," Miss Rosie said. "That would be anger, and it erases denial and guilt. I called down to the convenience store and told Frankie to make us a pizza and bring it up here for dinner. Give me that baby. I've been itchin' to hold her. We'll go on in the kitchen with Birdie and the kids. When the pizza comes, I'll bring it back to you."

"Thank you." Jodie handed over Bella into Miss Rosie's care.

Hannah threw up her palms defensively. "Why? Why am I so mad? I felt guilty because I didn't have any guilt in the courthouse. All I had was a total sense of relief, so why would I be angry?"

"What happened?" Liz asked.

"Marty showed up at the door to harass her," Jodie answered.

"And?" Liz went slightly pale.

"And I put him going, but he tried his damnedest to put me down, and it made me angry," Hannah said.

"Don't let him take away the serenity you've found or you'll be taking steps backward instead of forward. I've been reading this book about coping with divorce." Liz held up a hardback copy. "I brought it so I could show it to y'all. I bought it so I'd understand the emotional upheaval associated with all this. No, if I'm truthful, I skipped a lot of it and went to the part about abusive situations. So I wouldn't let him talk me out of leaving if he comes back."

"Can I borrow it or at least write down the title? Y'all have one thing easier than me. You don't have kids, Liz, and Hannah's sorry ex didn't want Sophie. I'm going to ask for restricted visitation and hope that he never sets foot in Kentucky to see my girls," Jodie said. "My brother says that our hill relatives can make sure he's never found if he comes around."

"You can have it. I'm done with the part I wanted to read." Liz handed it over to Jodie. "Now talk, Hannah. Did you ever get this mad at him before?"

"No, I was too afraid of him," she admitted.

Liz pointed at the ceiling. "Listen."

"What?" Jodie asked.

"The sound of a plane overhead," Liz said. "That means he's bought the plane and left."

Hannah pulled her phone out to call Cal.

Cal answered on the first ring. "He's gone. Travis did not kill him, because I wouldn't let him come out of the office. I made fifty grand more on the plane than I gave you for the property, so I'm putting it in a 529 for Sophie's college."

"Thank you, Cal, but you will have kids of your own someday," Hannah said.

"And I will take very good care of them and never let them have Darcy's maiden name. And don't you dare look at her right now, or she'll know we are talking about her. The 529 is what I want to do and I already have my lawyer working on it."

"She's not here so I can't look at her, Cal. Then thank you again, but save back ten thousand. I'll discuss it with you later," Hannah said.

"Jodie?"

"That's right," Hannah said.

"Gotcha." Cal's tone said he was smiling. "Now, go on and bitch with the girls. Travis and I are headed toward Aunt Birdie's for lunch. I promised to let Travis read to Sophie because he was a good boy and didn't sabotage the plane like he wanted to."

"Will do," she said and ended the call.

"So?" Liz asked.

"He sold the plane back to Marty for a lot more than he paid for the property, so the profit is going in a fund for Sophie's college. And right now I wish I would have put a bomb on that plane," Hannah said.

Jodie tucked her chin to her chest and broke out in a guffaw. "I didn't know you had a vengeful side in you."

"Why didn't I think of that?" Liz tapped a finger on her forehead. "We could have looked up the instructions on the Internet and detonated the thing in the sky."

Had they all lost their minds? There wasn't one thing funny about the whole situation, and yet—it started as a weak giggle, developed into laughter, and soon they were all wiping at their eyes.

"God, that felt good," Liz said.

Someone rapped on the bedroom door and then opened it. "Pizza is here. I tossed in some napkins and there's three bottles of root beer in the paper sack." Miss Rosie carried the box in and set it on the dresser.

"Thank you, Miss Rosie," Liz said. "For everything."

"Lord, honey, I ain't had this much fun since Woodstock."

"You went to the real Woodstock?" Jodie asked.

"Oops, that slipped out slicker'n bacon grease on a glass doorknob. You kids enjoy this." Miss Rosie grinned.

"I'm over the anger and the guilt about no guilt. What's the next step?" Hannah asked.

"Depression," Liz said.

"Well, I ain't doin' that one. I done been down that road and I don't like it," Hannah declared.

"Me, neither. I might even skip all of them and go back to enjoyin' my life in Kentucky," Jodie said.

"Sounds like a good plan to me," Liz said.

Chapter Nineteen

Hannah picked up her phone and didn't have the sudden adrenaline rush of fear that Marty would be angry about the mess in the house. When he'd shown up that morning, she'd automatically scanned the living room and fought the panic when she saw how cluttered it was. But now she didn't give a damn. She'd come a long way in such a short time. Liz needed a project, and she was going to have a messy house by nightfall. Those quilting scraps had been shoved up in the corner of the dining room. Cutting and putting together pieces would give Liz something to do and help pass the waiting time for Jodie, too.

Liz answered on the first ring. "Please tell me you are coming down here. I am going stir-crazy."

"Whoa." Hannah stopped her with a word. "I was thinking more that you two would come down here and we'd do some quilting. We all need a project today. Even Jodie is getting crazy with this waiting."

"What about Sophie?" Liz asked cautiously.

"We won't make a big deal of it, and she has Laurel to keep her busy for the rest of the week. There's barbecued chicken in the Crock-Pot, so we don't even have to stop and cook at noon. We'll just make some pulled chicken sandwiches," Hannah said.

"You are so good at organizing things," Liz said.

"I took a class called Living with OCD 101. I don't recommend it. I'll have the sewing machine up when y'all get here. You might ask Miss Rosie if she wants to join us and bring extra scissors. I only have one decent pair."

Liz got so tickled that she snorted when she laughed. "And I bet they don't have a sharp point."

"Why is that funny?"

"Think about it," Liz said, and the phone went dark.

Bella looked like a little blonde-haired toy as she crawled into the kitchen, flipped around, and sat up. She pointed at Lullaby, hidden behind a table leg, and jabbered.

"If we could understand her, that cat would be in so much trouble." Jodie laughed. "What's the matter? You look like you can't remember something."

"Oh!" Hannah suddenly smiled. "It was what Liz said about not having sharp-pointed scissors. Now I get it. I might have been tempted to stab Marty with them."

"You did have kitchen knives, though," Jodie said.

"Yes, I did, and the thought entered my mind many times. If I could have figured out a way without going to jail, I would have probably put a plan in motion," Hannah said seriously. "We are going to drag that bag of quilting scraps out today and start a project to give Liz something constructive to do. You ever do any quilting?"

"Grew up going to quilting bees with my granny. Can I take whatever I make with me?"

"Sure you can. There's tons of fabric scraps down at the hangar and over in Aunt Birdie's storage shed, too. Aunt Birdie suggested we make throws instead of full-size quilts so we can quilt them without a frame."

"I could just make a pretty top and take it with me on Saturday," Jodie said. "I'm sure this fabric is a lot nicer than the scraps we get in our part of the world, which are usually just the good parts of clothing that has worn out. Do you think that would be all right?"

"I'm here," Liz yelled right after she knocked on the door and let herself inside the house. "Are you sure about this, Hannah? I'm not completely healed up."

Hannah raised her voice. "In the dining room. We're about to dump the scraps on the floor. And I'm sure."

Liz headed for the refrigerator. "I want a beer, and I don't care if it's early in the morning." She opened the bottom drawer and pulled out a long-neck bottle. "I've been thirsty for one of these for two days."

"Where's Aunt Birdie? I thought she might come with you," Jodie said.

"She said that she and Miss Rosie were going to drive into town to grocery shop since—oh, my sweet Lord! Look at all that pretty stuff," Liz said.

"Let's make quilt tops for Jodie to take home to Kentucky this week. We'll always be able to make throws for our own use," Hannah said. "And I've given this a lot of thought, Liz. Sophie is going to see abused women coming and going."

"Don't shield her but don't make her afraid," Jodie said. "That's my advice. Just treat it without a lot of emotion."

"Okay, then." Liz set the beer on the cabinet and moved to her place at the table. "I can sit right there and cut the pieces. Jodie can pick out the way she wants them to go together and you can sew them up on the machine. I bet we could top out two a day if we just do a simple patchwork."

"Oh, my goodness!" Jodie clamped a hand over her mouth. "Y'all would do that for me?"

"Honey, I'd try to run a marathon even in the shape I'm in to have something to do other than read books or watch television," Liz said. "I keep worrying that Wyatt will change his mind about it all and refuse to give me a divorce."

"Aunt Liz!" Sophie ran into the room and wrapped her arms around Liz's neck. "I haven't seen you in a long time. What happened to your face?"

"I had an accident, but I'm going to be all right."

Sophie kissed her gently on the stitches and both bruised cheeks. "There, that will make it all better. Do we need to go out on the porch and sing the twinkle song?"

"I think I'll be all right." Liz smiled.

"Okay, but if you change your mind, you just call me or else come in my room and we will sing. Can me and Laurel have a cookie, Mama? And can we take it to my room? We're playin' McDonald's with our Barbie dolls."

Hannah handed each of them two cookies. "One for y'all to eat now and one to pretend to buy later."

They chased off to the bedroom, giggles following in their wake. Liz inhaled and smiled, and Hannah nodded. Words weren't needed. They had gotten past upsetting Sophie, and now Liz could come and go as she wanted. Hannah picked up the bag from the corner and dumped out an array of gorgeous fabric scraps, ranging in size from a few inches to half a yard, onto the table.

"Hey, where is everyone?" Darcy yelled from the front door. "I was out here with one of my loan officers looking at a piece of property, and my lunch hour is in fifteen minutes, so I stuck around." She scooped Bella up in her arms. "I want a dozen just like this precious little girl."

Bella cooed and reached for the bright colors, so Darcy set her right in the middle of them.

"That would make the most beautiful picture for Cal's baby campaign," Liz said.

"Oh, no!" Jodie threw up both palms. "Her face cannot be on anything or my ex will come looking for her."

"I'm so sorry," Darcy said with a surprising blush.

"I bet you'll be so glad to be back in Kentucky, where you feel safe," Liz said, smoothing things over.

"Yes, I will," Jodie said. "Why don't we do a six-inch patchwork? It goes together pretty fast. That sound good to you, Hannah?"

Liz picked up a piece of bright-turquoise fabric. "My granny used to make them with diagonal colored pieces, and they were so pretty. I'll help cut squares and stack them up and then I'll figure out the way they'll go together to get the diagonal stripes from the bottom up."

"Granny is going to love this," Jodie said.

"We can all cut squares until we use up what's here, and then we'll start sewing," Hannah said.

"Not me." Darcy shook her head. "If it's all right with Jodie, I'm taking Bella down to the hangar. She can use some fresh air, and I want to see Cal. And Miss Rosie sent her cutter so one of you can use it. She says that it'll make things go twice as fast and the squares will be perfect. She did send an extra set of scissors, so someone can cut threads as you sew things together, Hannah. It's in the brown bag over there by the door. I dropped it when I saw Bella."

"You can't take her outside. It's too dangerous," Hannah said. "First rule in the safe house book."

Darcy clamped her hand over her mouth. "I forgot about that. Then I'll run down to the hangar and be back in five with a report on how things are going."

Jodie smoothed a piece of hot-pink material. "Would any or all of you like to relocate to Kentucky? I'm going to miss you so much. This has been such a wonderful place to get my bearings before my brother comes. Sophie called it right when she said the name of the house was Lullaby Sky. It makes us feel like we're being rocked to sleep out in the backyard with the stars and moon smiling down on us. It takes away the turmoil from our hearts."

"That's so sweet," Hannah said.

More and more, she was convinced that she was doing the right thing and Lullaby Sky was a wonderful name for her house. Patchwork House fit the shelter, because it was the place where women could patch their lives back together, but Hannah's safe house was where they could come and find tranquillity.

"See y'all later. And she's right, Hannah. I don't know if it's the house or if it's you, but I always feel good here." Darcy disappeared from the room.

Hannah knew how to operate the cutting tool, since it was so much like the paper cutter she used at school when she helped the kindergarten teacher. After the first couple of cuts, she figured out that the fabric should be ironed to get the squares cut perfectly, so Jodie took on that job. Liz stacked and counted them, pinning a sticky note on the top of each pile as they finished with a color.

A cross-eyed monkey could be trained to do the work, and Hannah's mind wandered as she made the cuts. Liz and Jodie were talking about letting go of the anger and moving on to the next phase of their lives. Hannah still had a burst of pure old rage every time she thought about those cameras, bugs, and the tracking device on her old cell.

But then when she thought about that kiss she and Travis had shared, everything disappeared but joy. *Comfort and joy, like the Christmas carol,* she thought. *Why couldn't fate have put me and Travis together in the beginning?*

"You are arguing with yourself, and you know what Jerry Clower says about that?" Liz poked her on the upper arm.

"I cut my teeth on Jerry Clower and on Patsy Cline and Dolly Parton music. Granny still listens to the old classic country music, as well as the Kentucky bluegrass stuff," Jodie said. "And I know that story that Jerry used to tell. If you're arguing with yourself, you're fixin' to mess up."

"Aunt Birdie and Miss Rosie love his humor, so we all sat through it," Liz said. "Why don't we cut out and label today and start sewing tomorrow?"

"Hey, ladies." Travis rapped on the door and came in without waiting. "I've got to run into Gainesville. Need anything?"

"Three spools of white thread," Hannah answered.

"Okay, anything else? Want to go with me, Hannah?" he asked.

Lord, yes, she wanted to go with him. She would love to spend time in the cab of his truck alone with him on the ride down to Gainesville and back. To see just how wild those sparks would get in tight quarters. But she couldn't leave Sophie like that, or leave her girls in the middle of a project.

She shook her head. "We've got a pretty good assembly line going here. If you're getting the thread at Walmart, you could pick up a quart of potato salad and one of that pasta salad that Sophie likes. Oh, and a package of hamburger buns for our pulled chicken. You and Cal can eat with us, since Aunt Birdie and Miss Rosie are out of pocket today."

"Will do. Thread, two kinds of salad, and buns. I'll see y'all at noon," Travis said.

He'd barely cleared out of the house when Hannah felt two sets of eyes boring into her heart and soul. "What?" she asked.

"There were vibes," Liz said.

"I could almost see them," Jodie chimed in.

"You are both crazy. We're all getting out of bad stuff, so how can you even think about . . ." She couldn't say the words *relationships* or *love*.

CHAPTER TWENTY

Hannah closed her eyes, but she couldn't sleep. She beat on her pillow and drew the sheet up over her shoulders, but that didn't work. She tried counting backward from one hundred but all she saw was stacks of quilting squares. Finally, she threw back the covers and crawled out of bed to pace from one side of the room to the other. Jodie would leave on Saturday morning, and Travis would have no reason to be in the house. She'd miss Jodie but was glad that Travis had planned something to keep Sophie from being sad. Not even Lullaby would be able to keep her occupied after she had had a little girl to play with 24-7.

Pulling back the curtains and looking out over the backyard, she sighed loud enough that the moon and stars probably heard her. She finally pulled on a pair of jean shorts and tiptoed from her bedroom and out onto the front porch, where she sat down on the steps and looked up at the sky. Tonight it wasn't a lullaby sky at all. Tonight there were as many questions in her heart as there were stars and she had no idea if there were even answers to be had.

"You couldn't sleep, either?" Travis asked as he made his way from the screen door to sit beside her. He handed her a cold beer, and she took a long sip.

"I worry and try to analyze everything to death," she answered. "It doesn't make for a peaceful night's rest sometimes."

"We need to talk," he said.

"It was just a kiss. It doesn't have to be more than that. We are two adults." She sipped her beer again, more to shut herself up than to actually drink.

"That's not what we need to talk about," he said. "But FYI, it was more to me than just a kiss. I've waited more than twenty years to kiss you, and it was a big deal to me."

"Why did you wait so long?"

"Look at me. I'm just a lanky old carpenter with glasses and a horse face. You are movie-star beautiful, and you deserve something a hell of a lot better than me," he said.

She laid a hand on his knee. "I've never saw you like that."

"How do you see me now?" He turned to face her.

"I see strength. Your face has angles that a sculptor would die to be able to create. In or out of your glasses, I see soulful eyes that would melt a woman's heart. And I know you have a heart of gold, Travis, so don't ever talk about my friend like that again." She smiled.

"Is that all I am? A friend?"

"Do you want to be more?" She held her breath and hoped that she knew the answer.

"I have for years and years."

She reached for his hand and laced her small fingers in his big, callused ones. "I need some time."

"I'm more than willing to wait, as long as you'll tell me if someone else comes along." He brought her hand to his lips and kissed each knuckle.

"I promise I will, but I don't think you have a thing to worry about," she said breathlessly.

"We should talk about another thing." Travis chose his next words carefully and slowly. "You ever read anything by Teresa Walters?"

"Just everything she's ever written. She may be my favorite romantic suspense author. I absolutely love her. On one of the rare occasions when I was in Dallas with Marty, I got to go to one of her book signings. You can find that book in the old antique secretary in the living room. I didn't even read it but bought another one at Walmart so I wouldn't break the back binding on the signed one. Why would you ask that?"

He squeezed her hand. "Because I am Teresa Walters."

Hannah's mind did a couple of quick spins trying to figure out what he'd just said. He couldn't be Teresa, because she had bright-red hair, blue eyes, and a round face, and she was short, like Hannah. There was no way he could be her even in drag. So why would he say that?

"When my first book hit it so big eight years ago, my agent wanted me to do all that promo work, and I just couldn't. I'm not cut out for that kind of stuff, so we hired a model and she signs books, smiles pretty, and is the face on the back of my books," Travis said.

"You write romance?" Hannah gasped.

He dropped her hand and wrapped both of his around his beer bottle. "I knew it would make a difference. You'll never look at me the same now, but I couldn't keep the secret from you any longer."

"No, I won't look at you the same. Now I'll be looking at you in total awe, Travis. My God, you are amazing," she said.

He whipped around to stare at her. "You are the inspiration for Harley O'Rourke."

"No way! She's fearless." Hannah could feel her eyes getting wider and wider.

"Yes, you are, always have been. So you aren't going to add sissy to my list of undesirable qualities."

"Do you know Leigh Greenwood?" she asked.

Travis shook his head.

"I thought the author was a woman for years, but then I found out that it's a guy. His name is Howard and he writes western romance. And I love his western stories."

"Please don't ask me to come out of the closet. I like it in here just fine," Travis said. "The money is great. I love to write in the evenings, but I also like being a man's man in the carpentry world."

"I would never do that. You do what you are comfortable with, Travis. Will you sign all my books? I'll never tell, not even Liz and Darcy. I still can't believe it."

"For you, I'd do about anything. I'm so glad you didn't kick me off the porch when I told you."

She reached for his hand again. "Does Aunt Birdie know?"

He shook his head. "Only my agent, publisher, Cal, and now you. Not even the model who poses as Teresa knows who I really am, and I'd sure like to keep it that way. No one knew where my first book would go or how it would do, so I chose a pseudonym and that was that. Then it hit pretty big and the publisher wanted a picture on the back of the next book and they started talking about book signings. That's when my agent and I came up with the actress idea."

"If that's what you want, then that's what we will do," she said.

"Thank you." He looked up at the stars, evading her gaze. "Hannah, this is one of those nights."

"I know, Travis. One where good memories are made. Thank you for trusting me with your secret."

"I would trust you with my heart, my life, and my soul, Hannah."

"That's a lot of promise." She smiled.

"It's the truth, darlin'. When you are ready to take this thing between us to the next level, all you have to do is let me know. Until then I'll be waiting," he drawled. "But right now I expect we should be getting some sleep. We've got a party to get ready for tomorrow. The girls told me they want to go to a movie."

"That can't happen because of—"

He put a finger on her lips. "I know, but it doesn't mean I can't fix them up with a movie here, does it? Cal and I are going to make a theater in the hangar and we'll have popcorn and Cokes and candy bars. Not to worry. I cleared it with Gina."

Hannah didn't want to go inside. She wanted to sit on the porch, look at clouds shifting across what little bit of moon was showing that night, and rethink every sentence and every nuance of the whole evening. She wanted to go over and over that business of him trusting her with his heart and soul.

"Mama?" Sophie's thin voice cut through the night. "Where are you?"

"Out here on the porch talking to Travis," Hannah called out.

The screen's hinges squeaked when Sophie pushed it open. She crawled up in her mother's lap and laid her head on her chest. "I had a bad dream. Daddy came in the house to take Laurel and Bella away from us."

Travis rubbed her back gently. "Your mama would put them running, darlin'. She wouldn't ever let anyone take Laurel and Bella, but remember their uncle is coming on Saturday and it's okay if he takes them back to Kentucky to live with their kinfolk."

"Okay," Sophie said. "Mama, when is my granny coming to Crossing to see me? Laurel says her granny is real nice. I told her that mine is, too, but when will we see her? And can she stay in our house this time instead of Miss Rosie's? She can sleep with me in my rainbow room."

"I'm trying to talk her into coming to Texas for the Fourth of July," Hannah said, wincing at the memory that her mother had not even been able to stay with Aunt Birdie when she came for fear that Marty would find out.

"Really?" Sophie asked. "That's not very far away, is it, Mama?"

"No, it's not, and yes, she can stay in our house. She can sleep with you or in one of the upstairs rooms, either one," Hannah said.

"Uncle Travis can fix anything," Sophie said. "Mama, can I sleep with you? Laurel is in her mama's bed and I'm lonesome."

"Of course. We've got a big day tomorrow, so let's go get you tucked in." Hannah stood up.

Sophie wrapped her arms around her mother's neck and her legs around her waist.

"That is one beautiful sight." Travis grinned.

❧

Travis sat down in front of his computer, and the next scene appeared on the screen as if by magic. An hour later he'd written more than a thousand words and was so satisfied with the scene that he saved it, backed it up, and went to bed. He'd dreaded telling Hannah about his other job, but now that it was done, a weight had been lifted off his chest. He didn't tell her that he'd kept a first edition of every single one of his books already signed to her just in case he ever got up the nerve to tell her. Or that her reaction was far better than anything he'd ever hoped for.

Finally, he went to sleep and dreamed of growing old with Hannah and Sophie right there in that house. He would love to have a yard full of children looking like his beautiful Hannah, but he would be content to be a father to Sophie if that's what Hannah wanted.

The sun was a big ball of heat outside his window when he awoke the next morning. He could hear two little girls giggling and smell the aroma of breakfast and coffee drifting up the stairs. The soft drone of female voices said that the whole crew was there, not just Jodie and Hannah, but Darcy and—he cocked his head to one side. Yes, that was Aunt Birdie and Miss Rosie, too.

A few years ago, he'd given up on ever being a part of Hannah's life. No matter what a scumbag she'd married, she would be one who took her vows very seriously and would never leave him. So Travis had closed that chapter in his life and moved on. He and his father remodeled a house for a schoolteacher, and he'd asked her out on a date. His father adored Angela. She adored his father, and it looked like she might be the right woman for him.

Right up until he asked her to move in with him. She'd smiled sweetly and said that she would, but there was already someone somewhere in his past that was first in line.

"How do you know that?" he'd asked.

"Women know these things, sweetheart. You can't give me what you don't have to give. You still dream about her and call out for her in your sleep," she'd answered. "Don't try to replace her with someone else."

Travis had started to argue, but he knew Angela was right. He'd left her at the door with a quick kiss on the cheek, told his dad that he was moving back to Crossing to do odd jobs in Cooke County, and started packing up his truck that very night. He gave himself one year to get over Hannah and to write two more books. He'd gotten three books written, much to his agent's delight, but he had not gotten over Hannah.

And then six weeks ago, she'd gotten the divorce papers, and his whole world turned around. There was hope—a possibility—and he wasn't going to sit on his hands and let it get past him again.

The ringtone said his father was calling. He crossed the room in a few long strides and picked it up from the nightstand beside the bed. "Hello, Dad. What's going on?"

"I got married today," he said abruptly.

"It's about time. Congratulations?"

"I'm going to do remodeling jobs around Panama City Beach and this area. Guess I'm following in your footsteps." He laughed.

"Congratulations. Are you coming home for July Fourth?"

"Not this year. We're on our honeymoon cruise, and it's one of those long cruises that lasts a month. I just wanted to let you know because we won't have phone reception all the time. How are things with you and that O'Malley gal?"

"I'm taking one step at a time. Did you tell Miss Rosie that you got married?"

"Naw, but you can. Tell her I'll be home for Christmas like always. Crossing—it don't have such good memories for me, son. But that don't mean you can't be happy there. Good luck with Hannah," his father said.

"Thanks and enjoy the cruise. I'm happy for you, Dad. And for Linda. It's time to hang your hat on the same nail every night," Travis said.

"I think it might be. See you at Christmas. I'll call every chance I get. They tell me cell phone service is spotty in the places we'll be. Who would have ever thought an old carpenter from Crossing, Texas, would be off to places like Italy and France?"

Travis chuckled. "One never knows what might happen to the folks in Crossing. Hug Linda for me. 'Bye."

He dressed, checked his reflection in the mirror, decided against shaving that morning, and picked up his glasses. Today was Friday. He and Cal had work to do and a theater to whip up in part of the hangar for the girls. His stomach growled as he started down the stairs, and he was thinking about bacon and biscuits when he looked down and there she was.

The lyrics of an old country tune popped into his head. The singer said that he looked up and an angel stood across the crowded room. Well, Travis looked down and there was his angel, Hannah, standing at the bottom of the stairs.

"Cal is pitching a fit to get down to the hangar. I thought you might be 'reading.'" She made quotation marks in the air with her fingers. "So I held him off as long as I could."

"No, I read too late and forgot to set an alarm." He winked.

Cal poked his head out of the kitchen. "I sent Hannah to see if you'd died up there. I'm the one who sleeps until noon and works until the wee hours of the morning, not you."

"Guess you are contagious."

Travis brushed his hand against Hannah's as he passed by her, and the whole room lit up like a Christmas tree.

Christmas!

Only six months away.

The season of miracles and magic.

Could he give her an engagement ring by then? Would that be too soon?

Chapter Twenty-One

The buttery scent of popcorn floated on the night breezes from the hangar to the backyard as Hannah, Liz, Jodie, Darcy, Aunt Birdie, Miss Rosie, and the three children started out to go to the movies that evening. They'd only broken the rule about leaving the house a couple of times, and it made Hannah nervous that evening, but she'd rationalized that it was dark, there were no neighbors who could even see them, and it was the last night Jodie and her daughters would be staying with them. Still, she was glad when they were inside the hangar and no angry ex had popped up out of the grass to cause a fight, or worse yet, start firing a gun at them.

Everyone had their movie ticket in their hand except Bella, who probably would have eaten hers. The tickets were a nice touch and made the girls feel like they were really going to the movies to see the Chipmunks playing in *Alvin and the Chipmunks: The Road Chip*. Cal had not only rented the show, but he'd printed the tickets and delivered them to the door that morning.

Travis met them at the door, and immediately Hannah's heart kicked in an extra beat at the sight of him in starched jeans, a white pearl-snap western-cut shirt, and a bolo tie with the Lone Star emblem at his neck. His dark hair was slicked back and his boots shined. And sweet Jesus, he smelled like heaven. Hannah wished she'd dressed up and worn makeup.

He bowed from the waist and said, "Your tickets, please, princesses, and then the usher will show you to your seats."

"Oh, Uncle Travis, we're just Sophie and Laurel." Sophie giggled.

"But Sophie and Laurel are royal princesses." He lowered his deep voice. "I know you are sneaking in so the paparazzi don't know where you are." He paused and looked around.

A camera flashed several times from behind the curtains hanging over the doorway into the office.

"I guess you didn't get past them, but I promise our guards will keep them out of the movie room," Travis said.

Sophie giggled again. "What's the poppytotzie?"

"It's the people who take pictures of famous princesses and movie stars and then sell the pictures to magazines," Travis said as he held up his finger and answered his ringing phone. "But wait a minute, I have a phone call. Cal says he caught the sorry sucker trying to take your pictures. He is your bodyguard tonight and won't let anyone or anything near you."

Laurel giggled. "Here is my ticket."

Sophie put her ticket in Travis's hand. "Can we go inside now?"

"Yes, you may. Your seats and popcorn are waiting." Travis slung open the curtains, allowing them entry into the semidark theater room.

"Oh. My. Goodness," Jodie said. "It looks so real."

"We aim to please here at the Hangar Movie Palace." Travis smiled.

Two long black leather sofas flanked by three recliners were arranged in a semicircle around two hot-pink beanbag chairs for Laurel and Sophie. A small playpen was set up at the end of one of the sofas and had half a dozen toys ready to entertain Bella.

"Seats have been assigned," Cal said. "Jodie, you will sit on the end of this sofa so that you can take care of Bella. Darcy will sit in the middle, and I will take the other end. The recliners are for Aunt Birdie and Miss Rosie, and the one right beside Jodie is a recliner slash rocking chair in case you need it for Bella. The other sofa is for Liz, Hannah, and Travis. Liz, if you need it, just flip that handle on the side and the end becomes a recliner."

The adults took their places, and Travis passed out drinks and popcorn. A huge plastic bowl of miniature candy bars was sitting on the floor between the two little girls, who were whispering behind their hands.

"This is the best movie place ever," Laurel said.

"Yes, it is." Sophie reached inside the brown bag for a handful of popcorn. "And this is better than the show downtown. It's got more butter on it."

"I only been to the movies one time," Laurel said softly.

"It's true," Jodie said. "Any spare money that we had went into beer. This is a real treat."

Cal used a remote control to start the movie on the biggest television screen Hannah had ever seen. Where on Earth he planned to put that thing in his small loft apartment was a complete mystery. It started off with two previews and then went straight into the movie about the famous chipmunks who were afraid that Dave was about to marry his girlfriend. If he married the woman, the chipmunks would get a horrid stepbrother in the deal, so they had to stop the proposal.

Five minutes into the film, Travis laced his fingers with Hannah's, and he held her hand on his leg throughout the whole movie. Could he be her soul mate? Or would she ruin their friendship by letting it move to another level that didn't work out? She could never forgive herself if things suddenly became awkward.

❧

With the kids in bed that Friday evening, the four women all wound up in Hannah's living room. Jodie sat on one end of the sofa with her broken leg outstretched toward the end where Liz sat. Hannah and Darcy faced them, sitting cross-legged on the floor on the other side of the coffee table.

"What was your first thought about that movie?" Hannah asked.

"That it was crazy funny, but it sure hit a sore spot with me," Liz answered. "I'm not sure I'll ever trust anyone enough to dive into a relationship with him. With kids or not."

Jodie threw her two cents into the conversation. "I'm young, but I wouldn't want to get involved with someone who has kids for fear that mine and his wouldn't blend. Maybe I'll wait to even think about that until they are grown. Right now, I'm just grateful to be going home to my roots."

A long, pregnant silence filled the room. Finally, Darcy broke the quiet with a giggle. "Can we adjourn this meeting and talk about a good man before we tell Jodie good-bye tonight?"

"Yes, we can," Jodie said. "I want to hear about Cal. Did you hang back for a good-night kiss?"

"Yes, I did. Every single time he kisses me, I swear, my feet float and my whole body tingles."

Hannah was about to nod in agreement but stopped and rolled her neck as if she was getting kinks out. Travis affected her the same way, and it would be really easy to be jealous of Darcy and Cal and their ability to fall in love without baggage.

Jodie clapped her hands. "If a man like Cal ever comes along and makes me feel like that, I'll rethink my stand."

"Your husband didn't?" Darcy asked.

Jodie shook her head slowly. "Truth is, I didn't even like his kisses so much. I hate cigarette smoke and he kept one lit all the time. Beer and cigarettes came before groceries and electric bills."

Darcy frowned. "And you married him?"

"Sometimes a young girl doesn't listen to her heart. I wanted out of Kentucky. Besides, I was pregnant," Jodie said with a shrug.

"I just wanted to be married," Liz said. "And Wyatt had moved into that house here in Crossing and he was a little bit charming. Until the first time he came home and I'd rearranged the furniture and took down some pictures. The charm was gone and the first bruise appeared."

"And you?" Jodie looked at Hannah.

"I've been divorced less than a month. Too soon to call shots right now." Hannah sidestepped the issue. "Changing the subject here. What time is your brother arriving tomorrow?"

"He'll get into Dallas at seven in the morning, rent a car with a car seat, and pick me up by eight thirty. Nine at the latest. I want as little fanfare as possible with the good-byes. Laurel is going to be so sad about leaving Sophie, and yet it's been wonderful for her to have this experience. I have my suitcase packed and my quilt tops ready to go," Jodie answered.

"I want you to take Sophie's old car seat and some books for Laurel," Hannah said. "It's a long way to Kentucky, and Laurel will need things to keep her entertained."

"Thank you—again," Jodie said. "And if any of y'all are ever in Kentucky, you just ask around in Harlan about the Bennett family. They'll put you in touch with my granny, and she'll tell you how to find me. We live way up in the hills and the last three miles is dirt road, so don't drive a fancy car."

Liz pulled her feet off the coffee table and turned to face Jodie. "For real. I may go home with you tomorrow. Do they need schoolteachers or principals in your town?"

A chuckle came from deep in Jodie's chest. "We graduate about ten kids a year at our school, and believe me, they'd grab someone up like you in a hurry. But you'd probably be the principal and also teach a mixed class of two grades. So come on. We'll make room in the backseat for you."

"No! You can't leave. You have to be one of my bridesmaids in a few months and once you got up there in those mountains, you'd never come back to Texas. You know you loved *Justified*," Darcy argued.

"Oh, I'm not going anywhere. I love it here, but someday I might get an urge to go to Harlan, Kentucky, just to see if the men all look like Raylan Givens," Liz said.

"If you do," Jodie said, "call me and we'll haul him up into the hills and keep him for ourselves."

"Deal." Liz stuck out her fist.

Jodie popped it with hers. "And on that note, I'm going to bed. Thanks again for everything, ladies. I really do think that Sophie named this house right."

"And it's time for me to go down to Miss Rosie's," Liz said.

"I'll walk with you," Darcy said.

"I'm not afraid of the dark," Liz protested.

"Me, either. But I am afraid of what might be hiding behind a bush. We're not taking any chances. Which reminds me, when you get well, we are going to take some self-defense classes. All three of us," Darcy said. "Too bad you won't be here to take them with us, Jodie."

"Honey, there's a shotgun, two pistols, and a rifle waiting for me at my old house. I'm a fair shot, but my granny is better. That's why my sorry husband wouldn't allow a gun in the house," she said. "Good night, ladies."

"She's so sassy. I wonder what made her stay with him," Darcy said after they heard the bedroom door close.

"Fear of losing her kids. The same reason I stayed with Marty," Hannah said. "That is the worst fear in the world. Marty would threaten to take Sophie and put her somewhere I'd never see her again. Since she was a girl and I knew how hard his heart was, I had nightmares about him giving her away to some foreign family in private adoption, or worse yet, selling her."

"Sweet Jesus!" Liz murmured. "Did you ever tell Aunt Birdie or your mama? I can't imagine either of them letting him live if they'd known."

"I was afraid to say a word. If they killed him, then his parents would blame me and take Sophie. He had me in total submission. I imagine that's the same way Jodie was, only when she got ready to leave, she didn't have a tracking device in her cell phone. I hope that her ex never tries to track her down," Hannah said.

"I hope that he can't even find her to file for divorce until the kids are grown. She can jump over a broom or do some handfasting rather than have a courthouse marriage if she ever wants another husband," Darcy said.

"You've been reading too many historical novels." Liz laughed. "Come on. You can walk me home. If Cal is sitting on Aunt Birdie's porch, you can stop and talk to him, but remember, midnight is your curfew. And I don't know if you've been told, but Travis said we can all go with y'all to entertain Sophie tomorrow, Hannah."

"The more the merrier," she said. "Darcy, lock the doors when you come back. See y'all at breakfast."

Travis poked his head around the kitchen door after the room emptied. "I hope you aren't upset that I told them they could all go with us tomorrow. Liz needs a day away from Crossing, and Cal and Darcy love Sophie so much that they wanted to spend time with her."

"Of course not. How long have you been standing there?" Hannah asked.

"Just long enough to catch that last thing that Liz said. I was on my way for a Coke and I didn't want to butt in, so I'd started back to my room. I enjoyed the night, Hannah, even the chipmunks."

"Me, too. Thanks again for setting that all up. You made Laurel and Sophie's world tonight," she said. "I'll see you at breakfast if you don't 'read' too long."

Travis pushed his shoulder away from the doorjamb. "I'm done for the night. Finished a scene that had been on my mind, and now I'm going to take a shower and go to bed, too. I guess I'll be moving back across the street tomorrow, but I really don't want to. I keep hoping that Gina will bring another guest and you'll need me to stay awhile longer."

"I do feel safer when you are here. Abusive husbands or boyfriends are control freaks, Travis, and they hate it when they lose that. Any time I have guests, please move right in." She smiled.

He crossed the room and took her in his arms for a tender hug, then tipped her chin up with his rough knuckles and brushed the sweetest kiss across her lips. "Good night, Hannah."

"'Night, Travis," she said as she took a step back and turned around to leave.

When she was in her bedroom, she touched her lips. Crazy—they weren't nearly as warm as they felt.

CHAPTER TWENTY-TWO

*W*as it normal in a marriage to go without sex or any physical contact for a whole year? Hannah looked in the mirror that Saturday morning as she dressed and wondered whom she could ask such a personal question. Certainly not Liz, because her marriage had been every bit as dysfunctional as Hannah's. And not Darcy, because she'd never been married, but Hannah doubted seriously if she'd gone a year without sex since she was sixteen.

Her phone rang, and she checked the ID before she answered it. "Hello, Mama," she said.

"I'm the bearer of bad news and good news. Which one do you want first?" Patsy said.

"Give me the bad first. Do I need to sit down?"

"No, it's not that bad. Your grandmother fell this morning and cracked a hip. The doctor insists that she is going to a nursing home when she leaves the hospital. He says she'll need all kinds of equipment that I don't have. I'm tired, Hannah, and I've done my best, but now it's time," Patsy said.

Hannah hated hearing that her grandmother would be in a nursing home. "Mama, if you can get her on a plane and bring her here, I'll take care of her."

"Honey, the doctor says we're past that option, and besides, she wants to be in Virginia. She likes it here among her old friends and what family is left. This is her home. That's the reason I moved back to Virginia after your dad died and she had her first hip replaced. Some of her friends are even in the same nursing facility, so truth is, she's kind of excited about the whole thing. You'd think it was an extended slumber party that she's going to," Patsy said.

"Okay, and the good news?"

"I'm coming to Crossing for the Fourth of July and I'll try to stay a week. Travis called and told me that Sophie was fussing for me. I didn't think I could get away, but with this change I'm going to give it a try. But only for one week. I wouldn't want to leave your grandmother any longer than that."

Hannah sat down on the bed with a thud. "Oh, Mama, that is wonderful, wonderful news. I don't think Sophie could be a bit more excited than I am. I'll pamper you and we'll have long talks way into the night. I can't wait to see you."

"Okay, then. What's going on in your world this week?" Patsy laughed and changed the subject.

Hannah quickly filled her in on everything about Jodie and the kids, up to and including the movie the night before. But she didn't mention the kisses she'd shared with Travis. Lord have mercy! She certainly couldn't tell her mother that she'd been kissing Travis only two weeks after her day in divorce court.

"Sounds like you are keeping busy and doing something fulfilling. I'm proud of you," Patsy said.

"Mama, is it normal for a man not to have sex with his wife for a whole year?" She blurted out the question and felt her face burn with shame at asking. "I googled it but only found a million ladies' magazine answers. And now I'm fire-engine red."

"Don't ever be embarrassed to ask me anything. And the answer is yes, especially if he is cheating," Patsy said. "And he'll get mean as a snake so he can think that it's your fault that he's doing something he shouldn't. Then when the affair is over, he'll get sweet for a little while until he starts up another one. Is that what happened with Marty?"

"Yes, it is, but I thought something had to be wrong with me. Who could I have asked? Liz is in the same boat I was, and Darcy hasn't been married," Hannah said.

"Again, my child, you can ask me anything," Patsy said. "Marty had to be in control. I'm sure it was like that even in the bedroom, right?"

"Yes," Hannah answered honestly.

"That sure don't make it pleasant for the partner."

"How do you know all this?"

"I read everything I could find on men like him when you finally broke down and told me about his threats. I couldn't figure out a way to get you out of there. I thought he had someone on his payroll watching you. I had no idea about the cameras and the tracking stuff. But why are you askin' now?"

"We can wait and talk more about that when you are here. It's only a couple of weeks."

"Yes, we can, and I'm so looking forward to the visit," Patsy said. "I wish Mama would have agreed to move to Crossing rather than me having to come here, but at the time I was alone and all her friends were in her part of the world. Got to go now. The nurse is here with papers for me to sign. Love you."

Hannah tossed the phone on the pillow and crossed the room to look out the window. Today Jodie was leaving, and Sophie would be lonely for sure. They'd all miss having a baby in the house, but more than anything Hannah would miss Jodie's insight and sweet smile. Part of being a host for the shelter was not getting so attached that the guest or Hannah would want to keep in touch. Ties like that could be dangerous. She wished she and Jodie had met under different circumstances so they could be friends for longer than a week.

Daylight was breaking, giving the trees and houses dimensions, bringing them to life. Lights were shining from the kitchen windows, which meant Aunt Birdie was up puttering around in the kitchen. She owed Aunt Birdie so much for being her confidante and for letting her use her phone to call Mama every week.

Something akin to ice water running down her spine made her shiver as she visualized what Marty would have done if he'd ever heard the conversations she'd had with her mother over the past few years. She reminded herself that she'd never have to see him again. But a tiny little niggling space in her heart still worried that there would come a day when he'd make even another run at ruining her life.

Wrapping her arms around her body, she crossed the room and slung open the closet. Jeans and a shirt would do fine, and sandals. They were going to the zoo, not to a formal dinner.

Formal dinner.

That made her think of the clothing that hung in the penthouse apartment in Dallas. Things that she only wore when she went to the bank's black-tie affairs, usually at Christmas when Marty and his father were the big shots who gave out bonus checks. She wondered what Marty had done with them. Had he sent them all to Goodwill, or were they still hanging in the closet?

She was trying to decide which pair of sandals to wear when her door burst open and a yawning Sophie made her way to her mother's bed and curled up in it, pulling the sheet up to her chin.

"Good morning," Hannah said as she slid her feet into a pair of pink sandals that matched the shirt she'd chosen.

"I don't want this day to be here, Mama." Sophie sighed with all the dramatic ability of a little girl.

"Me, either, but we knew when Laurel arrived that it was only for a week. We'll be thankful for the week, not be sad that it's over." Hannah sat down on the bed and pulled Sophie into her arms.

Sophie buried her face in her mother's shoulder. "I wish Laurel was really my sister. Lullaby and me, well, we're going to miss her."

"I know," Hannah said. "You and Lullaby can love on each other, and that will make today easier."

"Mama, can we have sausage gravy and biscuits for breakfast? I like pancakes better, but Laurel likes biscuits and gravy. Since it's her last day, she should get to choose."

"How 'bout if we have both? It's your last day with her *and* her last day with you. And we'll even let Lullaby have a little bit of gravy on a plate so she can share the good-byes with you. But promise me—no tears. It will make Laurel even sadder if you cry," Hannah said.

"Okay, no tears. But that don't mean my heart won't be cryin'." Sophie bounded off the bed and ran to her room, yelling for Laurel to wake up.

"Out of the mouths of babes," Hannah murmured as she made her way to the kitchen.

Travis was already in the kitchen and holding a cup of coffee out to her. "What's that all about?"

She wrapped her hands around it and took a sip. "I'm making pancakes plus biscuits and sausage gravy for breakfast. One little girl needs pancakes to help with the pain of separation and the other needs biscuits and gravy."

He nodded and opened a cabinet door. "I'll start making biscuits."

"You cook?"

"When I want to or have to. Remember, darlin', I lived alone or with my dad. That's it. Of course, now he's got a new wife to help him with the cookin'. He called to tell me that he got married and is on a honeymoon cruise. Can you believe that? He's not coming home for the Fourth of July, but he will be here at Christmas." Travis measured two cups of flour into a bowl. "And I do make a mean pan of biscuits."

Hannah poked him on the arm. "You are full of surprises. I'm happy for your dad. I've often wished Mama could find someone, but I don't think it's going to happen."

"Take you a whole lifetime to figure out all my surprises. Maybe your mama has had her hands full with your grandmother," he said.

"Mama, Mama!" Sophie yelled. "Can I give Laurel one of my Barbie dolls to take home with her?"

"Of course, and maybe a couple of outfits, too," Hannah hollered back.

"Yay!" Sophie squealed. "Which ones do you want, Laurel?"

Travis added baking powder to the flour and stirred. "That little girl is going to flourish in Kentucky."

Holding hands, Laurel and Sophie skipped into the kitchen.

"We need a bag to put my new Barbie in because Mama says there's not room in the suitcase. Besides, I want her in the backseat with me so I can show her everything out the window," Laurel said.

Hannah handed over a grocery bag. "You two might want to pick out some books for Laurel to take, too, after breakfast."

Laurel hung her head, and her small shoulders sagged. "I don't have anything to give you back."

Hannah quickly crossed the room, knelt beside the two girls, and hugged them both. "You gave Sophie a whole week of friendship. She's had someone to play with and have a weeklong sleepover with in her new room with the clouds and twinkle stars. That's a lot, Laurel."

The little chin came up, and her bright-blue eyes twinkled. "We gave that to each other, and when I get home to 'Tucky, Mama says that she will paint clouds and rainbows and stars on my wall like Sophie's and then at night"—she stopped and sucked in more air—"we can look at the wall and Sophie can look at hers and we'll remember each other."

"That's right," Hannah said hoarsely.

When she turned around, Travis had both arms open, and she was about to walk into them when Jodie and Bella arrived in the kitchen. Lord, she needed that hug so badly right then, but she didn't feel comfortable embracing him in front of her guests.

With the baby on her good hip and her crutch firmly planted under her other arm, Jodie made her way slowly to the table. "Good morning. What can I do to help?"

Travis reached for the baby. "You can finish making the biscuits if I can spend a little more time holding Miss Bella. She doesn't look like she's hardly awake."

"She could have slept longer, but we've only got an hour and a half before Donnie gets here," Jodie said.

"I believe that's the first time you've said his name," Hannah said.

"It's one of those things that the television psychiatrist would have a ball with. I was afraid if I said his name out loud that this would all fall through. Gina called me on the house phone to tell me to be ready at eight thirty—he called her," Jodie said.

"Any news from your ex?" Travis dragged a wooden rocking chair in from the living room and reached for Bella.

Jodie put the baby in his arms and leaned her crutch on a kitchen chair. "Gina told me that he called a bit ago and asked if I was there. He cussed and ranted when she told him I was not. He wanted to know if I'd gone to Kentucky. She told him she had no idea what he was talking about and he hung up on her."

Travis sat down and started humming a lullaby, and the baby snuggled right down against his chest.

Jodie added oil and milk to the flour mixture and deftly completed the biscuits. "I keep praying that nothing happens before Donnie gets here. I hope things are better when I'm in the car and headed home, but I'm still afraid. Does it ever go away?"

"I'm still wondering the same thing." Hannah stirred up pancake batter.

"Laurel told me last night that she didn't ever want a daddy again. She only wants an uncle Travis and an uncle Cal. Daddies are mean people to her," Jodie said softly. "I'm not interested in another man in my life, but I hope I haven't ruined her heart for love when she's a grown woman."

"All you can do is your best to give her a happy life and hopefully her uncle Donnie will be a good male role model," Travis said from the other side of the room.

Hannah's blood ran cold. Did Sophie feel the same way about a daddy? She'd never suffered at Marty's hands, but she'd lived in a tense world when he was home. And she'd seen bruises on Hannah many times. Would she grow up to be drawn to abusive men?

"It won't happen," Travis said.

"What?" Jodie asked.

"What Hannah is worrying about. If anyone ever mistreats Sophie, they won't live to see daylight. Cal and I will take care of it," he said.

"How did you know that's what I was thinking?" Hannah asked.

"I know you." Travis smiled. "Your girls will be fine, ladies. With a lot of good nurturing from y'all and help from your families, they will grow up to be independent and smart just like their mamas."

Donnie knocked at eight fifteen. When Hannah opened the door, he crossed the floor and wrapped his arms around Jodie. A tall, muscular man with blond hair clipped close to his head, big blue eyes, and a round face, he finally pushed her back and really looked at her.

"You should have left sooner, sis." His voice was hoarse with emotion.

Tears rolled down her cheeks. "I should have never left Kentucky. I should have stayed home, had the baby, and been a single mother."

He wiped her tears with the back of his broad hand. "We'll move on to the future and let the devil have the past."

"That sounded just like Granny." She smiled through the tears.

"I haven't seen her in three years and the first thing I see is her crying. And she was always the tough one in the family, all full of sass." He grinned over his shoulder at Travis and Hannah. "Now, let me see

Laurel, take a peek at my new niece, Bella, and get you loaded. I can't get out of this state fast enough."

Jodie nodded and, tucking the crutch more firmly under her arm, started for the bedroom. "I'm packed and ready. I need help with the suitcase and quilt tops. Can you take the baby? She's crawling around in the living room."

"Three years?" Hannah asked.

"Last time I came to Texas, I got into it with her husband. I wanted her to leave with me, but she wouldn't. We've talked a few times, Christmas and on her birthday. Then that lady called and told me what had happened. I arranged for leave right then, but it took time for me to get the paperwork done and the plans made," he said. "Thank you for doing this for her. She was a good kid who believed a man with a slick line."

"She helped me as much as I did her," Hannah said around a lump in her throat. "There is a check in this envelope. I want you to give it to her when y'all get to Kentucky. I would have given her cash, but you don't need to travel with that kind of money. It's just a little seed money to get her on her feet this first year." She wiped the tears from her eyes. "Travis, will you and Donnie get Laurel and Bella situated while I help Jodie with the baggage?"

"Thank you," Donnie said. "Not taking charity has been ingrained in us, but I'll see to it that this gets cashed when we get home."

Hannah wiped a few more tears away as she went to Jodie's bedroom. The bed had been stripped and remade; the dirty sheets were on the floor beside the door. Jodie turned at Hannah's entrance to give the room one more scan.

"I should take those sheets to the laundry room," she said.

"Leave them. I'll do that. You've got a long, long day ahead of you and possibly part of the night. Remember, no tears, no good-byes, or we'll both be weeping all day. I'm not even going out on the porch with y'all." Hannah picked up the suitcase with the folded quilt tops lying on top.

She carried them out to the porch, and Donnie took them to the car. When he finished he got both children strapped into their seats, then motioned for Jodie.

Jodie held back for just a moment and then hugged Hannah tightly. "I will never forget you."

"And I won't forget you, either. Now go and don't look back. The future is yours, girlfriend. Make it beautiful."

Jodie nodded.

Hannah went into the house and straight back to the bedroom, where she sat on the bed and waited. In a few minutes, Sophie came into the room and put her tiny hand in her mother's. Without saying a word, they sat there until Travis peeked into the room and told them that the car was gone and out of sight. Then Sophie broke down and sobbed like only a child can do.

"I hate daddies," she said. "If it wasn't for her daddy bein' so mean, we could have been forever friends."

"If her daddy hadn't been so mean, you never would have met Laurel." Hannah held her on one side.

Travis knelt beside the bed and hugged her from the other side. "And not all daddies are mean," he said.

"The ones I know are. Sometimes they aren't even daddies and they are mean. Look at Aunt Liz." Sophie sobbed harder.

"Well, you don't know all the daddies in the world. My daddy is a pretty nice guy, and your mama's daddy was a nice guy, and Cal's daddy is nice. I bet a lot of your little friends at school have nice daddies," Travis said soothingly.

Sophie shot a puzzled look at her mother. "Then why didn't you get me one of them kind?"

"Because," Travis said before Hannah could answer, "your mama thought your daddy was a good man, but he fooled her. When you get to be a big girl, me and Uncle Cal will make sure that no one ever fools you, okay?"

"Okay." Sophie sighed.

"How would you like to go to the petting zoo and maybe to the movies or the park and play?" Travis asked.

Her eyes brightened. "Can we take fried chicken for a picnic and a blanket to put on the ground at the park by the zoo and then have ice cream on the way home?"

"You drive a hard bargain, but if you won't cry anymore, I think we can do that if it's okay with your mama," Travis said. "It breaks my heart when you cry, princess."

Sophie giggled. "You'll be a good daddy, won't you, Uncle Travis?"

"I hope so, darlin'. I really hope so," he said.

She broke free of their embraces and ran to her bedroom. "I'll get my shoes on and then we can go, right? Who all is going with us? Is Aunt Birdie going?"

"No." Travis sat down on the bed beside Hannah and covered her hand with his. "But Aunt Liz, Darcy, and Cal are all going, too. And we're taking Cal's van so we can ride together."

"This is going to be a wondermous day," Sophie yelled.

"I would do anything for you and Hannah," Travis declared.

Chapter Twenty-Three

Travis went right into the petting zoo pen with Sophie, and together they scratched baby goats' ears, ran their fingers through the baby lambs' wool, and even touched a skittish little fawn that barely came up to Sophie's waist. He'd purchased two paper bags of feed from a vendor and the little animals followed them around, making Sophie laugh.

"Now, Spotty Boy, you have to share." Sophie pushed a goat away and fed the fawn from her hand. "This is Bambi and he is hungry. His mama went to the store and she'll be back soon with his special treats, right, Uncle Travis?"

"That's right." He nodded. Lord only knew where that fawn's mama was—most likely killed on the road or back in another part of the zoo wondering what happened to the baby she'd birthed a few weeks before. Maybe at night they took the little critter to her, but he wasn't going to go into that subject with Sophie. Right now, the fawn's mama was at the grocery store.

That stupid Marty had no idea what he'd missed out on with his daughter. She was such a delightful, imaginative little girl who brought joy just by walking into a room. But then, if Marty had been a stand-up guy, Travis wouldn't have a chance at spending the day at the petting zoo with Sophie.

Darcy, Cal, and Liz found a bench under a shade tree, and from the expressions Travis caught every few minutes, they were deep in a serious conversation. The way they kept glancing at Hannah, who was standing behind the petting zoo fence, her cute little chin propped on a post as she watched Sophie with the animals, it was evident that they were worried about her. But then, so was Travis. The safe house idea was good in one aspect, but Hannah had a soft heart, and whether she liked it or not, she did get attached to her guests.

Sophie steered the little fawn over toward the fence where Hannah was watching. "Mama, Bambi sure would like to go home with me. Uncle Travis could build a fence in the backyard and I would feed him every day and I just know Anna Lou and Nadine would like to play with him, too."

"The zoo doesn't let anyone take the animals home. If they did, the little children wouldn't have anything to pet," Travis answered for Hannah. "All of our food is gone, and I see a whole busload of little kids arriving. You think maybe we could let them have a turn while we go to the park and have our picnic?"

"Yes!" Sophie handed Travis the last empty feed sack and pumped her fist in the air. "I'm almost hungry to death."

Travis raised an eyebrow toward Hannah.

"That's the ultimate hunger. Hungry as a bear is a close second." She smiled.

"Well, then I expect we'd best get to the park, send someone for chicken while we spread out our quilt under a shade tree, and feed this princess before she turns into an ogre," Travis teased.

"Oh, no!" Sophie clamped a hand on each cheek. "I might turn into Fiona from *Shrek* if I don't get fried chicken real soon. Let's get out of here in a hurry."

With the park less than fifteen minutes away, Cal, Darcy, and Liz all volunteered to go for the food while Hannah, Travis, and Sophie staked out a claim with the quilt. They drove away, and Sophie bounded on ahead, checking out three spots before she found the right one closest to the swings.

Travis flipped the quilt out, and it fell right into place. "There you go, ladies. This is our home for the afternoon. You get to pick the first room, Sophie, in our new home."

Sophie sat down in the middle of it and fell back to stare at the sky. "Silly Uncle Travis. This is a quilt, not a house. But if it was, I'd want this room right here in the middle. I can see the clouds. Look, Mama." She pointed up to the sky. "It's a lullaby sky today. Let's sing 'Twinkle.'"

Without hesitation Travis led the song in his deep voice. Sophie giggled and then joined him on the second line, and Hannah's sweet soprano came in on the chorus.

"Hey, hey," Aunt Birdie called out from behind the tree. "The song brought me right to you."

She and Miss Rosie carried a cooler between them and set it down on the edge of the quilt next to the gnarled oak tree trunk. Wearing jeans, sneakers, a ball cap, and a T-shirt with palm trees on the front, Aunt Birdie looked like she'd just gotten off a cruise ship. Miss Rosie, in her floral muumuu and a straw hat with silk daisies glued to the brim, looked more like she'd just flown in from Hawaii.

They eased down onto the quilt, removed their hats, and fanned almost in unison.

"Goin' to be a hot one, but we shouldn't burn if we stay under this shade tree," Aunt Birdie said. "Last time I went to that damned skin doctor, he tried to fry my whole nose right off my face."

"Quit your bitchin'," Miss Rosie chided. "If he didn't burn them precancer things off you, then you'd get the real thing and it would eat your nose plumb off. We brought a cheesecake, water, and soda pop. Y'all can go on and push Sophie on the swings and we'll hold down the camp."

"Aunt Birdie and Miss Rosie! Now the day is perfect." Sophie inched back a foot so she could lay a hand on both their knees.

"Yes, it is, baby girl." Aunt Birdie nodded. "And I brought your favorite—cherry Coke."

"Yay! Fried chicken and my favorite pop. I didn't think this would be a good day, but it is. Mama, come and swing with me until our chicken gets here," Sophie said.

"Go on, Hannah. We'll keep all intruders out of this house until you get back," Aunt Birdie said.

Sophie giggled. "It's not really a house but a 'tend house, Aunt Birdie."

"Well, then we'll keep the pretend critters out of it. You won't find a single dinosaur or ogre on it when you get done swinging," Aunt Birdie said.

Hannah rolled up on her knees and then popped up to her feet. "I thought y'all would be at the church most of the day."

"We got our meeting over with at the church and decided to join y'all," Aunt Birdie told her.

"I'll be over there in a minute and push both of you," Travis said.

Aunt Birdie waited until Hannah was out of hearing distance and said, "Is she going to be okay with all this? The only concern I had in the beginning of her taking in abused women was that she'd get too attached to them."

"It's a sad day, because she and Jodie really bonded this week. These women are bringing closure to her, though," Travis answered.

"Well, she needs that, for damn sure." Miss Rosie settled the hat back on her head. "You go on now and push them. Hannah needs this day as much as Sophie does."

⁓

The last time Hannah remembered swinging was high school graduation night. All five of them had wound up at this same park, swinging and playing on the slide, drinking beer and having one last night together.

Liz was going to college in Gainesville, Hannah had gotten a full-time job overseeing the volunteer organization at the Gainesville hospital, Cal was off to New York to study design, Travis had decided to go into construction with his father, and Darcy had been offered a position at the bank where she'd been working part-time in the summers. Change was in the wind that hot summer night, but not as much as it was this day.

Travis gave Sophie a high push first, and then he moved over and put his arms around Hannah's waist, pulled her back, and let go. His touch and the warm summer breeze stirred emotions that both scared and exhilarated her.

"Remember the last time we were here, all together?" Travis asked as he gave her a gentle push each time the swing took her back to him.

"Graduation night," she answered.

"Life has made a big circle."

"Boy, has it ever. You guys followed your dreams. Darcy kept moving up in the bank. Liz came back to teach in Crossing, and me—well, enough said," Hannah said.

"I'm glad we are where we are right now. And speaking of today, you look every bit as beautiful now as you did that night we graduated," he flirted.

Hannah's pulse quickened. "You are making me blush."

"And you look adorable with pink cheeks." He gave her another push.

"Uncle Travis, I'm getting real slow," Sophie called out from the swing beside Hannah.

Travis took a couple of long steps to the side and sent Sophie flying so high that her giggles could be heard all over the park. Then he went back to Hannah's swing.

"Is it all right if I stay on at your place one more night? Seems like late Saturday night or Sunday morning is the time for womenfolks to walk away from bad situations."

"Seems that way. Must be the Saturday night drinking that causes some of it. You can live at my house as long as you want," she answered. "In my case it was Friday afternoons."

"Friday?" Travis asked.

"That's the day Marty came home, if he did. He always left on Sunday night or early Monday morning, so those weren't bad days. On Fridays I still wake up, realize it's what day it is, and get an anxiety pain for a couple of seconds until I realize it's all over and done with."

"My turn again," Sophie yelled.

Travis pulled back on the chains until she was chest level. "Yes, ma'am. High as last time?"

"Yes, yes, yes. If there were stars out right now, I could touch them." She sang part of "Too-Ra-Loo" and then segued off into the chorus at the top of her young lungs as she soared in the air.

"We may have to play that song at her wedding." Travis chuckled.

"We won't talk about that today." Hannah frowned.

"It will arrive before we know it. Today we'll just enjoy her being almost six and talk about something else," he agreed. "I hated Fridays, too, Hannah."

"Why?"

"Because I could tell that you were nervous about him coming home, and I hated thinking about you over there with him. Miss Rosie kept telling me that the end was in sight, but I have to admit, I thought it would never get here," Travis answered.

"How did she know?"

"She and your aunt Birdie know everything," he said seriously. "Do you realize I've been back in Crossing one year this month and Marty was only home three times the whole year? And I wasn't in your house until the divorce, because I knew that it made you nervous for anyone to be inside."

"But you came over all the time," she said defensively.

He nodded. "I was over there nearly every day that Marty was not there, but we always sat on the porch. Same with Darcy and Liz."

"I have a confession. I didn't want any of you in the house," she said. "At first I thought it was fear that someone would move his lamp a quarter of an inch or that they wouldn't dry the sink in the bathroom after they'd washed their hands and that would set him off. But I have thought about it—I felt comfortable with you all. I didn't want to spoil that by exposing the feelings in my house at that time. Thank God I did." Her shoulders twitched in a shiver. "I'm sorry if I hurt any feelings."

He reached across the distance and wrapped his hand around the swing chain, bringing it closer to him. "Nothing to be sorry about. And darlin', if you ever have a gut feeling about something, you follow it down to the letter. That sure kept you alive."

"Look, Mama, there's our fried chicken. I want a leg and a wing. Oh! Oh! Uncle Cal is carrying a box of doughnuts, too. I hope he got a chocolate one." Sophie jumped out of the swing, landed on both feet, then took off in her usual run mode.

"You think they'll make it all the way to the altar someday?" Hannah nodded toward Darcy and Cal.

"Oh, yes, I do. They've been in love since high school, but it's their time now. I'll bet you ten bucks and a steak dinner that they tie the knot at Christmas." Travis stood up and offered her his hand.

She took his hand and shook on the deal. "I bet you the same that it's at Thanksgiving or before."

He kept her hand in his. "Either way, I win."

"So do I?"

"I will say grace, because y'all pray too long and I'm hungry to death." Sophie sat down on her knees on the quilt and bowed her head. "Father up in my lullaby sky, thank you for this food and for all my friends. Amen."

"And now that it is blessed, we will dig right in." Miss Rosie opened the cooler and brought out soda pop for everyone.

"I haven't been in this park since"—Cal paused and picked up a chunk of chicken—"graduation night."

"Beers and tears," Darcy said. "I cried all night because nothing would ever be the same."

"And here we are back again without beer or tears." Liz eased down on the quilt and opened the box of chicken. "I wonder how far along on the trip that Jodie is. I looked it up on the map, and it's about sixteen hours of driving. That doesn't include food and gas stops."

"Maybe about a third of the way," Travis said. "Donnie said he hoped to be there by one or two o'clock in the morning. He wasn't planning on making a two-day trip out of it. He wants Jodie back in the hills with her relatives as quick as possible."

"Smart man," Cal murmured.

Liz yawned. "I wish I'd brought a pillow."

"There's one in the backseat of my van if you can talk Travis into getting it for you," Cal said. "I'm not moving an inch from this gorgeous masseuse."

Travis rolled up on his feet, and in a few long strides was back at the van. He opened the door and brought out a bright-red velvet neck roll.

"Ahh, that is perfect," Liz said. "Good man you got there, Hannah. You'd do well to hang on to him."

"He's not my man. He's my friend," Hannah argued.

"Your mouth can say that, but your heart knows better."

"I've only been divorced less than a month," Hannah protested further.

"You've been divorced for more than a year. It's the legal part that's only a month old. Don't shut the door to an opportunity before you see what's on the other side. That's what you always tell us," Darcy said.

"That's right," Aunt Birdie said.

"I think this might be a conspiracy," Hannah said.

"Can't be. If it was, we'd invite you and Travis into it." Cal grinned.

"Aunt Birdie and Miss Rosie, when we get done eating, you can come with me and I will push you in the swings," Sophie said when she'd cleaned all the meat off the last chicken leg in the bucket.

Aunt Birdie patted Sophie on the shoulder. "Darlin' girl, you are not big enough to push us on the swings, but we can take turns going down the slide."

Miss Rosie clapped her hands. "It's been years since I've been on a slide." She slapped her hat on her head and grasped Sophie's hand. "I call dibs on going first."

After they'd finished eating, the three of them skipped along from quilt to the slide, one energetic little girl in the middle. Her giggles echoed off the big white puffy clouds floating in the sky.

Liz claimed a side of the quilt and the pillow that Travis had brought from the van and fell asleep. She looked better than Hannah had seen her since they'd lived together when Liz was in college and Hannah worked at the hospital.

"I want a whole houseful of kids with Sophie's energy. She's an amazing kid. Gets along with kids her age and older folks just as well." Cal yawned. "That heavy meal is weighing down my eyelids."

"Then put your head right here in my lap and take a nap." Darcy leaned back against the tree and patted her thighs.

"Don't mind if I do." Cal stretched out.

Darcy splayed out her fingers and dug down into his thick blond hair to massage his scalp. "Shut your eyes. This is guaranteed to put you to sleep."

"Ahh," he moaned. "That feels so good."

"Thanksgiving," Hannah said.

"I'll still win," Travis mouthed.

"What are you two talking about?" Darcy asked.

"A bet we've got going. We'll tell you all about it when we find out who wins."

Before long Darcy's head had dropped to her chest and everyone but Travis and Hannah was either asleep or playing with Sophie.

Travis laid a hand on Hannah's knee. "We should do this more often. Maybe make it a Sunday afternoon thing when nothing else is happening, instead of a Saturday like today. I don't *read* very often on Sundays." Travis winked. "I was so afraid you'd have a problem with that."

"Why?" She could feel the heat all the way through her jeans, and sparks flitted around them like fireflies in a late-summer evening.

"It's not masculine and it's . . ."

"I'm proud of you, Travis. Actually, it goes beyond that. I'm in awe. And any time you need to work to meet a deadline, just tell me and we'll respect that."

"Really?"

Before she could answer, her phone buzzed. She pulled it from her hip pocket, saw that it was Gina, and smiled at Travis. "Looks like you might need to stay tonight rather than just want to stay." She hit the "Answer" button on her phone.

"Hello," she answered.

"I have a guest for you for two nights at the most. I can bring her after five tonight, if that's convenient. Her name is Arabella. This is a strange situation, but your place is the best for her."

"Then bring her on. We're out right now, but we'll be home by five with no problem," Hannah said. "Are there children?"

"No children," Gina answered.

"Sophie will be disappointed."

"I talked to Jodie this morning, and she sang your praises for giving her and the children such a wonderful welcome. You are quite an asset to us, Hannah," Gina said. "I'll see you in a couple of hours."

Travis raised an eyebrow when she put the phone back in her pocket.

"I was right. We've got company. Her name is Arabella. Sophie can play another hour, and then we'll have ice cream on the way home before Arabella arrives."

"No kids from what I heard, right?"

"No kids, and she'll only be with us two days at the most."

Travis nodded. "Poor Sophie."

Hannah pointed to Miss Rosie and Aunt Birdie taking turns with her on the slide and then swung her finger around to include all five of the folks on the quilt. "She has someone all the time."

Sophie's little eyes were drooping when they arrived back in Crossing late that afternoon. "I think maybe Lullaby needs to take a nap," she said.

"I wouldn't be a bit surprised if your kitten has waited all afternoon on you to get home so that she wouldn't have to sleep all by herself." Travis opened the van door and got out. "How about I carry you in the house?"

Sophie wrapped her arms around his neck. "I'd like that, Uncle Travis."

She was asleep before he made it to the front door, her little head lying on his chest. He carried her to her room, laid her gently on the bed, removed her shoes, and pulled a soft throw over her feet.

Hannah stood in the doorway and wished for the millionth time that Marty had had half the paternal instincts that Travis or even Calvin had. Travis kissed Sophie on the forehead and tiptoed out of the room, easing the door shut behind him.

"I'm going to put a pan of brownies in the oven so the house will smell good and I'll have something to offer the new guest if she wants to sit and talk a little while," Hannah said.

"I'm going up to my room to give you space and time." Travis dropped a kiss on the top of her head. "See you later."

The house smelled like warm chocolate when Hannah heard the first crunch of tires on the driveway. Her hand was on the knob when Gina knocked. She pasted on a brilliant smile and swung open the door.

The smile faded quickly, and her big brown eyes came close to popping out of her head. Her chest compressed when she forgot to inhale, and her hands had grown damp and cold. Surely to God this was a joke. She blinked half a dozen times, but the woman did not disappear.

Right there, with only a screen separating them, was Marty's pregnant girlfriend, wearing a white satin wedding dress over a bulging baby bump.

Chapter Twenty-Four

Gina peeked over the redhead's shoulder, concern written on her face. "Are you all right, Hannah? You look as if you are about to faint."

Hannah finally sucked in enough air to ask, "Do you have a cell phone?"

The woman shook her head. "I threw it away."

"A suitcase or a purse?" Hannah asked.

Another shake. "Just the clothing on my back."

Hannah opened the door. "You'd better come in out of the heat in your condition."

Gina and Arabella stepped inside the house, but Hannah couldn't make herself welcome them. Why, oh, why would Gina ever bring this woman to her house?

Because she has no idea who the woman is, Hannah's conscience said bluntly.

"I'll leave," Arabella said. "I can stay in a hotel. I have enough cash for one night."

"What is going on here?" Gina asked. "Do you two know each other?"

"This is Marty's girlfriend. Or is it wife?" Hannah asked.

"Ex-girlfriend," Arabella announced stiffly. "I didn't know that we were coming to your house. I'm as shocked as you are." She turned to Gina. "Please take me to the nearest cheap hotel. I have a hundred-dollar bill tucked into my bra."

Gina laid a hand on Arabella's arm and motioned toward the door with a nod of her head. "I'm sorry, Hannah. I didn't even tell her your name. I just said that you had a little girl who called this place Lullaby Sky and the last two women that left here said it had done them a world of good to spend time with you. I'll figure something else out."

Hannah shook her head. "He'd never think to look here, so this is the perfect place. But why did you leave on your wedding day?"

"Last night, after the rehearsal dinner, he brought out the prenup. He'd had too much to drink and he said some things." Arabella paused as if trying to decide what to say next. "About you and not having a prenup. How he'd had complete control over you so he didn't need one, but he wasn't making that mistake twice. I didn't want to sign it without reading it, and he got furious and slapped me across the cheek."

"Sit down," Hannah said. "You look like you are about to fall. And Gina, we'll be fine for a couple of days."

"I didn't sleep all night. I signed that paper because the look in his eye scared me. This is Saturday, right? Last night was Friday and today we were supposed to get married. June 25. It had to be today, because that is his parents' anniversary and it was going to bring good luck into our marriage. I'm sorry, I'm rambling." Arabella sank down on the sofa. "And then he signed it and left my copy for me to give to my lawyer after the wedding was over. I read the thing over and over and over all night. There was a loophole, though. Everything in it would go into effect the minute *after* we were married."

Gina took a seat on the other end of the sofa. "I'm not sure about this, Hannah."

"I am," Hannah said. "I signed on to help abused women. I haven't changed my mind, and I want to do this."

"Why?"

"Because I firmly believe things happen for a reason. Arabella's only chance to escape may lie in this house. If she or her baby was hurt because of my selfishness, I would never forgive myself," Hannah said.

"Then I'm going to leave," Gina said. "And if either of you changes your mind, you have my number."

Silence filled the room after Gina left. Dozens of questions clogged Hannah's mind. She didn't know which one to ask first.

"I'm sorry," Arabella finally said. "I had no idea he was married until he told me that I was going to court with him because he was getting a divorce. By then I was very pregnant and my baby needed a father. I'm finding out that there are worse things in the world than being a single mother."

Hannah paced from one end of the floor to the other. It would be so easy to blame Arabella for everything. But if she was honest, she owed that woman her new life and freedom.

"Thank you," Hannah said softly as she sat down on the other end of the sofa.

"For what?"

"For getting me out of a marriage that I'd tried and tried to escape. I'd like to be angry with you, but what I had with Marty was fear, not love. The love part lasted about a month after we were married. If that long. The fear—now, that was a different story."

Arabella shivered. "Why didn't you just leave and take your daughter with you? She wasn't Marty's child, after all."

So that was his story.

"She is Marty's child, and that was the hold he had on me. With his money, he could have taken her from me. He threatened to frame me as an unfit mother, or worse yet convince people that I was crazy and have me committed. Then I would lose her and I never would have seen her again," Hannah said.

"Oh. My. God!" Arabella gasped. "I believed every word he said."

"You were smart to get away from him."

Arabella shook her head. "The prenup was horrible. I have a lot of money—more than he has—and the language said he would have complete and total custody of our child and I would pay him an exorbitant amount of child support if I ever left him. And that I would have supervised visitation for our child at his discretion and only when he or his mother could be there."

Hannah wasn't at all surprised. Strangely enough, now that the shock was fading, she was glad that God had sent Arabella to Crossing. She truly wanted to help this woman, and the fact that it was Marty who'd abused her really didn't matter.

"Someone was with me the whole day," Arabella went on. "The hairdresser. The lady who did my nails. He made sure I wasn't alone until thirty minutes before it was time to stand before the preacher. I was about to go crazy trying to figure out a way to get out of the house." She paused and locked gazes with Hannah a second before blinking. "I don't know if you believe in God, but I do, and I'm convinced that he gave me a way out. Marty's mother came to the room and said it was time for me to go downstairs to wait in the master bedroom until I heard the music and then his father would be right outside the door to escort me into the ballroom for the wedding."

"And?" Hannah asked when she stopped.

"I tucked what cash I had into my bra along with my cell phone. I called a cab and slid open the doors to their patio, kept to the brush along the road until I saw the cab, and stepped out. I was afraid after what all he'd done to you that he had a tracker on my phone, so I tossed it in the back of a passing pickup truck just before I got into the cab," Arabella said in a hollow voice.

"That was one smart decision. But now you have no identification."

"All that can be replaced once I'm in Mexico," Arabella said. "Gina let me call my grandmother before we left to come here. My *abuela* lives in Mexico City, and she is making arrangements to bring me home."

"That's very good. Now, about that wedding dress," Hannah said.

"It's all I have until I get to Mexico City."

"My friends help run a little clothing closet out of our church. Would you take that off if I could get you something else?"

Arabella smiled for the first time. "I would trade it for a burlap bag if you can find one."

Hannah picked up her phone from the end table and called Aunt Birdie. When she answered, she said, "I need some things from the church clothes closet. The lady is pregnant." Hannah looked at her and cocked her head to one side, studying her round stomach. "Six months, I'd guess."

"Eight and a half," Arabella said.

"Okay, then two weeks away from delivery, probably. She's tall and thin and she needs enough for a couple of days. Maybe two outfits. Bra?" Hannah asked Arabella.

"I have one on that will work."

"No bra, just underpants and a nice big nightgown in the mix so she can be comfortable while she sleeps."

"I'm on it. Did the bastard hurt the baby?" Aunt Birdie asked.

"No, she got away before too much damage was done."

"Good. Me and Rosie will be there in half an hour. Does she need anything else?"

"I think I've got it covered. Thanks, Aunt Birdie." She hit the "End" button and turned to Arabella. "Hungry?"

"Starving. I haven't had anything all day. I was too nervous to eat breakfast, and by lunchtime I couldn't force food into my mouth for fear of throwing it all right back up."

Hannah stood up and motioned for Arabella to follow her into the kitchen. "I'll make you a sandwich and then we'll have brownies as soon as they come out of the oven. Do you like pimento cheese or ham better? And milk or sweet tea?"

"Pimento cheese sounds great, and I love milk. I thought I smelled chocolate. This place reminds me of the way my grandmother's house smells. She has a fantastic cook. She is sending two of her best bodyguards to take me home to Mexico. I wish I'd never gone to that party where I met Martin. He was charming and sweet at first."

"Until you got pregnant and then things changed, right?"

Arabella nodded. "I hope I never see him again. My *abuela* wanted to send her personal plane, but I'm afraid to fly this close to delivery, so we'll drive back and Martin will never see her. I'm talking too much. I do that when I am nervous."

Hannah whipped around. "Don't be nervous. The baby is a girl?"

"Marty thinks it's a boy, but the first ultrasound was a mistake. The recent one, taken last week, shows that the baby is definitely a girl. I didn't tell him because I didn't want to disappoint him right here at the wedding time. But I think the biggest reason is that I was afraid to tell him." Arabella followed Hannah.

"I have one thing to ask. Please don't tell Sophie that the baby is her sister. She wants a sister so badly."

"I won't tell her. How old is she?"

Hannah set about making a sandwich and pouring a glass of milk. "Almost six. She's napping right now, but she'll be excited that we have a guest. She loves to have people in the house."

"When they are grown-up ladies, can we tell them then and let them decide whether they want to meet or not?" Arabella asked in shyness.

Hannah's dark brows knit together in a frown. It had not been arrogance or uppitiness that she'd seen in the woman that day in the courtroom. Marty had already started the process of teaching her submission. The fact that Hannah was not rich and didn't have the upper-class social skills had nothing to do with the situation. Arabella had those things, but he'd still managed to control her.

"He looks for vulnerable women. I bet you are basically pretty shy, right?" Hannah asked.

"Always have been."

"And you have money?"

"My mother's people were very wealthy, from oil. My dad was a professor in Mexico City. I moved to Fort Worth for a year to help set up an oil company. I wanted a change—look what it got me."

Hannah set the sandwich and the milk in front of Arabella. "And he sweet-talked you, sent flowers and candy and expensive presents?"

Arabella bit into the sandwich and chewed fast. She swallowed and sipped the milk. "Yes. All of the above. My first present was a lovely diamond necklace with my and his initials interlocked together. He insisted I wear it to the wedding, but I ripped it off and threw it on the floor before I walked out."

"He's upped his game. I didn't get diamonds." Hannah smiled for the first time. "Does he know your grandmother's name and where she lives?"

Arabella nodded. "He knows. But Mama Lita—that's what we call my *abuela*—would love to take care of him in such a way they would never find his body."

"Enough said." Hannah pulled the brownies from the oven and set them on a hot pad in the middle of the table.

"Not quite enough said. I've been a fool. You are a very kind woman for letting me stay and believing my story. I don't think I could do that if the tables were reversed. I want you to know that if he ever makes things rough for you, all you have to do is call a number I will leave with you. I will send two very responsible people to bring you and your daughter to Mexico or Mama Lita will take care of it permanently. Your choice."

The laughter that escaped Hannah was both edgy and nervous. "That sounds . . ."

Arabella nodded. "I know, but it is the truth. She is very, very powerful. I hope I can learn how to be more like her and less gullible in the future."

"Hey, anybody home?" Travis poked his head in the kitchen.

Hannah smiled. "This is Arabella. She is here until Tuesday morning. And to get it all out in the open, she was about to marry Marty and got smart at the last minute. Arabella, this is one of my lifelong friends, Travis."

Travis stopped in the middle of the floor. "And you are fine with this?"

"Yes, I am," Hannah said. "Aunt Birdie has gone to the church to get her something to wear other than that wedding dress. I just hope Sophie doesn't wake up until she gets changed out of it."

Travis pulled out a chair and sat down. "Better hide it or Sophie will want to play dress-up in the thing."

"Can I send it down to your church clothing closet?" Arabella said. "I don't ever want to see it or the shoes again."

Hannah brought out a knife and cut the brownies into squares. "Milk, coffee, or tea."

Travis poured himself a cup of coffee and sat down at the end of the table. "I don't know if I'm pleased to meet you, but if Hannah is comfortable with you staying here, then I trust her judgment."

"Well, I'm very glad to be here. Away from Martin and that horrible paper I signed. I'm such an idiot," Arabella said.

"Hey, we don't allow that kind of talk in this house," Hannah said. "You are free from abuse from this moment on. Life is what you make it. You can fall back into the hands of another man like Marty, or you can learn from this experience and raise your daughter to be independent and sassy." She quoted the words from her handbook almost word for word, but they came straight from her heart.

"You sound like Mama Lita. I hope my daughter is just like her. My folks were killed in an accident when I was thirteen, and she finished raising me. She and my mother were both very strong willed, but my father was a shy man. I wish I'd gotten more of Mama Lita's strength and a little less of my father's introverted qualities," Arabella said.

"You have almost no accent," Travis said.

"I came to Texas to go to college and afterward stayed to run a portion of our business here. Little by little I lost the accent and replaced it with Texan," Arabella said. "Martin's family did some of our banking, and I was invited to one of their parties last year. I didn't decide to go until the very last minute. How did you meet him, Hannah? At a party also?"

Hannah smiled. "Oh, no. He was in a minor fender bender and came to the emergency room to get checked. I wasn't even supposed to be working the admissions desk that night."

"What are you going to name the baby?" Travis lifted the first brownie out of the pan.

"My grandmother is Isabella Gonzales and my mother was Maria Fiona, so her full name will be Fiona Isabella Gonzales. I will choose her christening name on the day that we take her to the church or when *Abuela* brings the priest to the house to do that ceremony. I hope my daughter gets your kindness in her heart and my grandmother's sass in her head. Then she will never be led astray by a man like Martin Ellis," Arabella said.

Travis chuckled. "Well, that's as good as a slap in old Marty's face. But I thought the baby was a boy. That's what Marty told Hannah when he filed for divorce. He said that he found a woman who was equal to him in society and that y'all were having a boy."

It was Arabella's turn to giggle. "He was wrong on both counts. Martin Ellis is nobody in my grandmother's world."

Aunt Birdie carried a paper bag of clothing into the kitchen. "We're here."

Miss Rosie trailed along behind her. When she saw Arabella, she clamped a hand over her mouth. "Oh. My. Goodness. You look like you are about to have that baby right now."

Hannah made introductions. "This is Aunt Birdie, my great-aunt, and this is Miss Rosie, Travis's grandmother." She turned and nodded toward Arabella and introduced her.

"I'm pleased to meet you both. I'll be in Mexico in a few days, so keep your fingers crossed that my baby doesn't come before then."

Aunt Birdie handed off the bag to Hannah with a nod to Arabella. "You'll be a lot more comfortable if you get out of that dress."

Hannah motioned for Arabella to follow her. "I'll show you to your room."

Arabella made her way out of the chair with one hand on her stomach and the other on her back. She was almost a head taller than Hannah, and her red hair, styled in a crown of curls, had begun to fall. As she made her way down the hall, she removed the pins holding it in place.

"I haven't gotten the bed remade. My last guest just left this morning, but you can get dressed and I'll do that later," Hannah said.

"It's a lovely room, so light and airy," Arabella said. "Will you stay and help me get out of this thing? It's got so many buttons up the back that I can't begin to reach all of them."

"Of course." Hannah stepped behind her and began undoing all the tiny satin-covered buttons. "It's a lovely dress. Some girl who can't afford a nice wedding dress will be delighted to get it."

"I hope it brings her more happiness than it did me." Arabella pulled a pair of maternity shorts from the bag and a brightly colored, flowing top that looked as if it came straight from the islands. "And look, they even brought me flip-flops."

"The right size?" Hannah finished the last button.

"I wear an eight and these are nines, which gives my swollen feet more room. I'm forever in your debt, Hannah."

Hannah dumped the rest of the clothing on the bed, folded the dress as carefully as possible, and stuffed it into the paper bag. "There, now Aunt Birdie can take this with her when she leaves."

"I feel human again, but I have to admit, I'm lost without my phone," Arabella said. "Before we go back out there, I want to say something. I think fate brought me here to prove that I did the right thing."

Hannah laid a hand on her shoulder. "I think fate brought you here to show me a lesson. I thought it was because I wasn't as wealthy or as high on the"—she stopped and swallowed hard—"social ladder as Marty that he treated me like he did. Now I realize that it had nothing to do with status or money. It's his problem. Not ours."

"I shouldn't feel this comfortable with you," Arabella said.

"Crazy, ain't it?" Hannah laughed.

❧

It was near midnight when Hannah heard a gentle rap on her bedroom door. She peeked out to find Travis standing there with two bottles of beer and wearing a big smile. He held them up and nodded toward the stairs.

"Can we go out on the porch and talk?" he asked.

She tiptoed down the steps and out onto the porch and sat down beside him. "What do you want to talk about?"

He handed her a bottle of beer. "Arabella."

"I feel sorry for her. No woman needs to get tangled up with the likes of Marty."

"But she's the one who broke up your marriage."

"For that I can never thank her enough." Hannah laughed. "My marriage was over long before she came into Marty's sight. I just couldn't figure out a way to end it and keep Sophie. I owe that woman."

"Do you even know who she is?"

Hannah turned up the bottle and gulped twice. "She's the one who saved my life, my heart, and my soul."

"She is Isabella Gonzales's granddaughter."

"And that means what?"

"Just that Isabella is the grand matriarch of a powerful family down there. Nobody messes with her. Marty had better leave Arabella alone," Travis explained. "Remember my second book?"

"Oh!" Hannah gasped. "You researched her grandmother, didn't you?"

Travis nodded. "I even met her once for a short interview. She's short and very proper, and she's got red hair like her granddaughter. It was like meeting the queen. And believe me, her dark eyes don't miss a thing."

"Do you think Marty knew?"

"Of course he knew. To have a woman with that kind of background and standing under his thumb would have been a big thing in his eyes," Travis said. "But he was an idiot. When her grandmother finds out that he slapped Arabella, he could be a dead man. But that's not the only reason I wanted to talk to you. I want to know if you are all right with this. You've been doing so good, Hannah. I don't want you to take two steps back."

"It's brought me more closure than anything." She took another drink from the bottle. "Money and social class have nothing to do with him treating either of us like that. So it's him, not me."

He scooted over closer to her, draped an arm around her shoulders, and used the other hand to tip her chin up. "Then I appreciate her being here." He lowered his lips to hers.

The kiss started off sweet but deepened into a hot, passionate blending of two lonely hearts. Hannah forgot about Arabella, Marty, and the past in that moment and thought only about the lanky carpenter and author who had been at her side for months. She set the bottle of beer on the porch and shifted her position so she could wrap both arms around his neck and tangle her fingers in his dark hair.

It might not be right so soon after a divorce, but it felt right. With so much serenity in her soul, how could anything be wrong with what they had?

Chapter Twenty-Five

Sunday morning Hannah made blueberry muffins for breakfast and had just poured herself a cup of coffee when the house phone rang. She answered it on the second ring and hoped that it didn't wake Arabella. Poor lady needed some uninterrupted sleep after the previous day.

"Hello," she said.

"It's Gina, and I have good news and bad news. The bad news is that someone saw that cab leaving the Ellis place in Dallas and Marty tracked it to the shelter. He didn't show up, but one of his people did, and I assured them that Arabella was not here," Gina said.

"And the good news?" Hannah asked.

"Arabella's grandmother called. She is sending a private jet with bodyguards and a doctor to the Dallas airport today. She does not want her granddaughter riding that far in her condition and would rather take a chance on the baby being born on the plane than in a car on the side of the road."

"What time does she need to be ready to leave?"

"A car will pick her up at noon. That's all I've got. Did things go all right?"

"Talking to her was a blessing, Gina. I'm glad for her stay. Her Mama Lita must love her as much as Aunt Birdie and my mom love me. 'Bye, now," Hannah said and hit the button to end the call.

"Hey, do I smell muffins?" Travis asked as he headed for the coffeepot.

"Yep," Hannah said. "And Arabella is leaving at noon. I'm not going to church. I'll stay here with her. You think Aunt Birdie would mind taking Sophie? They're getting things ready for the Fourth of July celebration in her Sunday school class."

"You know Aunt Birdie. She'd take custody of that child if you'd let her."

"What child?" Sophie yawned as she crawled up in Travis's lap.

He wrapped his arms around her. "You, of course. Everyone loves you so much that they wish you were their little girl."

"Even you?" Sophie looked up at him with her dark eyes.

"Especially me. Your mama has to stay with the guest today, but Aunt Birdie will take you to church so you can make your Fourth of July stuff. Did I hear that you are riding on the church float?" Travis asked.

"I am," she answered seriously. "I get to hold a sparkler all by myself."

"I'll have to take a picture of you," Travis said. "Your mama made muffins. Blueberry. Isn't that your favorite?"

Sophie giggled. "Yes, it is, and chocolate chip pancakes. Can I have one little sip of your coffee to wake me up?"

"She's a charmer," Arabella said as she followed her nose to the coffeepot.

"Good news," Hannah said and told her about Gina's call.

Arabella looked up at the ceiling. "Thank you, God! I was dreading that drive down there."

"God ain't up in the bedrooms, Bella. It's funny, ain't it, Mama—we had a baby Bella in the house last week and now we got a big person Bella. I wish she could stay until her baby gets here so I could play with it. Me and Lullaby would be real careful when we held it. I like that it's a girl. I wish I had a sister." Sophie sighed.

"You'll make a great big sister someday." Arabella touched her cheek as she sat down at the table with Travis. "And I bet the baby would have dark hair just like you and your mama."

"I bet your baby has red hair like you," Sophie said.

"That would be wonderful. I'm so glad I get to fly home. That means I'll be there by supper time and Mama Lita and I can have a long visit."

"Mama who?" Sophie asked.

"That is what we call my *abuela*, which is Spanish for 'grandmother.' What do you call your grandmother?" Arabella asked.

"*Abuela*. Can that be our word for the day, Mama?"

"Yes, it can," Hannah answered.

"I like the way that the word sounds, but I think I'll just keep calling my grandmother Granny. She is coming to visit us real soon and she gets to stay in our house this time. She didn't stay with us before, because it made Father mad to have people messing up the house, but he's gone now. I thought I'd be sad that he wasn't coming home anymore, but I'm not," Sophie said. "I haven't even told Granny that we named the house, so it's going to be a surprise. And she hasn't seen my room and you didn't say if I can have a sip of your coffee, Uncle Travis."

"I hope my daughter is just like her." Arabella laughed.

"Yes, you can have one sip of Uncle Travis's coffee, but no more than that," Hannah answered. "Little girls need milk to make their skin pretty and their bones strong."

"And big girls need coffee so they will be smart, right?" Sophie asked.

"Absolutely." Arabella raised her cup. "And you can go to church, Hannah. I'll be fine right here until my people arrive."

"No, ma'am," Travis said. "We'll be here to wave as you leave Crossing. That's the way we do things."

❧

At nine thirty, Travis walked Sophie across the street. She wore a cute little sundress and her best white sandals. Her dark ponytail swung from side to side as she skipped along beside him, her hand in his.

"That is one good man," Arabella said as she waved from the doorway with Hannah right beside her.

"How would we know that with our history?" Hannah asked.

"Maybe since we had such a lousy experience, our eyes have been washed clean and we're given a clearer vision. Did you ever see Martin hold Sophie like Travis was doing or let her drink from his coffee cup? Did he ever walk her across the street with her little hand tucked in his?"

"No to both," Hannah answered with honesty.

"I didn't think so. He talked all the time about interviewing nannies after the wedding so that the baby wouldn't tie us down and we could continue our lifestyle. That day in divorce court when I saw the fear in your eyes, and then the prenup and the way he slapped me—it all convinced me that I was making the biggest mistake in my life." She paused. "Travis is a good man who is in love with you."

"What makes you think that he loves me?"

"It's written all over his face every time he looks at you. How long have you known him?" Arabella flipped her red hair up in a messy ponytail and secured it with a rubber band.

"All my life. We grew up together right here in Crossing."

Hannah watched until Travis put Sophie in the backseat of Aunt Birdie's Caddy and buckled her in. Then he waved until the three of them, Birdie, Rosie, and Sophie, were completely out of sight. After that, he jogged back to Hannah's house and went straight to his room, saying that he had some reading to catch up on.

The phone rang, and Hannah answered it on the third ring.

"Hello, Gina. Is something wrong?"

"Yes! Arabella's grandmother called again. Things moved faster than they thought and they will be at your house any time now. Tell her to be ready to go right then. Martin Ellis showed up here ten minutes ago and said that he knew for a fact that the cab let Arabella off here, because he watched it through the cab webcam thing. I put him off by saying that a lady did show up here, a tall redhead in a wedding gown, but there was no room at Patchwork, so she called another cab," Gina said.

"And?" Hannah held her breath.

"He left to go talk to the local cab companies. He asked what color cab picked her up and I told him I wasn't sure," Gina said. "I'm so glad that her transport is on the way."

"Me, too," Hannah said.

After she hung up the receiver, she turned around to find Arabella so close that she almost ran into her. "You will be leaving as soon as possible. Martin has been to the shelter, so he knows you were there."

"I'm ready. I don't even need to take anything with me. We'll be out of Dallas and in Mexico by supper time."

"Why didn't your grandmother come to the wedding?" Hannah asked.

Arabella went back to the door to watch but stood far enough back that she couldn't be seen. "She did some digging into his family and she said they were dishonest and if I was marrying into that mess, she didn't want to witness it. They are here. Oh, she's sent Rodney. He's my favorite of the bodyguards," Arabella said. "Good-bye, Hannah, and thank you one more time."

She walked out of the house with her head held high and got into the black vehicle. One burly black-suited man walked a step behind her and two waited beside the car. They made sure she was inside, and then she was gone, just like that, with no pomp or fanfare.

Hannah waved from the door, but the windows of the SUV were tinted so she couldn't tell if Arabella waved back or not. She waited until they were out of sight and then went back to the bedroom to strip the sheets off the bed. Unless the next visitor couldn't climb steps, she'd give the next folks one of the upstairs bedrooms.

The extra clothing that Miss Rosie and Aunt Birdie had brought had been carefully laid on the bottom of the bed. Beside the stack was a sticky note:

This is to buy something special for Sophie.

A hundred-dollar bill was attached to it with a paper clip.

Hannah sat down on the bed and sighed. Sophie would have a precious sister that she could never know. Maybe, like Arabella said, they could get acquainted later in life.

Travis sat down beside her and pulled her into his arms. "What's the matter? Where is Arabella?"

Hannah wiped the tears away with the back of her hand. "She's gone home to Mexico. They came for her earlier than expected, which is good, because Marty tracked her to the shelter after all." Hannah laid her head on Travis's chest and drew comfort from the steady beat of his heart. "Sophie will have a sister, and she'll never know it. It's painful knowing how much she wants one and I can't even tell her."

"Some things are what they are, darlin'. Let's drive down to the bait store and get some minnows and take some sandwiches to the river. We can fish or just lie back under that big old willow tree and watch the water flow by. I'll text Aunt Birdie and tell her to bring Sophie to us when she gets out of church."

Hannah sighed. "You always fix everything. I love you for that, Travis."

He flashed a brilliant smile. "So you do love me."

"Always have," she said.

"That's a step in the right direction."

"What does that mean?"

"You think about it and you'll figure it out." He hugged her gently.

❧

Hannah hated cryptic messages. She was still analyzing everything Travis said when Sophie showed up on the beach. Aunt Birdie had walked her down to the river and waved at them before she disappeared back into the willow trees.

Hannah watched the red-and-white bobber dance around on the top of the slow-moving, clay-colored water. With the fishing rod in her hand, she kept a close eye on Sophie, sitting right beside her with her own line out in the water. It wasn't long until Sophie grew tired of the monotony of waiting for a fish to bite and started to fuss that they weren't biting.

"Well, then why don't you and I take a walk up the river a little ways and throw rocks in the water," Travis said. "I bet that would scare them down this way and they'll bite one of our lines. Then your mama can reel him in for our supper. I'll prop my line and yours up on a stick so she can watch them."

"Yes!" Sophie pumped her fist in the air.

"Y'all have fun." Hannah adjusted her wide-brimmed fishing hat and began watching all three bobbers.

What's the difference? She asked herself as Sophie ran along beside Travis, each of them throwing stones into the river. *He's taking over a spot in my life just like Marty did, and I'm comfortable with him. Would things change with Travis if we got into a serious relationship? And what did he mean this morning when he said for me to figure it out? I do love him. I've always loved him.*

But, that niggling voice inside her head said, *there is a difference in loving someone and being in love with someone. You love Aunt Birdie and Darcy and even Cal, but you are not in love with them. Travis wants you to go to the next level someday in the future and be in love with him. He's left bread crumbs. Follow them if you want to see where it leads. Kick them*

*off to the side if you don't want to trust him with your heart. Simple as that
and up to you.*

She shook her head to get rid of the voice, but it came back in the
form of her mother's soft southern drawl.

"Need some help managing these poles?"

She frowned. Although she couldn't control the inner voice and it
often sounded like her mother, this was the first time it was that loud
or clear or that it brought a presence with it.

Her first thought was that Travis and Sophie had managed to sneak
upon her, but then she glanced over that way and her mother was sitting
right there, almost touching her.

"Mama?" She blinked half a dozen times in rapid succession.

"Surprise!"

She threw the rod on the sand and hugged her mother in a fierce
embrace. "How did you get here?"

"Darcy and Cal picked me up in Dallas. I decided to stay two weeks
instead of one." Patsy hugged her daughter and held on for a long time
before she finally pushed back and really looked at her from head to toe.
"You look good, my child. There's life in your eyes again. And I think
you've put on a few pounds. They look good on you."

"There's life in my heart, Mama. And Aunt Birdie and Miss Rosie
have been popping in and out with food ever since that day in court."
Hannah hugged her mother again. "I'm so glad you are here. How's
Granny?" Hannah picked up the fishing rod but kept a hand on her
mother's knee.

"She's doing great and said I needed a break, that she would be fine
in the new assisted-care center. She actually thinks she's on vacation,
too," Patsy said.

"I wish you could stay longer," Hannah said.

"Me, too, but not this time," Patsy told her.

"I'll take what I can get, but if she's happy there, then that means
you can come back more often, right?"

"Or you can come to Virginia anytime and bring Sophie to see her. I was thinking maybe Thanksgiving would be a good time. Sophie will have a week out of school and our house has extra bedrooms, so bring whatever friends want to tag along with you," Patsy said.

"Freedom." Hannah sighed. "It's a beautiful thing, Mama."

"Yes, it is!" Patsy agreed as she reached for Travis's fishing rod and quickly reeled in a five-pound catfish. Together, she and Hannah removed the hook and put the fish on a bed of ice in the cooler Travis had brought along for that purpose.

"Supper in the making," Patsy said. "I haven't been fishing since I moved away from here." She baited the empty hook and tossed it back out into the water. "If we catch enough, Travis can clean them and we'll have fish and fried potatoes for supper tonight."

"Hey," Darcy yelled as she and Cal made their way down the steep bank and to the river. "Did we surprise her, Patsy?"

"Yes, you did. How did you keep this a secret?" Hannah asked.

"Cal and I had to stay away from you or we would have told for sure. Did you tell your mama about Arabella yet?"

"Give me that spare fishing rod and I'll hold it for you," Cal said. "Where's Travis and Sophie?"

"Look down the river and you can see two tiny dots right at the bend. They're on their way back now, I think, but they've been throwing rocks in the river to scare the fish this way," Hannah said.

"It must be working." Patsy slipped the lid off the cooler and pointed. "Supper."

"I love your fried fish," Darcy said. "Got an extra rod and reel? I'll help."

"Arabella?" Patsy asked.

"It's a long story, which I'll tell you over a big fish fry tonight," Hannah said.

"Granny!" Sophie squealed when she was close enough to recognize the woman sitting beside Hannah. She churned up the dust behind her as she left Travis behind. When she was close enough, she made a dive and landed in Patsy's arms.

Cal grabbed the fishing rod that hit the ground and settled in between Hannah and Darcy. Sophie kept squealing the whole time that she planted kisses on her grandmother.

"Mama, Granny is here!" she finally said. "Is she still staying at our house? I want her to meet Lullaby and see my new pretty room and did Mama tell you that our house has a name? It's Lullaby Sky now and we get company and sometimes they have a little girl like Laurel and she can play with me. Oh, Granny, I love you!" Sophie settled into her grandmother's lap.

"Not as much as I love you," Patsy teased. "You scared up a fish and I caught it on your rod and reel. Think me and you should take a walk up the river again and see if we can make another one swim down here?"

"Yes, yes!" Sophie clapped her hands. "And I can show you the big old tree that just fell over. Now we can use it for a bench to sit on when we get tired. Only I didn't get tired. I found more rocks and threw them in the river while Uncle Travis talked on the phone."

Travis slipped in between Cal and Hannah, his bare knee touching hers. "Surprised?" he asked.

She nudged him on the shoulder. "You rat. You knew, didn't you?"

"I did, and I don't ever want to know another secret that I'm not allowed to tell you about." He grinned. "It wasn't easy. I didn't like keeping things from you."

Patsy stood up and took Sophie's hand in hers. Hannah could see a few more gray hairs around her mother's temples, but she still did not look sixty. Patsy's brown eyes sparkled when Sophie tugged at her hand to get her moving.

"Y'all have fun and send a lot of fish this way," Travis said. "Did she really surprise you?"

"She really did. And you are all forgiven for keeping the secret, because I'm so glad to see her," Hannah answered.

Her line tightened, and she reeled it in a bit. The end of the rod bent forward and started to slip from her hands. Travis quickly moved behind her, one leg on each side of hers, and closed his big hands over hers. "Give him some slack and then reel him in a little at a time. It's either a big fish or a rotten old gar."

"It had better be a fish or the rest of you are going hungry. I haven't had Mama's fried fish in years, and I'll eat that five-pounder all by myself," Hannah said as she reeled in the line, just like Travis said.

It wasn't easy to think about a fish, no matter what kind or how big, with Travis's bare skin against hers, his hands covering hers, and his warm breath on her neck. She wanted to throw the rod and reel out in the river and flip around and kiss him right there.

"That reminds me of fishing for blue marlin," Cal said.

"Only a marlin would be mounted, and this one is supper." Hannah could see the tip of the fish's head, and it was a catfish, a nice big one that would feed the whole family. She couldn't let it get away.

Finally, she and Travis together brought the fifteen-pound specimen to shore. It was too big to fit in the cooler, so Travis and Cal immediately set about cleaning both fish, filleting them and putting the pieces on ice while Darcy and Hannah manned the poles again.

"Hey, y'all." Liz gingerly made her way down the pathway. "I figured I'd find you right here, and I see that Patsy made it all right."

"You knew, too?" Hannah yelled back over her shoulder.

"We all did. I see you have an extra pole there. I'll use it if the guys are going to clean fish on the banks," Liz said.

"You sure you feel like fishing?" Darcy asked.

"If I catch something bigger than the palm of my hand, there are two strong men who can haul it in for me. What's Patsy and Sophie doing?" Liz pointed upstream.

"They are throwing rocks in the river to scare the fish down this way so we can catch them. It's working," Travis answered.

"Looks like it." Liz grinned. "So Arabella left this morning?"

"She did, and I'm glad for her visit. It made me face the fact that it wasn't my fault that Marty treated me like he did. It wouldn't have mattered if I was rich as Midas or had the manners of a queen," Hannah said.

"Well, halle-damn-lujah!" Darcy exclaimed. "We've been telling you that for years. Why couldn't you listen to us?"

"Because, darlin's, you all love me. Arabella and I were not friends, at least not at first, and, well, crap, I can't explain it. But it brought more closure than anything else. I hope you can get to this point, Liz."

"My Arabella will come along someday," Liz said. "Right now I'm just glad for sunshine on my face, the promise of a fish fry for supper, to see you happy and Darcy getting her wildest dreams fulfilled. And I'm real glad that I get to go back to work after the Fourth. I'm about to go stark raving stir-crazy."

"Do we need to quilt some more?" Darcy asked.

"No, but I do intend to spend lots of time at Hannah's while Patsy is there, so get ready for it. You have to share her," Liz said.

"You are all welcome anytime." She looked back over her shoulder and caught Travis staring at her.

He would move out that very day since there were no shelter guests, and the house would be empty without his presence. Her full heart suddenly had a hole in it. She didn't want him to go, and right now was the time to say so. "Travis, you don't have to move in and out all the time."

"Thank you. I've got stuff spread out everywhere, and I hate to move." He used the tip of one finger to push his glasses up on his nose. "Besides, this is going to be a very busy week for me and Cal. We'll be working from sunup to sundown. Some of our hired hands are only available this week. Family vacations and all. So I won't interfere with your visit."

"Mama will pout if you don't interfere some of the time." Hannah smiled.

"I'm planning on doing my fair share of getting in the way," Darcy declared. "I'm staying at Aunt Birdie's this week. I'll commute. It's not fair for y'all to get to be together every day and me to be left out. Save the good stuff for when I get there."

"I feel like we're back in high school," Cal said.

"Wouldn't it be nice if we could hit a 'Delete' button and get a redo?" Liz said wistfully.

Hannah considered what Liz had said and decided that she didn't want a redo. It was all the experiences, tough as they were at the time, that brought her to this day and made her appreciate her place in the universe. Her friends had proven that they could help her through anything. Her mother was there, and she had Sophie. Life was pretty damned good.

CHAPTER TWENTY-SIX

A falling star. Make a wish," Travis said from the shadows.

"We both saw it, so we each get a wish." Hannah smiled up at him as he padded across the wooden porch in his bare feet and sat down beside her. She handed him her glass of tea, and he took a long drink before handing it back.

Patsy had been dragged into Sophie's room to read her a bedtime story. Liz had gone home after supper to Aunt Birdie's place, and Darcy was down at the hangar with Cal.

"Remember that song about a falling star by Jim Reeves? I think Aunt Birdie still has it over there on vinyl," he said.

"The title was 'A Fallen Star.'"

He stood to his feet and held out his hand. "Yes, it was. Dance with me, Hannah."

She put her hand in his. "Where's the music?"

He started to hum the tune to the old country song as he guided her hands around his neck and looped his around her waist. The words played through her mind as they moved over the green grass in their bare feet.

The world disappeared, and they were the only two people on Earth. Hannah wished that the song could go on forever and that she never had to leave the warm feeling that she had in Travis's arms.

"I got my wish," he drawled. "I've wanted to dance with you for months."

"I got mine earlier, so I'm saving my fallen star for later."

"Want to share?" he asked.

"Maybe later. Right now I just want to dance one more time with you out here."

"Yes, ma'am." He began to hum another old country tune, "I'd Love to Lay You Down."

She pushed back and looked up into his eyes. "I know that song from Aunt Birdie's old vinyls, too."

"I'll hum, then, and you fill in the words. It's the way I feel about you. Do you remember all the lyrics?"

"I do," she said softly as she fought back the tears. Not once when Marty danced with her at those fancy parties had she felt the way she did right then with the soft grass under her feet.

It would be so easy not only to love Travis but to fall in love with him.

❧

Hannah arose early on Thursday morning to a quiet house. The week had gone by in a flash, but then, the whole month had done the same thing. Could it have really only been a short time ago that she was petrified in that courtroom? And after June was finished and July began, would she stop counting the weeks, the days, and the hours since that day?

She tiptoed down to the kitchen and found a note propped up on a box with ten doughnuts left out of the original dozen that let her know that Travis had filled his coffee thermos and the machine was ready to turn on for the second pot of the morning. Evidently he'd made a run to the convenience store that morning before he headed off to the hangar to get to work on Cal's new place. Things were coming along so well that Cal was hoping to get moved into his loft apartment by July Fourth.

Every other word out of Darcy's mouth was *Cal,* or else something about the new apartment. Hannah didn't need a road map to know that the bed in the loft was what Darcy was most interested in.

She raised the lid to the doughnut box and removed one, eating it standing up while the coffee dripped into the pot. She licked her fingers and reached for a second one.

"Good morning. We finally get a minute alone?" Patsy ran her fingers through her hair, pulling it up into a ponytail on the top of her head. "Anything planned for this day, or do we get to stay home and visit?"

Hannah ran water over her fingers and dried them on a paper towel and then poured two cups of coffee and carried them to the table. "We're having everyone over for hamburgers and hot dogs tonight. Travis and Cal are grilling, but it will be a late supper, because they're working until at least six thirty. The only plan I have is to walk down there and see how the new business and apartment are shaping up. You got something you want to do?"

"I do." Patsy nodded. "Did you get up early and go buy these?"

"Travis did," Hannah answered.

"He's a good man. Don't ever make the mistake of judging him by Marty's standard."

"I won't," Hannah said. "What do you want to do today?" Hannah set the box on the table and removed a third one.

"I have about six old friends who have planned a get-together in Gainesville. We are going to meet there at two o'clock, take in the antique stores downtown, and then have supper and go back to the closest one's house for coffee and dessert. I need to borrow your car and I may be late getting home."

"No problem with you taking my car, but we can talk right now, right? I don't feel like I've had nearly enough one-on-one time with you," Hannah said.

"We can talk. You never did get around to telling me about this Arabella person. I heard all about Jodie and Elaine but not the last one." Patsy fished out a doughnut and dipped it into her coffee.

Hannah started at the beginning and tried to tell Patsy about the emotional roller coaster as well as the order of the events of that evening and the next morning. "It felt like much longer, Mama. And yet, by the time she left, I'd made a friend from what I thought was an enemy. My heart is broken because Sophie will have a sister and never know her."

Patsy reached across the table to lay a hand on Hannah's arm. "It's best that way. Fate brought you and Arabella together. One never knows how it might bring Sophie and her half sister together. Maybe another one of Marty's women will shoot the son of a bitch, and then the way will be open for Sophie and her sister before they are adults."

"Mama!" Hannah chided.

"One can only hope. Now, let's talk about Travis. Y'all looked like you belonged together out there dancing under the stars. But don't get in a hurry about anything. Follow your heart, but go slow."

"You saw us?" Hannah blushed.

"I looked out the window and it was a beautiful sight." Patsy smiled.

"I could fall in love with him. He's so good to Sophie and me both," Hannah said honestly.

"But what happens when you are in his arms—sparks or just a nice comfortable feeling?"

"Fire. Pure, white-hot blazes like I never ever felt with Marty," she said.

"Then it's worthwhile. I thought he was the one for you in high school."

"You never said anything." Hannah frowned.

"My mother refused to let me date or marry the love of my life. I married your father and she loved him. He was a good man and a wonderful father, but the spark that I felt with the other boy was never there. I promised myself I would never interfere in your love life, much to my dismay for the last few years. I thought I would die when I found out that Marty was abusing you." Patsy paused and then went on. "I saw my daughter go from a slightly shy woman with a big heart to one who would hardly lift up her head."

"He had a pretty good hold on me with Sophie," Hannah said.

"I know that, and it's the only reason he's still breathing. I want to see you happy, and I have no doubt that Travis can make you happy. But for his sake as well as yours, you need to be whole again before you make a major life-changing decision about anything."

Hannah laid her hand over her mother's. "I agree with you, Mama."

"Good, now let's go outside and watch the grass grow while we drink our coffee. It's a beautiful morning. When Sophie crawls out of bed, we'll go take a look at the hangar." Patsy squeezed her hand and swallowed. "I have a confession before we go."

"Which is?" Hannah asked.

"Travis helped me keep tabs on you, so I've known how he feels about you, and my advice is still the same." Patsy picked up her cup and headed outside.

"So y'all have been talking behind my back?" Hannah didn't know whether to be angry or love both of them even more for caring so much about her.

"We have, darlin'."

"Well, all I can say is that I'm just glad for the progress I've made and for the friends and family who've gotten me to this point."

"Me, too, Hannah."

❧

July Fourth sneaked up on Hannah. She'd gotten so used to having her mother with her that she hadn't given herself time to think about the day that Patsy would go back to Virginia. So that Monday morning when Sophie bounced on her bed and woke her up just after sunrise, she finally had to face the fact that today was Patsy's last full day in Texas.

"Oh, no!" She buried her face in her pillow.

"What is oh, no, Mama?" Sophie asked in a worried voice.

"Your granny goes home tomorrow."

"Oh, no!" Sophie fell face forward into the extra pillow. "Say it ain't so, Mama."

"It is, Sophie, but she wants us to come to her house for Thanksgiving, or if not then, maybe Christmas. You've never been to Virginia, so what do you think?"

"Would it take a long time to get there?"

Hannah cut her eyes over at Sophie, but all she could see was a mop of curly black hair covering her face. "Only a few hours, because we would probably fly in an airplane."

"Nooooo!" Sophie sat up so fast that her little eyes took a moment to adjust. "We can't get in an airplane. It might take us to Father and he'll be mad at us."

Hannah quickly popped up and drew Sophie into her lap. "Not Father's airplane. That's gone. This would be a big airplane like what your granny came on. They go all different places."

Sophie's dark-brown eyes locked with Hannah's. "Promise."

"I promise, and you'll get to see your great-grandmother. That's Granny's mama."

It had been six years since Hannah had been out of the state of Texas. She and her mother used to go to Virginia every year during Christmas break and for a week during the summer. After Hannah graduated from high school and got a job in the admissions office at the hospital, she and Liz rented the apartment in Gainesville. Hannah's father died, and her mother moved to Virginia. She still went to see her mother and grandmother at Christmas until Marty came into her world and life changed drastically.

My life in a nutshell, she thought as she rocked back and forth with Sophie in her lap as if she was still a tiny baby.

"Granny has a mama!" Sophie gasped. "How old is she? Did she ever see a dinosaur?"

Hannah stiffened her lip to keep from laughing. "You'll have to ask her sometime when we go to Virginia, or better yet, when Granny gets home, maybe she could take her computer to the place where your great-granny lives and you could talk to her on the Internet. I bet she'd like that. But today we have the parade and the fireworks this evening and the Crossing festival. Maybe we should get dressed and go make breakfast so you don't miss riding on the church float."

It took two leaps for Sophie to leave her mother's lap and land on the floor. "I'll wake Granny up. I want to wave right at her when I'm on the float, so she'll need her coffee to get awake."

Hannah stretched, rolling her neck from side to side. The weatherman had said it would be a sunny, hot holiday, which was exactly what Independence Day should be. Sophie would be ecstatic over the small carnival set up in the lot beside the convenience store. There were several kiddie rides along with ponies and a few vendors just waiting to take money to win a stuffed animal or a rubber duck.

She threw off her nightshirt and dressed in khaki shorts and a bright-red tank top before heading to the kitchen in her bare feet. Travis was already there, and the coffee was ready.

"Good morning, beautiful." He poured a cup and handed it to her. "Big day in Crossing. How long has it been since you've had cotton candy?"

"Our senior trip to Six Flags. We shared a bag, remember?" she answered.

"It was purple, and you got more than I did," he teased.

She touched him on the upper arm. "I'll let you have the lion's share today to make up for it."

He drew her to his side and kissed her on the top of the head. "I already have the lion's share just being here with you and Sophie. Where is the princess? I heard her running in the foyer."

"In Mama's room. I told her that we might go to Virginia sometime, maybe Thanksgiving or Christmas. I didn't set a date in stone, because we don't know who's going to win that bet about Darcy and Cal's wedding. I did tell her that she could see her great-granny on the computer screen. She's all excited about it."

"Yes."

She looked up at his strong jaw and his twinkling eyes. "Yes to what?"

"If you go to Virginia, I want to go with y'all."

Hannah smiled. "Of course you are invited."

"When I'm with you, all is good. When we are apart, I'm lost. I do not like that feeling," he drawled.

"That may be the most romantic thing I've ever heard." She rolled up on her toes, cupped his face in her hands, and brought her lips to his in a passionate kiss that left them both speechless.

"That meant something," he said. "At least it did to me."

"It did." She laid her head on his chest. "It means that I know the difference in loving you and being in love with you. I know what you were talking about, Travis. I'm looking forward, but I need to do it slowly. And it means that I doubt if the fireworks tonight will be nearly as spectacular as your kisses or having you in my life."

"When did you know?" he asked.

"I'm not sure. It wasn't one of those instant moments. At the river that day when we were fishing, I listened to what my heart was telling me, and it was like a warm blanket around me on a cold night. But don't think for one minute that what we have is just a comfortable feeling. You leave me breathless when you kiss me, and there's sparks all over the room when you look at me," she said softly. "But I cannot rush into this, Travis."

"We can go at a snail's pace as long as I know you're right there beside me."

"Always," she said.

Epilogue
Thanksgiving

Hannah awoke to the aroma of cinnamon rolls baking in the oven. She quickly threw on a robe and tiptoed down the stairs, through the living room, and into the kitchen. Warm spiced cider waited in the Crock-Pot and cinnamon rolls were cooling on the table, along with a carafe of milk and a pot of coffee. Patsy wore an apron with a turkey on the front over a lovely burnt-orange dress.

"Happy Thanksgiving!" She hugged her daughter. "You're the first one up and around, but I expect the smell of cinnamon will wake the others before long."

"It's better than an alarm clock, Mama. Are we eating at four?"

"Tradition," Patsy said.

"Good morning," Aunt Birdie and Miss Rosie said in unison as they came in the back door. "This looks wonderful. Is that spiced cider?"

"It is. Help yourselves," Patsy said. "It's so nice to have a houseful on Thanksgiving. This is the way it should be."

"And you will come back at Christmas, right?" Aunt Birdie asked.

"If the airports aren't closed down with ice or snow. I've also promised Sophie that Hannah will bring her to Virginia for spring break. Her great-grandmother wants to meet her." Patsy nodded. "She loves their video chats, but she says she can't hug Sophie on a computer screen."

Hannah could feel Travis's presence long before he slipped his arms around her waist and pulled her back to his chest. She'd thought that the effects of his touch might lessen as the months went by, but they only got more intense.

"Good mornin', beautiful," he whispered in her ear.

"Good mornin' to you." She wiggled around so she could wrap her arms around his neck and give him a proper Thanksgiving kiss.

"I think they are in love." Miss Rosie chuckled.

"In love is different than loving," Travis echoed Hannah's often-repeated phrase.

"Of course it is," Patsy said.

"Thanks, Mama." Hannah stepped away from Travis. "Now, what can I do to help?"

"You and these folks can sit down and have warm cinnamon rolls for breakfast. This is your day, and you aren't going to help do much of anything. Besides, everything else is ready except the big old bird. I'll put him in the oven after breakfast and cook him slowly while we go take care of business. Ten o'clock will be here before you know it. Pull up a chair."

"Ten? I thought you said four," Miss Rosie said.

"We have a little surprise up our sleeves for ten this morning." Patsy's smile looked as innocent as a newborn lamb.

"We are taking pictures of the whole bunch of us. So after breakfast everyone needs to get dressed," Hannah said.

"You are saying that we can't take pictures in our pajamas?" Liz teased.

"I'm framing one to go above the credenza," Hannah said.

"Enough said." Liz smiled.

"This is a very special day," Patsy said.

"Hey! Oh. My. Sweet. Lord! I have not had your cinnamon rolls since we were all in high school." Cal quickly pulled out a chair and sat down. "And is that mulled cider I smell? This is heaven."

Darcy stopped in the middle of a yawn and sat down in Cal's lap. "It is cider. I helped Patsy put it together last night." She kissed him on the cheek. "Can you believe it's only a few more weeks until I get to marry this man?"

"The only reason that she's marrying me is because she got tired of running away from me." Cal separated a roll from the others and put it on a plate. He fed the first bite to Darcy, who rolled her eyes in appreciation.

"Just like I remembered. You have not lost your touch, Patsy."

"Good! I was telling the rest of them that Hannah and I have a little surprise ready at ten this morning. We want to take a few pictures before the Thanksgiving Day parade starts."

"Pictures of the whole bunch of us," Patsy said. "We've got a professional photographer coming. Y'all pull up a chair and have a cinnamon roll."

"Would not turn down an offer like that for anything," Aunt Birdie said.

"We should have pictures of all of us. This is our first Thanksgiving all together since we were seniors in high school," Darcy said.

Patsy took a second pan of rolls from the oven and set them on the table before she sat down. "So, Liz, how's school going this year?"

"Wonderful. And I love living in Aunt Birdie's house—I can't tell you what it means to me that it is now the safe house."

"But Mama, we don't say anything about it in front of Sophie. She went to church and told her friends about her new friends who lived in our house. That's why we had to move the operation," Hannah explained.

"I'm not a bit surprised. I bet everyone thought she was talking about her imaginary friends, didn't they? But it is much safer for the women to be across the street, especially when school starts and Sophie is with kids every day."

Travis chuckled. "We were saved by Sophie's imagination."

"We were saved by Liz. The fact that she's living in and taking care of that big house for me means me and Rosie can go places in our 'retirement.'" Aunt Birdie made air quotes around the last word. "It's nice to be able to go on a cruise or a senior citizens' trip up through the East Coast to see the foliage. Things are working out in Crossing, even if it did take a while to get it all done."

Miss Rosie poured a second cup of coffee and reached for her third cinnamon roll. "We are getting to be regular old gadabouts."

"I think that is wonderful." Patsy laughed.

"Who's got a secret?" Sophie wandered into the room and crawled up in her grandmother's lap. "When does everyone come for the pictures?"

"After breakfast." Hannah poured a small glass of milk and slipped a cinnamon roll onto a plate for Sophie.

Sophie put a bite of the gooey bun in her mouth and rolled her eyes dramatically. "Did you make this, Granny, or did God?"

"Now, that's a charmer." Cal chuckled. "But I have to agree with her. They are heavenly."

"Granny, promise me the pictures won't take too long and make me miss the floats in the parade. They are my favorite part," Sophie said.

"I promise. Only about half an hour, tops," Patsy answered. "So, Darcy, you are planning a Christmas wedding? What day should I book my flight?"

"We are getting married on the twenty-third. That's the Friday before Christmas, which is now less than a month away. I would be so happy if you could be there. Would you help Aunt Birdie and Miss Rosie cut and serve the wedding cake?"

"I'd be honored," Patsy told her. "How big is the cake?"

"Huge," Cal said. "It'll be four feet from top to bottom. But it has to feed the whole town of Crossing and about half of Gainesville."

"And I'm quitting my job a week before the wedding. I'll be working full-time for Cal as his financial adviser," Darcy said.

"And I understand he designed and made your dress?"

Darcy beamed. "He did, and it fits beautifully, but he still can't see me in it until the wedding. His assistants did all the fittings."

Cal kissed her on the neck. "You are knock-down gorgeous in jeans, sweetheart. I can't even begin to imagine you in that beautiful creation I made just for you."

"Jealous?" Travis teased.

"Hell, no," Hannah murmured.

❧

Everyone had changed into their Sunday best promptly at nine forty-five. They filed into the living room, where the photographer was setting up a tripod with a camera on the top.

"Y'all go on in and have a seat. I've got to run up and help with Sophie's hair. It's being a blister to get fixed this morning," Hannah said.

"I'll go with her. We won't be long," Travis said.

Patsy was busy combing Sophie's hair and putting a wreath of white baby rosebuds on her head like a crown when they arrived in her bedroom. "Well, what do y'all think of this princess?"

"I think she needs to put on the dress before she's a real princess." Travis grinned.

Patsy unzipped a clothes bag and fluffed out a taffeta dress with beading at the top.

"Oh. My. Goodness." Sophie clamped her hands over her cheeks, mimicking Darcy to a tee.

Hannah dropped down on her knees in front of Sophie. "And I have something I really need to ask you. I want you to be real honest with me and tell me the truth."

Sophie crossed her arms over her chest. "I did tell the truth. Laney was at our house and she wasn't one of my friends that nobody can see but me. And so was them other folks."

"It's not about that. It's about Uncle Travis. I love him very much and I want to marry him today, but . . . ," Hannah paused.

"Oh. My. Sweet Jesus." Sophie squealed as she dramatically slapped a hand on her forehead. "Then he will be my daddy, right? Do I get to change my name again?"

"What do you really, down deep in your heart, think of that?" Patsy asked.

"I think I'm the luckiest girl in the whole world and this is the bestest day of my whole life," Sophie said. "Do I get to call him Daddy?"

Travis ran his forefinger across his eye. "I would like that, but you don't have to."

"Well, I want to. Do I get to be in the wedding like I get to be in Aunt Darcy's?"

Hannah slipped the dress down over Sophie's head. "I thought you might like to wear this new dress and stand in the front of the living room with me and Travis when we get married. What do you think of that? It's Thanksgiving, and I'm thankful for you and for Travis and my mama and all my friends. We thought we'd get married today right here at Lullaby Sky."

Sophie shucked out of her boots and skirt and tossed them in the corner. "I love this day, Mama. Now can I please have a baby sister?"

"We'll see about that later on down the road." Hannah smiled and straightened up to give her mother a hug. "Mama, thank you so much for arranging this."

"I'm delighted to do it and that you are wearing my dress. It means so much to me."

A phone rang, and Travis automatically reached for his hip pocket then shook his head. "It's not mine, and I need to go get dressed. See you in the living room in a few minutes." He brushed a kiss across her lips.

"And it's not mine," Patsy said.

"It's Mama's phone," Sophie said as she fished around in Hannah's purse and handed it to her. "Answer it, Mama."

"Hello," Hannah said cautiously, since the number came up as unknown.

"This is Arabella. I have some news. Marty and his dad have been arrested for tax evasion. The government has finally got enough on them to bring down their whole banking system. Everything they own, including their bank accounts and all their credit cards, has been frozen. He's looking at years in prison if he's found guilty, and his parents will be right in the same boat with him."

"What does this mean for us?" Hannah asked.

"It means that you were wise to get your child support in a lump sum, because if you hadn't, there wouldn't be anything at all. And it means that neither of us has to worry about this anymore. Mama Lita says he is going away for a very long time. He can't even afford a lawyer. They've appointed one of those free lawyers for him."

Hannah fell back on the sofa. "Oh. My. Gosh."

"Do you think that once the trial is over I could bring my daughter to see you and Sophie?" Arabella asked.

"I'd like that. I wish you were here today. I'm about to marry Travis," Hannah said.

"I wish I was there, too. I'm not one bit surprised that you are going to marry him. I could see the love in his eyes for you," Arabella said.

"And your daughter?"

"She's doing so well," Arabella answered. "You go get married and have a wonderful Thanksgiving."

"Thank you, Arabella, for everything," Hannah said.

Closure had been hers for months now, and she wasn't sure how she should feel about all the news, but she would not let it spoil the best day of her life.

"I felt so guilty at first, because I was happy that he finally got what he deserved for the way he treated both of us," Arabella said. "Now I just feel guilty that I don't feel guilty. Does that make sense?"

"Yes, it does." Hannah said. "I felt the same way that day when I left the courthouse after the divorce. And I kind of have that same feeling today. There's a sense of relief that I don't ever have to worry about him kidnapping Sophie."

"Or Fiona." Arabella sighed. "*Abuela* said that we should call her by her first name, and she does look like a Fiona with her red hair. I hope you don't mind that I named her after you when it came time for her christening name."

"I'm honored, and I really would love to see you again."

"When you are ready to tell Sophie, let me know and we will arrange for you to come to Mexico. I never intend to set foot outside my country again. Good-bye, now, Hannah, and thank you one more time. Oh, and I'll give you the number you can reach me at any time."

Sophie twirled out of Patsy's reach. "Look, Mama. I'm a princess."

Later Hannah would get in touch with Arabella, but today, right now, she was about to get married, and that was enough for that day.

"What was that all about?" Patsy asked.

Hannah gave her mother a very short version while Patsy helped her into her wedding dress. "You were right. Now Arabella's daughter and Sophie can get to know each other. But today is my wedding day, and I want to give Travis all my attention and not think about that."

"Smart girl. Miss Rosie is going to be so happy, because she is going to win the bet today." Patsy grinned.

"What bet?" Hannah asked. "I didn't know anyone but me and Travis had one going about when Darcy and Cal would get married. And he won that one."

"She and Aunt Birdie had a bet going about when you and Travis would get married. Miss Rosie is the closest." Patsy turned Hannah around so she could see herself in the mirror.

"That is so funny. There is never a dull moment around those two old gals." Hannah's breath caught in her chest when she saw her reflection. "I'm almost as pretty as you, Mama."

"You are much more beautiful than I ever was, because today you get to marry your soul mate."

❦

Everyone looked up with questions on their faces when the preacher from the Crossing church appeared from the kitchen and took his place at the front of the living room. Travis had been waiting at the door, and now he crossed the room to join the preacher.

"Hannah and I have decided to get married. We didn't want anything big, but we did want all y'all to be here with us, so thank you all." Travis grinned.

"You ornery devil." Aunt Birdie shook her finger at him.

"I win. You owe me a hundred dollars." Miss Rosie clapped her hands. "And I figured this had to do with more than pictures, so I brought a bottle of Pappy Van Winkle." She pulled it from her oversize purse sitting on the floor beside her.

"What?" Darcy asked.

"We've had a bet for the past month. Birdie said Easter and I said Halloween. It's closer to my date, so she owes me," Rosie explained. "And she still has to pay up. And we've been saving this bottle for this occasion for years."

Slow piano music started playing, but it wasn't the traditional wedding song. "A Fallen Star," played in true Floyd Cramer style, filled the room as Hannah walked across the living room with one hand in her mother's and the other in her daughter's.

"Dearly beloved, we are gathered here to join this family together in holy wedlock." The preacher's big booming voice echoed off the walls. "Who gives this woman to this man?"

"I do because he is going to be my daddy," Sophie piped up before Patsy could say a word.

"Enough said." Patsy smiled and sat down beside Aunt Birdie.

In less than fifteen minutes, the preacher told Travis he could kiss the bride. He bent her over backward in a true Hollywood kiss, and when they were both upright again, he picked Sophie up on one arm while the other was draped around Hannah's shoulders.

"From the courthouse to the Lullaby Sky," she murmured. "I like this place much better."

"But we had to have the courthouse before we could get to this wonderful day. I will always cherish you and love Sophie, too." He kissed her again.

"Always and forever," Hannah said.

Sophie stretched out her arms to Hannah for a three-way hug. "This is the bestest day of my life."

Acknowledgments

Dear Readers,

I finished writing *The Lullaby Sky* with misty eyes. It's been said that family doesn't have to have blood ties and sometimes a friend is closer than a brother, and these characters sure proved that to me.

Sometimes life deals us a tough hand. Each of the five friends in this book had obstacles to overcome, maybe in love, maybe in trust, or maybe with abuse. But with the help of one another, they came through the course set before them and finished with victory.

As with all my books, there are those who deserve recognition for helping take this from an idea to a finished product. My deepest appreciation to my publisher, Montlake, for continuing to believe in me; to my Montlake editor, Anh Schluep, and my developmental editor, Krista Stroever—you are amazing; to everyone on the team at Montlake who work so hard behind the curtains, and a special thanks to Jessica Poore for all that she does to make me smile.

Special gratitude to my agent, Erin Niumata, and my agency, Folio Management, Inc. Hugs to all of you!

I'd also like to thank Mr. B, my husband, who doesn't complain when we order pizza or burgers two nights in a row so I can finish one more chapter. It takes a special person to live with an author, and he does a fine job. And once again, a big hearty thank-you to my fans, friends, and family, who buy and read my books.

And a very special thanks to everyone who helps with shelters for abused women. You are appreciated beyond what words can say.

Until next time,

Carolyn Brown

About the Author

Carolyn Brown is a *New York Times* and *USA Today* bestselling author of contemporary, historical, and western romance and a RITA Award finalist. *The Lullaby Sky* is her eightieth published novel. She and her husband live in the small town of Davis, Oklahoma, where everyone knows everyone else, as well as what they're doing and when—and they read the local newspaper on Wednesdays to see who got caught.

Carolyn and her husband have three grown children and enough grandchildren to keep them young. When she's not writing, she likes to sit in her gorgeous backyard with her two tomcats, Chester Fat Boy and Boots Randolph Terminator Outlaw, and watch them protect the yard from all kinds of wicked varmints like crickets, locusts, and spiders.